Dear Reader,

I've always loved cowboys and romance and so I've combined these two elements in my BRIDES FOR BROTHERS series, four books about the Randalls, a family of men in Wyoming. I fell in love with these four brothers: Jake, Pete, Brett and Chad and am happy that they are alive on the page once again. In *Wyoming Winter,* you'll find Chad's and Pete's stories, and in May, you'll be able to enjoy Brett's and Jake's stories in *Summer Skies.*

Readers have asked me what makes these men so wonderful, and I've concluded that the Randalls are special because they know what is important in life: their women, their babies. And when my editor requested I return to the Randalls in the Harlequin American Romance line, I jumped at the chance to tell the stories of the next generation. You see, Jake was so successful at his matchmaking, there have been a *lot* of babies. Which Jake thinks means he needs to do some more matchmaking.

Wyoming Winter also contains an original prologue, never before published, that I wrote for the series.

So get cozy and get set to enjoy the original Randalls all over again.

Happy reading,

Judy Christenberry

THE RANDALLS

WYOMING WINTER

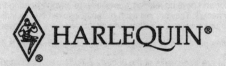

HARLEQUIN®

TORONTO • NEW YORK • LONDON
AMSTERDAM • PARIS • SYDNEY • HAMBURG
STOCKHOLM • ATHENS • TOKYO • MILAN • MADRID
PRAGUE • WARSAW • BUDAPEST • AUCKLAND

ISBN 0-373-83526-4

THE RANDALLS: WYOMING WINTER

JUDY CHRISTENBERRY,

bestselling author for Harlequin American Romance and Silhouette Romance, has been writing romances for over fifteen years because she loves happy endings as much as her readers do. A former high school French teacher, Judy now devotes herself to writing full-time. Her spare time is spent reading, watching her favorite sports teams and keeping track of her two adult daughters. A native Texan, Judy now resides in Arizona.

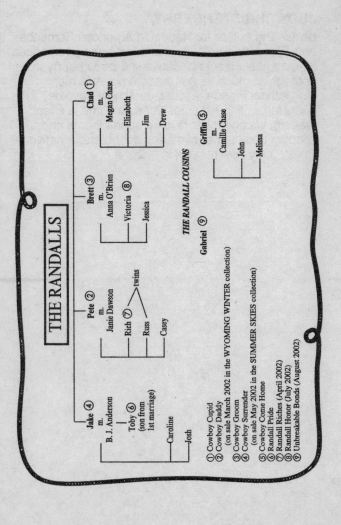

THE RANDALLS

Jake ④
m.
B. J. Anderson
Toby ⑥
(son from
1st marriage)
├─ Caroline
└─ Josh

Pete ②
m.
Janie Dawson
├─ Rich ⑦ ┐ twins
├─ Russ ┘
└─ Casey

Brett ③
m.
Anna O'Brien
├─ Victoria ⑧
└─ Jessica

Chad ①
m.
Megan Chase
├─ Elizabeth
├─ Jim
└─ Drew

THE RANDALL COUSINS

Gabriel ⑨

Griffin ⑤
m.
Camille Chase
├─ John
└─ Melissa

① Cowboy Cupid
② Cowboy Daddy
   (on sale March 2002 in the WYOMING WINTER collection)
③ Cowboy Groom
④ Cowboy Surrender
   (on sale May 2002 in the SUMMER SKIES collection)
⑤ Cowboy Come Home
⑥ Randall Pride
⑦ Randall Riches (April 2002)
⑧ Randall Honor (July 2002)
⑨ Unbreakable Bonds (August 2002)

COWBOY CUPID

Prologue

"Would you like to come visit my ranch?"

"All the way in Wyoming?" the blonde cooed, batting her lashes at him.

Dumb question, but his brother Pete liked pretty blondes. She was certainly pretty. "Yeah. In Wyoming."

"Well, this is so sudden. I mean, we just met," she said, peeping at him from under her heavy lashes.

Realization struck Jake Randall like a punch right to the chin, almost taking him out for the count. After blinking several times, he said, "Uh, Carol, I'm not interested—I mean, I wanted you to come meet my brother."

"Well, of course. And you should meet my parents," she said, smiling.

His collar seemed to be cutting off all circulation and breathing was growing more difficult. "No, you don't understand. I'm looking for a wife *for my brother*. Not me."

She glared at him. Then, without warning, she slugged him.

Man, she sure packed a wallop for such a little woman, Jake Randall decided, rubbing his jaw, as he watched her stomp from the room.

THIS TIME HE'D TRY the direct approach.

He sure didn't want anyone thinking *he* wanted a wife. After all, he'd already tried marriage...with disastrous results. In fact, he blamed his divorce as part of the reason his brothers hadn't married.

But he was head of the family now, since his father's death

last year. He and his three brothers lived on the Randall ranch in Wyoming, no females around. After his father's death, however, Jake had become concerned that there were no heirs, no next generation.

So he was going to change things. He'd come to Denver to find wives. Or at least one. Pete, the next eldest brother, was thirty-one. Time to be married. He'd been dating a local girl, one of only a few in town, but they'd recently broken up.

"Howdy, ma'am," Jake said, tipping his hat to a buxom young lady.

"Hi, cowboy. What's your name?"

"Jake. But I'm looking for a wife for my brother." That was better. A clear statement of his objective. No one would think he wanted a wife.

She did a double take, then her eyes narrowed. "What's wrong with him?"

"Nothing!"

"Then why can't he find his own wife?"

"'Cause he doesn't know he needs one."

"Has he got any money?"

Jake stared at her. "I beg your pardon?"

"I just wanted to know what he's got to offer."

She was pretty. But she had a greedy heart. That wasn't the kind of wife he wanted for Pete, or any of his brothers.

This matchmaking was harder than he'd thought.

"HOW MAY WE HELP YOU?" the turban-wearing woman asked after Jake sat down on her Victorian sofa.

"We?" he asked cautiously, looking around the room.

"Just an expression of speech, dear boy. Though I frequently feel I am guided by the spirits." She let her fingers flutter in the air, as if signaling someone.

Jake shivered, feeling as if a ghost had run fingers up his spine. He wondered if contacting Love Connections had been such a good idea, after all.

"I want to find a wife for my brother."

"Wonderful. What kind of wife do you want?"

"He wants, uh, would want, a nice girl."

"Naturally. Do children matter?"

"Of course! I want someone for him who can have children." That was important. An heir to carry on the Randall tradition.

"No, no, dear boy, I meant must she be childless now?"

He shrugged. "Doesn't matter, I guess."

"Excellent. Do you have a picture of your brother?"

Jake frowned. "Why?"

"Well, naturally my ladies wouldn't marry without seeing a picture."

"That's all they require, a picture?"

"They'd need a financial statement, of course."

His stomach was beginning to roll. "And they'd agree to marry him, just like that?"

"Of course. I'm a marriage broker. I deliver a bride."

"What happened to love? That's in your name, isn't it?"

"Dear boy, if you are looking for romance, not marriage, then you've come to the wrong place."

Obviously.

WHAT WAS THE MATTER with him? Jake questioned as he left the building. He should go right back to Love Connections and have that old witch find him a woman. Then he could take her back to Wyoming and present her to Pete as his future wife.

Except that Pete would slug him harder than that little blonde.

No, he had to sneak up on Pete. Let the woman persuade him. How was he going to do that if he couldn't get the lady to Wyoming?

He walked down the Denver sidewalk, pulling his sheepskin jacket against him to keep out the sharp winter wind. Somehow, he had to find a reason to bring a woman to the ranch.

His mind racing, he scarcely noticed the stores he passed until something he'd seen a couple of windows back had him turning around. He moved to the display that had snagged his attention.

Rolls of fabric stood in one corner. A sofa, with several swatches displayed on it, filled most of the window. There were several decorative lamps, and a display board with the services of the interior design firm spelled out.

An interior designer. Woman's work.

He could hire an interior designer to come look at the house. It needed work. Hell, it needed a complete makeover. Chloe, his ex-wife, hadn't been interested, and not a stick of furniture had been changed since his mother's time, twenty years ago.

He spun around and entered the design store. Only to be greeted by a man.

"Uh, I'm looking for an interior designer."

"Wonderful. How may I help you?"

Jake eyed this person with misgiving. "I need to see an interior designer," he repeated.

"Of course. I'll be glad to help you."

"Look, I want to see *her*."

"Her? *I* am the designer. Maurice Wells, at your service."

All Jake could do was growl in frustration before he charged out of the store. A man! He didn't need a man. He needed a woman. For Pete. Surely there were some *female* interior designers in Denver. He hurried back to his hotel to do a little research.

Because he wasn't going home without at least one female to tempt Pete into marriage. Then he'd start working on Brett and Chad.

Chapter One

Chad Randall took another sip of coffee, watching his brother Jake pace the kitchen floor.

"What's up, Jake?" he finally asked.

His brother's head jerked around as if Chad had roped him. "What?"

"What's got you so stirred up? You've been walking the floor the last ten minutes. Has the bottom fallen out of the beef market?"

"No. Where are your brothers?"

"They went to the barn. Said they'd be back in a little while." It wasn't like Jake to be so antsy.

Jake checked his watch and walked to the window over the sink.

"It's Sunday afternoon, Jake. Our one time to relax. Even if there's snow on the ground, the sun's shining. Everything's doing fine." When his brother didn't answer, Chad prodded, "Right?"

"Uh, yeah, right."

"Good thing you're not trying to sell me anything," Chad drawled.

Again Jake whirled around. "What do you mean?"

"You're not very convincing. Come clean."

Jake stared at Chad, reminding him of times in the past when he'd incurred Jake's censure. He frantically searched his memory to see if he was in trouble, but he could remember nothing that would upset Jake. At least not much.

"Okay, here's the deal," Jake said at last with a rush of breath. "We're going to have company."

"So?"

"Female company."

Jake's blunt words stunned Chad. "Female company?" he echoed. "You been seeing someone, Jake?"

"No!" he roared. "No, of course not, you idiot!"

"Well, hell, Jake, what was I to think? What female company are you talking about?" The Randalls weren't women haters, by any means. In fact, Chad, the youngest of the Randall boys, loved women—*all* women. But after Jake's divorce, none of them had gotten serious about women.

"Do you remember me going to Denver?"

"'Course I do. That conference in pasture management."

"Well, I also hired some decorators."

Chad looked around him. He didn't see anything wrong with their home. "Why?"

"The place needs fixing up."

"Okay. But why from Denver?" There was something going on here, Chad was sure, but he couldn't figure out what.

"Why not? We want the best."

"Hell, Jake, it'll cost you twice as much as a decorator from Casper or Cheyenne. This lady might even expect to stay overnight."

"*These* ladies," Jake muttered.

Chad slapped his cup down on the table. "Two? You've got two ladies coming?"

"Three."

His eyes widening in surprise, Chad leaned back against the chair and stared at his brother. "Three?" he repeated faintly.

"Yeah. We had to have a choice." Jake paused, frowning. Before Chad could question his strange statement, he added, "A choice of decor, I mean. Each decorator will draw up some plans, and we'll choose the one we like best."

"Okay. Have you told Red?" The old cowboy who took care of them would be the one most affected by the changes.

"Just that we were having visitors."

"So what's the plan? We show them around this afternoon, then they go back to Denver and draw up their plans?"

"Uh, not exactly."

Again that feeling that something was going on that he didn't yet understand filled Chad. "What do you mean?"

"They'll have to stay a little longer."

"Tomorrow? They'll go back tomorrow."

Jake shook his head.

"How long are we going to have to have these women here, Jake? And what in hell are we going to do with them? We're not used to having women around."

"A week. They have to stay a week."

"A week? Three women here for a week?" Chad demanded, rising to his feet. "We can't—" He broke off as a thought occurred to him. "What do they look like? You got designs on any of these women?"

He did a double take when Jake didn't offer him an immediate no. He'd been teasing, sure Jake would reject such an idea. The fact that he didn't left Chad uneasy. Was Jake back in the marriage market?

MEGAN CHASE'S GAZE MET the lady's next to her.

"Bit remote, isn't it?" Adele Paxton observed, one eyebrow rising.

She nodded. "Were you given much information about the job?"

Adele started to answer, but the young woman sitting across from them in the limo interrupted. "It's a complete redo for a wealthy rancher. We're competing against each other, you know." Her self-satisfied smirk made Megan think Rita Larson was confident she would win.

"Yes, I know, but did you get any more details?" she asked.

"No, but even if I had, I wouldn't tell you," Rita replied. "After all, why help my competition?"

"I wasn't told any more," Adele added. Her gray hair was cut short and stylishly coiffed. "Though I understand Mr. Randall requested we all be single. My boss thought it was strange, but Mr. Randall explained that he didn't want any jealous husbands upset because everyone on the ranch is a man."

Megan had also thought that request was a little bizarre, but her employer had assured her everything was on the up-and-up. She'd been with the interior-design firm since her graduation a little over three years ago, but this was her first solo project.

"You must have a lot of experience," she murmured to Adele. The woman appeared to be around fifty, though she'd aged well.

"Yes, I suppose so."

"It's the creative spark that's important, not experience," Rita snapped, frowning at both of them. Then she looked directly at Megan. "Of course, you, poor dear, probably don't have either."

Megan raised her eyebrows and smiled slightly. If Rita Larson thought she could intimidate her competition, she had another thought coming. "Really? You've seen my work, Rita? I've seen yours."

Though she had carefully said nothing offensive, Megan wasn't surprised when Rita got upset. Sputtering, she tried to protest.

"Look," Adele said in a warning voice, "if we're going to be here a week, we'd best put aside any petty behavior and cooperate."

Megan appreciated Adele's words. She had let her temper get the better of her. Still, she had no intention of allowing Rita Larson—or anyone—to verbally assault her. Megan was nothing if not assertive. Over the years, she'd learned to look out for herself. She had to: her mother had married five times. Good for Lila, as each husband got progressively wealthier.

While Megan had enjoyed helping her mother with the redecorating—with each marriage, a total redo was imperative, according to Lila—she'd hated dealing with the heartache of each divorce. She learned the only reliable person in her life was herself—and she'd promised herself she'd never marry and allow anyone to do such damage to her heart.

"How much farther?" Rita demanded of the driver.

"According to the map, the turnoff should be soon." He kept his eyes on the road, scarcely paying them any attention.

That behavior suited Megan, but Rita seemed peeved by it. "Can't you tell us something about the area?" she asked.

"No, ma'am. I just moved to Casper last month."

"It doesn't matter," she snapped back. "I've done my research." She turned a triumphant look on the others, as if it wouldn't have occurred to them to check out some facts about Wyoming.

Megan tried to hide her grin. She wasn't going to purposefully irritate Rita Larson if she could help it, but the woman certainly did offer herself as a prime target.

The limo slowed down and turned off the main road. All three women leaned forward to catch the first sight of the ranch house they were going to be working on. All they saw was pastureland with mountains in the background.

"Where's the house?" Rita demanded of the driver.

"I don't know, ma'am. We'll just follow this road and see if we find it."

Megan exchanged a smile with Adele. The driver's words were polite, but there was a note of impatience in them.

"I hope we get to ride horses. I've never been on a ranch," Rita told them.

Adele only raised an eyebrow in response, and Megan said nothing. Her mother's second husband had had a ranch in Colorado. That's why Megan had chosen Denver after college. She'd fallen in love with the area.

She wouldn't mind doing some riding while she was here, but she doubted there would be time. Redoing an entire house would take a lot of planning.

"There's the house," Adele said quietly.

"It's large," Megan murmured, training her eyes on the small speck on the horizon.

"Look, there are some other buildings, too." Rita pointed, bringing another grin to Megan's face.

"There usually are on a ranch. Bunkhouse, barns, storage sheds."

"How do you know so much about it?" Rita demanded, frowning at Megan.

Unable to resist, Megan smiled and said, "Research."

WHEN CHAD HEARD FOOTSTEPS on the back porch, he straightened in his chair. He couldn't wait to see how Jake informed his brothers of their guests' arrival.

"Hey, Jake," Brett said as they entered the kitchen. "Did

you put the bill for the feed on my desk? I didn't find it, and the delivery is here.''

"Bill hasn't come yet."

Pete ignored everyone and headed for the coffeepot. Since he'd broken up with Janie, a neighbor, he seldom spoke to anyone. Chad knew his brothers, as well as himself, were worried about Pete, but the second brother shrugged off any attempt to cheer him up.

Maybe that's why Jake had decided to have the house redone, Chad thought. To take Pete's mind off Janie. Chad didn't think silk pillows and fancy lamps would do it, but you never knew.

"What are you grinning about?" Pete growled as he sat down beside him.

"Uh, nothing. 'Cept maybe your reaction to Jake's news." A quick look at Jake had Chad wishing he'd kept his mouth shut.

"What news?" Pete demanded, looking at Jake.

Jake gave a succinct account of his plan.

Red entered the kitchen, vacuum cleaner in hand, just in time to hear the news. "Hey, Jake, does that mean the kitchen will be redone?"

Jake pulled his gaze from his brothers'. "I guess, Red, if there's anything you want changed."

"Hellfire, boy! Of course there's things I want done. Some modern equipment wouldn't hurt. A new floor that's easy to clean. An up-to-date dishwasher would be a miracle."

The brothers all stared at the man who had essentially been their mother since Chad was born.

"Why didn't you say anything before?" Brett asked.

"I didn't want to cause no trouble. And I don't know what I want 'cause I'm never in a store. 'Ceptin' the grocery store to buy more supplies for you human vacuum cleaners."

Jake patted him on the shoulder. "You can have whatever you want, Red. You deserve it. When the ladies get here, we'll tell 'em to work with you." After Red happily left to put away his cleaning equipment, Jake turned back to his brothers.

"I expect you all to be on your best behavior. And Pete, since you're second-in-command, I thought maybe you'd show the ladies around. Explain the setup."

"Brett or Chad can do that," Pete growled, not looking up from his coffee.

"I think you'd be the better man for the job," Jake insisted. "Those two can't be trusted around a bunch of pretty women."

Pete frowned even more. "I'm not interested in any ladies."

"Exactly. So you'll be the perfect host," Jake agreed, a gleam in his eye that reminded Chad of his earlier suspicions.

"Don't worry, brother," Brett said, slapping Pete on the shoulder. "If they're good-looking, you won't be alone."

Jake stepped closer to the table. "You and Chad are to take care of business and leave the women to Pete."

Brett started to protest, but Chad interrupted him. "They're probably all married, Brett."

"Nope." Jake's unequivocal response had everyone staring at him.

"How do you know?" Chad asked.

"Because I made that a requirement," Jake said. "Since we're all men here, I didn't want any complaints from a lot of husbands."

Chad looked at his three brothers. He could understand what Jake was saying. They were an impressive quartet, even if he had to say so himself.

Even more than his good looks, Jake had a reputation for honesty and strength throughout the state. Chloe may have considered him poor husband material, complaining that he worked too much and led a boring life, but Chad figured if Jake so much as hinted that he wanted to remarry, there'd be a line forming all the way to the state border.

"I hear a car," Jake suddenly said. "Come on. I want all of you out front to greet our guests."

Force of habit had his brothers following Jake. Chad was certainly curious to see the women who would invade the all-male environment on the Randall ranch.

And he couldn't wait to see which woman was going to be the first in line to try to rope and hog-tie Jake. Was their male bastion about to change again? Chad only hoped Jake made a better choice this time.

The limo came to a stop, and Jake moved down the steps to open the door to the long vehicle, eager expectation filling his face. He looked like a lottery player, his ticket clutched in his hand, waiting for the right numbers to be called.

One long, silk-stockinged leg came through the open door, and Chad took a deep breath. Maybe Jake had hit pay dirt after all.

Chapter Two

Megan was the first out of the limo. She didn't see the reception committee until she'd moved aside for the other two women to emerge. Then her gaze collided with four pairs of brown eyes.

"Oh, my," she murmured, stunned by the sight of four large, handsome men, casually dressed in tight jeans, boots and flannel shirts, staring at her. They were an impressive array of testosterone.

"Well, well, well," Rita crooned as she joined Megan. "I think I *love* Wyoming."

"Glad to hear it," one of the cowboys said, moving forward. "I'm Jake Randall. Welcome." He extended a large hand first to Rita and then Megan.

When Adele emerged from the limo, Megan noticed a frown appear on the man's handsome features. But it quickly disappeared as he welcomed the older woman, too.

"Let me introduce my brothers." Each of the men tipped his hat to the ladies as Jake presented him, much like the cowboys in movies, Megan thought with a smile. In fact, any of the four men would make a good living in Hollywood, she surmised, whether they could act or not. Women would pay money just to look at them.

"Come on in out of the cold," Jake invited.

Megan noted that the four men wore no coats, while she and the other two city ladies were bundled in overcoats. It was a sunshiny January day, but the high hovered somewhere around freezing.

The limo driver was unloading their bags, and two of the Randall brothers stayed behind to collect them. Jake and the fourth brother escorted them into the house.

When one of them touched Megan on the shoulder, she turned to discover him smiling, his brown eyes warm as he said, "Hey, pretty lady, can I take your coat?"

"Yes, thank you." In spite of the way her heart leapt at his sexy tones, she kept her voice as cool and crisp as the mountain air. Just because a good-looking cowboy paid her some attention, she wasn't about to lose her head. A flirtation wasn't on her list of things to do.

Rita, on the other hand, cozied up to the man, leaning toward him. "Which one are you? You're all so gorgeous I forgot to pay attention to the names."

"I'm Chad, ma'am," he said with a grin, helping her out of her coat. "And I think the word *gorgeous* might be better used for you ladies. We haven't had such attractive visitors in a long time." His gaze slid to Megan's, as if checking her reaction to his flattery, but she turned away.

Megan discovered Adele staring at their surroundings, and she was reminded of their reason for being there. It didn't take long to realize their work was cut out for them. The entry hall was wide, well proportioned, but it had a neglected air to it. The delicate table along one wall seemed out of place, uncared for.

Jake gestured for them to come into the first room on the right, and Megan couldn't hold back a gasp when she entered. The huge room, clearly the living room, had picture-frame windows along the front of the house. The other end was dominated by a huge stone fireplace. In between were odds and ends of furniture worn out by, she suspected, the size of the four men.

A decorator's dream.

She and Adele exchanged excited smiles.

"We thought you might like a cup of coffee to warm you up before going to your rooms," Jake explained as he invited them to sit down.

An older man, with the stamp of cowboy on him in spite of his gray hair, entered the room carrying a large tray. He was followed by the other two brothers.

"I'd like you to meet Red. He takes care of us," Jake said, looping an arm across the smaller man's shoulders. "And he wants you to fix up the kitchen, as well as the rest of the house."

Adele and Megan nodded, smiling at Red. Rita, who was momentarily distracted from Chad, said, "Oh, I know the perfect thing. Tile imported from Italy with hand-painted flowers on them. It's the latest rage. You'll adore it!"

Megan and Adele looked at each other but remained silent. Rita hadn't done enough research if she thought these men would be swayed by the latest rage. They reminded Megan of her first stepfather. A practical man, he opted for what worked, not what other people thought would be best.

Red stared at Rita, a puzzled frown on his face. "Why would we want anything from Italy?"

For once Rita had nothing to say.

"There are a lot of other choices," Adele assured Red, smiling.

"Good. Here. Try my coffee cake. It's a special recipe." Red handed Adele a plate with a slice of cake on it, then offered one to Megan and Rita. It only took one bite for Megan to know they were in good hands for the week. She looked up to find Chad watching her, and she corrected her thought. They were in good hands as far as food went. Imagining Chad's hands anywhere near her sent chills all over her body.

"This is delicious, Red," she hurriedly said.

"Glad you like it," the cook said, beaming as he passed around cups of coffee.

Chad slapped the man on the shoulders. "Red, here, is a lot better cook than he ever was a cowboy." The men laughed, as if Chad's teasing was an old joke.

"Mr. Randall," Adele began, when Jake interrupted her.

"Make it 'Jake.' All of us answer to 'Mr. Randall.' It gets too confusing."

"Of course. Jake, how extensive are you wanting the plan we each present? Just a few rooms? The entire house? We'd like some guidelines."

Jake waved one hand to the room around him. "As extensive as you want to make it. The place hasn't had much done to it since our mother died more than twenty years ago. We're not

big on socializing, so it hasn't really been a problem, but—but
I think it's time we bring things up-to-date.''

One of the other brothers stood abruptly, nodded to the ladies
and muttered, ''I need to get some work done,'' then left the
room before anyone could say anything.

Jake frowned, and the other two looked uneasy. Chad cleared
his throat. ''Don't pay any attention to Pete's bad manners.
He's got woman troubles.''

''Don't pay any attention to Chad, either,'' Jake said, glaring
at his brother. ''As usual, he talks too much. Pete's starting a
new business and has a lot on his mind.''

Megan wondered what was going on between the brothers.
Somehow Chad had displeased Jake.

''I'm servin' lunch in an hour. Best you take these ladies to
their rooms,'' Red said, rounding up the dishes from their
snack.

''Right,'' Jake agreed. ''Brett, you and Chad take the ladies
upstairs. If there's anything you need,'' Jake added, turning to
them, ''just let me know.''

As they stood, murmuring polite responses, Chad appeared
at Megan's side. ''Right this way, Megan.''

She was almost overcome with the urge to tell him her name
was Miss Chase, but to deny him the familiarity Jake had offered them would be unspeakably rude. Besides, she was never
standoffish. So why did she feel that way?

He took her arm, and Megan had the answer. Somehow this
man threatened her serenity. A shiver engulfed her from his
innocent touch. ''Thank you,'' she said, and swiftly moved
ahead of him.

Their luggage was waiting in the hall.

''If you'll each identify what's yours, we'll bring it to your
rooms,'' Brett explained.

When Megan pointed out the two black pieces of luggage
that belonged to her, Chad immediately picked them up.

''I can carry the smaller one,'' she insisted, reaching for the
handle.

''Nope,'' Chad returned, one dark eyebrow slipping up. ''I
wouldn't dream of letting you do that. Here in Wyoming, we
take care of our women.''

Megan took a step back from him, holding back the urge to

assure him she wasn't "his" woman. "But then you'll have to make two trips."

"We'll carry up yours and Adele's and come back for Rita's, since she brought more. It won't take us but a minute," Brett said. He was as handsome as his brother, but somehow Megan felt more at ease with Brett.

"Two of you will have to share a bath. The other room has its own. Does it matter to any of you?" Brett asked as he led the way up the stairs.

"I'll take the private bath," Rita quickly said, smirking at Adele and Megan.

When they reached the top of the stairs, Brett showed Rita to her room. "We'll bring your bags up in a minute."

The other two rooms were toward the front of the house. Chad led Megan to the room at the end of the hall, overlooking the porch.

Megan looked longingly at Brett and Adele, who were entering the room next door. She didn't want to be alone with Chad. Stepping into her room, she turned around and said, "Thank you. I can manage now."

Chad didn't seem ready to go, however. He carried the two bags across the room and set them down on a cedar chest. "Do you like the room?"

"It's very nice." She looked away from his brown eyes, hoping he'd leave while she could maintain her standoffish attitude. He was much too potent a package of male virility.

"You from Denver?"

"I live there now."

"But you weren't born there?"

"No." She walked to the front window, hoping he'd get the idea that she didn't want to talk.

"How long have you been a decorator?"

"Three years."

"Any boyfriends?"

Shocked by his sudden change of subject, she spun around to stare at him. "I beg your pardon?"

"Just checking to see if you were paying attention. You seemed a little distracted," he said with a self-assured smile. "But if you want to answer the question, I don't mind."

"No, thank you," she said, keeping her voice neutral.

"You don't like to give out too much information about yourself, do you?" He wandered across the room toward her.

What did she say now? No? That would be the truth. She cleared her throat. "I didn't realize you'd be interested."

He leaned against the windowsill and grinned at her. "Oh, yeah, I'm interested. We don't get such pretty visitors very often."

Then there must not be any women left in Wyoming. She couldn't imagine any other reason the Randall men would be suffering from loneliness.

When she said nothing, he moved a little closer. "Anything I can do to make your stay more...enjoyable, just let me know."

"Thank you, but I'll be busy working."

"All work and no play is bad." He reached out to finger the collar of her coat. "Besides, you might get lonesome."

She jerked away as his finger touched her cheek. She didn't know if she was misreading his offer or not, but she wanted to put an end to any ideas he seemed to have.

"Thank you for bringing up my bags, Mr. Randall. I'll try not to be a bother while I'm here."

Her deliberate formality had its effect. He straightened from his slouched position and stared at her, his gaze cool. "Oh, you'll be a bother, Miss Chase," he drawled, "one way or another. But I reckon we'll survive it." With a nod of his head, he left the room, and Megan sagged against the wall.

She only hoped *she* did.

CHAD WENT BACK DOWN the stairs for the other bags, a puzzled frown on his face. Megan Chase hadn't responded to his flirting at all. In fact, she'd seemed downright antagonistic. What had he done?

Not that it mattered, he hurriedly assured himself. After all, she wasn't the only beautiful woman in Wyoming. But there'd been something about her that drew his interest. Other than her looks, of course.

Brett was already picking up two of Rita's bags. "Where have you been? Chatting up the ladies?"

"Just being friendly. Left the two heaviest for me, didn't you?" he asked, noting the size of the bags.

"You're the youngest. We old folks have to be careful."

Since Brett was only three years older than Chad's twenty-six, he ignored his brother's dig.

"Besides, the lovely Rita will appreciate all your muscle. You'll probably be thanking me by the end of the day. She's definitely your type," Brett assured him as he started up the stairs.

Brett was right. Rita looked like the women he partied with occasionally at the bars in Casper. So why was he still thinking about Megan's reaction? There was no question about Rita's willingness to strike up a flirtation.

After escaping Rita's determined friendliness, Chad discovered his brothers all in the kitchen, sitting at the big table while Red prepared the meal.

"Aha! Here's our Romeo," Brett announced when he entered.

Jake sent Chad a sharp look.

"Cut it out, Brett," Chad protested at once. "Rita's on the prowl. I don't think she's too particular about who she catches as long as she catches someone." He pulled out a chair and sat down.

"That's not too gentlemanly a thing to say," Red criticized from the sink.

Chad shrugged. He figured if none of his brothers offered Rita their company, Red would have a good chance of getting lucky.

"So what do you think of them?" Jake asked. Chad noted his gaze went first to Pete.

"I guess they'll do a fine job," Brett answered first. "Though I don't think Red likes the idea of Italian tile."

"What do I need foreign stuff for?" Red demanded.

But Jake seemed to have no interest in a discussion of tile. "I'll expect everyone to clean up good for dinner each evening."

They all groaned.

"Damn," Brett groused, "it'll be like when the evil Chloe lived with us."

Chad noted the stricken look on Jake's face and felt for his brother, but Brett was right. These women were going to disturb their peace.

Jake turned to the one brother who'd remained silent. "Pete? What did you think of the decorators?"

Looking up from the column of figures he was adding, Pete gave his brother a puzzled look. "What?"

"The women. What did you think of them?"

Pete just shrugged his shoulders.

"I thought you liked blondes," Jake insisted. "Rita is pretty."

"If you like that type," Chad added. When his brothers, even Pete, turned to stare at him, he asked, "What?"

"Blondes are your speciality," Brett said, grinning. "You and Pete always go for the blondes. Have you changed your mind?"

Chad started to tell Brett he was leaning more toward light brown hair and hazel eyes, but he stopped himself. His brothers might recognize his description of Megan Chase, and he didn't want them thinking either of the ladies mattered. Not to him. He never let women interfere with his life.

"Variety is always good," he said, shrugging his shoulders like Pete.

"I guess you haven't changed, after all," Brett teased, and they all laughed.

The conversation reminded Chad of something else. "By the way, Rita is already asking about nightlife. I told her I'd ask you if you'd planned something," he added, looking at Jake.

"I hadn't really planned anything. I thought we'd show them the ranch, things like that. You'll help out, won't you, Pete?" Jake asked.

"I don't have time for that, Jake. The vet is coming soon to look at the house we've set aside for him. And I've got—"

"Hey, a good idea, Pete. You need to show the decorators that house. They might have some ideas for fixing it up. Why don't you do that this afternoon?" Jake stood. "Yeah. That's a good plan. I'll explain to the ladies over lunch."

Before Pete, staring at his brother openmouthed, could complain, Jake left the room.

"What's got into him?" Pete demanded, staring at the other

three. "He knows I'm trying to start my new business. You two are sitting around doing nothing, and he picks on me."

Chad was wondering the same thing. Oh, not that he and Brett were doing nothing, but the winter months were their less active period.

A sudden reason occurred to him. "Maybe Jake thinks you need a little cheering up since Janie's—" He stopped right there as Pete sent him a steely look that warned him he might have his nose broken again if he continued.

Pete shoved back his chair. "You can handle the social hour, little brother. That'll teach you to mind your tongue." He stomped out of the room toward the back porch, the opposite direction from Jake.

"Whew! That was close," Brett said. "You ought to know better than to mention Janie's name."

"Damn it, she's an old friend. I went to school with her. Just because Pete and her parted doesn't mean I can't even say her name."

Brett grinned at Chad. "Then I'd up my medical insurance if I were you. Come to think of it, when Jake finds out Pete dumped his guide role on you, you may be in trouble all over again."

"Why is Jake wanting Pete to spend time with the women? I thought he might be interested in one of them himself, but now I'm not so sure."

Brett shrugged, but Red agreed with Chad's earlier theory. "I think you got the right of it, boy. Pete's not been the same lately. I think Jake's tryin' to cheer him up."

"I don't think it's working," Chad said.

"Maybe not, but these ladies are going to do wonders for your social life," Brett teased. "Seems to me, for all your talk, you've been slipping lately. You stayed home last night—on a Saturday night!"

"There were snowstorm warnings," Chad said defensively. He'd been going into town less and less lately, and that fact bothered him. Was he getting old? Losing interest in women? It wasn't a good sign when a book held more excitement than a warm, willing woman.

A mental picture of Megan Chase immediately reassured

him. No, he hadn't given up women. Maybe he was becoming more particular in his old age.

"You boys better go get cleaned up for lunch," Red warned. "I'm ringing the bell in five minutes."

When Chad returned to the kitchen a few minutes later, everyone except Pete was already at the table.

"You're late," Jake declared. Before Chad could round the table and take the seat beside Megan, Jake gestured to the empty place between Brett and Adele. "Come join Adele, Chad. She attended the University of Wyoming, too."

Chad wasn't sure what he would have in common with the lady who had attended his alma mater, since she was old enough to be his mother, but he obeyed Jake. Besides, that chair put him across the table from Megan, where he could see her much better.

He grinned at her. All she did was look away. What had he done? Had he offended her in some way? Rita, on the other hand, made a point of greeting him.

"I was afraid you weren't going to join us for lunch, Chad," she purred.

"I don't miss many meals, ma'am," he assured her, but he kept his gaze on Megan.

For several minutes, everyone was silent as they passed the dishes around. Chad couldn't help noticing the polite strain that filled the air. It was in such contrast to their normally noisy meals. Women complicated life. And that was why he shouldn't be interested in the woman across from him.

But he was.

He looked at Megan again. She acted as if he didn't even exist. He didn't like being ignored. Leaning forward, he asked, "How do you like Red's cooking, Megan?"

Not looking at Chad, Megan turned to Red. "The food is delicious, Red."

The old man grinned with pleasure.

Chad ground his teeth. And tried again. "Ever been on a ranch before?"

"Yes," she replied, no warmth in her voice. And she kept her eyes on her plate.

"I haven't," Rita enthused.

Chad had to endure several minutes of vapid conversation

from the blonde before he could try again. "You're not a city girl, Megan?"

Her hazel eyes brushed over him, sending unexpected chills over him. She pushed a silky strand of hair behind one ear, and the urge to trace the path of her fingers was undeniable.

Jake interrupted his thoughts. "This afternoon you ladies will take a look at a nearby house. A new vet is going to move in, and I wouldn't mind a few suggestions about fixing it up."

Despite the repercussions, Chad was happy he'd traded the job of tour guide with Pete. He'd get to spend more time with Megan. Just the thought of getting her alone in the barn filled him with anticipation—and a feeling he hesitated to name....

He had to get a grip on these fantasies, he admonished. Or else—like Jake with Chloe—he'd find himself in a heap of trouble.

Chapter Three

"Well, that's the nickel tour," Chad announced to the three women. "Anyone want the dollar version through the barns?"

The smell of hay always invoked happy memories of Megan's years on her stepfather's ranch, and in spite of her vow to avoid Chad, she immediately agreed. "Oh, yes, I'd love to see the barns."

"If it won't offend you, Chad," Adele said, "I'll return to the house. I'm not the outdoor type."

Chad grinned. "Of course I don't mind. Not everyone is agreeable to getting manure on their shoes."

Rita had moved to Chad's side, taking his arm again, but she stepped away at his words. "What? You mean there is actually such disgusting stuff in your barns?"

"The barns are where we keep our best animals during cold weather, Rita," Chad explained.

"But doesn't someone clean it up?"

He stiffened as if she'd impugned his honor. "Yes, ma'am, every day."

Rita looked down at her expensive heels and then glared at Megan. Before leaving the house, Megan had changed into wool pants and loafers.

"You'd better come back to the house with me," Adele said. "You're not dressed for a trip to the barn. I'm sure Chad will show it to you later."

After sending another antagonistic look Megan's way, Rita turned to Chad. "Will you give me a personal tour later, Chad?"

"We can probably work it in," he said, but Megan noticed he didn't meet Rita's gaze.

It amused her that Chad, whom she'd already classified as a consummate flirt, had more than met his match in Rita. He was backing away as fast as he could without tripping over his boots.

"Then I'll see you later," Rita said, patting his arm and batting her lashes at him.

Megan was so amused with Rita's antics, it didn't occur to her that she, too, was going to receive a personal tour until Rita and Adele opened the door.

"Wait! I'll go back with you. There's no need for Chad to waste his time showing me the barns now. I'll see them some other time."

Chad grabbed her arm as she headed for the door. "No problem. I don't have anything else I need to do. You two go ahead."

There wasn't anything Megan could say now without sending up a flag saying she didn't want to be alone with Chad Randall. And she wasn't willing to expose her fears to the man. So she just nodded to Adele.

"Yes, go ahead. I'll be back at the house soon."

Chad held her beside him until the door closed behind the other two, as if he were afraid she'd change her mind at the last minute. Then he released her.

"Well, shall we go?" she hurriedly asked, moving toward the door.

"There's no hurry. I'd rather get to know you."

He moved closer, and Megan remembered how he'd touched her cheek in her room earlier. The last thing she needed was to get close to one of the Randall men.

"I'm not very interesting. How many barns do you have?"

"Lady, you don't understand men if you think you wouldn't stand out, even in a crowd." With his words came a sexy smile that sent shivers over her.

He just wouldn't get the message. Turning toward the door, she asked over her shoulder, "Which way?"

A large hand closed around her upper arm. "Now, darlin', don't be in such a hurry. We've got plenty of time."

His touch only confirmed what she'd already discovered.

This man was potent, one who would encourage any woman to lose her head. She pulled from his grasp. "Stop!"

"Stop what?" he asked, a frown replacing his flirtatious grin.

"Stop playing games."

"Games?" he questioned, one eyebrow rising to emphasize his puzzlement. "What do you mean?"

She wished she hadn't decided to be honest. But it was too late now. "I'm talking about your flirting."

His brown eyes narrowed. "You been talking to my brothers?"

"No, I haven't. I don't have to ask anyone." She gestured in the direction Rita had gone. "I've seen you in action. You certainly wouldn't act like this if I were a man."

"I *hope* not," he responded with a grin. "If I flirted with a man, my reputation would be ruined!"

"I didn't mean that, and you know it!" she exclaimed in frustration. "But I'm here as a professional, not as your date."

He took another step closer. "Just because you're here to do a job doesn't mean we can't be friendly. I haven't had any complaints from other 'friends.'"

"I'm sure you haven't, but I'm not interested."

"You already got a man?"

Megan blew out her breath in frustration. "Is that all you think I meant? Must I have a man if I don't fall at your feet? You certainly have a large ego, don't you?"

He moved closer to her, and she backed to the wall. "You think you know all about me in one afternoon?"

She raised her chin. "I think you expect women to play along with you. Look at what you're doing now. You're cornering me, using your strength, your size, against me."

His eyes widened as if surprised by what she'd said. "I'm not— Well, maybe it seems that way. But what if I just wanted to be close to you?"

"Don't you think I should have some say in that decision?"

CHAD HAD NEVER THOUGHT about the woman's point of view. He'd never had to. The women he'd spent time with invited his closeness.

Damn it, she was right! He had pressed her against the wall, without ever touching her. And he knew she didn't want him close to her. He felt like a heel, and he didn't like it. "Come on," he growled as he turned away. "Let's go see the barns."

He wasn't sure she'd come. Opening the door, he stood back and waited. If she hightailed it back to the house, he wouldn't stop her.

"Are you sure you don't mind?" she asked again after he closed the door to the house.

"I said I didn't."

"But that was before I—"

"Look, contrary to your opinion, I've heard the word *no* before. Let's go."

He watched out of the corner of his eye as she tugged her overcoat closer around her. Megan Chase had Rita beat all hollow in the looks department. She wasn't flashy, but there was a sheen, a polish, to her that gave the impression of pure gold.

"How many barns do you have?" she asked again.

Chad noticed she was almost running to keep up with him, and he slowed down. "Four. Actually one of them is an indoor arena."

"An indoor arena? You mean like a rodeo?"

He grinned reluctantly at the enthusiasm in her voice. "Yeah, sort of. You like rodeos?" This Megan, eager and smiling, was more enjoyable than the antagonistic one he'd just faced.

"Yes, though I haven't been to all that many."

"And you aren't worried about the mistreatment of all those animals?" His grin widened as she recognized his mocking of one of Rita's earlier inane statements.

"Shame on you!" she said with a laugh, the first time she'd relaxed in his presence.

He wanted to kiss her. That thought stopped him in his tracks. She'd just pushed him away, told him to get lost and he wanted to kiss her. Real bad.

"What? Did I offend you?" she asked, stopping when she realized he wasn't keeping up with her.

"Nope. I just thought of something. You want to see the

arena first?" He automatically took her arm and then paused again. "Is this all right?"

She looked at him, surprised. "Of course. You're just guiding me in the right direction, aren't you?"

"Yeah, but I'm touching you." *And liking it.*

Her cheeks flushed. "But it's out of courtesy, not—not a come-on."

"Oh. I guess I got confused." And still was. If Megan thought he could touch her and not have a sexual response, she was naive. Right now he was fighting the urge to pull her into his embrace.

He released her arm when they reached the arena. She eagerly entered the building, her gaze darting all around. Her interest seemed to be real.

The main area of the barn consisted of a large corral where the cowboys could practice their skills even when the ground was covered in snow. At the moment, several men were training some cow ponies in the art of cutting out cattle.

Megan crossed her arms over the top rail and propped her foot on the bottom one as naturally as if she'd been raised on a ranch.

"You like horses?" he asked, keeping his voice casual. She seemed reluctant to share anything about herself, but he hoped if she didn't notice his questions, she'd be more forthcoming.

"Yes," she said, but her gaze remained on the horses in the corral.

"Ever owned one?"

"Yeah. Jim gave me a sorrel mare. I named her Baby Doll," she added, grimacing at him as if daring him to criticize her choice.

He was more concerned with the identity of Jim than he was with her choice of names. An unexpected surge of jealousy filled him. To put her at ease, he said, "I named my first one Blackie. Not too imaginative."

She acknowledged his comment with a smile and looked at the work going on in the corral again.

"Who's Jim?"

"My stepfather," she murmured. "Wow! Did you see that move?"

"Yeah." Stepfather. Chad took a deep breath of relief before asking another question, but the cowboys stopped work and rode over to the rail.

After introductions and a little talk, Chad said goodbye and led Megan to the next barn. "We keep the mares ready to foal in here," he explained, then stood back to watch Megan make friends with his horses. She was a natural, he decided, stroking the mares, crooning to them.

"So, do you still have Baby Doll?"

A sad look crossed her face. "No."

"What happened?"

"I moved away," she said in clipped tones, and walked to the next stall. The mare occupying it was a favorite of Chad's.

"Let me introduce you to Maybelle," he said, pretending he hadn't noticed her terseness. "And in the corner is the latest addition to the ranch, her baby." He scratched the animal's forehead while Megan leaned over the half gate to see the foal.

"Oh, it's beautiful. A filly or a colt?"

"A filly. Want to name her?"

She whirled around, a gleam of excitement in her eyes. "Doesn't she have a name already?"

"Nope. She was just born last night."

"But your brothers might not like my choice."

"Doesn't matter. Maybelle belongs to me. What's a good name for the little lady?" He leaned against the gate and watched the delight on her face. It made him feel good all over.

"Oh, I think she should be named— No, you'd hate it."

"How will I know until you tell me?"

"I just thought—she's tiny. Would you consider 'Tinkerbell' too silly?"

He would have agreed to any name to receive that smile from Megan, but he considered 'Tinkerbell' more than appropriate. Matching her smile, he said, "I like it."

"You do? I would've thought you'd want something more...serious." She watched his face for a reaction, as if she didn't believe his earlier agreement.

"Serious? When her mother's name is Maybelle? What did you expect, National Velvet?"

"Did you watch that movie? I saw it when I was small, and I loved it," Megan said, still smiling.

He liked this Megan so much more than the earlier one, who

put him in his place. "Yeah, I saw that movie. In fact, I think we have a copy of it. Dad bought us one of the first VCRs and started building a film library. It comes in handy when we're snowed in with nothing to do."

"Do you get snowed in often?"

"Yeah," he told her with a laugh. "In fact, the weather we've been having the past couple of days is rare. I think you brought Denver's weather with you. Beautiful weather and a beautiful woman. Jake got a real bargain."

The smile immediately disappeared, and she gave him a cold stare before walking toward the door of the barn.

"Megan? What's wrong?"

"I'm ready to go back to the house."

"I can tell. But I don't understand why."

"I told you I'm not interested in flirting."

"Flirting? Flirting includes an honest compliment? Are you telling me you don't know you're beautiful?" He couldn't keep incredulity from his voice. "Or that men haven't told you how beautiful you are?"

"You're exaggerating," she said huffily, standing by the door, waiting for him to join her.

He strolled over to her, determined not to apologize for thinking her beautiful. "Lady, you don't take a compliment well, do you?"

"I guess not. So you should forget about paying me any more."

Gone was the laughing, relaxed young woman who'd named his newest filly and talked about her own horse. Instead, the stiff, formal Megan was beside him again.

He swung open the door and waited for her to go back out into the cold sunshine, then followed her. "I'll try to keep that in mind," he muttered, irritation filling him.

Though the sun was shining, there was almost a foot of snow on the ground. The path had been cleared between the barn and the house, but it was narrow.

Chad slammed the barn door to relieve his frustration, and the noise must have startled Megan because she tripped over the mound of snow next to the cleared path and went sprawling into it.

He grabbed her arm and tugged her back to her feet. "Are you all right?"

Snow was caked on her coat and even in her hair. He began brushing her off.

"D-don't," she protested, shoving his hands away.

"I'm just trying to help," he protested, continuing to remove the snow.

She backed away and again fell, this time on her back. "What are you doing to me?" she yelled at him. "Trying to turn me into a snowman?"

He pulled her to her feet again. "You wouldn't have fallen if you'd stood still. Now you've got snow all over you."

"I can—"

"Hold still!" he roared, his patience at an end. "If I take you into the house like this, Jake will have my hide."

Finally she followed his orders and allowed him to brush her off. When he ran a hand through her hair, he saw uneasiness fill her eyes, but she didn't move—until she suddenly squealed and leapt forward into his arms, knocking him into the snow on the other side of the path and falling on top of him.

Chad lay there stunned until her warm, squirming body on top of him got his attention. He'd better get her off him fast before she felt how attracted he was to her. Without warning, he dumped her sideways in the snow.

"Lady, do you *want* to die of pneumonia?"

"No! Of course not!"

"Then do you mind explaining what happened? First you don't want me to touch you, and then you leap into my arms."

She struggled to a sitting position. "I didn't leap into your arms," she assured him indignantly. "Some snow fell onto my neck and—and it shocked me. I didn't intend to—I'm sorry." She struggled to her feet, again covered with snow. "Aren't you going to get up?"

"I don't know. Are you sure it's safe?" He stared up at her, wishing he could pull her back down against him.

Something in his eyes must've given his thoughts away. She backed toward the house.

"Wait," he called as he got up. "I still can't let you go back to the house covered with snow. I don't want Jake to think I mistreated you."

"It's all right," she said, moving farther away. "I'll explain that I fell."

"That won't satisfy Jake. Come on, Megan. It won't take but a minute." Since she stopped moving, he assumed she accepted his words. He began the process of removing the snow all over again, turning her back to him and brushing her derriere gently. Then her back and, with a warning, her hair.

His fingers tangled in the silky strands, now a little damp, and grazed her warm neck beneath them. Heat surged through him. Spinning her around, he discovered she'd been working on the front of her coat and it was almost clear. Damn. Too bad. He'd been looking forward to covering that territory.

"You have some snow on you, too," she said, surprising him. "Turn around."

Automatically he did as she asked. But as her hands slid over his backside, he realized her touching him wasn't a good idea. Even through his jeans, he felt her fingers. Or maybe he just had a good imagination.

Whirling back around, he had to reach out to grab her arms as his abrupt movement had her losing her balance all over again. "No, you don't! Not again."

She surprised him, bursting into laughter, her hazel eyes sparkling above flushed cheeks.

Adorable.

And irresistible. Almost with a will of their own, his hands pulled her against him and his lips touched the softness of hers.

He didn't intend to deepen the kiss, to plead for her to open her lips to his. He was sure he didn't. But somehow, before he even realized it was happening, her arms were around his neck and her curves were pressed into his flesh.

Just as he decided he'd found heaven, that nothing could be sweeter than Megan's lips, she wrenched her mouth away from his and gave a mighty shove. The next thing he knew, both of them were sitting in the snow. Again.

"You—you—" Megan sputtered, glaring at him. "See? I told you! You're a flirt!"

"You didn't exactly stop me!" he roared back at her, frustration filling him.

"Of course! That's just like a man! Blame me for *your* behavior."

"Hey! That's not what— Wait, Megan!" he suddenly called as she got to her feet and stomped toward the house.

He jumped up and set off in hot pursuit, but she'd gotten a head start. "Wait! Let me dust off the snow."

"I don't care if I look like Frosty the Snowman," she said between clenched teeth, "I wouldn't let you touch me again."

He was only a step behind her as she rushed through the back door. Just close enough to realize their entrance was going to be observed by his brothers.

Megan seemed unaware of their audience until she came to a screeching halt two steps into the room.

Unfortunately Chad wasn't able to put on the brakes quite as soon and bumped into her, his arms automatically coming around her.

She angrily pushed him away just as Jake spoke.

"Hi, Megan. Did you—? What the hell happened to you?"

Chapter Four

"You made a pass at Megan?" Jake demanded, frowning ferociously at Chad, making him want to slink down in the chair.

After his and Megan's abrupt entry to the kitchen, Chad had known he'd have some explaining to do. Jake hadn't bought the falling-down-in-the-snow story Megan had lamely offered. An actress she wasn't.

Jake had ordered Chad to his office.

"Not exactly." He hadn't intended it as a pass. It had just…happened.

"Why don't you tell me what occurred on your little tour? You obviously dumped the other two. They turned up back here over an hour ago."

"I didn't dump them. They decided they didn't want to see the barns. But Megan did. So I gave her the extended tour." He sounded defensive and decided to try another tack. "Look, Jake, I didn't intend any— It just happened!"

"What I want to know is just exactly what 'it' is."

Jake's steely glare reminded Chad of a few other sessions in his big brother's office. Jake had taken on his father's duties frequently, especially where his brothers were concerned.

"I kissed her."

"And then buried her in snow?"

"No! First she fell down and—and then she fell down again. I was trying to brush her off and we both fell and—and I kissed her."

"That's all?"

"Word of honor." Chad breathed a sigh of relief when Jake nodded. His brother's trust was important to him.

"Well, you can't do that anymore."

Wondering if he'd heard right, Chad stared at Jake. "What did you say?"

"You heard me. I don't want you messing around with Megan."

Chad's earlier suspicions resurfaced. Was Jake interested in Megan? "Why?"

"I can't explain right now. But tonight, after dinner, you follow along with my plans. And keep your thoughts on Rita. She's much more your type." With that, Jake strode from the office.

Damn. Chad was getting tired of everyone telling him Rita was his type. He could pick up a woman like Rita any day of the week. But Megan... He abruptly halted his straying thoughts.

Jake didn't ask much of him. And it wasn't as if he had any serious thoughts about Megan. After all, marriage wasn't something he ever contemplated, and Megan would be gone back to Denver before he could do much more than— He'd better stop right there. If he thought about touching her, kissing her...

He sprang up from the chair as if he'd had a shock. Time to occupy his mind with work. Not a certain hazel-eyed beauty who could drive him crazy in no time at all.

AFTER DINNER that evening, when Rita wanted to know what entertainment was available, Chad discovered Jake's plan. Chad and Brett were assigned the task of watching a movie with Rita while Pete and Jake played forty-two, a domino game, with Adele and Megan.

Since Pete didn't looked thrilled with the prospect of dominos, Chad hurriedly offered to switch places.

"That's generous of you, little brother, but I think Pete will enjoy the game." The tone of Jake's voice told Chad he wasn't pleased.

"Sure. Just thought I'd offer." When Rita threaded her arm through his, Chad gave her a jaunty smile, as if she'd just fulfilled his life's dream, but out of the corner of his eye, he watched for Megan's reaction.

Nothing.

"What movie shall we watch?" Rita asked.

"Whatever you want," he replied, and reluctantly led her down the hall.

MEGAN BREATHED a sigh of relief as Chad and Rita left the kitchen. She'd done her best to ignore the irritating man ever since they'd gotten back to the house and made their embarrassing entry.

She'd also tried to put their kiss out of her head. But anytime she got within ten feet of Chad Randall, a tingling surged all through her. And she wanted to throw herself into his arms.

"Ridiculous!" she muttered.

"What did you say?" Pete asked as they walked to the living room.

"I said I love forty-two." And that was the only thing she was going to love. It wasn't just that she was wary of charming, flirtatious men because of her latest stepfather's roving eye. No, Megan had seen it all firsthand—from her very own fiancé.

While he was engaged *to* her, he was also engaged *with* other women—in secret little rendezvouses. Lucky for her they weren't all kept hush-hush and she'd found out just what kind of man he was *before* she walked down the aisle to him.

Her mother hadn't been as lucky, nor had she learned from her mistakes. And Megan had spent her life shuffling from one stepfather to another. But when her mother had married the rancher in Colorado, Megan had become part of a large family for the first time in her life. She'd been in heaven. For four years.

Then her mother had packed their bags and took her away. She'd never been able to recapture that elusive feeling of being part of a family—and now she envied Chad for his loving brothers. But once Megan had gained control of her life, she'd vowed she'd never again offer her heart to anyone. And that included Chad Randall.

"I'm glad you like the game. 'Cause we play to win around here." Pete's wicked chuckle interrupted her thoughts. "The last time I lost to Jake, he had me rubbing down his horse for a week.''

"Then I wouldn't mind losing. I'd love to be around horses again.''

"You like to ride?'' Jake said from behind her.

"I love it. I'd love to try some of the cutting horses I saw in the barn today.''

"That can be arranged if you want to meet me in the barn in the morning,'' Jake said. "Pete and I will put you through your paces.''

"That would be great!'' Anything to keep her mind off another Randall and his wickedly sexy kiss.

An hour later, the hair on the back of her neck stood on end, and she turned around to discover Chad standing in the door of the room watching her.

"Movie over?'' Jake asked.

"Nope. Red told me to ask if you're ready for some chocolate cake.''

Megan heard him move closer, but she refused to look at him again. She couldn't. Slapping her domino down on the table, she looked at Pete instead. The startled expression on his face had her looking at her domino again. "Pete, I'm sorry,'' she said with a groan. She'd out-trumped her own partner.

"No problem,'' Pete responded with a smile, carefully hiding his true reaction.

There was only one more round of play, and they made their bid. Then Jake pushed back his chair. "Maybe it's time for a break. This game can get a little tense.''

Megan felt about two inches high. They were kindly making excuses for her boner play. "Pete might like a change of partners, as well as a piece of cake.''

As the two older Randall brothers protested, Chad spoke up. "Maybe Rita would like to play.''

Adele, who hadn't said anything, leaned forward. "It would be my guess that Rita has never heard of the game, much less want to play it.''

"Good,'' Pete said, slipping an arm around Megan as they all stood. "'Cause I wouldn't want to change partners. We're in the lead.''

Chad glared at both her and Pete, and Megan looked away.

When they finished their dessert and returned to play, Megan was able to relax. Chad had been banished to the movie again. Indeed, Jake had ordered him to return to Rita and Brett.

Before Megan could think about that fact, the game began and she was determined she wouldn't embarrass her partner again. As a testament to her concentration, and maybe a little luck, they ended the game an hour later with her and Pete declared the winners.

"Good job, Megan!" Pete exclaimed. "I think I'll have Jake ride fences this week as payment."

"You're going to get your pound of flesh, aren't you?" Jake said with a wry grin that Megan found charming.

In fact, all the brothers were charming. Warm-hearted, polite, with a generous sense of humor, they were the answer to any woman's prayer. Even more attractive to Megan was the love the four men shared with no embarrassment.

She'd wanted to be part of a big family all her life. In Colorado she'd had that feeling for a short while. She knew that craving for connections lurked deep within her. Another reason to avoid the Randalls. She couldn't trust herself.

"I'll ride fences with you, Jake," Megan offered.

"You really do want to ride, don't you?" Jake said with a laugh. "No need to be so sacrificial, Megan. You can ride in the indoor arena. In winter it's the best bet."

"You've got a deal. If you'll excuse me, I think I'll go up to bed now."

"How about a cup of hot cocoa before you go upstairs?" Pete offered.

"No, thanks." She wanted to be safely in her room before the movie ended.

She started up the stairs, deep in thought. Jake and Pete were wonderful. Why did they not affect her the way Chad did?

She rounded the corner at the top of the stairs and gasped as she bumped into a broad, muscular chest. Chad's arms went around her, and she found herself in a repeat of their snowy encounter.

But this time, when she pushed away from him, her feet didn't go out from under her. "Excuse me," she murmured, and tried to go around him.

"Wait a minute. Are you through playing?"

"Yes."

"How about something to drink? We could go to the kitchen and—"

"No!" She drew a deep breath and tempered her response. "Thank you, but I'm tired." Again she tried to go around him. He shifted his large body to intercept her.

"Listen, Megan, I wanted to tell you that I'm sorry for what happened earlier."

His words were all that was polite. The look in his eyes started her to trembling. The fire she could see there stirred the coals of her attraction to the man...and her memory of his touch. "Thanks," she managed to choke out.

"Normally I wouldn't treat a guest like that."

"Okay." He still didn't move to let her pass.

"It was the close proximity that caused—"

"I see. I should keep my distance, is that it?" She hadn't wanted the embrace, but she resented his explaining it away with "proximity."

"Well, I only meant—"

"You've made your meaning quite clear. I'll warn Adele and Rita to keep their distance, too, unless they want to be mauled." She regretted her choice of words at once, but refused to admit it. Shoving against his arm, this time she succeeded in bypassing the sexiest blockade she'd ever seen.

"Ow!"

Chad stared in shock at the blood oozing from the cut on his hand.

"What happened?" Brett asked, looking over the back of the horse he was saddling.

"I cut myself on a piece of barbed wire some fool left laying about!" Chad shouted, anger at himself filling him. He hadn't been paying attention, or he would've noticed the wire hung over the bench.

Brett came around his horse and took Chad's hand, examining it. "Doesn't look too bad. You'd better go let Red look at it, though."

Chad wasn't about to go back in the house. He didn't want to chance facing Megan. Last night was enough. The upstairs hallway had felt colder than the barn this morning. "It's okay. Where's that first-aid kit we keep in the barns?"

With a dryness that called Chad to order, Brett said, "Where it always is. What's wrong with you this morning?"

"I guess I had my mind on other things." If a man could call Megan Chase a "thing." A major distraction. A teenager would call her a hot babe. That would do.

"Chad? Chad!"

He turned to his brother with a frown. What was he yelling for? "Yeah?"

"Hey, bro, you'd better clear your head before we mount up. You're going to get both of us in trouble if you don't." While he was talking, Brett had fetched the first-aid kit and now began to clean the gash.

Chad cringed with Brett's rough treatment. "Maybe I should've gone to Red after all. Red wouldn't be so rough."

"So why didn't you?"

Brett's brown-eyed gaze, like his own, stared and Chad had to look away. "No need to disturb anyone."

"Uh-huh. Seems to me you might find several angels of mercy just waiting to bandage you."

His brother's remarks were too close to the bone. Chad jerked his hand away. "I can handle it from here."

"Hold still and don't act any dumber than you are." Brett's grin took the sting out of his words, and Chad obeyed. Brett unwrapped a bandage and covered the cut. "That ought to keep it clean for a while at least. We'll take a couple of these with us."

Once they were in the saddle, hats pulled low and coats zipped high, Brett asked another question. "What do you think's going on?"

Chad looked sharply at his brother and then let his gaze roam over the snow-covered range. "What do you mean?"

"You know what I mean. These women. If all Jake wanted was a new paint job and some furniture, he wouldn't bring in three women from Denver. And he sure as hell wouldn't give half his time to entertaining them."

"Maybe he's feeling the isolation this winter. Things have changed since Dad's death."

"Do you think Jake is thinking of remarrying?"

A coldness filled Chad. He'd shied away from thinking about Jake's order to leave Megan alone. It didn't much matter why if Jake asked something from him. But the idea of Jake and Megan…Chad shut down his wayward thoughts.

He cleared his throat. "Uh, I don't know. What do you think?"

Brett shrugged his shoulders. "I think we can eliminate Adele. She's a nice lady, but a bit long in the tooth for any of us. And Rita is too obvious to be believed. That leaves the lovely Megan."

"And?" Chad said harshly, anxious to hear what Brett had to say.

"Well, I think either he's interested in Megan, or he wants Pete to be. After all, you and I were sent to baby-sit Rita."

"Maybe he was just trying to be a good host." Even to Chad, his remark didn't have much merit. He wasn't surprised when Brett chuckled.

"Yeah, right."

They rode on in silence. Chad's thoughts lingered on the attraction he felt for Megan Chase before he considered the other part of the equation. Jake and Pete were family. They'd been surrogate fathers, as well as brothers. He could sacrifice a little pleasure—maybe a lot of pleasure—if either of them was interested in Megan.

Couldn't he?

CHAD FIGURED he had his answer. Jake had invited the three decorators out to a steak dinner in Rawhide, the nearest town. He'd also made it clear, one way or another, that Rita was Chad's responsibility tonight, while Pete would take care of Megan.

That meant it was Pete whom Jake had in mind for Megan. And it looked as if his plan was working. On the way to the restaurant, Pete and Megan kept their heads together, talking so quietly he couldn't hear a word they said. Especially not with Rita chattering away incessantly.

When they reached the restaurant, he managed to maneuver himself next to Megan.

"What were you and Pete talking about?" he asked her. It

was the first time he'd spoken to her since their meeting in the
hallway last night.

She raised one eyebrow. "Why?"

"Just curious. Pete's not much of a talker."

"So he said."

The waitress passed out menus and told them the night's
specials. Megan leaned toward Pete and asked him what he
recommended, and Chad clenched his jaw. She was ignoring
him.

"Chad, sweetie, what should I order?" Rita crooned. "You
know what a small appetite I have."

"Have a salad." He didn't care what she ate as long as it
kept her from bothering him.

Several men stopped by the table to greet the three Randalls,
but Chad wasn't misled by their friendliness. Three new
women, all of them good-looking, even if Adele was older,
stirred a lot of interest in their neck of the woods. He could
tell by Jake's frown that he wasn't too pleased about the circling of the wolves, either.

"People are very friendly here," Megan said after a third
group had left the table.

Pete snorted with smothered laughter. "Yeah, that they are.
But they're not as friendly when it's just us Randalls, you
know."

"Wait until we get to the dancing," Jake added gloomily.
"They'll be all over us."

"How wonderful," Rita enthused, ignoring the Randalls'
unhappiness. "I love to dance."

A little over an hour later, Jake's prediction came true. The
minute the band began warming up, several men drifted over
to their table to extend invitations to dance. Jake told them all
to back off until the Randalls had a few dances with the ladies.

There was a lot of laughter in the room, and even Pete
seemed more relaxed than Chad had seen him in a long time.
Why shouldn't he be? He had Megan beside him. Chad tried
to dismiss his jealous thoughts, but he couldn't keep his gaze
from Megan.

The first dance began, and Chad, after Pete led Megan out
on the dance floor, took Rita's hand.

He scarcely noticed when Rita pressed against him. He was

too busy watching Megan dancing at a discreet distance from Pete. She was a good dancer, with a natural rhythm.

"Chad? Did you hear me?"

"Um, no, Rita. What did you say?"

"I wanted to know how long the band will play. Until midnight?"

"I don't know." He hoped not. It was going to be a long night. At least he knew Rita would have a lot of offers to dance. That would leave him free. He could have at least one dance with Megan. That would be expected of him. To do otherwise would be impolite. He was sure Jake would understand. He'd wait awhile, bide his time. He didn't want to seem too anxious.

Pete and Megan moved away from them, and Chad swung Rita in that direction so abruptly that she protested. "Sorry," he apologized, but he didn't drop his pursuit of the other two.

When the music stopped, he managed to be right next to Pete and Megan. The earlier decision to wait seemed silly when the opportunity presented itself. His rationale couldn't quite disguise the raging need to touch her again. "Shall we change partners?" he suggested casually to his brother.

"Sure," Pete said gallantly, extending his hand to Rita.

Chad gathered Megan into his arms with a hunger that disturbed him. She was just a woman. He didn't *need* her. But she was the perfect size, her head coming just above his chin. He leaned his cheek against her silky hair and inhaled a delicate, flowery scent.

"Nice perfume," he murmured.

She pulled back and looked up at him. "Thank you. It's gardenias."

"And you," he added with a smile.

"And me," she agreed. "Is this place always so crowded?"

"There aren't too many other places to go. You must dance a lot."

"Why?"

"'Cause you're good." He dared pull her a little closer, reveling in the feel of her soft curves against him.

"My mother insisted on dancing lessons. She thought that skill was much more important than something that would provide me with a job."

"And what did your father teach you?" he asked, hardly even realizing what he'd said until she stiffened.

"That happiness doesn't last."

He pulled back and looked down at her. "Your parents are divorced?"

"No. He didn't come back from Vietnam."

"And your mother remarried."

"Yes."

She was as tightly strung as a new barbed-wire fence. "You don't like your stepfather?"

"My newest stepfather, the fourth since my father died, is only ten years older than me. I consider him to be a gigolo. No, I don't like him." Her voice had tightened with each word.

"Sorry. Bad subject, I guess," he whispered, tucking her head to his shoulder.

She didn't let her head rest there. "It doesn't matter."

Something about the tone of her voice now and the way it had sounded earlier, when they'd argued at the foreman's house, made his eyes narrow. "Is your stepfather a flirt?"

"The worst."

He pulled back from her again. "You weren't comparing me to him, were you?"

Watching her gaze, he knew when she figured out his question, and her cheeks flushed. "You were flirting."

"Not like a gigolo," he protested.

"Flirting is flirting."

"Lady, you've got a lot to learn."

"Probably, but you're not going to be the one to teach me." She stiffened in his arms, her body no longer pliant.

"You're thinking Pete will? Listen, Pete's had a hard time. Don't give him any more heartache." She'd upset him with her words, but he hadn't meant to talk about Pete's personal business. He wished he could take the words back.

"What do you mean?"

"Nothing."

They finished the dance in silence, Megan stiff and tense in his arms. He regretted their entire conversation. If he'd paid attention to Jake's plan, he wouldn't have asked her to dance and then—and then he wouldn't have held her against him again.

As soon as the music ended, she pulled away from him and hurried back to the table. Before she could sit down, however, she was surrounded by eager cowboys.

Chad joined his two brothers as the music started again. All three ladies were on the dance floor.

"You okay?" Jake asked.

Chad managed a smile. "Sure. Looks like we won't have to worry about dancing our feet off."

"True," Pete agreed. "And I was worried."

"You didn't want to dance with Megan?" Jake asked, a frown on his face.

"Dancing with Megan was fine. I might not even mind dancing with Adele. It's Rita I'm staying away from."

"Well, she'll be real popular tonight, then. I just hope she doesn't upset anyone bad enough to fight."

"It's too nice a night to do any fighting," Pete assured his brother, leaning back in his chair and watching the dancers.

Chad watched them, too, wondering if he should ask Megan to dance again. Actually he knew he shouldn't. But he wanted to. When the music ended, he rose to meet her as she left the floor.

"Dance with me," he whispered in her ear, his arms going around her.

Before she could protest, he looked over her shoulder, and what he saw made him change his mind. "No. Dance with Pete."

Chapter Five

Megan was primed to protest Chad's sexy invitation—no, command—and his embrace, in spite of her racing heart. Before she could do so, however, the flirtatious cowboy had figuratively dumped her in his brother's lap.

She stood gaping at him, unable to come up with a single word. Every time he got near her, she couldn't think.

"Dance with Pete!" Chad hissed under his breath, and sidestepped her.

Somehow the intensity in his order, a sense of life or death that couldn't possibly have anything to do with a simple dance, impelled her forward.

"Pete, will you dance with me again? All these strangers…" She let her voice trail off, sounding overwhelmed, appealing to his gentlemanly side.

"You bet, Megan," Pete agreed, though he looked puzzled.

Chad touched her shoulder briefly, as if in approval, and walked away. She released an exasperated sigh even as Pete led her to the dance floor. Chad Randall was enough to drive a woman crazy.

She didn't want him to flirt with her, but he did anyway. Sometimes. And just when he was pressing her, ordering her to dance with him in a sexy whisper, enveloping her in his embrace, suddenly he rejected her.

As she went into Pete's arms, she looked over his shoulder to see Chad talking to a beautiful young woman. Dark like the Randalls, the lady was tall and fit, an outdoors woman with the stamp of Wyoming on her. And unhappy.

Megan was filled with unexpected jealousy. What was wrong with her? She'd rejected Chad every time. But she didn't want to, she finally admitted. She wanted to lose herself in his strong arms, feel his big body pressed against hers…all night long.

She was so intent on her thoughts that she missed Pete's lead and zigged when he zagged.

"Sorry," she said breathlessly, hoping he wouldn't notice her distraction.

"Probably my fault. I'm no Prince Charming," Pete said with a chuckle.

She leaned back to look at his strong, handsome face. "Don't be ridiculous, Pete Randall. All four of you would qualify as a prince in any woman's book."

His cheeks actually flushed, and he gave her a sheepish look. "Aw, come on, Megan. You know I'm not a ladies' man. That's all I meant."

Smiling, she only said, "You'll do." And he would. But not for her. For whatever reason, the man across the room, chatting up a local lady, was the only one who pushed all her buttons, including jealousy.

Chad had been joined by Jake, the two of them standing side by side, facing the young lady. Megan's eyebrows rose at the show of strength. Poor lady. If she'd upset one Randall, Megan suspected she'd have to fight all four of them. And that would be a formidable task.

While she watched, the woman pushed past the two brothers, and Megan noticed for the first time that she was accompanied by another man. Who was she? Ex-girlfriend of Chad's?

Pete swung Megan around, and she couldn't watch the unfolding events. "Pete, has Chad recently broken up with his girlfriend?"

This time Pete leaned back to look at her. "Chad? He hasn't been dating anyone in particular lately. He's kind of the love-'em-and-leave-'em type. Why?"

She should've known. "He seemed upset when a young lady entered the restaurant."

Pete lifted his head to scan the room. Megan knew the moment he found his brothers and the unknown woman. He came to an abrupt halt and the hand holding hers turned into a vise.

"Pete? Pete, are you all right?" Megan grew more concerned as she realized his cheeks actually paled.

He began dancing again, but without his fluid cowboy grace. It was as if he'd received a blow. Megan turned her head to see that the unknown lady had sat down at a table, joined by her escort, and the two Randall men were standing beside the table, still talking to her.

"Who is she?"

Pete, his teeth clenched, muttered, "Janie Dawson."

"Is she from around here?"

He nodded, his steely gaze never leaving the young woman.

Whatever she'd done, she'd upset the entire Randall clan. "Is she an old flame of Chad's?" she asked again, acid eating at her stomach.

"No!" With his sharp response, Pete swung her around so his back was to the young woman.

Finally the light dawned. It was Pete who had recently had his heart broken, according to Chad. Janie Dawson must be the culprit. "I'm sorry, Pete," she whispered. She truly felt sorry for him. She also felt dismayed—at the relief that filled her when she discovered the beautiful brunette wasn't Chad's old flame. How could she be so selfish to feel joy while Pete suffered?

"Nothing to be sorry for," he assured her in icy tones that made it all too apparent there was.

The music ended, and Pete led her back to the table, his gaze never straying to the other group. Before she could even sit down, another cowboy asked her to dance. Her declining response was broken off by a sudden scuffle across the room. It was loud but exceedingly brief. By the time she looked, the young lady's escort was on the floor, rubbing his chin. And Chad stood over him, glowering.

Even as she watched, Jake stopped Chad from continuing his brawl. Pete stood, and she quickly grabbed his arm. "Pete, stay here. Jake will take care of it." He didn't act as if he'd heard her, but he remained beside her.

Megan watched the other two brothers, her heart sinking. Chad must be more involved with the other lady than she'd thought.

When Jake and Chad joined them, Pete demanded harshly, "Is that the greenhorn from Chicago?"

Chad and Jake exchanged a glance, then Jake replied, "Yeah."

"Damn him," Pete muttered under his breath.

Megan laid her hand on his clenched fist in a comforting gesture. At her touch, he looked down at his hand and forced himself to relax his fingers, linking them with Megan's.

Relieved, Megan smiled at him and then encountered Chad's gaze. The fierce glint in his eyes was difficult to interpret.

What did he have to complain about? He'd been fighting over another woman. She lifted her chin and glared at him. He had no claim on her.

When Jake decided to call it a night a few minutes later, she breathed a sigh of relief.

TWO HOURS LATER, Megan wasn't feeling relief. After a silent drive home, everyone had gone to their rooms, grateful for the evening to be over. But Megan hadn't been able to forget any of it.

Not the immense attraction she felt for Chad Randall, nor the jealousy that had surged through her. What was she doing? There was no future in a relationship with him. His own brother had called him a love-'em-and-leave-'em type.

And she wasn't interested in putting her heart on the line anymore. Not for anyone. She just had to keep telling herself that.

After trying to read and seeing the image of Chad in place of the words, Megan finally tossed the book aside and shoved back the covers.

Maybe she could blame her restlessness on her muscles stiffening from the horseback riding she'd done that morning at the arena with Jake. It had been fun. But she'd spent the time wondering where Chad was. There was that forbidden subject again.

Snatching up her robe, she quickly wrapped herself in it and headed for the door. A glass of milk would cure everything.

The soft glow of a tiny light at the head of the stairs guided her down the hall. She tiptoed, hoping not to awaken anyone.

The stair third from the bottom creaked as she stepped on it. She'd have to remember that when she returned. It echoed through the house, magnified by her apprehension. Pausing, she waited for any response and was gratified when she heard nothing.

It was darker after she'd started down the hallway to the kitchen, but she saw a light under the kitchen door. Was Red still up?

Just as she got near the swinging door, the light under the door disappeared and the door itself swung open. For the third time, she bumped into Chad Randall.

Only this time was different. He was naked.

CHAD STOOD under the hot water, letting the steam build up around him. He'd hoped a shower might help him relax. He hadn't been this tense in a long time.

So far, it wasn't doing him a hell of a lot of good. Maybe because his head was filled with thoughts of Megan. He should've gone for a cold shower instead of a hot one. But in winter in Wyoming? Even he wasn't that much of a masochist.

With a sigh, he reached for the bottle of shampoo. By having his shower tonight, he wouldn't have to bother in the morning, which would give him an extra half hour of sleep. He'd need it at the rate he was going.

When nothing came out of the shampoo bottle, Chad stared at it and then shook it again. Damn! Nothing about this night was going right. First he'd had to watch his brother and Megan together, then he had to hold her in his arms and pretend it didn't affect him…and now this.

With another muttered expletive, he shut off the water and stepped from the shower. He eyed his jeans, but he didn't want to dress and undress again just to go downstairs to the storage closet. If the women hadn't been in the house, he would've just gone downstairs stark naked. Instead, he grabbed the towel off the rack and wrapped it around his body.

When he came out of the kitchen, carrying the bottle of shampoo, he was grateful for his forethought.

His arms went around Megan, and her body pressed against his was all that kept the slipping towel in place.

"Turn loose of me!" Megan protested.

"Uh, Megan, I can't," he whispered, holding her against him.

"Don't be ridiculous. Of course you can. This bumping into each other is getting to be silly."

"If I let you move, I'm going to be standing in front of you in all my glory," he returned, chuckling slightly. His glory was increasing all the time with Megan in his arms. When she stared at him, uncomprehending, he explained, "My towel will fall if you move."

He watched the movement of her throat as she swallowed, and longed to trace its slender grace with his lips.

"What—what are you doing down here in a towel?"

"Getting shampoo," he said, carefully lifting one hand from her back to show her the new bottle of shampoo.

"Oh."

"What are you doing down here?"

"I wanted a glass of milk."

She swallowed again, and he thought he'd die of hunger to touch her throat, to caress it, to nestle there against it.

"Having trouble sleeping?" he asked hoarsely.

"Yes. It was an exciting evening."

The way her gaze skittered from his told him she was referring to his brief fight.

"I couldn't help it."

"Help what?"

Her voice was cooler now, in contrast to her warm body.

"You know what. The fight."

"Where I come from, gentlemen don't settle their differences with fists."

He continued to hold her against him with the hand holding the shampoo bottle, but his free hand circled that throat and slid up to her jaw to lift her face to his. "Maybe where you come from, men aren't men," he growled.

"Don't be absurd! They certainly are."

"Then why did they let you escape?" he muttered, and did what he'd been waiting all evening to do. He kissed her.

Megan had been wondering what to do with her hands. From the moment Chad had pulled her against him, she'd tried to

find an answer to that question. She couldn't rest them against
his bare chest, as tempting as it was.

If she touched his skin, she knew she'd give herself away.

Once his lips covered hers, however, she had no choice. Her
fingertips skimmed that warm, sculpted skin, covered with a
trail of black hair. Like a blind woman reading braille, she
learned the pattern of his muscular chest, tracing the curves,
brushing across the pebblelike nipples, feathering against his
strong neck and descending again.

Meanwhile, her lips were responding to his, opening to his
urging, receiving his seeking tongue, her own responding.
What this man could do to her in the space of seconds was
incredible. This time, unlike yesterday in the snow, there was
no soft approach, no brushing across her mouth. Chad went
into high gear at once, and Megan couldn't keep from meeting
him halfway.

She scarcely noticed when the shampoo bottle hit the floor
with a thud. Vaguely she felt both of his hands urging her
closer. Then one was undoing the belt that held her robe closed.
She gasped when his warm hand slid inside and encircled one
breast. With a moan, she folded both arms around his neck and
pressed closer.

His lips left hers and joined his fingers as they pushed the
buttons of her top through their holes. Then he passionately
kissed each inch of skin as it was revealed.

Freed from his intoxicating lips, Megan's head began to
clear. What was she doing? She shouldn't— As if he'd heard
her thoughts, his lips returned to hers, to demand even more
cooperation. They were magic, carrying her to another world,
where all was perfect, loving and, of course, forever.

That word rattled around in her head until his lips departed
again. Forever? *Love 'em and leave 'em*, Pete had said. Her
eyes fluttered open just as he lifted her against him and used
those lips on one breast, freed from the pajama top.

"Chad!" she gasped, not sure if she was protesting or urging
him on.

He let her slide back down his body, a journey filled with
incredible pleasures. "Megan," he whispered in her ear. "Let's
go upstairs."

His words shook her. He was asking for more than a kiss.

He was offering a night of mind-altering sensations, she knew. But morning would come.

It wasn't easy, but Megan shook her head no.

"Megan?" Chad whispered, and she heard the confusion in his voice.

She could understand his confusion. Her body wasn't too happy about it, either. But she couldn't face another heartbreak. "No. No, I can't."

Without worrying about his modesty, she pulled away and ran back down the hall and up the stairs as if she were being chased. And she was.

Temptation was on her heels all the way back to her room.

LIFE ON A RANCH began early. But if she hadn't planned a meeting with the other decorators, Megan wouldn't have appeared outside her bedroom before noon, since it was dawn before she'd gotten to sleep after the debacle in the hallway.

But she was a professional. She dragged herself from bed, her eyes almost as heavy as her heart, and headed for the shower.

Megan, Adele and Rita had their meeting, not necessarily a felicitous one, right after breakfast. When Rita left the table, Adele looked at Megan.

"This is going to be a huge project."

Megan nodded. "I know. It could drag out over several years."

"What would you think about a joint proposal, half by your firm, half by mine? I know your people do quality work, and I could work with you."

Surprised, Megan sat up straight, thinking about what Adele said. It might mean her company could benefit without her having to spend much time at the ranch. "You know, that might be a very wise plan." She continued to mull over the ramifications. Then she looked warily at Adele. "But we should include Rita, shouldn't we?"

"Not if I'm going to be a part of it. That woman is a pain."

Red, working at the sink behind them, almost cheered. "Good for you. I'd rather give up a new dishwasher than have that lady hanging around here."

Megan and Adele exchanged guilty looks. "You weren't supposed to hear that, Red," Adele said.

"I'll keep my trap shut," he promised. "How about some more coffee?"

"I'm floating already," Megan complained with a grin. "Besides, I'll need to talk to the head of our firm before I can promise to make a joint bid. I'll go call her now."

Half an hour later, Megan had her employer's approval. Megan was the only decorator available to work on the Randall project, and Geraldine agreed that it would be better to split the work, since there was so much to be done.

She returned to Adele, and they worked out a fair division of labor. Then Adele returned to the work area she'd confiscated in the living room.

Megan looked longingly out the kitchen window. The good weather had held, providing lots of sunshine, though the temperature remained around freezing. She'd love to spend some time outdoors.

"Go ahead, girl," Red prompted, as if he'd read her mind.

"What?" she asked, startled.

"Go for a walk or something. All work and no play, you know."

"I really shouldn't—" She stopped and grinned at Red. "All right, I will. And if anyone wants to know why I'm not working, I'll tell them I'm only following orders."

"Good enough," Red agreed.

Already dressed in jeans, a sweater and boots, Megan grabbed a coat and stepped outside, taking a deep breath of the crisp, cold air. It helped dispel her tiredness.

Then she began a brisk walk to one of the barns Chad had shown her two days ago. She wanted to visit Tinkerbell again. After spending a few minutes with the mare, Maybelle, making friends, Megan was thrilled when the filly allowed a brief pat on her little nose before dashing behind her mother.

Feeling more content than she had all morning, Megan left the barn, her gaze roaming the view. How could anyone be sad living here? Then she thought about the man who'd seldom left her thoughts. She couldn't be happy here unless— She dismissed such thoughts. Chad wasn't interested in anything more than a roll in the hay—or the bed, as the case might be.

She determinedly turned her thoughts to other things. Pete hadn't seemed happy last night. Unlike Chad, Pete wasn't a flirt. He'd said he wasn't a ladies' man and, by the normal definition of the term, he was right. But he was a man many a woman would've been glad to claim.

Yet Megan felt at ease with him, as if he were a brother. And she didn't want to see him suffer.

Her mind on Pete, she didn't notice a pickup truck coming down the long driveway. It hadn't quite reached the ranch house when the noise it made intruded on her thoughts. She watched, expecting it to stop by the front door. However, it veered to the left and headed toward the foreman's house she'd inspected with Chad.

The new vet.

Curiosity drew her in that direction.

As Megan reached the cottage, the truck drew to a stop and the driver's door opened. The tall brunette who emerged was a little older than Megan, probably somewhere around thirty, a striking beauty. Could she be the vet? Pete had explained earlier that a large-animal veterinarian had to be strong, and the woman didn't appear to be a weakling. But there was a soft, feminine air about her, even so.

"Hello?" Megan called out just as a little boy scooted out of the truck. She couldn't hold back a smile as he eagerly began looking around him.

"Hello," the brunette returned, smiling. "I hope I'm not too early."

"You're the new vet?" Megan asked even as she looked around for a man.

She walked over to Megan, extending her hand. "Yes, I'm B. J. Anderson. This is my son, Toby, and my aunt, Mildred Bates."

"I'm delighted to meet all of you. I'm Megan Chase, one of the decorators looking at the main house."

"That explains it. Pete said there were no women on the ranch," B.J. said. "Is he around?"

Megan looked out over the pastures and saw a couple of horsemen in the distance. "He and Chad had to move a herd early this morning. That may be them returning now. Can I help you with anything?"

"No. The moving van is supposed to be here this afternoon. We just thought we'd get a head start."

"Why don't you come over to the main house and have a cup of coffee? Red won't mind. He might even have some cookies, if anyone's hungry," Megan added, grinning at the little boy. He was adorable, holding on to his mother's leg and half hiding behind her.

B.J. smiled her thanks. "If you're sure no one would mind, I'd love a cup of coffee. Aunt Milly?"

"We don't want to be intruding," the older lady said with a frown. "Toby and I will go on in the house, if it's all right. I packed us a picnic lunch."

"I'm sure that will be fine." Megan turned to B.J. "Come on. I'll introduce you."

Red made the woman welcome. "Make yourself useful, Megan, and pour the lady a cup of coffee."

Noise on the back porch signaled someone's arrival, and Megan tensed. She hadn't seen Chad since last night.

"Red," Pete called before he appeared in the doorway, "have you seen—?" He broke off as he saw that the answer to his question was seated at the table. He strode across the room, his hand extended. "There you are, B.J. Your aunt said she thought you were here."

Chad came in after his brother, his hat in his hand, his sheep-skin coat unbuttoned. His gaze met Megan's and then returned to the newcomer.

"I'm Chad, Pete's brother," he said, extending his hand to B.J. also.

Megan discovered her jealousy wasn't limited to old friends. She'd liked B.J., but she couldn't stand seeing Chad's admiring look for the newest arrival.

Before Megan could gain control of her emotions, they all heard more steps on the porch. She wasn't surprised to see Jake in the doorway, but she noticed Pete's concern and wondered what was wrong. She might be jealous of B.J., but that wouldn't be Jake's reaction.

"It's getting colder out there," Jake said, taking off his hat and hanging it up. He slipped out of his heavy coat, his back still to the company. "You get that herd shifted?"

Obviously he hadn't looked too closely at the group around the table.

"Uh, yeah," Pete assured him.

Jake swung around and started to the table before realizing there was a stranger in the group.

"Hello! The new vet must've arrived. I'm Jake Randall," he said to B.J., extending his hand.

She stood and met him halfway.

Jake, a warm smile of welcome on his face, said, "Your husband already at work?"

B.J. stared at Jake and then looked at Pete, uncertainty on her face. Megan searched desperately for a tactful way to break the news to Jake, but B.J., seemingly unaware of the tension, said, "I'm a widow."

With a dawning look of displeasure, Jake asked for confirmation of his thoughts. "Then who's the vet?"

"I am," B.J. assured him.

Jake stared at her, then turned to his brother and rapped out, "Pete, I want to see you in my office!"

Chapter Six

The kitchen was silent until Brett walked in. It seemed to Megan that everyone drew a relieved breath when he greeted them. Chad performed the introduction to B.J.

"Glad to meet you. Where's Jake?" Brett added, bringing back the tension.

"Uh, he needed to talk to Pete. Lunch about ready, Red?" Chad asked, turning his back on everyone else.

Megan fought a rising irritation. The man was ignoring her. Yes, he was absorbed with a situation right now, but other than that glance in her direction when he came in, he'd ignored her.

And that was what she wanted, of course, she reminded herself. But he'd wanted to take her to his bed last night. How could he so completely turn off the attraction they'd both felt? She certainly wasn't very good at it.

Even now she could imagine him shirtless, letting her run her fingers over him, pressing against him—

"Megan?"

She snapped to attention. "Yes, Red?"

"If'n you'd set the table, we'll be ready to eat in about five minutes."

Getting up, she sailed past Chad as if he didn't exist and opened the drawer that held the silverware. He immediately moved to the other side of the room.

She was vaguely aware of Brett chatting with B.J., but all her attention was centered on the contrary man across the room. When Jake and Pete reentered the kitchen, however, they held even Megan's attention.

Though Jake's voice was stiff, he nodded in B.J.'s direction. "Welcome to the ranch, Ms. Anderson. Will you join us for lunch?"

Megan couldn't help but admire B.J.'s calm. "No, thank you, Mr. Randall. My aunt is waiting for me at the house. I'm glad to have met all of you." With a nod, she strolled to the back door.

"I'll walk you back to the house," Pete hurriedly offered, and followed her out the door.

Megan returned to her chore of setting the table, but she heard Chad's comment.

"I gather that was a surprise."

"You could say that." Jake rubbed the back of his neck, his gaze still fixed on the door.

"Maybe the boy thought you wouldn't mind since there's other women around," Red said, and nodded toward Megan.

She found that remark curious. After all, she and the other decorators would only be here a few days. The veterinarian would be a permanent fixture. Jake's frown in Red's direction did nothing to clear her confusion.

"Are we ready to eat yet?" was his only comment, however.

"I reckon, soon as Pete gets back and the other ladies come down."

Having finished setting the table, Megan volunteered to call the other women to lunch. Red thanked her as he carried steaming platters to the table.

Pete was just coming in the back door when she, followed by Adele and Rita, returned to the kitchen. After a wary look at Jake, Pete took his place at the table, saying nothing.

Silence reigned for several minutes as dishes were passed around the table. Suddenly Jake raised his head.

"I almost forgot. While Pete and I were in the office, Mike Caine called. When he was flying over the area this morning, he came across a herd of cows up in the foothills. Not a large one, but maybe thirty, forty head. Who's available to send up there to check it out?"

Brett swallowed his food and said, "I can go if you need me, Jake, but I'm up to my eyeballs in tax stuff right now."

"Pete and Chad can go, I guess. I'd like a third rider, but

the hands are working that new herd we bought in the east pasture. Okay?''

Chad nodded, though Megan noticed he didn't show any enthusiasm. Pete, too, agreed.

"I could go," Megan murmured, looking longingly at Jake.

"This would be a tough ride, Megan," Jake said, frowning at her.

"I know, but you saw me ride yesterday morning. I might be of some help to them. And I'd enjoy being back in the saddle again."

"It would be too hard, Megan," Chad protested, really looking at her for the first time.

So he thought he could tell her what to do when it suited him and ignore her the rest of the time? She had some news for him. "I'm tougher than I look."

"Why not come along?" Pete said, ignoring his brother's response. Turning to Jake, he added, "If this is a wild bunch, it might be easier to have a third rider."

"Do you mean it?" Megan asked, excitement bubbling in her smile. "I've even done some herding when I was younger. I'll do whatever you want."

"You're not going to finish your recommendations if you go off playing cowboy," Rita warned.

Megan looked at Adele. "I'll work evenings to get finished, Adele, I promise."

"I'm sure you'll manage," Adele responded calmly.

Megan, thinking about what she'd need to take with her— and, she had to admit, enjoying the consternation on Chad's face—paid no attention to the sudden silence that fell.

"Why would you need Adele's permission?" Rita demanded.

Megan exchanged a look with Adele before answering, "Adele and I are doing a joint proposal for Jake since it's such a big job."

"Why wasn't I included?" Rita demanded again, her voice rising.

It was Adele who again took the wind out of Rita's sails. "Because the job isn't big enough to be split three ways. Besides, you've indicated you wouldn't enjoy working with us." She continued with her meal, as if nothing was wrong.

Before Rita could complain again, Chad turned to Jake. "I don't think it's a good idea for Megan to go. It'll be an overnight trip probably. Could be dangerous."

"Overnight? I haven't been on a camp-out in years," Megan exclaimed.

"Megan, it'll be too cold. And you haven't ridden much."

"You're wrong," she said, staring at him. He was still trying to avoid her, was he? "I ride frequently at a stable near Denver. I just haven't herded cattle in years."

Jake ran a hand through his hair, looking distracted. "Are you sure, Megan?"

She nodded, grinning.

"Okay. Looks like I have a new ranch hand. Red, can you pack some supplies for them?" At Red's nod, he looked at Pete. "You'll need to leave right after lunch. Take a truck and trailer until you get to the trail up Tucker's Divide. The cattle were in a small valley a few miles away. You might find them by nightfall."

"Right. Put on your long johns, Megan," Pete advised. "You're in for a cold night."

"I don't have a sleeping bag."

"No problem. We've got plenty," Pete assured her.

Chad sat there and steamed. He didn't want Megan riding with them. He didn't want a threesome that would tear his insides out. He'd decided last night that his only recourse was to avoid her.

He tried to think of other reasons to leave her behind. Like her need for privacy. They'd have to pack two tents.

A sudden thought almost doubled him over. Suppose Pete and Megan decided to share one of the tents? Chad didn't think Pete and Megan were that friendly yet, but he knew that was what Jake intended. Even so, Pete wouldn't be that open about—about courting Megan. Would he? He was still too sore over Janie, wasn't he?

What if Megan offered you the chance to share her tent? What would you do? he asked himself. And knew his immediate answer. Cold, rocks, small space, none of it would stop him from making love to her.

Could he blame Pete if he did the same?

He shoved away from the table, unable to remain in the room with Megan and Pete. "I'm going to get my gear together."

"You've got time to finish lunch," Pete said, a puzzled look on his face.

At least Pete hadn't figured out what was wrong. And Chad hoped he never did.

MEGAN STEPPED into the shadowy barn, saddlebags thrown over her shoulders. Jake had given them to her to pack her necessities, though he'd warned she should take as little as possible.

"What's wrong with you, Chad?" Pete's irritated voice floated through the shadows.

"Nothing. But I don't think taking Megan is a good idea."

She stiffened in anger and almost called out to Chad to challenge him. But she thought better of it.

"An extra rider may come in handy. And we won't let her come to any harm. Pick out a good mount for her. Maybe Buck. He's reliable."

"Me? You—" He stopped abruptly and spun on his heel, stomping away from his brother.

Megan grew angrier. He clearly didn't want her along, though she didn't know why, since he was so good at ignoring her. But she wasn't going to let him keep her from going.

"Hello?" she called as if she'd just entered the barn.

Pete turned and walked toward her. "Megan! You made good time. We're almost ready. While I'm loading the other horses, why don't you mount Buck over there and see if he suits you? He's a pretty good cow pony."

As Pete was talking, Chad had brought over and unlooped the reins of a buckskin pony standing quietly with two other saddled horses and a pack mule.

"I'm easy to please. If you think he's okay, I'm sure he will be." She smiled sweetly at Pete, ignoring Chad.

After dropping her saddlebags by the door, she followed Chad and the horse out of the barn, into the cold air.

"Where's your hat?" Chad snapped.

She reached in her coat pocket and pulled out a wool cap,

along with leather gloves. "I thought this might be warmer than a cowboy hat."

He grunted—she assumed because he could find nothing to complain about.

After pulling on the cap, she walked to the horse's head and introduced herself, scratching his forehead and giving him a chance to get used to her. Then she pulled on her gloves, took the reins from Chad and swung into the saddle. Again she patted the horse, talking to him all the while, before easing him into a walk. A minute later, she pushed him to a canter, circling the open area before bringing him to a stop in front of Chad.

"Well?" she asked, a challenge in her eyes.

"That was great," Pete called from by the trailer. "He suit you okay?"

"Oh, yes. He's as smooth as silk." She kept her gaze on Chad.

Instead of speaking to her, he crossed to his brother's side, and she watched as an animated discussion ensued. Pete won, as she expected him to, because Chad didn't have a leg to stand on. She was a good rider.

"Bring Buck over so we can get him loaded, too," Pete called after a brief word to his brother, smiling at her. "Then I think we're ready to be on our way."

Chad was scowling as she approached and dismounted, but she ignored him. Or tried to. Why couldn't she feel the same way about Chad as she did about Pete—brotherly?

Instead, the man sent her up in flames. She wasn't going to give in to the fire, of course. But she wouldn't mind tormenting him a little in the process. She wanted him to know he couldn't almost seduce her and then act as if she were a bag of cow feed.

"You pack a bag?" he growled.

"A bag? No, Jake gave me saddlebags," she said, stepping back inside the barn to pick up the leather pouches connected to fit over a horse's haunches.

"Hey, a lady who's a light packer. You're a rarity, Megan," Pete said, grinning.

She handed the item to Chad, who continued to look un-happy. In fact, Pete was the cheery one today. Chad had no reason to be upset. Ignoring the turmoil in her stomach, she decided to change the subject. "What did you think of B.J.?"

Like a Geiger counter, she registered very little response in Chad at the mention of the vet's name.

"She seemed okay."

"Will Jake be okay about her being a woman?"

Pete answered that question. "As long as she can do the job, Jake won't have a problem. He's just concerned that she's— she's too feminine." He grinned at Chad. "And beautiful."

"Jake noticed, huh?" Chad asked, for the first time sounding like himself.

"Yep," Pete replied. "It's hard to slip a beautiful woman by the Randalls." He grinned at Megan, then abruptly sobered. "Even if we don't know what to do with her afterward."

FOR A WHILE, the trail they were following was wide enough for two horses, and Chad let Megan and Pete ride together while he followed with the pack mule. The sight of Megan astride a horse shouldn't have disturbed him, but he found it sexy as hell.

All he could think about were long rides, the two of them together, then stopping and making love under a tree.

In the summertime, of course, he reminded himself as the cold wind whistled down his neck.

He was turning into a sick character, he decided, since whatever Megan did or said made him think of making love with her. He hadn't been this randy since his teenage days. He was going to have to start getting out more.

The sun was almost down when Pete stopped to make camp. They'd have to hurry. Once the sun disappeared in the mountains, it got dark in a hurry.

Pete instructed Megan to gather firewood while he and Chad put up the tents. Chad had to admit she did a good job clearing a space for the fire, even digging a hole with a sharp rock. Before they finished the tents, she had a fire going in front of them.

"You're a good camper, Megan," Pete praised as he turned around. "This tent is yours if you want to move your stuff in there. I'll get dinner started."

"I'll see to the horses," Chad mumbled, coming out of the other tent.

"Better get those two lanterns going, too," Pete called out.

Chad hauled their packs to the fireside so Pete could start cooking. Then he extracted the two kerosene lanterns, filled and lit them.

"Megan, you need a lantern in there?" Pete called.

Her head appeared in the opening of the tent. "No. I was just unrolling my sleeping bag. Want me to fix yours?"

"Sure," Pete agreed.

"No!" Chad snapped. The other two stared at him, and he felt his face grow red. "I mean, no need to put yourself out."

"No problem," Megan said mildly, staring at him.

He hadn't lost his mind. But he was going to find it hard enough to sleep tonight, knowing she was in the next tent. If he could smell her scent on his sleeping bag, he'd be in hell all night long.

Turning away, he tended to the horses, tying them to a nearby tree on a long rope. Then he set out some oats. There wasn't a lot of grazing in the winter up here.

By the time he returned to the fire, Pete had grilled some steaks and warmed up baked beans. Chad discovered Megan had made some quick biscuits for the Dutch oven.

"This little lady is handy around a camp fire," Pete said, smiling at Megan.

"She's handy everywhere," Chad declared, sarcasm heavy in his voice. He regretted his loss of control as Megan stared at him, hurt in her hazel eyes, and Pete gave him a piercing stare.

After that, Chad ate in silence, concentrating on his food, while the other two chatted quietly across the fire.

After they cleaned up their dishes, Pete stood. "I'd better take one of the lanterns and see if I can find some more wood. We'll get out of here faster in the morning that way."

"I'll help you," Chad said, jumping to his feet. He didn't want to be left at the camp fire alone with Megan.

"Nope. I'll manage. Megan might get nervous here by herself," Pete said. Without waiting for any argument, he disappeared into the darkness, only the lamp he carried making it possible to follow his progress.

The two remaining sat staring into the camp fire, saying nothing. Finally Megan shifted and then looked at Chad. "I'm sorry you're unhappy that I came along."

"What makes you think that?" he snapped.

He was surprised when a chuckle escaped her. "Really, Chad, I'm not an idiot."

"What do you mean?"

"You've been acting like a bear with a sore paw. You tried to convince Pete I shouldn't come. You even made an ugly remark about my biscuits. I make good biscuits!" she added.

"They're damn good. But I don't think you coming was a good idea. I'm sorry if I've been difficult, but this ride is going to be tough."

"Did I complain today?"

"No. But we had an easy ride up here. Herding cattle out of these mountains is going to take a lot more riding skills than today's ride. And it's going to take all day. We can't all ride back in the truck, you know. Someone's got to herd the cows."

"I did figure that out," she said dryly. "Don't worry. I won't slow you up. You might even find I can be helpful."

He didn't have anything to say about her helpfulness. Somehow, since he had trouble concentrating when she was around, he didn't think he'd consider her presence a benefit.

After several minutes of silence, she looked away from the fire. "Shouldn't Pete be coming back by now?"

"He can take care of himself. Don't worry about him."

He hadn't meant his words to sound so sharp, but Megan said nothing else, and he worried he'd insulted her again.

When she spoke next, he wished he had. He didn't want to answer her question.

"The lady last night. Was she the one who broke Pete's heart?"

Chad turned his head, searching for Pete. Finally, with no sign of his brother to keep him from answering, he nodded.

"Tell me about her."

"Why?"

"I was just curious. She's pretty, seems perfect for a rancher."

"What do you mean by that?" he growled. Janie was a friend of his. He wasn't going to stand for her being insulted.

Megan raised her eyebrows in surprise. "I just meant she seems the outdoor type. Doesn't she live on a ranch?"

"Yeah."

"Well, I thought Pete would want a wife who could share in ranch life."

"Of course he does. We all want that."

"You want a wife?" The skepticism in her voice bothered him.

"No! I mean, I haven't thought about it." And he didn't intend to, either, he assured himself. Pete and Brett might change their minds, but he and Jake would remain bachelors together. Where was Pete?

No sign of him.

"Well, you'd better think about it before you get caught by someone like Rita," Megan warned, arching one brow. "I can't see her living on a ranch."

Surprising laughter escaped him. "You've got a point there, but I can assure you Rita doesn't tempt me in the least."

"She's very pretty."

"If you like Barbie dolls."

"What do you like, then?"

He stared at her, wondering how she could ask such a question. "You have to ask?"

She turned bright red. "I meant for a wife," she returned sharply.

"I don't want a wife. I prefer staying single."

Her gaze turned stonier. "Then you'd better think before you act like you did last night. You might get trapped."

"I didn't—" he began, wanting to defend his behavior, but he didn't know exactly what to say. He couldn't say he regretted holding her, because he sure as hell didn't.

The sound of Pete moving through the woods halted their conversation, and Chad was glad. Megan had a knack for turning the most innocuous topics into something personal.

"Found plenty more wood," Pete called as he approached the camp fire. He dropped a load of branches nearby and came over to them. "Megan, if you need to, uh, you know, excuse yourself, there's a bunch of bushes right up the hill that will offer you some privacy."

"Thanks. May I take a lantern?"

"Sure." Both men watched as she made her way up the hill. When she disappeared behind the bushes, only the faint glimmer of her lantern through the greenery revealing her whereabouts, Pete spoke again. "Megan's a good companion."

"Yeah."

"You've been acting kinda funny ever since we started out. Is anything wrong?"

"Nope. Think we'll find the herd early tomorrow?" If not, they might be faced with another night camping out.

"I hope so. I promised B.J. I'd take her around and introduce her to people."

"Hope she works out," Chad muttered, his gaze fixed on the hill behind them. When the light began moving again, coming toward them, he released the breath he hadn't realized he was holding. What was wrong with him? She was perfectly safe twenty yards from the camp fire.

"You go next," he told his brother. "I'll build up the fire so it won't die out too soon."

Pete stood and took the light from Megan as she reached the camp fire. "Okay?"

"Sure. I'm fine."

"I'll be back in a minute. Chad'll be here, though."

Megan looked at Chad and then turned back to Pete. "I'm going to turn in. I'll see you in the morning."

Pete nodded and left the campsite. Megan looked at Chad. "Can I use the lantern a few minutes to get organized in my tent? Will you have enough light with the fire?"

"Sure. Keep the lantern with you. Pete will be back in a minute."

"Thanks." With a sweet smile that left him hungry, she turned and entered her tent.

Pete came back, and Chad left with the lantern. When he returned, Pete was already in the tent. He noticed the lantern was still lit in Megan's tent. She knew to extinguish it before she went to sleep, didn't she?

Just as he was about to approach the tent to warn her, he came to an abrupt stop. Her silhouette played against the side of the tent, a dark shadow against the light.

With several sensuous wiggles, she removed her jeans. Then

she crossed her arms and grasped the sides of her sweater and pulled it over her head.

"Dear God, don't let her remove anything else," Chad moaned to himself, his gaze glued to the striptease she was innocently performing.

She leaned back and shook her head, running her fingers through her hair, and his hand unconsciously reached out as if to touch her. Then she collapsed on the bedroll and extinguished the lamp.

He wished he could as easily extinguish the desire that filled him.

Chapter Seven

Megan shifted in her sleeping bag, trying to find a soft spot on the hard earth. She'd done the same thing several times during the night.

"I'll take the horses to the stream for water," a quiet voice said, and Megan immediately recognized Chad's deep tones.

The sound of two pots clanging together indicated Pete was starting breakfast. Time to get up.

Even though her bed was hard, Megan had no complaints about warmth. She'd been snug in her long johns and sleeping bag. With reluctance, she unzipped the bag and scrambled out, hurriedly pulling on her jeans and sweater, then her boots.

"Megan, you up?" Pete called softly.

"Yeah," she answered, stepping through the tent door, running her fingers through her hair as she did so. She excused herself and went up the hill. When she came back to camp, Chad still hadn't returned. "Is it okay if I go down to the stream and wash my face?"

Pete grinned at her. "Sure, as long as you go upstream from the horses."

She grimaced. "I know that much, mister."

"Figured you did."

Walking down the hill, Megan marveled again at the easy camaraderie she shared with Pete. As she approached the stream, however, the other Randall who tied her in knots, awaited her.

"Good morning," she said cheerfully, hoping to start off better than they had yesterday afternoon.

He turned to glare at her.

"Didn't you sleep well?" She noted shadows under his eyes.

"Not exactly," he said, snorting in disgust.

Confused, she stared at him. He acted as if his poor night was her fault. Did he intend to blame her for everything? "What are you talking about?"

Instead of answering, he shrugged his shoulders and turned his head away.

"Was I snoring?" she persisted. The man was driving her crazy. It only seemed fair to return the favor.

"Nope. Forget it, will you?" He turned his back on her again.

"Stop that!" she yelled in frustration.

He turned around, seemingly surprised. "Stop what?"

"Turning your back on me," she explained, finishing lamely. "I don't like it." And felt silly complaining about his behavior.

"What would you prefer? That I stare at you all the time? Tell you you're beautiful?"

The fierce gleam in his eye brought back their encounter in the hallway two nights ago. All her plans to avoid this sexy man would go up in flames if he came near her again.

"No! No, but I'd like us to—to act normal around each other."

His gaze roamed up and down her body, bringing a flush to her cheeks. He seemed to select and then discard several responses before muttering, "Yeah, right."

Without waiting for her response, he turned on his heel and led the horses back up the hill to camp.

Megan knelt by the stream and bathed her face in the frigid water, all the more shocking because of the heat that lingered in her cheeks.

When she returned to the fire, she clung to Pete's side, unwilling to be left alone with Chad again. It was too stressful.

Breakfast was over quickly. With the tents packed and the fire safely out, they mounted and headed up the trail. Again she rode with Pete, leaving Chad to bring up the rear with the pack mule.

"Do you think we'll find them?" she finally asked Pete.

"Maybe. Mike was able to give us pretty good directions.

If they stay put, we should find them. Problem is cows don't usually stay put.''

"Why are they up here? Isn't it too cold for them to be this high up?"

"Yep. We must've missed them when we moved the big herd down below for the winter. It's fortunate we've had an easy winter so far. Otherwise, they wouldn't be alive. Between the cold and the wolves, they couldn't survive.''

"Wolves?" Megan asked in surprise.

Chad called from behind them. "Yeah, wolves. The government was concerned the wolves were dying out. They've reintroduced them to the state.''

"But don't they kill calves?"

"Yeah. But they're a protected species," Pete told her. "There's nothing we can do about it.''

An hour later, they had reached the top of the pass and started down the trail. Megan suddenly reined in her horse, causing Chad to stop just as abruptly.

"What are you doing, woman?" he roared.

"Listen!" She thought she'd heard the lonesome sound of a cow lowing. It came again, and she turned to grin at Chad. "Did you hear that?"

"Yeah. Looks like we've found our herd. Can you see them, Pete?"

"Not yet. But there's only one way to go." He continued down the trail.

About halfway down the mountain, Pete called a halt. "I think we're moving away from them. Seems to me the sound is coming from over there," he said, motioning to his left.

They all listened, then Chad agreed. "You're right." He looked around them in frustration. "There's no way to go left here. I saw an animal trail a little way back. Want me to go check it out?"

"We'll all go," Pete decided.

"It might lead nowhere," Chad warned. "Maybe you and Megan should wait here or go on. You might find another way in.''

"No, I don't think we should split up."

With a shrug, Chad pulled his mount around, followed by the pack mule, and headed back up the trail. Megan followed in his wake, her gaze now fixed on his strong shoulders, making it difficult to concentrate on her riding.

"Pete," she said, over her shoulder, "I don't know much about cows, but—but they sound like they're in trouble." The constant lowing had grown louder as they had moved down the trail.

"Yeah." Pete didn't offer any explanations.

Chad came to a halt. "Here's the trail. It's not a big one."

Megan smiled slightly at his understatement. The trail was extremely narrow, just barely wide enough for one animal. She looked at Chad to find him watching her.

"Maybe Megan should wait here."

She stared at him, about to protest, when Pete spoke. "Why?"

"This trail could get tricky. And we don't know what we'll find."

"I don't want to stay behind," she said, turning to Pete, knowing he was her best hope to continue.

"You're not. Get going, Chad. We'll be right behind you." Pete's authoritative tones left no room for argument.

Megan held her breath while Chad stared at his brother. When he finally urged his horse down the animal trail, she breathed a sigh of relief.

For half an hour, they slowly descended, winding back and forth down the side of the mountain. Then Chad called a halt and pointed downward. "There they are."

With the last twist of the trail, a small canyon was revealed where the herd of cattle milled around.

"Why are they going in circles?" Megan asked, puzzled. "Why don't they leave?"

Chad moved his horse a little farther along the trail. "There's the reason. This is a box canyon, and there's been a slide of rocks and trees that fenced them in."

"Damn, they're half-starved! Look at them," Pete said, concern in his voice. He turned to Megan. "Cows aren't the most rational of animals at any time, Megan, but these are going to be a little crazy. Be careful."

"Do they have water?" she asked.

"Yeah," Chad said, pointing. "There's a stream. That's all that saved them." He urged his horse forward and completed the several more zigzags down the mountain. Megan followed, but she wondered what would happen now.

"Can we drive them up the mountain?" she asked Pete.

"Looks like it's our only choice."

When they reached the bottom, Pete ordered Megan to one side and he and Chad tried to drive the cows up the animal path. But the bottom of the path wasn't very clear, half-hidden by several bushes.

"We're going to have to lead them," Chad finally said.

"What does he mean?" Megan asked.

Ignoring her, Pete looked at Chad. "You or me?"

"Flip you for it," Chad said with a grin, reaching into his jeans pocket. He tossed a coin in the air, and Pete called heads.

"Tails. Looks like you get to lead the way, big brother."

"But if you won, why does Pete get to lead?" Megan asked, confused.

Pete grinned as he explained. "Leading isn't the fun part, Megan. The cow I'll rope is going to be mad as a hornet. She's going to resist or charge me. Either way, it won't be a picnic."

It sounded highly dangerous to Megan as she thought about the narrow trail leading up the mountain. "Be careful," she urged.

"Never mind," Chad said abruptly. "I'll lead."

"Wait a minute!" Pete roared. "You won fair and square. I'll lead. You and Megan get to push 'em up. And keep an eye on Megan."

"I'll be fine."

Neither man responded to her assertion. They were discussing the best cow to choose as the lead. Once they'd selected it, the two men cut the cow out of the herd, and Pete's rope sizzled through the air to settle around its horns. Rodeo cowboying at its best.

Pete set out for the mouth of the trail. When the cow resisted, Chad rode behind it, slapping its flanks with his coiled rope. The rest of the herd scattered, and Megan pulled Buck out of the way.

It was a struggle, but Pete finally got the cow on the path and started up the mountain. Realizing that they'd need to move quickly while the other cows could still see the leader, Megan began pushing the herd toward the path.

Chad turned around and discovered the animals already in place and looked at Megan in surprise.

"Out of the way, cowboy!" she called, a grin on her face. It felt good to show him she could be of assistance.

He circled the herd, joining her in the rear. She breathed a sigh of relief when first one and then others began the steep climb. Their only difficulty came when the animals, finally reaching something to eat, most of the small valley having been stripped, wanted to stop.

"Keep pushing them, Meggie," Chad called as he swung his coiled rope.

Meggie? She hadn't been called that name since she'd lived on the ranch with her stepfather Jim. Distracted, she almost fell from Buck's back when he darted off to chase a recalcitrant heifer.

"You okay?" Chad called, worry in his voice.

He *would* have to be watching the minute she slipped up, she thought in irritation. She waved at him to let him know she was fine and went after the stray.

When they finally convinced every last animal to save itself by climbing the trail, the horses were weary, as were the riders. Looking up the mountain, they could see Pete way above them, now leading the subdued cow.

"Whew! They were a stubborn lot," Chad complained. "You as tired as me?"

His question made it easy to admit her exhaustion. "Yes."

"Well, I hate to break it to you, but I think we'd better walk our horses part of the way up. Think you can make it?"

She swallowed hard and stared up the trail. Then, with a weary sigh, she slid from the saddle. "Yeah, sure."

Much to her surprise, Chad stepped closer and patted her shoulder. "You did a good job, Meggie. It would've taken me a lot longer working by myself."

She couldn't help beaming at him. His praise meant a lot. With a surge of energy, she smiled and thanked him and then led Buck to the trail. "Shall I go first?"

"I'd better go first. Can you lead the mule? Some of those cows might change their minds and try to come back down."

"What do we do if that happens?" she asked anxiously as she reached for the reins to the pack mule.

"Try like hell to get out of the way."

Fortunately none of the herd tried to return to the canyon. However, when they reached the main trail, Chad and Megan discovered some of the cows had started down the trail instead of following Pete up. Luckily, they were too interested in grazing to go far.

Mounting, the two of them rounded up the strays and pushed them up the mountain.

Megan's stomach grumbled, and she looked up at the sky to see if it was near noon. The sun was still visible, but unlike the day before, there were a lot of clouds moving in from the west.

"Chad, I think a storm may be coming."

He jerked his head up before looking at her. "Yeah. We'd better push a little harder. Once we get them down the other side, we can leave 'em if we need to, but we've only got about four hours before dark."

This time she checked her watch and discovered it was already after one o'clock. He was right. And they hadn't reached the top of the pass yet. At least the cows could climb two or three abreast now that they were on the main trail. That would speed up the process somewhat.

Four hours later, tired and sore, Megan could have cried in relief when she caught sight of the truck and trailer they'd left parked at the start of the trail. She hoped she could hang on long enough to reach it.

Pete was waiting for them, leaning against the pickup, his horse grazing nearby. "Glad you made it," he called as they rode up.

"That was a tough haul," Chad said.

Megan decided that was another understatement. She sat slumped in her saddle, not anxious to dismount because she was afraid she would embarrass herself by crumpling to the ground.

Chad swung out of the saddle and came at once to her side, surprising her. "Come on, Meggie. You need to get in the pickup and get warm. Go start the heater, Pete. She's worn-out."

Before Megan could actually move, Chad put an arm around her waist and pulled her down into his arms.

"M-my legs are shaking," she muttered against his chest.

"It's okay, Meggie. I'll carry you."

As he swung her up into his arms, she sagged in relief. "Sorry," she mumbled. "You must be tired, too."

"Just a little. And ready to eat one of those ornery cows. I don't like skipping lunch."

Megan thought she might be too tired to eat. When they reached the passenger side of the truck, Pete had the engine running and the door open.

"She okay?" he asked softly.

"Yeah. But she's exhausted."

"I didn't quit," she tried to insist in a strong voice. It irritated her that it came out a whisper.

Chad gave her a little squeeze before he released her. "You sure as hell didn't, Meggie. You can ride with me anytime."

She flashed her gaze to him, trying to determine his sincerity. "Do you mean it?"

"Yeah. I mean it." He touched her cheek with one finger and then backed away. "We'll see to the horses."

CHAD FELT GUILTY. He hadn't meant to respond to Megan quite so intimately. He looked over his shoulder to see if Pete had witnessed their little exchange, but his brother was already working on loading the tired horses.

He hurried over to help.

"How's Megan?"

"Okay. She was a gamer."

"Yeah. She was a lot of help. Aren't you glad she went with us now?"

Chad shrugged. "Think it's going to start snowing before we get back to the ranch?"

"Probably. I've been watching the clouds while I waited for you two. It had me worried."

"Yeah. I should stay with the herd, actually, and bring them in tomorrow," Chad offered reluctantly.

"You're as tired as me. They'll probably be all right. I don't think the snow will be heavy. Jake can send some of the men out to round them up."

Chad shook his head. "I think Jake will expect one of us to

stay. And you should be the one to take Megan back.'' He must be crazy, he decided. But guilt made him insist that he stay.

Pete looked at him, maybe questioning his sanity. ''Are you sure?''

''Yeah.''

''I hate to leave you here, but I agree that Jake would want the herd brought in in the morning.'' Pete paused to think. ''Okay, you go get in the truck and get warm while I load the horses. Then we'll eat some supper before Megan and I head back.''

Chad didn't argue. He needed to thaw out before he crawled into a sleeping bag, or he'd be cold all night.

When he reached the truck, Megan was curled up in a tight little ball, sound asleep. He couldn't hold back a smile. He didn't know of a single woman, except maybe Janie, who could've made such a rigorous ride.

He slid onto the seat and gathered her against him. Only to make room for both him and Pete.

It wasn't long before Pete joined him. He took one look at Megan and said with a grin, ''Sleeping Beauty.''

Chad said nothing, staring at her.

''Think we should wake her up to eat or let her wait until I get her back to the ranch and she can enjoy Red's cooking?''

Chad didn't want to turn her loose. ''I think she'd prefer to wait.'' Without ever waking, as if she agreed with him, Megan snuggled against him, her head on his shoulder. He looked at Pete out of the corner of his eye to see if his and Megan's intimate positions bothered him, but Pete was opening the pack that carried their food.

''This is cold, but I need something in my stomach,'' Pete said, handing one of Megan's leftover biscuits to him.

''Me, too.''

They added some lunch meat and shared a canteen of water. It wasn't gourmet food, but they were hungry.

''Has she stirred?'' Pete suddenly asked, staring their way in the dark.

''Nope,'' Chad said softly, trying not to enjoy too much the feel of her against him, the warm breath that caressed his neck.

"Who would've thought a decorator from Denver could ride like Megan? She didn't complain once, did she?"

"Nope. Never even asked about lunch," Chad said.

"Well, I don't care if she wants to use Italian tile, I'm going to tell Jake to let her have the job."

"Her and Adele. They're working together now, remember?"

"That's right. Without Rita. I'm ready for that lady to be gone. When are they supposed to leave?"

"They came on Sunday, so I guess next weekend." It was Wednesday night, so Chad figured he had a couple more days of resisting the attraction he felt for Megan. Then he could forget about her.

Except when she came back to work on the house.

"Do decorators do a lot of the work themselves or send someone else?" he asked cautiously.

Pete chuckled. "I imagine we'll see a lot of Megan for the next few months. Maybe Jake will even offer to have her and Adele live here while they're working."

Chad felt as if the ground had given way beneath his feet. "I'm sure that won't be necessary. They probably send other people to do the work."

"Uh-huh."

Their talking must've disturbed Megan because she shifted in Chad's arms, turning so that her breast pressed into his chest. He swallowed and concentrated on not responding to her softness. A half hour of this torture, and he'd be ready for the funny farm.

They sat in silence until, out of the blue, Pete asked, "What did you say to Janie the other night?"

Chad chose his words carefully, hearing the tension in his brother's voice. "I suggested she and her friend find another restaurant."

"Not much to choose from around there but Cassie's Chili Bowl," Pete said, naming a greasy spoon with a bad reputation.

"That's what Janie said," Chad agreed with a wry smile.

"We didn't have any right to ask her to leave."

"That's also what Janie said." Chad added with a sigh, "Don't worry. I told her you weren't asking. I was."

"So why did you hit the greenhorn?"

Chad gave a laugh that held little humor. "He thought he could order me around. And his opinion of the Randalls wasn't particularly flattering."

"Hard to believe, isn't it?" Pete drawled sarcastically. "Probably matched Janie's."

More silence. Chad thought long and hard before he asked the next question, but he wanted to know the answer. He liked Janie. And she hadn't seemed any happier that night than Pete had. "What went wrong?"

He thought at first Pete wasn't going to answer. Or would tell him to mind his own business. Pete wasn't much for sharing his innermost thoughts.

Finally Pete said softly, "I wish the hell I knew. I figure it's the Randall luck. Like Jake. I shoulda known better, but she was so—so sweet. I thought—I thought wrong."

"But Pete—"

"Forget it, Chad. She made it clear she's through with me. It's no big deal," he said in a patent lie. "There's other women."

Chad instinctively tightened his hold on Megan as Pete glanced their way, and then he forced himself to relax. He already knew Pete and Megan had something going, particularly if Jake had any say in the matter. It wasn't a surprise. Hadn't he watched them hold hands after the fiasco with Janie and her escort? Keep their heads together the entire ride back to the ranch, as if they were sharing secrets? Hadn't Pete been the one to include Megan in their ride?

Yeah. He already knew Megan wasn't for him, even for a night. So it was no big surprise.

"Guess I better get us started back to the ranch," Pete said with a sigh. "I hate leaving you here."

"Don't worry about it."

Pete grinned at him. "I'll put up your tent for you while you roast your toes another five minutes."

"You don't need to do that, Pete," Chad protested.

But Pete was already getting out of the truck. "I'll be back in a minute." The door closed, leaving Chad alone with Megan.

He looked down at her face, pale in the shadowy darkness. Sleeping Beauty.

Hell, why not? he suddenly asked himself. She wouldn't remember, and Pete would never know.

His lips covered hers in a wake-up call.

Chapter Eight

Megan awakened slowly, stretching her legs beneath the cover, feeling content. Until her muscles protested. The pain brought back the events of the past day. And night.

That seemingly never-ending ride down the mountain in the increasingly cold air had been difficult. She'd been rewarded by Chad's tender care when he helped her from her horse. Then his holding her in the cab of the truck while Pete loaded the horses had been paradise.

The sweet kiss he'd pressed on her lips had awakened her, but before she could respond, he'd gently laid her against the seat and disappeared. In just minutes, Pete had slid behind the wheel of the truck, and they had driven back to the house. Without Chad.

How could a man ignore her one minute, rejecting her at every turn, and then treat her like something precious the next? He was driving her crazy. And why hadn't he come back with them? She supposed he'd stayed to take care of the herd, but it seemed to her the weather was worsening.

That thought had her shoving back the cover and going to the window. Big, fat flakes of snow were drifting down until the occasional gust of wind blended them into a blur. Fortunately the wind wasn't constant, but the thought of being out in the storm made Megan shiver.

And worry.

Had Chad come back? Was he all right? Would he be loving and caring as he was last night? Or would he revert to the cold and distant man who ignored her?

In the shower, with the hot water easing her strained muscles, Megan admitted that her attitude might be part of the problem with Chad. Her head told her to stay away from the man, but her heart leapt every time he came near her.

"Silly thing," she muttered to herself. Didn't her heart have any sense of self-preservation? The man had no interest in marriage—or anything else long-term. He wouldn't mind having sex, but he didn't want to make love. And she couldn't settle for anything less than love.

With a resolve to strengthen her resistance to sexy Chad Randall, she dressed in several layers of warm clothes and ventured out of the safe haven of her bedroom. Her defenses remained strong…until she reached the kitchen.

"Hi, Red, sorry I'm up so late," she said, greeting the man bent over a mixing bowl.

"No problem, young lady. I understand you earned your keep yesterday. You could've slept all day and not heard any complaints."

"I'll bet Chad and Pete didn't sleep late, though, and they worked a lot harder than me." She'd kind of hoped they'd be in the kitchen, figuring the snowstorm would keep them inside.

"No, probably not. Pete was certainly out early," Red agreed.

Her heart faltered a beat. "And Chad?"

"Haven't heard from him yet. He stayed with the herd, you know."

Concern washed away her feeble attempt to dismiss the man from her thoughts. "But it *is* almost noon, Red. Wouldn't he be back by now?"

Something in her voice must've caught Red's attention. He moved away from the counter and said gently, "Now, sugar, that depends."

"On what?"

"On whether he ran into trouble…or had something else to do before he comes in."

Her voice growing more strident in spite of her efforts to control it, she said, "What could he have to do in a snowstorm? Have you looked out the window?"

Red grinned. "Megan, this is Wyoming. It's winter. We always have snowstorms. It's no big deal."

In spite of her liking Red, Megan wanted to bonk him on the head. Fortunately for him, a buzzer going off on the oven took him out of her range.

"Go tell the other ladies lunch is ready," he said as if everything was normal.

"What about the men? Aren't they going to eat?"

"They know what time lunch is," he explained. "If they show up, they eat. If not, we have leftovers."

Red's easygoing attitude didn't soothe Megan's concerns, but she did as he asked and sought out the other two women. Rita was working in her room, and Adele had her work spread out at the dining-room table. Since their arrival, the women hadn't had a meal in the more formal room. Megan preferred the kitchen, but the dining room was elegant in its proportions.

"How was your cowboying yesterday?" Adele asked as she accompanied Megan to the kitchen.

"Wonderful…and exhausting. I'm glad I don't have to do it every day."

"Especially not in this weather," Adele added.

"Did you see Pete this morning?"

"Why, yes, I came down just before he went to the barn," Adele said. "Why?"

"Did he say anything about Chad getting back?"

"No. Didn't he come in with the two of you last night?"

"No, he stayed with the herd."

Adele shivered. "Rather him than me. I don't know how they stand conditions like today."

Since they'd reached the kitchen, Megan didn't bother responding to Adele's comment. Instead, she eagerly looked for any of the Randalls. "The men haven't come in?" she asked Red.

"Nope. They called from one of the barns. They're eating with the crew today. Said they didn't have time to clean up for lunch with you ladies."

"Is Chad with them?"

"Didn't say, Megan. Quit worryin' about the boy. He can take care of himself." Red's kindly glance brought a blush to her cheeks.

"Of course! I—I just wondered."

In Megan's opinion, lunch was deadly dull and the food

tasteless, though she'd had no complaints about Red's cooking before. Perhaps the problem was that she could think of nothing but Chad's safe return.

After lunch Adele asked her to look over some ideas she'd had. Megan couldn't refuse since she hadn't worked on the decor for the past day and a half. But her heart wasn't in it.

After an hour's struggle, she left Adele and returned to her room.

"You've got to get control of yourself," she lectured as she stared out the window. "Chad means nothing to you."

Her heart whispered, *I'd feel the same if it was Pete.*

"Hah!"

Okay, okay, so she was lying. With a sigh, Megan gave in to her anxiety and swiftly changed her shoes for boots and gathered up a heavy coat, hat and gloves. She was going to the barns.

"Where you going, girl?" Red asked as she strode through the kitchen.

"I need some fresh air. Cabin fever." That was the best excuse she'd been able to come up with.

"You haven't been in the house even twenty-four hours yet. Cabin fever takes a little longer, I think," Red responded, a grin on his face.

"Maybe I have a new strain of cabin fever."

"I'll bet you do," Red agreed, grinning even more. "And I think its name is Chad."

Her cheeks flamed, and she couldn't meet his gaze. "Don't be silly, Red. I'm just going to the barns, that's all."

"Ah. Well, try the arena. I think that's where everyone is."

"Thanks, Red," she threw over her shoulder as she raced out into the snowstorm. Her heart was pumping with excitement, as if she knew she'd find Chad there.

She followed the path that led to the barns, but it had already been filled in with the falling snow. She estimated at least four inches had piled upon the old snow. The wind was stronger, too. She leaned into it as she struggled past the horse barn.

Once she reached the safe harbor of the arena, she slipped inside and leaned against the closed door to catch her breath. And then scan the arena for the one person she couldn't forget.

He wasn't there.

She rubbed her eyes, wondering if the wind had made her vision unclear. But no, she could pick out Pete along with B.J. They were both on the railing of a narrow chute at the other end of the arena. Thinking Pete might have some news of Chad, she hurried over to him.

When she got closer, she realized B.J. was inoculating Pete's rodeo herd. Each bull was run into the chute, and B.J., perched on the railing, would lean over and jab a large syringe into the animal. B.J. must be stronger than she looked, since Megan realized it would take muscle to do this job.

She gingerly climbed a nearby rail. It wouldn't be a good idea to get close enough to be the victim of the angry patients. Timing her call to the exit of the latest bull so she wouldn't disturb the other two, she signaled Pete.

"Hey! How's our cowgirl?" he called out, a grin on his grimy face.

Since the cowboy nearby forced another bull into the chute, Megan had to wait to ask her question. She admired B.J.'s efficiency while she decided she preferred interior design to B.J.'s job, even if she did like ranch life.

"We'll be through here after two more," Pete called out to her, and Megan took his words as a signal to wait. She spent her time scanning the arena for any more Randalls.

When Pete, along with B.J., appeared beside her, she almost fell from the railing in surprise.

"Hi, Megan. How are you feeling after yesterday?" Pete asked.

"What happened yesterday?" B.J. asked.

"Megan went with us to find that missing herd. The ride down the mountain wasn't one I'd want to repeat any time soon. And she stood it like a trouper." He grinned up at Megan as if he were a proud papa.

"Thanks. What about Chad?" She'd intended to slide her question into the conversation, so it didn't stand out like a neon sign in the middle of the desert. So much for that idea.

"Chad? What do you mean?"

She couldn't believe Pete's response. Hadn't he even noticed his brother was missing? "Has Chad come back?"

"Haven't heard." He casually turned to look around the arena.

Megan could tell him his youngest brother wasn't in sight. In fact, he was the only Randall apparent to her eye. "Aren't you worried about him?"

Pete put his hands on his hips and stared up at her. "It will take awhile to get the herd back."

"Yes, but it's two o'clock, and the storm is growing worse. What if he gets lost?"

Pete rolled his head back and let out a roar of laughter. Megan jumped down from the railing, her hands clenched into fists. She'd thought the Randalls were loving, caring men. Well, she'd just changed her mind.

B.J. touched Pete on the arm. "I think Megan is really worried, Pete."

As if that had never occurred to him, he stopped his laughter and frowned at Megan. "Are you? Really worried?"

Megan could only nod.

"Honey, don't worry about Chad. The boy's part Indian. He could find his way back home no matter what kind of storm hit him."

"Maybe Jake, I mean, Mr. Randall, has had word of him," B.J. suggested.

Pete looked at her impatiently, "Call him 'Jake,' B.J. If you want to wait, Megan, I'll go ask him. He's on the phone over there in the office."

Again Megan nodded.

Once he'd walked away, B.J. slipped her arm around Megan's shoulders. "Men don't understand the art of worrying, Megan."

She couldn't hold back a sniff, but at least she didn't sob out loud. "I guess not."

"I haven't been outside in a few hours. How bad is the storm?"

"I guess not that terrible, but there's been about four or five inches that have fallen, and the wind is picking up." Megan kept her gaze on Pete's back, willing him to walk faster. When he stopped to chat with one of the cowboys, she actually groaned and then shot a look at B.J. "I tend to overreact."

"Then you'll make a great mother. Once you have a child, you spend half your life overreacting," B.J. assured her with a grin.

"Then it's a good thing that I don't intend to have children."

"Why not?"

"Because I'm not going to marry."

B.J. took her arm down and stepped in front of Megan so she could see her face. "I know men are weird, but what other choice do we have?"

Megan shrugged her shoulders, trying to sound nonchalant. "Some people aren't cut out for marriage."

"I've heard that line before, but it usually comes out of a man's mouth."

"Especially the Randalls." Megan said, making her own attempt at humor.

One of B.J.'s eyebrows went up. "Thanks for the warning. I won't set my cap for any of them."

Megan sighed. "Then you'll probably be in a crowd of one. I think every woman in Wyoming has them at the top of her most-eligible-bachelor list."

"I can see why. Handsome, charming, wealthy. Those qualities are always in high demand."

"Well, they'd better add mule-headed, hard-hearted, love 'em and leave 'em...." She trailed off when she saw Pete emerge from the office. "Here comes Pete."

"Hey, Doc!" a cowboy called from over by the chute.

"Will you be all right until Pete gets here?" B.J. asked.

Megan felt ashamed that her distress had been so obvious. "Of course I will. Go do your work. And B.J....thanks."

The vet smiled and got back to work.

Megan couldn't stand to wait for Pete to saunter back to her side. Couldn't the man walk faster than a snail? She headed in his direction, eating up twice the distance he did.

"Well?" she demanded breathlessly when she reached him.

"He's not back yet. But Jake sent a couple of our best guys out to meet him and give him a hand. They should be back any time."

She stared at him, incomprehension filling her. "That's it? You're not going to do anything?"

Pete seemed taken aback. "What did you want us to do, Megan?"

"You could go look for him yourself. I'd go but I don't

know the area. I could come with you." She didn't realize how desperate she sounded until she saw the shock on Pete's face.

"Never mind," she gasped, and turned to run for the door to the arena.

"Megan, wait!" Pete called.

She guessed he could move fast when he wanted to because he caught her about halfway to the door. Unfortunately tears were streaming down her face. She'd shut her heart to so much that now that Chad had sneaked inside, the emotion was hard to control.

"Aw, Megan," Pete said with a groan when he saw her face. Without another word, he pulled her into his arms and laid his head on her hair. One large hand rubbed a big circle on her back, and he softly assured her of Chad's safety.

Feeling absolutely ridiculous, Megan brought her tears under control and wiped her eyes with the back of her hand. "You—you do that comfort thing awfully well." Her attempt to laugh didn't quite come off, but she tried.

"Thanks. Someone told me women like that sort of thing," he assured her with a wry grin. "You okay?"

"Yeah, sure. I'm not used to being out in the wilds, that's all. In the city, no one even gets in their car if there's a snowstorm, unless they have to, of course." She tried a smile this time and was more successful.

"Good for you." He leaned down and kissed her cheek. "If he's not here by dark, I can assure you Jake will have an all-out search going. We'll take the jeeps and bring him back. We Randalls take care of our own."

She nodded.

Before she could pull out of his arms, he gave her another hug. "Now, you go on back to the house so we don't have to worry about you."

"Thanks, Pete." She turned to follow his orders. But she couldn't quite bring herself to go back to the house. Instead, she stopped off in the horse barn. Somehow being there made her feel closer to Chad.

Mindful of her own worry, she called Red and told him where she was. Then she plopped down on a bale of hay next to one of the stalls and talked out her frustrations with the horses.

CHAD HAD SPENT a lousy morning. The herd, having found a little grass and shelter from the worst of the storm, wasn't interested in moving before daylight. It was well after sunup before he finally convinced them to move in the right direction.

By that time, he felt half-frozen, and the cold biscuit he'd had for breakfast didn't do much to fill his stomach. His mind played with the idea of a hot shower and a steaming bowl of Red's stew while his horse did most of the work.

About ten, when the two cowboys caught up with him, Chad was glad for the company. And even happier with the thermos of coffee and food they brought him.

"Thanks, guys. Did Pete and Megan get back okay last night?" He knew they must've, but he wanted to hear someone say so.

"Haven't seen Megan yet. Pete was down at the corral early. I think the new doc was going to start giving his bulls their shots."

"Good." Good, hell. The least she could've done was get up and show herself so he'd know she was all right.

"I think the storm's gettin' worse," one of the cowboys said. "We didn't think you'd have 'em this far along."

"It wasn't easy. They found a sheltered area and they weren't anxious to face the storm."

"Can't blame 'em. Let's push 'em a little faster now that there's three of us."

They made it back to the ranch a little after two, herding the cows into a large corral near the arena. The two cowboys hurried to the bunkhouse for a late lunch, offering for Chad to join them.

He refused, saying he'd check in with Jake and then call it a day. He intended to spend an hour or two in a hot, steaming shower, after he ate something.

Opening the door to the arena, where he figured everyone would be, he came to an abrupt halt. Not thirty feet away, Megan stood wrapped in Pete's arms.

It wasn't as if she was resisting or anything. She was cuddled right up against him. Chad watched as Pete leaned down and caressed her cheek. He almost doubled over from the pain in his gut. Without another word, he backed out of the arena.

Then he tried to decide what to do. He didn't want to go

back to the house now. Megan could return at any moment. He couldn't face her now that he knew what he'd suspected was true.

Megan was for Pete.

All the indications had been there. But somewhere in the corner of his heart, Chad had been harboring the hope that he was wrong. That Pete didn't care anything about Megan. That she hadn't been claimed by one of his beloved brothers.

Because no matter what he felt for Megan—and he couldn't quite identify it yet—he wouldn't let her come between him and his brothers. Chloe, Jake's wife, had tried that. She'd even flirted with Pete. And look where it had gotten her.

He turned his footsteps in the direction of the bunkhouse. He'd borrow clothes from one of the guys and have his shower there. Then maybe he'd be able to scare up a game of poker or something. Anything to avoid Megan Chase.

She was definitely off-limits.

MEGAN SAT in the growing darkness of the horse barn, not bothering to turn on any of the lights. She was becoming quite chilled, but somehow she knew Chad would look in on his horses before he went to the house. And she was too anxious to assure herself of his safety to do anything else.

This compulsion she had was like a sickness. She'd already decided pursuing any kind of relationship with Chad Randall would be like playing Russian roulette. Except there'd be five bullets and one empty chamber.

Over and over she promised herself she just wanted to be sure he was safe. That was all. Once she knew he was safe, she'd go back to the house and try to avoid him.

The longer she waited, the more tense she became. With the snow falling, she couldn't hear any noise. Surely she'd be able to hear an entire herd, wouldn't she?

When the door to the barn suddenly swung open and a light was flicked on, it took her a minute to be able to see who had arrived.

Then she leapt to her feet and charged down the barn. "Chad! You're safe!"

She wasn't sure what she expected, but it certainly wasn't

for him to back away from her, one hand extended to keep her at a distance.

"Of course I am," he growled.

"But I've been— When did you get back?"

"A couple of hours ago." His voice still sounded wary.

"A couple of— What?" she almost screamed. "And you didn't let anyone know?" Suddenly she couldn't stand it any longer. With a bloodcurdling scream, she went for him, her fists flailing the air. She intended to make him pay for her suffering.

"What's wrong with you, woman?" Chad roared as he tried to avoid her fists. Then they both tumbled into a pile of hay, and Chad wrapped his arms around her to keep her from hitting him.

"What in hell is going on?" he demanded again.

"I've been sitting here worrying about you for hours! And you weren't even suffering!"

"So you're trying to beat me up? Women! You never make sense!"

The hated tears filled her eyes even as she struggled against him. The last thing she wanted to do was cry and appear weak. She ducked her head, but he lifted her chin.

"Aw, Megan," he muttered, and his lips covered hers as he pulled her more tightly against him.

Chapter Nine

Megan knew there was something she should remember. But wrapped in Chad's embrace, his warm lips loving hers, she couldn't think what it was.

Didn't want to think what should stop their kiss.

Suddenly he pulled away from her, a look of horror on his face. Feeling bereft, cold, she stared at him.

"I'm sorry!" Chad gasped, his expression changing to one of self-disgust.

"It was just a kiss," she lied.

"One that shouldn't have happened. My apologies. I'd appreciate it if you wouldn't tell Pete."

There was a sternness about his features that drove away the image of the flirt, the young man who chased women, according to his brothers. Megan was mesmerized by it and almost didn't hear his request. "Not tell Pete?"

"That's right. I'd appreciate it."

"No, I won't tell Pete…or anybody," she promised. "But—" she paused to swallow and try to remove her gaze from his lips "—it shouldn't happen again."

"No, not again."

They stood there, staring at each other in the gloom of the stables. Megan felt as if she were resisting the pull of a powerful magnet. Her head told her she wanted nothing to do with the handsome man across from her, but her body pleaded to move back to his embrace.

"I'll—I'll go to the house now. I have work to do," she finally said, and forced herself to move.

"Good idea," he agreed harshly.

Even then, she hesitated before walking away. Why did this man have so much hold over her? Her mother's experiences had taught her well to avoid all handsome, arrogant men, those who played women like instruments. She'd identified Chad as a member of that group when she'd first arrived.

Memories of the heartache her mother had suffered, *she* had suffered, strengthened her resolve, and Megan walked out of the barn. The sky was overcast, as if it still hadn't emptied its offerings, and the wind blew sharply. Coldness surrounded her inside and out.

She needed to get away from the Randalls. They were an attractive family. Not only was Chad a temptation, but his brothers were, too. To have a family, a loving family, had been one of her childhood dreams. Each time her mother married she'd thought, as a child, that she had a chance to become part of one. Each time she'd been proved wrong.

No, the Randalls reminded her too much of the disappointments and heartaches she'd suffered. If she added to that pain the danger in falling for Chad Randall, she knew she faced major devastation.

Determined to gird her heart against such weaknesses, she trudged sturdily toward the house. It was time to think about her job. That was her lifeline. She'd concentrate on work and put any thought of Chad Randall behind her.

DARKNESS HAD FALLEN as Chad crossed the area from the horse barn to the house. He'd driven himself relentlessly for over an hour after Megan had left him, cleaning stalls that didn't need it, putting out more hay. He didn't go to the house for dinner. He'd had a late lunch, he assured himself.

He wasn't hungry. He didn't want to see Megan again. He couldn't bear to face Pete.

He had no excuse for his behavior. He'd known Pete was interested in Megan. His brother had shown him over and over again. And he knew Pete needed someone like Megan right now.

There were plenty of other women around. He didn't have to try for his brother's woman, he reminded himself in disgust.

Tonight he'd flirt with Rita if it killed him.

And it just might.

He entered the house with his head down, concentrating on redeeming himself.

"There you are, boy. We were getting worried," Red said, surprising Chad.

"Worried? Why? I was working."

"I know, but the weather's gettin' worse. And it's dark."

"I'm fine."

"Want any dinner? I've got some left over."

Chad gave him a weary smile and nodded. Red had played the role of caretaker all Chad's life.

As he sat down, Pete and Jake entered the kitchen. He mumbled a greeting, not looking either of them in the eyes. He was too ashamed.

"Chad, everything okay?" Jake asked, puzzlement in his voice.

"Yeah, fine. I'm having a snack."

Red put a bowl of stew before him, and Chad had an excuse not to talk, even after his brothers joined him at the table. The other two discussed the worsening storm and the necessary chores for the next day.

When Rita entered the kitchen, Chad remembered his vow.

"We missed you at dinner," she cooed, batting her lashes at him.

"I missed you, too, sweetheart, but the horses demanded my attention." The word of endearment stuck in his throat, but he was determined to undo any damage he'd done. His gaze flickered to Pete, but quickly returned to Rita.

While he finished his stew, he engaged Rita in conversation, listening to her long anecdotes about her popularity or her business successes. Red, working at the kitchen cabinet, sent him several disbelieving stares as he encouraged the woman, but Chad ignored him.

When he carried his bowl over to the sink, Rita asked her inevitable question, "What are we going to do this evening?"

Chad wondered if the woman went out every night in Denver. She certainly gave that impression. Even in his younger days, he hadn't been that dedicated a partier. But tonight he was ready with an answer.

"How about playing some pool?"

"Pool? You have a pool table?" she asked eagerly. "I'd love that. I'm quite good."

"How about Megan and I take you on, then," Pete said, rising. "I'll go get her."

Chad almost groaned aloud. He didn't want Megan in the same room with him, much less playing pool.

"Maybe she's too tired," he suggested hurriedly.

"Won't hurt to ask. She's had an easy day today. We didn't drag her out in the storm." Before Chad could stop him, Pete went in search of the one person Chad wanted to avoid.

"You okay?" Jake asked.

Chad pasted a smile on his face. "Sure. Looking forward to beating Pete. Right, Rita?"

"Of course. I'm very good," she assured him again with supreme confidence.

He avoided his brother's and Red's faces and escorted his modest partner into the back room, where a large pool table dominated.

They were selecting their pool cues when Pete and Megan entered.

"I'm not very good, Pete," Megan was saying as they approached.

Pete's arm rested across Megan's shoulders, and Chad looked away. He didn't need a repeat of the earlier scene he'd witnessed in the barn. He wasn't a slow learner.

"Then let's play for money," Rita said, an avaricious smile on her carmined lips.

"Against the house rules, my dear," Pete drawled. "But we could play for something else, like doing the dishes or mucking out the stalls."

Rita stiffened. "I don't *muck*."

Chad knew his brother well. To prevent the fight he knew would erupt from Rita to Pete's next words, he inserted, "How about the losers serve the winners breakfast in bed?"

"Okay," Rita agreed. "I might even think about making their task easier by sharing your bed," she added, her invitation blatant.

Pete muttered, "I don't think that will be necessary."

Rita pouted, but Chad breathed a sigh of relief. He wanted

to make up for kissing Megan, but he didn't want to get carried away with his guilt.

Pete helped Megan choose her instrument and selected one of his own. Chad racked the balls. "Shall we flip to see who breaks?" he asked his brother.

"Sure," Pete agreed.

"Or you could let me break, since I'm a lady," Rita said, batting her eyelashes at both brothers.

Pete shrugged. "Sure, why not."

Chad was disgusted with her ploy for an advantage. The Randalls played fair and square. He sent his brother a look of apology.

With the break, Rita knocked in the seven, a solid ball. When she tried her next shot, she missed. Visibly irritated, she stepped back from the table, a frown on her face.

"You go next, Megan," Pete said.

"I'm not sure which ball to aim for," Megan protested, looking worried.

Before he caught himself, Chad thought of smoothing away her frown, putting his arms around her, guiding her, soothing her. He turned away to rub chalk on his stick. Anything to take his mind from Megan.

"I think the best shot would be the thirteen." Pete explained how to sink it.

"I don't know—"

"Here, I'll show you." Pete stepped to Megan's side and put his arms around her to guide her cue.

Chad studied the shelves lined with books, trying to think of the last title he'd read. Anything to erase the image of Megan with Pete's arms around her.

"You can't do that, Pete. She has to do it on her own. This is a competition!"

Immediately his partner's protest irritated Chad, and he turned back to the others. "This is a friendly game, sweetheart," he said, using the endearment to soften his reprimand. "Of course he can help Megan."

He moved around the table, noting that Megan was again wearing tight jeans and a sweater. He shifted his position so he wouldn't have to watch her bend over the table. Pete, after a grin at his brother, pointed out the direction Megan's shot should take and then put his arms around her again to guide her cue.

"Fix your fingers like this," Pete showed her, forming a rest for the cue. Chad moved farther away as her scent surrounded him.

"I'm—I'm not sure this is a good idea," she whispered.

"What's the matter, Megan?" Rita asked. "Afraid you'll lose the bet?"

Megan responded by making her shot, then watching as the nine ball hit the thirteen, knocking it into the hole.

Megan spun around, excitement on her face. "We did it! We knocked it in!" She seemed totally surprised by her success.

Chad raised one eyebrow, a crooked smile on his face. "Why are you surprised? Didn't you know Pete's good?"

"Yes," she said, taking a deep breath, her gaze meeting Chad's and then looking away. "All you Randalls are good."

"Thanks, Megan," Pete said with a bow.

"It's still your turn, Megan," Rita urged, bitterness in her voice. "And I don't think you deserve any more help from your partner."

Chad gave the woman a cool stare. "Don't be a poor sport, Rita."

"No," Megan said. "Rita's right. Pete shouldn't be helping me. I'll manage on my own."

Rita's mood improved considerably when Megan missed her next shot. And improved even more when Chad hit three balls in a row before missing. Pete stepped to the table and began his first turn. His run lasted for five balls.

"I didn't think I was going to get another turn," Rita complained as Pete finally missed.

"I was hoping you wouldn't," Pete agreed with a rueful shake of his head. "I shouldn't have missed that one."

Rita sank two balls, drawing them even. When she missed the next one, she looked at Chad. "We've still got a chance if Megan doesn't get any help."

He gritted his teeth but said nothing. But he promised himself this was the last time he'd be on a team with Rita. His idea of flirting with her seemed more and more difficult.

"No need for anyone to help her. She'll do fine," Pete said mildly, but he sent his brother a smile of commiseration.

Megan lined up her shot under Pete's direction. Chad closed his eyes as she bent over the table right in front of him. He didn't need any more visual stimulation to feed his dreams.

Without opening his eyes, the plop of the ball as it went in the hole told Chad Megan had done a good job. Rita's growl also confirmed it.

"Now you have to sink the eight ball, Megan, and call what pocket it's going to. That will be a little tougher," Rita assured her, a hint of taunting in her voice.

Megan bent over the pool table again, and Chad found himself holding his breath, hoping for her success.

When the ball rolled into the designated pocket, Megan let out a whoop and spun around, her arms in the air. Pete and Chad joined in her celebration, as if she'd won a gold medal at the Olympics.

Rita glared at all of them.

Before Chad could say anything, she slammed her cue back in the rack on the wall and stomped out of the room.

"Looks like your partner is a poor loser," Pete said, smiling at Chad.

"Looks like it. Good shot, Megan. I'll be serving you both first thing tomorrow morning." The thought of seeing Megan still tucked in her bed, her cheeks flushed with sleep, filled him with such longing, he decided he'd better escape before anyone noticed his reaction.

He headed for the door.

"Come back, Chad. We'll play three-way," Pete suggested.

"I'd better not. I've got some work to do," he told him, looking over his shoulder but not turning around. He hurried down the hall and through the kitchen, not stopping until he was standing on the back porch in the cold night air.

"You hoping to get sick, boy?" Jake asked from the door.

He spun around in surprise. He hadn't seen Jake as he'd passed through the house.

"Just needed a breath of cold air."

"How'd the pool game go?"

"Pete and Megan won."

"Aha. So Rita wasn't as good as she thought?"

"Is she ever?" Chad growled.

"I thought maybe you were interested in her tonight after the things you said in the kitchen."

"Nope. Just being a good host."

"Good. I'd hate to see you get involved with her. She reminds me of Chloe in some ways."

"Then you shouldn't have been worried. You know how I feel about your ex-wife," Chad reminded him.

Jake rubbed his arms. "Come inside and have some coffee. It's too cold to stay out here."

Once they were seated at the table, coffee mugs before them, Jake said, "Megan's not like Chloe."

Chad took a sip of his coffee to give himself a little time. "No, she's not," he finally said.

"She and Pete seem to get along okay. He's happier now than he's been since—in a while."

"Yeah." Another swallow of coffee. "Too bad they leave Sunday morning."

"She'll be back. I'm not about to choose Rita to redo the house. So Megan and Adele will get the job."

Chad had known all along that Jake would choose them. It wasn't a surprise that Megan would be coming back to the ranch. But it was a strain on him just then. Later, after he'd had some time away from Megan, he'd be able to handle the prospect. But not now.

"I think I'll walk down to the horse barn and check on that mare. It's getting close to time." He stood and crossed to where his coat was hanging by the door.

"Need any company?"

"No, I'm fine. I'm a little worried about this mare since it's her first. That's all."

That wasn't all. He was worried about himself, too. He'd never wanted a woman as he wanted Megan. Every time she moved, she incited his arousal. When he got close to her, it took all his strength to keep his hands off her. She occupied his mind night and day.

And she was for Pete.

When he reached the barn, he hadn't resolved anything, but he had at least put some space between him and his problem.

He was hanging over the half gate of the stall when he heard the barn door open. Expecting Jake, a mother hen if there ever was one, he turned to discover his problem had followed him. But at least she hadn't come alone.

"Hi, Chad. Megan wanted to see the babies again. Hope you don't mind," Pete called out.

"Of course not," he replied, but he turned away from them, staring at the young mare.

Megan stopped to visit with Maybelle and Tinkerbell, but Pete came on down the barn to lean against the gate next to Chad.

"How's she doing?"

"Okay. But I don't think it'll be too much longer."

"The storm's getting worse. They always deliver at the most inconvenient times."

The phone by the front door of the barn rang.

Megan looked up. "I always forget you have such modern conveniences out here."

Pete, on his way to answer it, explained, "Jake had them installed a few years ago. Saves us some time."

As Pete answered the phone, Megan moved to Chad's side.

"You shouldn't have come here," he whispered harshly.

She looked at him in surprise. "Why?"

"You know why!"

"No, I don't. We agreed what happened earlier wouldn't happen again. I just wanted to look at the horses. Besides, Pete came with me."

"I know he came with you. That doesn't stop me from wanting to kiss you again," he growled.

Her cheeks flushed bright red, and she looked away.

"I'm beginning to think you're a tease!" he added, determined to drive her away.

She turned to stare at him in horror, her hazel eyes filled with hurt as tears pooled in them. "I—I wouldn't do that!" she exclaimed.

"I'm not so sure," he complained. "It would explain why you're down here now, after I left the two of you alone."

With a final reproachful stare, she turned and stalked toward the door of the barn. Pete, hanging up the phone, looked at her, puzzled.

"Where are you going, Megan?"

"Back to the house...where I belong!" she snapped, glaring once more at Chad.

Pete followed her to the door and watched from there as she crossed the open area to the house, but he didn't go after her. Much to Chad's regret, he turned and came back to him.

"What happened?"

Chad shrugged.

"What did you say to Megan?" Pete insisted.

Chad ground his teeth. Why did his brother assume *he* was the one to say something wrong? "Nothing. I was just surprised that the two of you came out here."

"Why? You know Megan loves horses. In fact, you two have that in common."

And they both loved Pete. They had that in common, too, Chad reminded himself.

"You didn't tell her not to visit the horses, did you?" Pete questioned.

"Of course not."

"Well, you must've said something to upset her. Megan's not like Rita. She doesn't get upset for no reason." Pete stood waiting, a stern look on his face, much like Jake's.

"I told her—I told her she was a tease," Chad finally confessed, feeling bad about his words. But he'd been desperate to put some distance between them.

"What?" Pete roared, shocked.

"Well, she is. She knows I— I'm sorry, Pete. I kissed her. I broke it off as soon as I remembered. I shouldn't have, but—"

"As soon as you remembered what?" Pete asked, frowning.

Chad snapped the stem of hay in his hands and threw it on the floor. "As soon as I remembered she's yours. It won't happen again!" He turned to walk away, ashamed that he'd betrayed his brother in such a way.

"What are you talking about? Megan's not *mine!*"

"I mean, I know you have feelings for her." Chad was getting a little put out by Pete's reaction. Chad was making a sacrifice for him, and he didn't even seem to appreciate it.

"Sure, as a friend. You think I'm romantically— Come on, Chad. You know about Janie."

"You and Janie are through."

"And you think it's that easy? That I can put Janie out of my heart, just like that?"

The pain on Pete's face made Chad uneasy. His brother was still hurting.

"Listen, little brother, don't hold back with Megan for my sake. But be careful. Games of the heart can really hurt." Pete slapped him on the shoulder and turned to walk out of the barn.

"What about in the arena this afternoon?" Chad called after him.

"What are you talking about?"

"She was in your arms. You kissed her."

Pete grinned at his brother. "Jealous? She was worried about *you*. I was just comforting her." Without waiting for a response, he left the barn.

Chad stared after him, his stomach, as well as his head, in turmoil.

Pete didn't want Megan.

A big smile broke across Chad's face.

He did.

At least for a while, he cautioned himself.

Right?

Chapter Ten

Megan woke before the alarm went off the next morning. Not surprising. She'd had a restless night. Her thoughts had centered around a certain difficult cowboy.

Today was Friday. One more day of avoiding him, and she'd be on a plane back to Denver. After his accusation last night, she didn't think she'd regret leaving, even though she'd come to love life on the Randall ranch. It made the thought of returning to Denver unattractive.

But it was for the best.

The alarm went off, and she reached out to turn it off just as someone knocked on her door. She sat up in bed and grabbed the silk wrapper that matched the thigh-high silk nightgown she wore. Hurriedly belting the robe, she opened the door.

"Breakfast is served, madam," Chad said, a smile on his lips.

He hadn't been smiling last night. She was still angry at him and shook her head. "No, thanks. I'll come down for breakfast."

Raising the tray a little higher, he said, "I've already got everything ready. And you won the bet, remember?"

She remembered. She'd won in spite of his partner's taunting. His friendliness with Rita hadn't made the evening fun for her at all. But it was a good reminder of his history with women. Love-'em-and-leave-'em Chad. She guessed he'd moved on from her to Rita.

"Why don't you take it to Rita? I'm sure she'd welcome you with open arms."

"Come on, Megan, let me serve you breakfast in bed. Rita didn't win the bet. She doesn't deserve to receive the prize."

"Fine, give it to me," she suddenly agreed, and opened the door wider to reach out for the tray.

"Nope. You have to get back in bed. That was the deal."

"Have you already served Pete his breakfast in bed?" she asked. She wanted to know, if he was going to insist she adhere to the bet.

"I would've, but he was up early. I poured him a cup of coffee," he added, a smile on his lips.

Those lips. She looked away, hoping she could forget how warm, how persuasive, those lips could be.

He nudged the door even wider. "Go on. Get in bed."

She finally did as he ordered, but as she pulled the covers around her, she asked, "Why aren't you still angry with me? Not that you had a valid reason, but last night you were angry."

Instead of answering, Chad set the tray on the end of the bed and reached for the extra pillow to slip behind Megan. She leaned forward to make room and then realized how close that put her to Chad. Her breathing speeded up, and she leaned back against the pillows.

"Thank you for breakfast. Don't let me keep you," she said, hoping the man would get out of her bedroom.

"Here's your hat, what's your hurry? Sounds like you're trying to get rid of me, Megan."

"I wouldn't want to be accused of being a tease again," she said, wishing she could've kept the bitterness from her voice, but she couldn't.

He picked up the tray and settled it across her lap, and she thought he would then leave, giving her a break from the tension she was feeling. Instead, he pulled a chair up to the side of the bed and sat down.

"What are you doing?" she asked.

"I thought you might like a little company."

He sounded the slightest bit uncertain, which made her more accepting of his presence than she should be. Not that he was easy to resist. His brown eyes were warm, his smile filled with charm. Tight jeans and a red plaid flannel shirt covered his physical attributes, and Megan's gaze traced his broad shoulders and narrow hips hungrily before she caught herself.

"No, thanks," she said, picking up the fork to take a bite of scrambled eggs.

"You're a hard woman, Megan Chase," Chad complained, but he was still smiling.

"And you haven't answered my question. Why aren't you still angry? Why are you— You're trying to repay me, aren't you? You're teasing me with your— You're trying to charm me."

He leaned closer, his lips only inches away. "I'm trying to say I'm sorry, sweetheart."

"'Sweetheart'? Aren't you confusing me with Rita? I heard you call her that last night. Or do you call all women 'sweetheart'? Saves remembering their names?"

"Megan, you're being difficult."

Anger was building in Megan. The past few days, when Chad had tried to help his brothers and had helped her on the trail ride, she'd thought she'd misjudged him. He hadn't acted like a conceited man, thinking every woman was waiting for him to cock an eyebrow at her in invitation. But now that arrogant flirt she'd first met was back.

"How kind of you to inform me," she said in frozen tones.

"Megan, why are you getting upset?"

"Stop flirting with me!"

"You're not comparing me to your latest stepfather again, are you?" Chad demanded, all the charm leaving his face as he frowned.

"Why not? You're flirting, aren't you?"

"Yeah, but— Damn it, Megan, I'm attracted to you!"

"That's not what you said last night!" she retorted, irritated.

"You're wrong! I told you I wanted to kiss you. And I still do!"

He leaned across the tray, one hand catching her chin, and those wonderfully warm, seductive lips moved in on hers. But Megan wasn't a masochist. The man would kiss her, then accuse her of seducing him. Without thought to the results, she drew her knees up in protest and shoved against him.

The breakfast tray, including a full cup of coffee, emptied

all over her. Fortunately, because of her stubbornness, the coffee had cooled off a little, but it was a messy way to warm up.

"Hey!" Chad yelled, trying to grab the tray and only making matters worse.

Megan's scream as the coffee hit her and then drained down her sides coincided with his protest. "Ooh! Yuck!" she added as she started scooping scrambled eggs off her chest.

"Damn it, Megan, why did you do that?" Chad demanded as he picked a biscuit off the floor.

"Why? Why?" she repeated, her voice rising. "Did it ever occur to you that I did it because I didn't want you to kiss me? Does that make any sense to your macho head?" The other biscuit was in her hand, and she couldn't stop from throwing it at his head as hard as she could.

Red's biscuits were notoriously light and fluffy, so her missile didn't do any damage, but it did surprise Chad. His eyes widened. Before she could apologize, something she actually considered, he stuck his finger in the strawberry jam Red had put on the plate and drew a line across Megan's forehead.

"What do you think you're doing?" she demanded.

"Retaliating," he assured her calmly.

"Retaliating? I'm the one sitting in a lake of coffee. How dare you!"

"If you are, it's your fault. You're the one who upset the tray."

"Only because you were trying to kiss me!"

"Well, how could I know you were opposed to the idea? You didn't protest before."

Because she guiltily knew he was right, she gave up on the argument. "Get out! Just get out of my room."

"Fine!" he agreed huffily, and rose to stride to the door. About halfway there, he stopped and came back.

She stared at him warily, not sure what he intended doing now.

"Go get in the shower. I'll pick up the dishes and strip the bed."

"What?" she asked in surprise.

"I said, go get in the shower. I'll clean up this mess."

Damn him. The moment she had dug up enough anger to

resist him, he had to do something kind. "I can clean it up. Tell Red I'll bring down the dishes—"

"I said I'd do it. It's my fault."

She couldn't argue with him any longer. If she did, she'd end up in his arms. And then she'd be in real trouble. With a muttered "Thank you," she gathered some clothes and escaped to the bathroom. And prayed that he'd be gone before she came back.

DAMN! That scene hadn't played itself out as he'd planned. In Chad's mind, Megan had welcomed him with open arms and invited him to share her breakfast and her bed.

A little overly optimistic, maybe, but a nice fantasy.

A fantasy that hadn't even come close to reality.

He entered the kitchen, expecting his brothers to still be at the breakfast table, but only Red was in sight.

"Where is everyone?" he asked.

"The latest weather report came through. Looks like this storm is going to be a big one. Jake said for you to hightail it to the barn and saddle up. They're going to bring all the herds in as close as possible. It'll save time for feeding them."

Chad shoved aside his concerns about Megan and hurried out. He met Pete halfway across the yard. "Where are you heading?"

"I've got to call B.J. She's already at her office in town. If she doesn't start for the ranch now, she'll be snowed in. Or maybe I should say 'out.'"

"Glad you thought of her. She wouldn't know, not being from around here."

"Actually Jake thought of her. You take Megan her breakfast? How'd it go?"

Chad looked away. "Fine. Gotta hurry. Jake's waiting on me." He knew he didn't convince Pete, since he heard him laughing.

As soon as Jake saw him, he ordered him to string the ropes from the house to the barns. "And add one to the vet's house," he added.

They'd used the rope system for years. When the snow was blinding, whoever took care of the animals could reach the barn safely by holding on to the rope. There'd been a number of cases of men getting lost between their houses and barns and freezing to death. Judd, their father, hadn't been about to let that happen on the Randall ranch.

The storm was building in its fury. Already Chad couldn't see the mountains. As he attached the rope to the front porch of B.J.'s, the front door opened and Mildred stuck her head out.

"Is everything okay?" she asked.

"Yeah. We're connecting ropes to all the buildings. If you need to come to the main house, just hold on to the ropes and follow them. Is B.J. on her way home?"

"Yes."

With the cold, wet flakes hitting him in the face, he told her to let him know if she needed anything and hurried to the horse barn. He had to check on the mare due to foal before he saddled up.

Everything seemed okay at the barn, and he crossed to the next barn to join the others. He was surprised to discover Red saddling a pony also. "What are you doing here?"

"Helpin' out. I left Megan in charge of the kitchen," Red added with a grin. "She wanted to come, too, but I talked her out of it."

"Good. You must be powerfully persuasive, though, 'cause I can't seem to talk that lady into anything."

Red laughed. "Maybe you're askin' too much."

Maybe he was. But her heart seemed about as cold as the snow this morning. Though he couldn't say the same for her kisses. They could heat all of Wyoming.

As he mounted and headed out to the pastures, he wished he had some of that heat right now.

MEGAN WORKED HARD on the redecoration plans until noon. Then, mindful of Red's charge, she went to the kitchen to prepare soup and sandwiches for the three of them. The fury of the snowstorm drew her constantly to the window, but she couldn't see much of anything. How the cowboys were able to work in such conditions she didn't know.

She began a fresh pot of coffee. Whenever they came in,

something hot would be their first need. Next she put on a huge pot of stew, knowing it would fit whatever time frame she needed. With the storm continuing to intensify, she couldn't believe they'd stay out much longer. She hoped not.

"They're not back yet?" Adele asked as she entered the kitchen after Megan had called to her and Rita.

"No. I'm getting worried."

"Yes. I don't think I've ever seen such an intense storm." Adele moved to the window to stare out at the whiteness when Rita entered.

She stared at the table. "Sandwiches? That's all?"

Megan shrugged. "I was working. And I made stew for later when the men return."

Rita sniffed but said nothing. The three women sat down, and Megan watched as Rita made a multilayered sandwich that Dagwood would've been proud of. When the men were present, she barely nibbled at whatever Red served.

"You must be hungry," Adele said, eyeing the sandwich, too.

Ignoring both of them, Rita bit into her creation and chewed, staring into space.

Adele and Megan chatted quietly as they ate, perfectly willing not to include Rita if that was what she wanted. A few minutes later, however, Rita deigned to speak to Megan.

"I suppose, with the storm, you didn't get breakfast in bed. Too bad."

Megan would have liked to ignore the catty remark, but Chad deserved his due. He had tried to fulfill the bet. "No, Chad brought me breakfast in bed."

Rita's eyes narrowed. "Oh? Well, I hope you enjoyed it. You didn't win fair and square, you know." When Megan said nothing, she added, "He would've preferred to bring breakfast to me. In fact, I'm sure he would've if it weren't for the storm."

"Probably," Megan agreed pleasantly. She stood and carried her plate to the sink and rinsed it. Adele did the same, but Rita left everything on the table and walked out of the kitchen. With a roll of their eyes, the other two cleaned up after the prima donna without a word.

"Adele, I'm going to bundle up and go to the horse barn."

"Are you sure? It looks pretty dangerous out there," Adele said.

"Red explained to me about the ropes. Someone has to check on Chad's mare. He can't since he's out bringing in the herds."

"What will you do if something's wrong? Do you know that much about delivering baby horses?" Adele asked.

"No. But I have B.J.'s number. She was supposed to come back. If she's here, she can come." She paused, thinking about the possibilities. "If she's not, I'll just have to do the best I can. I saw one born once, on my stepfather's ranch." But Megan prayed she wasn't called on to play midwife to Chad's mare. She'd be frightened to death.

But something was prompting her to go to the barn. Even if Chad had upset her, too many times to mention, she didn't want anything to happen to his horses. She pulled on her coat, gloves, hat and even a muffler, wrapping her face so only her eyes were visible, and slipped out onto the porch.

Even with the porch roof absorbing some of the fury of the storm, she could barely see. She grabbed the rope hooked to one of the posts at the edge of the steps and moved out into the storm.

Now she knew what they meant when the weathermen said visibility was zero. She couldn't see as far as the end of her own nose. Her eyes were useless, and she snapped them shut and ducked her head.

The important thing, the lifesaving thought, was not to let go of the rope. Whatever else happened, her hands were both wrapped around that lifeline.

The horse barn was the second building. The relief that filled her when she slipped inside the shadowy barn was almost overwhelming. Her breathing was ragged, and she leaned against the closed door, relishing the muffled sounds and the relief from the pounding of the snow and wind.

Finally she pushed away from the door and began brushing the snow from her clothing. The welcoming nickers from the horses pleased her, making her feel a part of the ranch, as silly as that sounded even to her. Then she heard the sound of a horse in distress.

Flicking on the electric lights, she hurried to the last stall on the left, where the young mare was kept. The horse was lying down on the straw, clearly in trouble.

"Oh, no!" Megan moaned, and began digging in her pocket for B.J.'s number while she raced back to the other end of the barn to use the phone.

It didn't work.

Trying not to panic, Megan pulled back on her gloves. Red hadn't said anything about a rope from the last barn to B.J.'s house, but Megan prayed there was one. If not, she didn't know what she'd do.

Her return to the storm almost took her breath away. But she had more on her mind this time than the rope. An animal was suffering, and she was the only one to summon help.

Relief filled her when she found the taut rope after the next building. Following it as quickly as the storm would allow, she reached the front porch of the vet's house. Then she climbed the porch and pounded on the door.

Though it was only seconds, Megan thought she pounded for several minutes before the door swung open and she fell into their entry hall.

"Lands' sake! What's wrong, girl?" Mildred demanded as she helped her to her feet.

"Is B.J. here?" she panted.

"I'm here, Megan. What's wrong?" B.J. answered before her aunt could, moving from the back of the house.

"One of Chad's horses. She's delivering, and I think something's wrong. I could see part of the baby, but the mare was down, and—and—"

"I'll get my bag."

Megan liked the way B.J. didn't waste any time. Mildred held her coat for her, and though she warned her to be careful, she didn't slow her niece down.

In no time, the two women were outside, B.J. following Megan as they traversed the yard through the blinding snow, guided by the ropes. Megan could only hope B.J. was behind her, because she couldn't see her.

Once she stepped inside the horse barn, she turned anxiously to wait for B.J. She panicked when B.J. didn't immediately appear. Just when she was ready to retrace her steps, the other woman entered.

They were both gasping, but Megan led the way to the last stall.

"Go to her head and see if you can calm her down," B.J. ordered, and Megan circled the mare to kneel in the straw and stroke her.

"The baby's leg is caught. I've got to try to reverse the process a little. Hold her tight, Megan," B.J. ordered.

Megan caught the halter with one hand and continued to stroke the mare's neck and talk soothingly. "Is it going to live?"

"I don't know. We could lose both of them," B.J. gasped as she struggled to free the newborn.

Megan closed her eyes briefly and sent a silent prayer for the animals' survival. Chad might make her angry, but he didn't deserve such a tragedy.

B.J. had thrust off her coat and rolled up her sleeves before she began working on the animal. Now she gave a cry of satisfaction and withdrew her arm, bloody past the elbow, as the mare strained under Megan's hand.

In almost no time, B.J. was easing the birth sac from a tiny colt, helping it to lie down in the straw before she turned back to the mare.

Megan watched, thankful B.J. had been home. Without the storm, she would've been in town and not arrived in time. Of course, maybe Chad could've done the same job, but Megan was glad *she* hadn't had to try.

"Are they okay?" she asked, her voice barely above a whisper.

"Looks like it. The next couple of hours will tell. I'm going to give mama a shot, so keep hold of her head."

When that was accomplished, they let the mare rest a few moments and then B.J. came to her head to try to get her on her feet. It took several tries, but finally the mare was standing. Megan stayed with the animal, stroking her, congratulating her on her first baby, while B.J. steadied the colt on his trembling legs and guided him to his mother's milk.

Megan moved to B.J.'s side, and the two of them admired the product of their work. They didn't hear anyone approaching until Chad called out, "Is everything all right?"

He was just inside the door, looking more like a snowman

than a cowboy, but he raced down the barn before either of the surprised women could answer.

Megan beamed at him when he came to a halt beside them. "Look, Chad. She had a colt, and everything's all right, thanks to B.J."

"And Megan. If she hadn't checked on them and come to get me, they'd both be dead."

Megan drew in her breath as Chad stared at her, suddenly fearing that he would kiss her in front of B.J. Instead, he grinned at her. "Well, Megan, looks like you've got another horse to name."

Chapter Eleven

"I think B.J. should have that honor," Megan said, dropping her gaze from Chad's.

"No way," B.J. protested. "If you hadn't come to check on the mare, she would've died, and the foal with her. You do the honors, Megan. And if you'll excuse me, I'm heading home. It's been a long day."

Before Megan could think of a reason to keep the vet with her, preventing a tête-à-tête with Chad, the woman had left the barn. Megan finally shrugged her shoulders.

"Okay. But I'd like to know the father's name this time."

"He's a champion named Black Demon," Chad said.

"And what's mama's name?" Megan asked, patting the mare on her forelock.

Chad's cheeks reddened. "Licorice."

Megan's lips twitched, but she kept her expression solemn. "Then I think he should be called Black Sugar."

"Black Sugar? Is that masculine?" Chad asked.

"Yes. Masculine things can be sweet," she assured him, her chin raised.

Chad laughed. "Black Sugar it is. You're good with names, Megan." He looked at her and then turned his gaze away. "Uh, I'd like to apologize for this morning."

He would, of course, bring up the one subject she'd like to avoid. "That's not necessary," she mumbled.

"Yes, it is. I shouldn't have forced myself on you. I washed the sheets myself so Red wouldn't know."

"Thanks," Megan returned, and anxiously tried to think of

some way to change the subject. "How bad is this storm going to be? Are we going to be snowed in?"

Chad shrugged his shoulders. "Probably. It's pretty normal around here for winter."

Megan couldn't think of anything else to say. Retreat seemed the best option, and she moved toward the door to the stall. Chad apparently had the same idea, because he almost crashed into her.

He reached out to ward off the collision and then jerked his hands back. "Uh, we seem to have a past history of bumping into each other."

"Yes," Megan replied, her voice strained. All she could think about was how warm and seductive his touch was, how easily she was lost in his embrace.

"I guess we can learn from our mistakes. At least we missed each other this time." His lopsided grin made her want to trace his lips with her fingers, to change the half grin into one that took over his face.

"True. And we should never get close to each other with a breakfast tray," she added, trying to join in the spirit of his remarks.

"Especially one that has coffee on it," he said, his grin widening.

"Or strawberry jam."

"I don't know," he said, his gaze going to her forehead, "I find strawberry jam particularly seductive."

Megan sucked in her breath and held it. "We're supposed to avoid these situations, remember? Not encourage them."

"Oh, right."

The mare nudged Megan's arm, as if asking for attention, and she automatically rubbed her soft, velvety nose. "I guess we should go back to the house. You must be half-frozen." Anything to end their togetherness.

"Yeah, I guess so."

He elaborately swung open the stall door and gave Megan a wide berth to pass through. She took one last look at the horse and colt before she headed for the door.

But she couldn't help thinking that in a year or two, when none of the Randalls could remember her name, they'd know Tinkerbell and Black Sugar. She would have contributed to the

Randall future in a small way. It left a bittersweet taste in her mouth.

"Don't be an idiot," she warned herself. The longing that filled her when she thought of the future was a weakness she had to root out. She'd made up her mind a long time ago that marriage wasn't for her. As if Chad had marriage in mind, she reminded herself.

"Did you say something?" Chad asked, catching up with her.

"No, nothing at all." After all, what was there to say?

"Well, brace yourself. The wind is awfully strong. We don't want any more falls, do we?"

She couldn't even respond to his teasing. Had she lost her sense of humor, as well as her heart? She gasped at the thought. She hadn't lost her heart. It may have suffered a little damage, but she hadn't lost it. Had she?

"If it's that bad out, how did you find your way back to the house?" Her question was a desperate attempt to distract her thoughts.

"It was hard. But we used compasses and fence lines. We didn't expect the visibility to get so bad so quickly, though. Jake wouldn't risk his men to save cattle."

While he was explaining, she pulled on her gloves and wrapped her muffler around her face again.

"Ready?" he asked, and she nodded. He opened the door and, with a hand on her back, guided her out the door.

Again she could see almost nothing in front of her. Hanging on to the rope for dear life, she inched her way toward the house. But she had to admit, Chad's presence behind her, even if she couldn't see him, was a comfort.

CHAD BREATHED a sigh of relief when they reached the back porch. His body was exhausted from straining against the strength of the storm. It was only early afternoon, but he felt as if he'd put in twelve hours of hard work.

He started brushing down Megan after they reached the porch, but she pushed him away and did her own dismissal of the snow covering her. She was an independent woman, he decided with a frozen smile.

Too independent. And hardheaded. After the morning debacle, he'd decided he'd better slow down in his pursuit of her. At least he'd won a smile or two from her in the barn. Maybe this evening, he could convince her he wasn't all bad.

"That's enough," he muttered, reaching for the door. "Come on inside and let's thaw out."

The minute the warm air hit them, Chad felt better. And the savory smell filling the room reminded him of how hungry he was.

"Wow. How did Red manage a stew? He was out with us most of the day."

"I cooked it while you were gone. Red left me in charge of the kitchen."

"Well, as the person in charge of the kitchen, would you allow me to have a bowl before I take a shower? I think I'd warm up faster from the inside out."

"Of course." She moved toward the stove.

"Hey, you don't have to serve me, Megan. I can serve myself. You want a bowl, too?"

Her eyebrows went up in surprise. "Yes, thank you."

"Why do you look so surprised?" he asked as he filled two bowls.

"I didn't know women's lib had made it to Wyoming."

He gave her a friendly grin. "We weren't raised with a woman hovering over us. Red raised us right. Everybody does his job and everybody shares."

He set the bowls down on the table, side by side, and pulled out a chair for Megan. Together they began eating, conversation falling a distant second to their hunger.

The steaming beef and vegetables, seasoned with thyme, immediately began to thaw out his insides. "Lady, you can cook one mean stew," he murmured, smiling.

"Thank you."

Before he could make any more comments to reestablish friendly relations with Megan, Rita strolled into the kitchen.

"Chad! I wondered where you were. I've been so bored without you around," she trilled, and took the chair on his other side.

"Uh, I thought you had work to do." He hoped she had something to do. Last night, when he'd had to avoid Megan,

Rita had proved useful. But tonight he didn't want to avoid Megan. Though he wasn't sure he'd have a choice as he felt her stiffen next to him.

"I finished already. Megan's the one who has to make up time. Don't you, Megan?"

"I'm afraid so. And a shower to thaw out my toes might be a good idea, too. If you'll excuse me…?"

Before he could protest her departure, Megan was out the door. Right behind her came Jake and Pete, with Red trailing after them. Though he greeted his brothers, his mind was still on Megan and how he was going to make any progress if she was holed up in her room.

"Chad!" Rita complained. "You're ignoring me!"

He expelled his breath and tried counting to ten before he looked at the woman. "It's been a long day, and I'm tired."

"But what are we going to do for entertainment this evening?"

Jake must've sensed that Chad was losing patience. He stepped in to answer Rita's question. "We're going to watch a movie this evening. We just received a new shipment a few days ago. I'm sure Chad will join us after he has his shower. Right, Chad?"

"Sure, Jake," he replied, and stood.

Adele entered the kitchen before he could leave. "You're all back? Nasty outside."

After general agreement to that comprehensive statement, Adele continued, "So how does this storm affect our travel plans?"

Rita hadn't realized the implications of the storm. She looked at Adele. "What do you mean?"

"We couldn't get you to the airport in this storm," Pete explained, "and it wouldn't do you any good if we did. Planes aren't going to take off in a blizzard."

"How long will the storm last?" Rita demanded, an uneasy expression on her face.

"We don't know," Jake said, "but at least a couple of days. We've had them go on for a lot longer."

Rita appeared upset by their responses, but she said nothing. Jake rose from the table and joined Chad as he walked to the door.

"I need to talk to you," he said quietly, nodding toward his office.

Chad wondered what his brother needed to talk to him about, but he didn't hesitate to follow him from the kitchen. After all, Jake was the boss.

"In spite of what you said, you seemed interested in Rita last night. At least she thinks so," Jake began, sitting on the edge of his desk.

"No, I—" Chad began. Then he remembered his behavior at the dinner table the evening before and flushed. "Well, maybe I seemed interested in her for a while, but, Jake—"

"Chad, you know how edgy everyone gets in a storm, trapped in the house like we are. Play along with Rita, just until they leave. Okay?" He stood, assuming Chad would go along with his suggestion.

"I can't do that," Chad protested.

Jake turned to stare at him in surprise. "Why not?"

"Because—because I'm interested in Megan." Chad watched Jake's eyebrows lower. He hadn't wanted to upset his brother, but he couldn't pretend to pursue Rita with Megan watching his every move.

"No, Chad, Megan is for Pete."

"No, she's not."

"They're getting along well. Pete isn't as upset as he was. I don't want you interfering. I'm planning on expanding our family with Megan." Jake stood with his hands on his hips, his jaw squared in determination.

Chad frowned in return. "What do you mean, 'expand our family'? You expected Pete to marry her?" His voice rose in surprise.

"Well, of course I did. Why do you think I invited a bunch of decorators here?"

Unexpected laughter bubbled up in Chad. "I don't know. To decorate?"

Jake grinned in return. "I guess it sounds crazy, put like that, doesn't it? Look, Chad, one of us has got to marry. We need descendents, someone to come after us. Dad's gone. It's time we began producing the next generation."

"I don't see you going out looking for a woman to have *your* children." The conversation had turned serious again.

"Of course not! I tried marriage. I guess I'm not cut out for it. But you and Brett and Pete, you'll be great at being daddies. And I'll be the best uncle your kids have ever seen." Jake stepped closer and clapped Chad on the shoulder.

"Whoa! Wait a minute here, Jake. Pete or Brett, maybe, but not me. I'm no more cut out to be a husband than you were." Just the thought made Chad's skin clammy.

"You're wrong. You'll make a fine husband." Jake paused and then looked more closely at Chad. "If you're not thinking marriage, then what do you have in mind for Megan? I didn't bring her up here for your entertainment, boy. If that's all you've got in mind, leave her for Pete."

Frustrated, Chad snapped, "Pete doesn't want her!"

"How do you know?"

"Because I was leaving her for Pete, but he said he wasn't interested."

"Damn!" Jake ran a hand through his dark hair and blew out a big sigh. "Now what? How about Brett? Does he have any interest in her?"

"She's not a platter of meat to be passed around, Jake!" Chad protested, his insides aching. He didn't like the way this conversation was progressing.

"I know that! But after all my trouble to matchmake, I'd like some kind of result other than you getting laid."

Chad's hands involuntarily clenched into fists, and for the first time since they were boys, he was filled with the urge to hit his hero. "Don't talk about Megan like—like she's a groupie at one of the bars!"

Jake studied him, waiting before saying quietly, "So tell me what you have in mind if you don't mean marriage. A friendship? Going to be pen pals?" Then his voice hardened. "Or was sex what you had in mind, brother? A fling? An affair? And if that's what you're planning, then why is what I said so wrong?"

Chad's face flushed. "There's nothing wrong with two people enjoying each other."

"I used to think that way. Now I'm not so sure."

When Chad would've protested again, Jake raised his hand to silence him. "I'll talk to Pete. If he really isn't interested in

Megan, then I'll back off. But you be sure the choice is mutual and that you're honest about your intentions.''

"Jake!" Chad protested, hurt by his brother's warning.

Jake ignored him and stomped from the room, muttering, "Damn matchmaking! I can't do anything right when it comes to women!"

Chad stared at the door Jake closed behind him.

Matchmaking? Jake was matchmaking when he'd invited the decorators to come? The man was crazy! He didn't even meet the women first.

And what was he, Chad, going to do now?

He felt guilty thinking about bedding Megan when Jake had intended her to be Pete's bride, to carry on the Randall family.

Jake was right, too. Pete had seemed more cheerful with Megan around. Had he denied interest in Megan too soon? Was he really interested in her but just didn't know it yet?

Chad suddenly felt selfish.

Selfish and unsatisfied. Damn, he wanted Megan. Every time he got near her, he had to fight to keep his hands off her. She seemed to occupy more and more of his thoughts. But marriage wasn't anything he'd considered.

He thought about Jake's miserable marriage.

No, marriage wasn't for him, just as it wasn't for Jake. And maybe Megan wasn't for him, either. Jake was right. Just taking her to bed to satisfy his urges didn't seem too honorable.

Damn.

MEGAN STARED at the big-screen television as she nibbled on popcorn. Seated between Brett and Pete, she'd kept her eyes on the movie from the very beginning, trying to ignore the cozy twosome on the couch across from them. Chad had returned to the kitchen after his shower and immediately begun flirting with Rita.

Proving Megan right.

He was a flirt, a man who chased after the nearest woman, without any regard to people's feelings. Just like several of her mother's husbands. Just like the man she'd planned to marry, only she'd discovered his true nature before she'd walked down the aisle.

Just like all men.

Unfortunately they were watching a romance. Jake had been intrigued by the title, *While You Were Sleeping*. The film had come out a year or two ago, and Megan had seen it then. And cried.

Not because of the romance in the movie, though it was satisfying. No, she'd cried because the heroine was all alone in the world and was tempted to lie because she coveted the hero's family.

Megan knew just how she felt.

This past Christmas, she'd spent the day alone. Her mother and her young husband were in the south of France. Not that her mother had forgotten her. No, Megan had received a box a couple of days before Christmas with instructions not to open until December 25. But a bottle of perfume, even expensive French perfume, couldn't replace family.

She'd kept busy. It wasn't the first Christmas she had spent alone, and it wouldn't be the last, she was sure. She knew all the tricks. New Year's Eve, she'd had a party, inviting everyone she knew. And she'd had the Christmas holidays to get ready for it.

"Can you imagine someone living in a city that big?" Pete asked softly.

"But there's so much to do in Chicago," Rita assured him. "You'd never be bored."

Pete shrugged. "I'm never bored here on the ranch."

Megan smiled at him. No, she couldn't imagine any of the Randall brothers bored.

When the main character, Lucy, gave her speech about loving the hero's family, Megan nodded. Yes, that must explain what had been happening. She was attracted to Chad, of course. There was no doubt that they had some kind of weird chemistry any time they got close to each other.

But she'd also wanted his family, just like the character in the film. She'd wanted to be a part of their closeness. And she'd wanted to move back to the country. Those years on Jim's ranch had been the best of her life.

No wonder she'd thought she was falling for Chad Randall. He was handsome, sexy and intelligent. He had a wonderful family. And he lived on a ranch.

She couldn't have concocted a more potent attraction if she'd tried.

Time to wise up, Chase, she warned herself. *These things never work out. Better to understand that now and not break your heart. Look at him over there flirting with Rita. If that's the kind of action he's interested in, then you're better off without him.*

There. She'd gotten things worked out. Now she could forget about Chad Randall and get on with her job. She'd make her employer very happy if she and Adele won the job. She might even get a promotion out of it.

Yes, she was lucky to have this opportunity.

So why did she feel like the unluckiest person in the world?

Chapter Twelve

Chad scarcely noticed the movie. He was much more intent on Megan, sitting between Pete and Brett. Was she interested in Pete?

Rita, seated beside him, reminded him of a persistent fly at a picnic. No matter how many times you swatted it away, it kept coming back. Not that he took the opportunity to swat Rita, tempting as that might be. He'd tried to discourage her interest in him, though, with no success.

She kept hinting about the size of her bed, her loneliness, her needs. He was surprised she hadn't had cards printed for advertising.

Too bad they couldn't take her back to the steak house in Rawhide. She'd find some willing cowboys there, but she was striking out at the Randall ranch. Especially with him.

When the movie ended, they all returned to the kitchen. Red had promised them hot apple pie.

"I can't believe anyone could eat more after the huge dinner," Rita complained. "Though, of course, I didn't eat that much, but with my delicate appetite, it doesn't take much to fill me up." She looked pointedly at the two other women.

Chad grinned as Megan ignored the catty remark. Adele wasn't as generous. "Maybe it was that huge sandwich you ate at lunch that really filled you up."

Rita pouted, and Jake hurried to change the subject, asking everyone's opinion of the movie. Under the cover of the conversation, Chad murmured, "You won't offend Red if you'd rather go on up to bed. He'd understand."

Her eyes opened wide, and she leaned closer to him. "Are you going to have dessert?"

"Yeah. Apple pie is one of my favorites." Rats. Maybe he should've given up pie if it would mean Rita's departure. But she probably would've suggested they do something together. The lady was nothing if not determined.

She reached out a finger to stroke his arm. "Maybe—" she paused to wet her lips "—maybe I'll go on up to bed, have a bubble bath, prepare—" a significant flutter of her lashes filled the pause "—for bed."

"Good idea," he replied enthusiastically. "A bubble bath would be relaxing."

"And sensual," she whispered. "Will you come…tell me good-night?"

"If it's not too late," he said vaguely, vowing to himself to stay up all night if necessary.

"Oh, it won't be. I'll be waiting."

Yeah. That's what he was afraid of.

Rita stood. "I think I'll pass on the pie, Red, though I'm sure it's delicious. My figure, you know." Again she ran her hands up and down her body and stared at Chad.

Finally, with a general goodbye to everyone and a heated look at Chad, she left the kitchen. Everyone ate in silence until Brett finally said, "You must not have any calories in you, Chad. The lady almost swallowed you whole right here at the table."

Chad wadded up his paper napkin and aimed at Brett's head as everyone laughed. "Any time you want to entertain the lady, just let me know. I'm only doing it 'cause Jake asked me to." He couldn't keep his gaze from Megan's face as he made his explanation. There wasn't any reaction that he could tell.

"I know," Pete said with a sigh. "It's a tough job, but someone has to do it."

"I haven't seen you making an effort with the lovely but obvious Rita," Chad complained.

"Of course not. Megan's my job. And talk about a tough one! The lady constantly wants to be entertained, waited on, flirted with. She won't leave me alone for a minute."

Megan, sitting next to Pete, dug an elbow into his side and grinned at him. "Watch it, mister!"

Chad was jealous as hell.

"I'm afraid Rita is a little spoiled," Adele said. "We're here as professionals. None of us should need to be 'taken care of.'"

Jake responded, "You and Megan have certainly conducted yourselves professionally. And I don't mind telling you that I will probably hire your two firms to do the job, so I hope you like spending time here."

Adele expressed her pleasure, but Megan remained silent, and Chad watched as her fingers tightened on the coffee cup she was holding. What did that mean? Didn't she like it here? Her enthusiasm had seemed sincere.

"And with Megan around for a while, all our animals will have terrific names," Pete murmured, sending a teasing grin her way.

"That's true," she said, relaxing, "and I've been thinking about asking Jake if I could rename the rest of you. I think Pete's name should be Teaser, Brett is Joker, and Chad... Womanizer."

The other two protested loudly, but Chad said nothing. He already knew her opinion of him.

"Of course, you got Chad right," Pete added. "He's known for his reputation with the ladies."

Chad groaned under his breath. Leave it to his brothers to sink him completely.

Brett, as if more sensitive to Chad's mood, said, "I don't know. He's been hanging around the ranch the last few weekends. I thought he was losing his touch until Rita came into our lives."

"I told you I'm only entertaining her because Jake asked me to. Isn't that right, Jake?" He pleaded with his gaze for his oldest brother to back him up.

"That's right, Chad, and you're doing a damn fine job. In fact, the way the lady was heating up, I think you might consider easing off."

There was more laughter and comments before Jake stood. "Well, I'm ready to call it a night." He carried his plate and cup to the sink.

Among general agreement, Chad panicked. It was way too early for him to go up. If he didn't go to Rita's room, she'd come knocking on his door. "I'm not ready for bed yet. Won't anyone keep me company?"

Chad figured there must've been some desperation in his voice, because Pete started a refusal and then changed his mind. "Why not? I guess we can sleep in until seven or so in the morning."

"I'll have another piece of pie," Brett said, getting up to cut a second slice.

"I'm not sleepy because I slept late," Megan said, "but I think you all must be masochists after the day you've had."

"Well, I'm not a masochist," Jake said as he walked past them. "You kids have fun. And don't stay up too late. We'll have to do a few chores tomorrow."

Adele accompanied Jake as he left the kitchen. Red, having finished rinsing their dishes, turned to the others. "Do your own dishes when you finish. I'm turning in, too. These old bones aren't used to being back in the saddle all day." He paused by the table to put a hand on Megan's shoulder. "Thanks for helping out today."

She smiled at him. "I enjoyed it, what little I did."

After Red left, Pete said, "I hope you're happy about getting the job here. We haven't upset you with our teasing, have we?"

"No, of course not. It makes me feel part of the—the family." She flashed a bright smile that Chad thought was a little uptight. "I was just thinking of the complications all the traveling will cause."

Megan stood and began picking up the dishes, and the three men joined her.

"Were you thinking about a boyfriend?" Pete asked.

Megan looked at him, puzzled. "What are you talking about?"

Chad's interest intensified, and he waited for Pete to explain.

"When you were talking about complications, were you thinking about a boyfriend? Someone who would be unhappy that you were out of town, here with four incredibly handsome, sexy bachelors?" He grinned at his self-description.

Though Megan smiled back, she only said, "No."

They rinsed the dishes, and then Pete asked, "No boyfriend, or no, he wouldn't be jealous?"

Chad was glad Pete was asking the question he couldn't ask,

until it occurred to him that Pete's insistence was proving his earlier speculation: that Pete was interested in Megan. He stuck his hands in his back jeans pockets and studied the floor.

"No boyfriend at the moment, Pete, though I would never let my personal life interfere with my job anyway."

"A career lady, huh?"

"Yes." Her answer was crisp and dismissing, as if she didn't want to answer any more personal questions.

Pete leaned against the counter, studying Megan. "Why isn't a beautiful lady like you married?"

Megan burst into laughter.

"What's so funny?" Chad asked.

"Look at you. Four eligible, handsome men, none of you married, and you want to know why *I'm* not married? You're probably all older than me. Why aren't *you* married?"

Chad held his silence, but Pete answered her. "Some of us aren't cut out for marriage."

"Oh, so all women are cut out for marriage, but not all men?" she returned.

"Well…" Pete paused.

"That's not true," Brett suddenly said, a frown on his face. "I think it's because there aren't too many women around here. We don't have that many opportunities to meet women."

"Then why don't you go where you *will* meet some women. Unless you're not interested in marriage."

"That's what Jake did," Pete muttered. "Didn't do him much good."

"Why did Jake end up getting a divorce?" Megan asked. "I know it's none of my business, but I'm curious."

"Because she was a…witch," Brett said with a grin. "At least that's what Chad named her—Chloe, Wicked Witch of the East."

"She made Jake's life miserable," Chad said in defense.

"I guess we Randalls aren't very good with women," Pete added, and Chad was reminded of Pete's failed romance.

"That's not true! I don't see why all of you aren't married. You're charming, handsome, kind. You must not be trying."

Pete tensed up. "I tried! It—it didn't work out."

Megan reached out to touch Pete on the arm. "I'm sorry,

Pete. I didn't mean— She must be nuts to let a guy like you get away," she finished with a warm smile. "But why—?"

"Jake chose the wrong kind of woman," Pete said. "He met her while he was in Casper on business and married her before he knew much about her. She was beautiful, but she didn't fit in here on the ranch. She wanted Jake to move to Casper."

"Leave the ranch?" Megan demanded, horrified. "Surely she couldn't expect such a thing?"

"Yeah, she did. She said it was sick, all of us living here together."

Brett chuckled. "She even hinted we were…strange," he said, pausing to wiggle his eyebrows at Megan.

She giggled. "Not a perceptive woman, I'd say."

"No, and a lot like Rita. She thought the world should revolve around her," Brett continued. "Because he worked long hours instead of entertaining her, she told Jake he was too dull to ever make any woman happy."

"He believed her?" Megan demanded incredulously. She surveyed the faces of the three men. "You all believed her, didn't you?"

Megan listened as all three men disclaimed belief, but the only one who sounded convinced was Brett. Shaking her head, she said, "I can't believe you let a woman like that persuade you that you weren't suited for marriage."

"Hell, Megan, as far as I can tell, she was right!" Pete exclaimed, sadness on his face.

"Why? Because you had a fight with your girlfriend? Everyone has fights, Pete."

"Why are you giving us advice?" Chad demanded. "You said yourself you didn't intend to marry. What makes you the next Dear Abby?"

"I choose not to marry, Chad, because I'm not interested. But the four of you are going around believing you're not suited to marriage."

Pete growled something in response, and Megan shook her head. "Sorry. You're right. I have no business giving you any advice. I'd better go to bed before I get myself in real trouble."

The three brothers stood watching her in silence. When the door closed behind her, Chad muttered, "Not the four of us," and then regretted his slip.

Pete's gaze whipped to him. "What do you mean, not the four of us? Who doesn't think marriage isn't for the Randalls?"

"Nothing," Chad muttered, and started toward the door, hoping to escape without explaining.

Brett, more curious than upset, unlike Pete, demanded, "Who, Chad?"

"Yeah, who?" Pete asked. "You must be talking about Brett here. He's the only one—"

"No. I'm talking about Jake. He thinks *he's* not suited to marriage, but he's planning on sending the rest of us down the aisle."

"Yeah, right," Pete said with a cynical chuckle. "How's he gonna do that?"

"Hire a decorator."

His brothers stared at him in confusion before first Pete and then Brett's eyes widened in comprehension. "No!" they said in unison.

"What are you saying, Chad?" Brett asked, as if wanting confirmation of his thoughts.

"He didn't," Pete protested, his stare fixed on his youngest brother also.

"He did. He told me."

"Wait a minute," Brett protested. "It doesn't make sense."

"He hired decorators so that we'd meet some women."

"You mean he really isn't going to have any work done?" Pete asked, suddenly appalled.

"Yeah, he's going to have the work done. Jake wouldn't be dishonest. But he intended— He hoped that one of us would…that is, he wanted— Hell!" Chad finished in frustration.

"Adele's too old," Pete mused aloud, "and Rita's too much like Chloe. It's clear Jake doesn't like her. I guess that leaves Megan."

"But why is Jake so intent on us marrying?" Brett asked.

"He's worried about the next generation," Chad explained. "Apparently, since Dad died, he feels responsible for continuing the Randall name. He wants us to have children."

Brett's face showed panic. "Kids? I'm not ready to have kids. We've got a few good years left, don't we?"

Chad slapped his brother on the back. "Don't get your shorts all twisted in a knot. You're not first on the list."

Pete stared at him. "That leaves you and me, little brother." Then comprehension seemed to come to him. "That's why you thought—" He stopped in midsentence. "Well, I've had enough soul-searching for one night." Before anyone could say anything, he shoved away from the kitchen counter and strode for the door. Brett followed him.

Chad stood alone in the kitchen, wondering how he was going to avoid going upstairs. He was afraid if he didn't go to Rita's room, she'd come to his. And he didn't have a lock on his bedroom door.

He didn't have long to contemplate his problem, however, because Megan reentered the kitchen, anger on her face.

"Megan? Are you all right?" All thought of his conversation with his brothers disappeared as he focused on her.

"Apparently all right enough to be a sacrificial virgin for the Randall brothers!"

He wouldn't have been surprised to see flames come from her mouth, her words were so hot. And accurate.

"What—what do you mean?"

"Don't act innocent with me, Chad Randall! I came back down to ask Brett a question about the office. I overheard you tell your brothers that Jake only hired decorators so he could find wives for all of you."

"Now, Megan—" His soft tone didn't soothe her.

"Are you sure he's going to have any work done? Or was this whole thing just a scam?"

"Surely you've been around Jake long enough to know he wouldn't do such a thing. Of course he's going to have the work done. And there were no strings attached to the job. He just thought— He was hoping— We don't meet many women out here."

"That's a pretty lame excuse, Chad. You could go some-where to meet women."

"Yeah, women like Rita."

She put her hands on her hips, still angry. "There are other women. Pete found one."

"Yeah. And all he got for his efforts is heartache."

"Oh, please!" Megan protested, and began pacing the floor. "Just because you stub your toe, you don't quit the game."

Chad couldn't help grinning, and Megan whirled around to see him. "What's so funny?"

"You sound like a coach. It's kind of surprising to hear something like that from a girl."

She rolled her eyes in exasperation. "This is a ridiculous situation. And now we're snowed in. How can I face Jake, knowing that he only hired us as potential brides?"

"Aw, Megan, you won't tell Jake I told you, will you?" He knew Jake would forgive him. After all, he hadn't really told Megan. But he'd told Pete and Brett.

Megan sized him up with her gaze. "You didn't tell me, technically. So I suppose I could keep quiet. But it means you owe me a favor."

"Anything." He suddenly remembered the dilemma he'd been facing when she entered the room. "Uh, Megan, I have another favor to ask." He unconsciously took a step toward her, not even aware of his movement until she backed away, a wary expression on her face.

"What favor?"

"I need protection." He tried to look helpless, but he didn't think Megan was buying that pose. Her expression grew skeptical.

"What kind of protection?"

"From Rita."

Megan made a production of looking around the kitchen. "I don't see her."

"No, she's waiting upstairs for me."

Megan rolled her eyes again. "I think you've gotten yourself into this particular jam, and you can get yourself out of it."

She turned to go, and Chad sprinted to the door to block her exit. When she saw him run, she hurried, too. They arrived at the door almost simultaneously.

"Not another collision!" she protested as he captured her shoulders.

"Nope, I won fair and square."

"What do you think you've won, Chad Randall?" she demanded, her chin raised in challenge.

Chad had to fight hard to resist the urge to kiss her, but he knew if he gave in to his wants, she'd leave him stranded, on his own.

"Okay, here's the deal. I beat you to the door, so now you either have to remain down here with me for a while, or let me share your bed...room," he hurriedly added as Megan's cheeks flamed.

Chapter Thirteen

"What did you say?"

Her full, pink lips opened in surprise, and he desperately wanted to close them with his. But this wasn't the time.

"I said you need to stay here with me or let me share your bedroom. Bedroom," he repeated, making sure he'd said it correctly this time.

"You're being ridiculous." She tried to unsettle him from his position, putting her hands on his chest.

His arms came around her. "No, I'm not. If I go up this early, Rita is going to expect me to come to her room."

She rolled her eyes in disgust. "Don't go. She'll catch on in an hour or two."

"Not Rita. She'll come to my room. And I don't have a lock on it." His temperature was rising from her nearness.

Laughing scornfully, she suggested, "So sleep with her."

"No, thank you."

"Why not? She wouldn't be your first, would she?"

"Look," he replied in frustration, "I know you don't have a very high opinion of my behavior with women, but I've never slept with a woman I didn't like or respect. And I'm not about to change now."

She dropped her gaze to his chest. "Rita's not that bad. She's a little pushy, but I heard she recently went through a bitter divorce. That does a lot of harm to a woman's ego."

Something in her voice got his attention. "Have you been married?"

Her gaze jerked up to his and then away again. "No! I— was engaged once, but I didn't marry."

"Why not?"

"This conversation isn't about me," she protested, and tried to step back out of his arms.

He held her fast. "Why didn't you get married?" He wasn't sure why he persisted with his question. He figured he already knew the answer. When she stubbornly said nothing, he prompted, "He was a flirt, right?"

At that, her gaze lifted to his, her eyes as icy cold as the world outside. "A flirt? He was a lot more than that. He had several women on the side. And believe me, he didn't care if he liked or respected them. And he also didn't understand why his infidelity would upset me!"

Without thinking, he hugged her close against him. "He was an idiot."

She pushed away from him, and this time he let her go. "I'm not letting you in my bedroom, Chad."

"Then stay down here with me a while longer."

"I don't want to play any pool. I'm not good at it."

"How about a computer game?"

She stared at him with exasperation written all over her face, and he tried to look innocent and vulnerable.

"This situation is all your fault," she said in disgust.

"Yes, ma'am."

"I should ignore you."

"Yes, ma'am."

"I won't play computer games with you. But I'll watch *National Velvet*."

He let out a whoop that had her shushing him, then he picked her up and spun around.

"Chad! You're going to have Jake down here fussing at us," she warned, "or maybe Rita."

He set her back down on the floor. "I'll be as quiet as a mouse." Then he took her hand and headed down the hall to the TV room.

SOME NOISE WAS DISTURBING his sleep. Chad shifted slightly, only to find his movement constrained by something heavy on his chest. His eyes slowly opened to stare down at Megan's sweet face, her warm body sprawled across his.

He was in heaven.

No, he was in the TV room.

Ah, last night. He remembered now. They'd started watching the movie, sitting circumspectly apart. Then, as the night grew chillier, he'd pulled out a blanket to cover both of them. They'd taken off their shoes and gotten comfortable on the extrawide sofa and the hassock in front of it.

Now Megan was stretched out the length of the sofa, her head on his chest, while his legs were propped on the hassock. He felt a distinct stiffness in his neck, but he wasn't going to complain.

Even as he wondered what time it was, considering trying to ease his arm from under Megan to look at his watch, the door to the TV room was thrown open.

"Aha!" Rita shouted.

Chad turned his head to warn her not to wake Megan and discovered she wasn't alone. Almost every other member of the household was right behind her.

"What's going on?" Jake asked, stepping past Rita. "Are you two okay?"

Megan's eyes fluttered open, and Chad grinned at her. A slow, dreamy smile spread across her lips, and he wished they were alone.

"Megan? Is everything all right?" Adele asked.

Awareness shot into Megan's gaze, and she bolted upright. "What?"

"We fell asleep watching a movie last night," Chad hurriedly explained to their audience. "That's all. What's wrong with everyone?"

"I couldn't find you," Rita said angrily. "I thought you were going to come...tell me good-night." She looked around self-consciously at her last statement, but Chad wasn't buying the act. The lady knew exactly what she was saying.

"No. I was busy." He didn't want to be cruel, but he was tired of, as Megan put it, playing that game, even for the sake of peace.

"Sorry we woke you," Jake said. "When Rita didn't find Megan in her bedroom or downstairs, she asked about you.

Brett checked your room. With both of you missing, I thought we should search the house before we went out to the barns.''

"Is the storm still raging?" Chad asked, unable to see out with the drapes closed.

"Yeah…inside and out," Brett said with a chuckle.

Rita sent him a killer look and stomped out of the room.

"Um, Red wants to know if you want breakfast. Everyone else has eaten," Jake asked, ignoring Rita's behavior.

"Yeah, sure. Give us a minute to wake up," Chad asked, already feeling the loss as Megan sat beside him now, her cheeks red.

As Jake shooed everyone out of the room and closed the door softly behind him, Chad sagged against the cushions in relief. "Sorry, Megan. I didn't mean to cause a scene."

"It's not your fault. I'm as guilty as you."

He noticed she didn't look at him. "Hell, we're not guilty of anything but being tired. Jake's not upset. The only one who cares is Rita. It's no big deal."

She gave him an awkward smile and stood. "Do you think I have time for a quick shower before breakfast? I feel… disheveled."

"Sure. But on you, disheveled looks good." And had felt good, too. In fact, her warm, flushed body pressed against his had felt sensational.

Blushing, she turned to the door. There, she paused to say, "I enjoyed watching the movie with you." Then she was gone.

He breathed out a deep sigh of frustration and longing. Enjoyed it? Oh, yeah. He only wished he hadn't fallen asleep. Then he could remember holding her. As it was, he only had those couple of minutes this morning.

MEGAN STEPPED OUT of the shower, dried off and wrapped the towel around her before opening the door to her bedroom. She came to an abrupt halt when she discovered a visitor.

"Hello, Rita. Did you want something?"

"Yes! I want Chad." The woman's face was tight with anger, and her arms were crossed over her chest.

"Then you need to talk to Chad, not me. He's not mine to give away."

"Not yet, but I'll have to give you credit for trying."

"I'd like you to leave so I can dress. Red is waiting to fix breakfast for me."

"That old man would fix you breakfast at midnight if you wanted it. You've certainly done your best to get in good with everyone around here. You think that will get you the contract, don't you?"

Megan chewed her bottom lip while she tried to decide on a response that would bring this conversation to an end. Finally she said, "Rita, I realize you're angry, but I have no interest in discussing any of this with you. Please leave."

"Keep your hands off Chad!"

"As I said before, you need to discuss your relationship with Chad, not me." She moved to the dresser and pulled out her clothes, trying to ignore the other woman.

"You were just playing hard-to-get, weren't you?" Rita demanded, following her.

"What are you talking about?"

"When we first arrived, you acted like you weren't interested in him, to draw his attention."

Wordlessly Megan gathered her clothing and went back to the bathroom, with Rita dogging her heels like a pit bull. The only way to get rid of Rita was to shut the door in her face.

"I'm not going to give up!" Rita screamed through the door, pounding it with her fist. "I want Chad!"

Megan dressed calmly, ignoring the muffled sounds coming through the door.

Why wasn't she more upset over the confrontation with Rita? she wondered. Maybe it was because she knew she hadn't tried to take Chad away from her. Not because she wasn't attracted to him, of course.

This morning when she'd awakened to his smile, she'd felt wonderful. It had taken her embarrassment to shake her from that enjoyment.

Now, of course, she remembered all the reasons to avoid Chad Randall. But she had enjoyed those few moments.

She unlocked and swung open the door, prepared to ignore Rita if she was still there.

She wasn't.

Chad was.

"What are you doing in here?" she demanded.

"I heard Rita berating you and thought I should rescue you." He grinned. "Want to reward me with a kiss?"

"No, I do not!" she protested, but she couldn't help smiling back. "But I do thank you. She seems to feel that I've stolen something from her. Namely, you."

"You couldn't steal what she didn't have. I've explained that to her."

Her gaze met his in surprise. "How did she take it?"

"Not well. She's downstairs right now demanding to be taken to the airport."

Megan's gaze turned to the window, noting that the storm hadn't let up. "I guess Jake's trying to explain to her why that's impossible."

"That would be my guess." Without any warning, he walked over and wrapped his arms around her. "Mmm, you smell good."

"Chad!" she exclaimed, taken by surprise. "What are you doing?"

"Giving you a morning hug. After sleeping together, I don't think that's too forward, do you?"

She pushed her way out of his embrace. "You're being ridiculous. We didn't sleep together."

"We most assuredly did. Unfortunately that's all we did… sleep." He followed her to the dresser where she was searching for socks.

"You shouldn't be in here," she told him, her fingers shaking as she finally pulled out a matching pair. He was unnerving her.

"What difference does it make? It's not like we're naked on the bed."

Megan frantically tried to dismiss the picture he'd drawn, but his fingers on her shoulders made it difficult. With her breathing becoming more and more shallow, she pulled away and sat down on the bed to pull on her socks.

Chad leaned against the dresser, his arms crossed over his broad chest, and watched her. "I've never thought putting on socks was sexy, but you've changed my mind, Meggie."

"Stop it!" She yanked on the second sock and stood. "I'm

sure Red has breakfast ready. I don't want to keep him waiting.''

"Where are your shoes?"

She looked around her, but concentration escaped her with Chad watching her every move. "I don't know!" she wailed.

He crossed to her side and hugged her again. "Shh, honey, don't get upset. You probably left them downstairs. Come on. We'll get them before we go to breakfast.''

WITH HER SHOES RETRIEVED from the TV room and a big breakfast in her stomach, Megan felt much more in control of things an hour later. Even more so because Jake had given Chad a list of chores to be done.

When Chad was in the same room, she had difficulty concentrating. She hoped the storm ended soon. If not, she feared constant exposure to whatever chemistry occurred when she was with him would result in her doing something stupid. Like loving him.

"More coffee, Megan?" Red asked, interrupting her thoughts.

"Oh, yes, thanks, Red. But you didn't need to wait on me. I could've gotten it myself.''

"Well, I thought I'd have a second cup with you.''

Megan waited as Red joined her, wondering if he wanted to say something to her. However, he simply sipped his coffee, remaining silent.

"How much longer do you think the storm will last?" she finally asked.

"Reckon another day or two. You're not anxious to leave, are you?''

She smiled, hoping he wouldn't notice the tension she was feeling. "I've enjoyed my visit, but I have a job to do, you know.''

"Are you one of these career ladies?" he asked, watching her intently, innocently repeating a question she'd been asked last night.

"I—I have to support myself, Red. And I like what I do.''

He grunted in response and looked away. "Well, I wanted to tell you that havin' you here has made a real difference.

We've been without any women for a long time. I kinda like a little feminine influence.''

Neither of them had noticed Jake at the door. "Glad to hear you say that, Red. Megan will be back a lot to fix up the house. Her and Adele. And then there's the vet and her aunt. We're going to have women all over the place.''

Megan looked at Jake, wondering if he knew that Chad had told them of his plan. She didn't think so. What would he think up next? Had his brothers figured out that he would come up with another scheme when this one didn't work?

"Red said he thought the storm would last another couple of days,'' she said, hoping Jake might have better news.

"If Red says so, then he's probably right. He's more accurate than the weatherman on television,'' Jake said as he poured himself a cup of coffee and settled down at the table.

"I'm going to sit down with Adele and put the final touches on our recommendation this morning,'' Megan told Jake. "Then, when the storm stops, you'll be able to ship us off at once.''

"You make it sound like we're going to be glad to get rid of you,'' Jake drawled, smiling at her. "Red was right. We've enjoyed having some ladies around the place.''

Megan took a sip of coffee. Then she impulsively said, "Look, Jake, it's not going to work.''

Both men stared at her, Red in puzzlement, but Jake's gaze grew hard.

"What are you talking about?''

"I know about your plan. I overheard Chad telling his brothers last night.'' As soon as she said the words, she wished she'd kept her thoughts to herself.

"Chad told them what?''

She finally lifted her gaze to his. "That you hired decorators because you hoped to—to matchmake.''

"Damn his hide, that boy's got a big mouth.''

"What's she talkin' about, Jake?'' Red demanded. "You mean you're not gonna redo the kitchen?''

The sight of this wizened old cowboy worrying about his kitchen caused a bubble of laughter to escape. She was relieved when Jake's smile matched her own.

"Sure, we're going to redo the kitchen for you, Red. We're going to redo the whole blasted house, right, Megan?"

She nodded. "But we don't have to do the entire house, Jake. You could just choose part of our recommendations."

"Then what was she talkin' about it not workin'?" Red was persistent.

"Megan's talking about my plan to find wives for those three scalawags I call brothers." Jake smiled ruefully at her. "It was a kind of crazy plan, wasn't it?"

Megan shrugged her shoulders. "It might have worked, Jake," she said softly. "You were a little unlucky, that's all. You four Randall brothers are prime choice. The women in Denver would have a feeding frenzy if they knew about you."

"But not you?"

She ignored his question. "Pete's not ready to think about another woman. I think he's still hung up on Janie."

"You got that right," Red inserted.

"I've got two other brothers. Care to take either of them off my hands?"

With perfect timing, the back door opened and Chad and Pete rushed in.

Chapter Fourteen

"It's mighty cold out there." Pete shook off the snow and rubbed his hands together. "Got a spare cup of hot coffee, Red?"

"Sure do." The old man filled two more mugs.

"You've finished all the chores?" Jake asked his two brothers.

"Yeah." Chad took the seat beside Megan.

"How's Black Sugar?" she asked, breathing in the mixture of cold air and masculine scent that covered him.

"Looking good. He's not as wobbly this morning. B.J. was in the barn when I got there, checking him out." Chad smiled at his big brother. "I think Pete did a damn fine job of hiring a vet."

Jake grunted. "How's her family settling in? The boy and her aunt."

"She hasn't said," Chad replied, "but she told me yesterday that her husband was killed in a storm. Makes her boy nervous when she's out in bad weather."

In a casual move, he stretched his arm across the back of Megan's chair and drank his coffee with his left hand. Though she liked the warmth that surrounded her, she leaned forward, away from him, and sipped her coffee.

Jake frowned but said nothing.

"Aren't you going to offer us a snack?" Pete complained

to Red, changing the subject. "I've been working hard. I need some sustenance."

"You've only been out there an hour or two, boy. What's wrong with you?" Red asked. But even with his question, he got up from the table.

"If you're going to serve cookies, I've got to leave," Megan said with a grin. She pushed her chair back, dislodging Chad's arm. "Any more of those cookies, and I won't be able to fit in my jeans."

"And that would be a real shame," Chad said softly, his grin cocky.

She glared at him before turning to Jake. "I'll go get together with Adele. We should be able to show you what we have in mind this afternoon."

"Great. I'll look forward to it," Jake assured her with a warm smile.

In fact, they were all smiling at her as she left the room, giving her a feeling of belonging. And one smile did more than that. It made her hot.

CHAD HAD RETURNED to the horse barn after a quiet lunch. Rita had decided to take all her meals in her room until it was possible to escape from the ranch. Red agreed to her request because, as he put it, that was a lot less trouble than having that blasted woman in his kitchen.

Megan and Adele were meeting with Jake this afternoon to go over their proposal, so Chad knew he wouldn't see her. He might as well check on his horses.

He spent the afternoon puttering around the barn, cleaning the stalls, polishing tack…and thinking about Megan. The woman turned him on like no one else ever had. If she were leaving permanently when the snowstorm ended, he'd have to make a decision about his feelings, his desire, soon.

But she'd be back. He had time to work out the fascination he felt for her. Time to gain control of the need that was building in him. A need that scared him spitless.

Even during his early romantic escapades, he'd never felt so out of control, so needy. Yeah, he had time to step back and strengthen his resistance.

He was feeling pretty good about his decision until the barn door opened and a snow-covered Megan came in. He watched her from the shadows where he sat mending a bridle, his body tensing.

"Chad?" she called.

"Yeah. What are you doing out here?"

His voice gave away his position, and she walked toward him. "I wanted to see the babies again."

"Didn't anyone tell you you shouldn't come out in this storm without a good reason?"

"The storm isn't as bad now. It's still snowing, but the wind has died down." She tilted her head to one side, staring at him. "Are you in a bad mood?"

"Nope. How did the session with Jake go? You get the job?" He watched as she turned away from him, moving to the door of the nearest stall to pet the mare kept there.

"Yes. We're going to do the work in stages."

"So when will you be back?"

She looked over her shoulder at him. "I haven't left yet."

"I know. But you'll leave as soon as the storm's over, won't you?" Somehow, saying that fact aloud made his gut tighten.

"I suppose so."

"You like living in the city?"

Shrugging her shoulders, she murmured, "It's okay."

"Brett tried it. He couldn't stand it longer than a year."

"And you?"

"Only when I was in college."

"But according to Brett and Pete, you go to town a lot, at least on the weekends."

He smiled slightly. "A man gets tired of masculine company all the time."

"Ah."

"You seeing anyone?" Pete had already asked that question, but he wanted to hear her answer again.

She turned and wandered farther away from him to the next stall. "No."

"Why not?"

She shrugged her shoulders again.

"You're not being very talkative." He didn't think he'd ever complained about a woman not talking before. But he wanted to know everything about Megan.

Instead of answering him, she walked toward him. "What are you doing?"

"Mending a bridle."

"Oh. It's almost dinnertime."

"Yeah." More brilliant conversation. Finally he decided to stop avoiding the topic on his mind. "What are we going to do about this?"

"This what?"

"This feeling. I want you so bad that if you said the word, I'd strip you naked right here." A visible shiver ran over her, and he felt his body responding.

"I don't think that would be a good idea."

"Oh, it'd be a great idea. We might be a little late for dinner, but that's okay." His gaze roamed her body, even though more than half of it was covered by her coat.

"Stop it, Chad. I don't bed-hop."

"You said you weren't dating anyone!" he protested sharply.

"I'm not. But that doesn't mean I'm ready to jump in bed with you."

She wouldn't meet his gaze. "I'll wait," he finally said.

"For what?"

"Until you're ready. You'll be coming back real soon. I'll be here waiting."

"Why?"

He stared at her as if she'd lost her mind. "I just told you why. I want you. And I think you want me, too."

"I might not be back that often. You should find someone around here. There were some other women at that restaurant we visited."

He was irritated that she wouldn't admit she wanted him, that she kept shoving him toward other women. "Maybe you're right. Maybe I'll find a real woman, one who is willing to admit attraction when she feels it. One who doesn't hide behind her past.''

''Look who's talking!'' Her voice rose in irritation. ''You and your brothers have let the past completely dominate your lives.''

''Look, lady,'' he roared, ''we were doing all right before you got here. We don't need you to point out our shortcomings.''

''Well, the same is true for me,'' she yelled back, taking a step toward him. ''I'm perfectly happy in Denver.''

''And I'm perfectly happy right here. Without you!'' he lied as he cast aside the bridle and stood. Then he grabbed her shoulders and pulled her against him, his mouth covering hers before she could protest.

Her lips were warm and pliant, molding to his, opening to his urging. Chad felt the pressure build in his body as they came together. She'd unbuttoned her coat earlier, and his hands slid around her inside it, pressing her closer. Her arms encircled his neck, her fingers weaving through his hair.

He felt as if he were going to explode. Never had he gotten so hot so fast. His hands slid beneath her sweater, stroking her satiny skin, loving the feel of it beneath his fingers. Breaking the kiss to gasp for breath, he muttered her name several times, drinking in her beautiful face. But he couldn't last long without her kisses.

Megan was drowning in sensations. Everywhere he touched her, she felt on fire. His kisses seemed as necessary to her existence as air and water, and she pressed closer, enjoying feeling buried in his strength. But she wanted more.

She wanted to be one with Chad. The attraction she'd felt the first time he touched her had grown, expanded at a rapid rate. When she'd awakened in his arms this morning, she felt as if she'd come home. As if she finally belonged. As if she'd be there forever.

Desire racked her body, causing her to tremble against his hardness. He pushed up her sweater as his hands sought her breasts, cupping, stroking them. She pressed closer, only wanting more of his touch.

He whispered her name as he lifted her against him to caress her breasts. Even as she clung to him, she wanted the same privilege, to touch his skin. When he lowered her to a pile of hay and began undressing her, she unbuttoned his shirt and slid her fingers over his hard chest, loving the feel of him.

Chad's mouth returned to hers, as a parched man to the well. Any conscious thought went spinning away. All she could do was cling, stroke, consume and be consumed in return. She became lost in a world filled with Chad.

He undid her jeans and slid them down, along with her panties. As impatient as he, she assisted him in unbuttoning his jeans, too. The power and strength of him only made her long for him even more.

When he pulled away from her, the loss was almost more than she could bear. "Chad?"

"Just a minute, Meggie," he whispered, his breathing rapid. When she realized he was preparing to protect her, removing a condom from his jeans, not stop loving her, she lay back and waited. Without his touch, sanity began to return. What was she doing? She couldn't— Before she could complete that thought, Chad's lips were covering hers again and taking her to incredible heights of pleasure.

When he entered her, neither could wait for completion. Mindlessly they each urged the other to that unique journey of two souls.

When their rasping breaths had softened to normal breathing again, Megan delighted in Chad's heavy warmth and a sense of peace that filled her. Had she found her home? Had Chad been as devastated by their lovemaking as she? She longed to ask him what the past few moments had meant to him, but she was afraid. Though she called herself a coward, she remained silent.

"Sorry, Megan. I didn't intend for that to happen."

Chad's rough whisper cut her to the quick. He was apologizing for their lovemaking.

He stood and pulled up his jeans, refastening them as he turned his back to her. Feeling like some discarded souvenir, she, too, stood, dressing as she did so.

"Me, neither." What else could she say? Afraid she'd burst into tears any moment, she grabbed her coat, shrugging into it as she moved and ran from the barn, ignoring Chad's call.

CHAD DIDN'T RETURN to the house right away. He needed time to compose himself…and to decide what he should do.

After promising himself he'd take time to get his needs under control, he'd blown it. He'd wanted Megan so bad, he'd made love to her on the hard floor, pleasuring himself without any thought of her.

Not that she hadn't wanted it as bad as him. He was sure of that. But he'd wanted their first time together to be special. Instead, he'd taken her on a haystack with her clothes half-on.

The tension that had sizzled between them since the day she arrived had short-circuited his system today. He only hoped she would let him show her how generous a lover he could be. Especially since even the thought of loving Megan again made him hard.

Finally he made his way to the house, wondering if Megan would make an appearance at dinner. Wondering if she'd talk to him. Wondering if he'd ever kiss her again.

Dear God, he hoped so.

His first question was answered at once.

Everyone was gathered around the table, staring at him as he entered. His gaze flew straight to Megan, and she turned a bright red. And looked more desirable than ever.

"We was beginning to worry about you," Red said. "Come on, boy, you're holding up dinner."

Chad washed at the sink and took his seat beside Adele, his gaze remaining on Megan.

"Everything okay in the horse barn?" Jake asked after saying the blessing.

"Uh, yeah," Chad muttered, distracted by the bowl of mashed potatoes Adele was passing him. "Sorry. I didn't realize it was so late."

"How's the storm looking?" Pete asked.

Chad stared at him blankly. The storm? The storm he remembered had taken place between him and Megan. And right now it felt just as cold. "I—I think it's letting up."

"Then if we get out early in the morning with the snowplow, ladies, you might be able to catch an afternoon flight to Denver," Jake said. "After dinner we'll check the forecasts and call for reservations."

Chad wanted to protest. But he couldn't figure out a good reason. He stared at Megan, but she concentrated on her food. He noticed, however, that she only picked at it, shifting it around the plate instead of eating.

"You off your feed?" Red asked, and Chad looked up, expecting him to be speaking to Megan. Instead, he was staring at Chad.

"Who, me? No! No, I was just thinking." He took a big bite of steak and chewed determinedly, his gaze drawn back to Megan.

"I checked with the men in the bunkhouse, and they'll be out at first light to see to the herds. Chad, you and Brett had better go out with them. Pete and I will clear things out here and get the ladies to the airport." Jake never looked up as he ordered their day.

"No!" Chad protested without thinking. When everyone at the table stared at him, he added, "I can handle the snowplow better than Pete. It broke down the last time he used it. Remember, Pete?" He stared desperately at his brother, hoping he'd understand.

"Oh, yeah, right," Pete said after meeting Chad's gaze. "You'd better do the snowplowing. I'll go chase cows." There was a thud from under the table as Pete turned to Jake. "That's okay with you, Jake, isn't it?"

Chad didn't know if Pete had kicked Jake or not, but he breathed a sigh of relief when his oldest brother looked at him and agreed. "Good idea. We wouldn't want the snowplow to break down tomorrow."

Brett stared at all of them, a puzzled look on his face. "I don't remember the plow breaking down."

"Doesn't matter," Chad hurriedly assured him, avoiding Megan's eyes now, in case she caught on to his scheme.

He didn't understand how he could be so vulnerable to this woman. He hadn't known her that long, but every moment around her was precious. He'd figured once they'd made love, his hunger for her would ease. But he'd been wrong. He wanted her more than ever.

He cleared his throat. "Well, I hate to sound like a certain blonde, but what are we going to do this evening?"

Adele expressed enthusiasm, commenting on how much she'd enjoyed forty-two that first night, which seemed like weeks ago to Chad. He looked at Megan again. "Megan? Will you be my partner?"

She kept her gaze on her plate. "Thank you anyway, but I believe I'd better go pack. And I have a few more additions to the plans we've made. Red, I like your idea about making a mud room."

"Yesiree, that mud room will keep my kitchen a lot cleaner."

Adele was more interested in the forty-two game. "Jake, will you and Pete make up the foursome? I'd really love to play."

"Of course. We'll be glad to join you and Chad."

Chad wanted to groan in his misery. Now he was trapped in a game of forty-two that would go on all night while Megan escaped. Maybe he'd be able to persuade Brett to take his place. But he couldn't ask until they were away from the table.

After that, conversation languished. And Chad thought everyone and everything moved in slow motion, while his heart raced at double speed. He felt he somehow had to talk with Megan tonight, to find out how she felt about what had happened.

When she excused herself from the table, he willed her to meet his gaze, to give him some encouragement. Instead, she left the room without even telling him good-night.

"You do something to Megan to upset her?" Jake asked as soon as the door closed behind her.

Chad looked up to find Jake staring at him. And shook his head no. It wasn't exactly a lie. She hadn't been upset until after they'd made love.

"Okay, then," Jake said, standing. "Let's go play some forty-two."

Chad had no choice but to join the game. But he was going to talk to Megan tonight. She wasn't getting away until they settled what had happened between them.

Chapter Fifteen

It took Megan all of fifteen minutes to pack.

What was she going to do the rest of the evening?

She paced the floor, trying not to think about what had happened in the barn. Trying not to remember Chad's touch. The man was all wrong for her. There was no future in their passion.

But there was a lot of heat.

"Stop it, Megan!" she ordered herself. Woman could not live by sex alone, she paraphrased. And Chad had made it clear he had no interest in a permanent relationship.

And she didn't, either, she hurriedly reminded herself. She'd watched her mother ride a roller coaster of heartbreak and passion. Even worse, she'd been an innocent passenger on the ride. She wouldn't do the same thing to a child of her own because Chad made her want him.

Already, after sleeping with him once, she knew it wouldn't be enough. She couldn't keep any distance, any perspective, if she was around him. She would lose all control—as she had in the barn.

And that frightened her most of all. Loss of control made a person vulnerable to another's whims.

She opened the door and cautiously peered into the hallway. Maybe she could find something to read without going into the living room, where Chad was playing. She'd go crazy if she couldn't keep her mind off him.

Walking softly, she headed for the kitchen, but found it empty. As she came back into the hallway, she heard the television. Easing open the door to the room, she saw Brett all alone watching the big screen.

"Brett, would you mind some company?" she asked.

"Of course not," he replied, smiling over his shoulder. "That is, unless you want me to change the channel. This is one of my favorite shows," he explained, gesturing to the sitcom.

"No, I like this program, too." She settled down on the sofa beside him and tried to lose herself in the story.

She was only partly successful. The banter between the couple on-screen, flirting madly with each other, made her think of Chad. The kiss they shared stirred her passions and made her shift uncomfortably on the sofa.

"Need more room?" Brett asked without looking at her.

"No, I'm fine." She willed herself not to move.

When the program ended, Brett offered her a choice of a romance or a detective show. She chose the detective program. She'd rather see someone get shot than kissed tonight. It would be less bothersome.

Halfway through the hour-long show, Brett suggested they have a snack. Though she wasn't hungry, Megan accompanied him to the kitchen. She wasn't willing to remain alone outside her bedroom this evening. Chad might find her.

Just as they were ready to return to the TV room with their leftover apple pie and coffee, the door swung open and Chad stared at them.

"What are you doing here?" he demanded.

Megan tried to ignore him, but when she walked past him, he grabbed her arm. "I thought you had to pack."

"I did. Excuse me."

But he wouldn't let her escape that easily. "Come play forty-two."

"No, thank you. Please turn loose of my arm."

He didn't move, staring at her.

"Come on, Chad, let the lady go. Our show is starting again," Brett complained.

"You're watching television?"

"Yes, we are." Megan yanked her arm free and hurried out the door, afraid he'd follow. If he did, she'd be relegated to her lonely room again.

"What's going on between you and Chad?" Brett asked once they were seated again.

She almost choked on her bite of pie. "What do you mean?"

"Come on, Megan. Anyone can see you react to each other. Kind of like two hot wires touching. Sparks fly. You interested in him?"

"Do you remember our discussion last night? Neither of us is interested in anything permanent. And I don't do one-nighters," she said crisply, her gaze determinedly fixed on the television, hoping he couldn't tell she just had.

"Chad's a good guy," Brett explained, "but he took Jake's divorce about as hard as Jake. We all love Jake, but I think Chad almost idolizes him."

Megan looked at the handsome man beside her. "Just because Jake's marriage failed doesn't mean yours or your brothers' would fail. Not that I'm interested in—in anything like that. But if Jake tried romance again, he might find things changed."

Brett laughed. "You may be right. But if there's one thing we can all count on, it's Jake not trying marriage again. He's a hardheaded cuss."

"I think it runs in the family," she said dryly, and turned back to the television. Watching someone else suffer was easier than continuing their discussion.

CHAD MENTALLY KICKED himself over and over again. Megan was sitting in the room across the hall with Brett, and he was trapped at the game table. How could he have been such an idiot?

"Chad, you just trumped your partner's trick," Jake reprimanded mildly.

"Oh, sorry, Pete." He was grateful when Pete sent him a sympathetic look.

"No problem. These sharks were gonna take us anyway," he said, gesturing to Jake and Adele.

"We're just having a good run of luck," Adele said.

Which was more than he was doing, Chad decided. He was determined to talk to Megan tonight, *had* to talk to her tonight—though his body wanted to do a lot more than talk.

Just thinking about what he'd like to do with Megan caused a reaction. He hunched over the table, hoping no one would notice, and tried to concentrate on the dominoes.

Good manners insisted, as well as Jake's stern eye, that Chad remain at the table until their guest had her fill of the game. He played quickly, preferring speed to skill, hoping the number of games racked up by Jake and Adele would satisfy her.

Around ten o'clock, he heard voices in the hallway and realized Brett and Megan were going upstairs. He lost all concentration at the thought.

"Your play, Chad," Jake ordered.

"Uh, what was led?"

"Fives," Pete answered with a grin. As if he'd read Chad's mind, he added, "Threes are trumps."

"I think that might be considered table talk, boys," Jake muttered, glaring at Chad.

He kept his gaze on his dominoes, trying to think about the game instead of a certain young woman going to her bedroom, taking off her clothes, brushing her hair—

"Chad!" Jake barked. "Pay attention."

He'd misplayed again. With a sigh, he offered his apologies for his boneheaded play.

As they finished the hand, Adele pushed back from the table. "It's late. I know you three worked a lot harder than I did today, so why don't we turn in?"

Chad could've hugged her. "I am a little tired," he muttered, smiling his gratitude at Adele. "I'll put things away," he added. He'd have to wait until everyone was settled down for the night before he could go to Megan's door.

And hope she didn't yell for him to go away.

"Want any help?" Pete asked as Jake and Adele left the room.

''Nope, but thanks for putting up with me tonight.''

Pete grinned. ''You tolerated my bad moods the past couple of weeks, didn't you?''

''But you're feeling better. You haven't been so down since the ladies arrived,'' Chad declared. He wanted Pete to recover from his heartbreak. Chad needed to believe recovery was possible. For him, too.

''Yeah, sure.''

''Unless Janie walked in the door?'' Chad prodded ruefully, having heard the doubt in Pete's voice.

''That's not going to happen, so we don't have to worry about it. Good night, little brother.''

Pete really had it bad. Sighing, Chad admitted he might be in as much trouble as his brother. That was a frightening thought.

He cleaned up and ran upstairs for a quick shower. In clean jeans and a flannel shirt that he left untucked, he opened the bathroom door and listened intently.

When he heard nothing, he tiptoed out into the hallway, pulling his door to behind him. He felt like a teenager, trying to sneak in past his curfew. Reaching Megan's door undetected, he rapped softly.

No response.

Could she be asleep already? It'd only been half an hour since he'd heard her come upstairs. Time enough for someone to fall asleep, unless she had something on her mind.

Like that encounter in the barn.

He rapped again. She couldn't be asleep yet. When he heard the slightest sound of movement beyond the door, he leaned against the doorjamb in relief.

''Who's there?'' she called softly.

''Chad. We need to talk.''

''No. We'll talk in the morning.''

''Megan, there won't be time. Let me in.''

''No,'' she whispered back.

But he wasn't accepting that answer. Without warning, he turned the doorknob, hoping she hadn't locked her door. It silently swung open, and he slipped into the room.

"Chad!" she protested in a hoarse whisper, moving rapidly away from the door. "You can't come in here. What if someone hears you?"

"They won't. Everyone's gone to bed." He moved toward her, but she continued to back away until she was pressed against the wall by the window.

He halted suddenly, remembering their discussion in B.J.'s house that first day. Instead, he just repeated his entreaty. "Meggie, we need to talk."

"About what?"

"How about the fact that you drive me crazy? I played forty-two like the village idiot tonight. Jake was ready to slug me."

She looked away. "I don't think I can be blamed for your poor play."

"Probably not. But my body reacts to yours like steel to a magnet. I can't resist the pull." He stepped closer again. "Just like now. I want to touch you so badly my body aches from holding back."

"We—we can't touch. It would be a disaster. We both know we have a problem. You'd better go to your room before we lose control." Her hands were clasped tightly in front of her, as if she didn't trust them.

"I think it may be too late. I'm afraid I'll start drooling if I don't get to kiss you soon," he said with a grin, trying a little humor to lighten the mood.

"Ugh. Very unattractive," she agreed, smiling in return.

"I can't think of anything that would make you unattractive, Meggie. Don't you see? We need to explore what's going on here. Neither of us could stop this afternoon. Whatever it is, it's pretty strong."

"You apologized."

Chad frowned, trying to figure out what her statement meant. "Yeah?"

"If you regretted it this afternoon, what makes you think now would be any better?

With a lopsided grin, he confessed, "Honey, I didn't apologize because it wasn't good. If it got any better, I'd die." Her cheeks flamed, and he wanted to pull her into his arms. "I apologized because I wanted it to be right for you."

She licked her lips, and Chad thought he was going to fall to his knees. "Don't do that."

"What?" she asked, startled.

He leaned forward and lightly touched his tongue to her bottom lip. Her hands came up to frame his face, but her fingers were shaking against his skin.

"Meggie, I can't stand this torment any longer. We want each other. We're both adults," he breathed, his mouth only inches from hers.

Suddenly Megan capitulated, closing the distance between them, her mouth taking his, her arms pulling him closer.

Not that Chad resisted. Once she'd shown her willingness, he devoured her with his lips, his arms, his entire body. Unlike this afternoon in the barn, when she'd been covered with a lot of clothes, tonight she was dressed in the same thigh-length silky robe and nightgown she'd been wearing the morning he'd brought her breakfast.

With eager hands, he slipped the robe from her shoulders while his mouth continued to caress hers. Their breaths mingled, and he could scarcely contain his desire to make love to her again.

"Meggie," he whispered, burying his face in her neck, his lips touching her skin. "I want to eat you alive."

Her fingers began working the buttons on his shirt, and soon her hot hands were stroking his chest, her fingers burrowing through the hair on his chest, rubbing his nipples with lightning touches.

His fingers slid to the hem of her gown, and he slipped it over her head. "It's only fair play," he assured her teasingly, his hands imitating hers.

Her breathing quickened, and his mouth covered hers again, as if to help her breathe. Their tongues parried and thrust while his hands wandered over her enticing figure. Chill bumps on her back gave him an excuse to move them to the bed.

"You need to be under the covers, sweetheart," he managed to say, his chest heaving as he yanked back the bedspread and eased her down on the mattress. He was reassured when her arms reached up to him, urging him to join her. Before he did so, he removed his jeans and briefs, then reached for her panties.

One part of him wanted to stand and admire her beauty. The other urged him closer. He slipped into bed beside her, loving the warmth she exuded against the entire length of his body.

He needed no encouragement to be ready to make her his. All it took was being within a mile of her and he was ready. As she whispered, "Please, oh please, Chad," in his ear, he moved over her, eager to please her.

Only then did he remember the condom he'd put in his jeans. Premeditation, he knew, but Jake had drummed responsibility into all their heads. "Wait, Meggie. I need protection."

She said nothing as he prepared himself, but there was no waning of desire when he returned to her side. Her mouth joined his again, and her body welcomed his touch.

When he entered her, her warmth closing around him, there was a second's peace, a momentary exaltation that filled him with greater happiness than he'd ever known. Then an urgency drove him, and he and Megan joined together in soul-shattering satisfaction.

When his heart slowed to a steady thud, he eased himself to the mattress beside her, then wrapped his arms around her to pull her close. "Are you all right, Meggie?" he whispered.

"Yes. Yes, I—I'm fine. You?"

He pressed her even closer to him. "I'm better than I've ever been in my life." The words he'd never said to a woman hovered in his mind, and he resisted the inexplicable urge to whisper those fatal words, *I love you.*

He was moved by the moment, he reasoned. If he said something like that now, she wouldn't believe him anyway. Hell, he didn't believe himself, he thought staunchly even as he held her against him.

One of her hands stole to his chest, her fingers playing against his skin.

"Didn't get enough before?" he whispered, his lips punctuating his question with kisses on her neck.

"I like to touch you," she whispered in return.

He pulled back to study her face, but she buried it in his chest, apparently unwilling to look at him.

"Meggie? Are you all right?"

"You already asked me that. I'm fine." Her hand trailed down his chest, heading in a dangerous direction.

Already his body was gearing up for a repeat performance, which pleased and startled him, but also brought problems. He'd only brought one condom with him.

Her lips were nibbling at his neck, sending shivers all over his body, and his hands cupped her hips, pulling her against him.

"Meggie," he whispered, desperately trying to control his response to her. "You'd better get to sleep. Tomorrow's going to be a long day."

There was a sudden stillness after he spoke. Then her hand withdrew from his body, and she turned her face away from his. "Yes, I am tired."

"Meggie," he pleaded without being sure what he was pleading for, "I don't want you to be embarrassed if someone sees me leaving your room. Jake gets up early."

"That's very thoughtful of you."

The words were fine. Her tone of voice wasn't.

He pulled her head back toward him and kissed her again, but her lips were cold, and her heart wasn't in the caress. He didn't know what to do. His first instinct was to make fierce love to her, convincing her he wanted her. But to do so unprotected would be wrong.

He had to leave. Even thinking about making love to her again had him pulsing with desire. "I'll see you in the morning."

He forced himself to slide from the covers and pick up his clothing. He slipped on the jeans but didn't bother with the shirt. Then he bent to kiss her one more time. She turned her head away just as his lips reached her face, and he touched her cheek.

"Good night," she murmured, her eyes closed.

"Good night," he returned, but he stared at her, frowning,

rather than leaving at once. She never moved. He crossed to the door, looking at her once more.

An unsatisfying ending to a very satisfying night.

MEGAN DIDN'T OPEN her eyes until she heard the door close. When she did look, she was glad to discover the room empty, because the tears that had gathered behind her eyelids now ran down her face.

So, a good time was had by all.

And that was that.

Chad had more mundane thoughts than the paradise he'd just shared with her. There was potential embarrassment and the need for sleep. Maybe the problem was their lovemaking hadn't meant to him what it had to her. She'd known it would be a mistake to get so close to Chad. And she was right.

After all her warnings to herself, she'd laid her heart on the line one more time. And again it was trampled. There was no protection left to her. She couldn't pretend he didn't matter to her.

She loved him. Totally. Completely. With all her heart. And he was concerned about embarrassment.

He wanted to hide what had happened from everyone. She wanted to shout it from the rooftop. What had happened between them had been the most glorious event in her life—and would lead to the most incredible heartache.

And perhaps even cost her her job.

She couldn't come back to the Randall ranch now. The decorating would have to be done by someone else in her firm. Or maybe Adele by herself. Megan just knew she couldn't return to Chad's home. She would come as a beggar, pleading for his love, his touch, even a smile.

What they had, what they'd shared tonight, would turn into a sleazy affair, with Chad eventually returning to his other women. Wherever he found them.

Better to cut off her association with the Randalls now and do what she could to protect her poor overworked heart. She couldn't avoid the pain, but maybe she could shorten it.

Too bad her decision only brought more tears.

Chapter Sixteen

Chad was in the kitchen at first light. "No time for breakfast, Red. I'll grab a cup of coffee and be on my way."

"What's the hurry, boy?"

"I want to be back and have breakfast with Meg—the ladies. I figure I can put in a couple of hours' work before then."

Red gave him a knowing grin. "I see."

He was on his way out of the house as Jake entered the kitchen.

"Chad wants to get a head start," Red said behind him.

Chad grinned. That would make Jake suspicious, for sure. Chad wasn't at his best in the mornings, though he could think of circumstances where waking up would be a pleasure.

For example, if he were in bed with Megan.

He regretted leaving her last night. Her response hadn't been reassuring. Had she been offended that he'd left? He didn't think she'd want everyone to know what had happened last night. For himself, he was ready to tell the world that Megan Chase was his woman.

The world. Denver. She was returning to Denver without him. No one in Denver would know she was his. Maybe he'd need to make a trip to Denver real soon. Yeah, that's what he'd do. She'd probably be back here in a month. So if he visited Denver in a couple of weeks, the wait wouldn't be so long.

Though his plans pleased him, he noticed they didn't satisfy the uneasiness he was feeling. He wasn't sure of the source of that uneasiness, but he thought it had something to do with the way he'd left Megan last night.

Driving the snowplow at a speed Jake wouldn't approve of, Chad turned back to the house after an hour and a half, with one lane clear to the road. He was anxious to see Megan.

When he burst into the kitchen, the table was full, Jake, Red, Adele and even Rita around the table. But no Megan.

"Hi, guess I'm in time. Where's Megan?"

"I knocked on her door," Adele assured him. "She said she'd be right down."

Chad gave her a smile and headed for the stairway. Bounding up the stairs two at a time, he rounded the corner to Megan's room just as the door opened.

"I thought maybe you'd overslept," Chad teased with a grin. She had a surprised look on her face, her full lips parted, her eyes rounded.

He didn't hesitate. The need to taste her again, to feel her against him, was so overwhelming he swept her into his arms. To his relief, she responded at once, her mouth opening to his, her arms around his neck.

"Wanna skip breakfast?" he whispered, his lips trailing down her neck. He noticed she wasn't wearing his favorite, jeans. Today she was the professional decorator again, clad in a suit and heels.

"I—I'm hungry. And we have to leave soon, don't we?" she asked breathlessly.

"Yeah," he reluctantly agreed, allowing her to take a step back. "You okay this morning?" She didn't meet his gaze as she straightened her suit jacket.

"I'm fine. We'd better go down. I'm late already." She started around him, but he caught her hand.

"There's not that big a rush," he assured her, and brought her hand to his lips. He frowned as she turned away from him and pulled him toward the stairs.

As quickly as she moved, he had to hurry to keep up. "Megan?" he questioned, but she never stopped.

As they reached the kitchen door, she pulled her hand from

him and entered in front of him. Once they were at the table, he had no chance to talk to her, of course.

"Your travel agent called before any of you were up," Jake announced as they took their places. "She asked me to tell you she got you seats on the eleven-o'clock flight. We'll need to leave for the airport as soon as you finish breakfast."

"Wasn't there anything later?" Chad asked.

"Why would we want to hang around here?" Rita asked with bitterness in her voice.

Chad shrugged, but his gaze was on Megan. She concentrated on her breakfast.

Something was wrong. It didn't take a rocket scientist to figure that one out, Chad concluded. And whatever it was had gone wrong last night, when he'd left her bed.

He hoped Megan would return to her bedroom one last time and he could catch her there alone. Instead, Jake sent him and Red up for the luggage. When he came down, Megan was speaking to Jake alone.

Okay, so he'd sit beside her in the Suburban. They could whisper without anyone overhearing them. He stored the luggage and turned to offer a hand to each of the ladies as they entered the vehicle.

"Why don't you ride out and see how the others are doing? They might need a little help," Jake said, coming to a stop beside him.

"I thought I was going with you," Chad said, surprised.

Jake looked at him, a sympathetic stare that confused Chad. Then his brother began pulling on gloves, staring at his hands. "Megan asked that you not go," he said quietly.

Chad looked at his brother, then Megan. She'd been watching him, but as soon as he looked her way, she leaned forward to say something to Adele.

"She what?"

"Megan asked that you not come with us. She said she would be uncomfortable." Jake put a hand on his shoulder. "Maybe you can straighten things out the next time she comes."

Then he got behind the wheel, waved a hand at Chad and Red and pulled away.

Chad stood, as frozen as the ground under his feet, too shocked to even think.

"You want some more coffee before you ride out?" Red asked. When he didn't respond, the old man nudged him. "You want more coffee?"

"Yeah." Chad finally turned and walked into the kitchen. With every step he took, he had a growing certainty he'd just made a huge mistake.

MEGAN WORKED VERY HARD at keeping her composure all the way into Casper. It helped that she didn't need to make conversation.

When it came time to tell Jake goodbye, she thought she was going to be professional about it. Then he hugged her.

"We'll be looking forward to your return," he said softly as his big arms enfolded her. "You feel like part of the family."

"Oh, Jake," she said, half sigh, half cry, and one tear escaped to trail down her face.

"You call us if you need help, Megan, okay?"

She nodded and ran for the airplane gate. Call the Randalls? Not likely, though she knew she'd want to. But they were the problem, not the solution.

Adele took the seat next to her. "We just made it. The plane leaves in ten minutes."

She looked out the window, saying nothing. She was still too on edge to speak.

"Are you okay?"

Nodding, she gave a brief glance Adele's way and then turned back to the window. *Please take off. Please take off.* She repeated those words in her head over and over again, like a mantra that would save her.

The plane engines revved up, and she closed her eyes in thanks. Her ordeal was almost over. She would leave Wyoming and never return.

A commotion at the front of the plane caused her to open

her eyes. She was suddenly consumed by fear that one of the Randalls would walk down the aisle. Instead, it was an elderly lady followed by an impatient attendant. Megan breathed a sigh of relief. She was being silly. She and the Randalls—*all* the Randalls—had parted company. This interlude in her life was over.

Completely over.

She tried not to cry again.

CHAD RAN THROUGH the airport. After having purchased his ticket, with the warning that the plane was ready to take off, he knew he had no time to spare.

Unfortunately a young mother with two small toddlers didn't know that. She'd allowed the smallest to wander right into Chad's path while she tended to the temper tantrum the older one was giving.

Chad's choice was to run over the child or come to a screeching halt and hope he wouldn't wipe out. He did his best to stop, but he scooped the child into his arms to protect him as he did so and set off a commotion as the mother assumed he was trying to kidnap her baby.

With the woman screaming so loudly that security guards came from all directions and the older child continuing his temper tantrum, Chad had no hope of catching his plane. In fact, he was going to be lucky if he didn't spend the night in jail.

After a long and tortuous explanation, and several phone calls, he was released.

With a determination that had only grown stronger with each moment since Megan's departure, he returned to the ticket counter. Too bad he hadn't come to his senses before she'd left.

By the time he had reached the kitchen for that cup of coffee Red had offered, Chad had known, with a surety that scared him, that if he didn't go after Megan then, right that minute, he might never see her again.

He couldn't let that happen.

With blinding quickness, he had also realized that if he

didn't claim Megan Chase as his in every sense of the word, his life would be useless.

He thought back to his talk with Pete. He didn't want to make the mistakes Pete had made. Pete had lost the woman he loved.

Chad wasn't going to do the same thing.

When he landed in Denver, Chad, with no luggage, made a quick exit from the airport. He hailed a cab before he remembered he didn't have Megan's address. "Take me to the nearest phone booth with a directory," he ordered.

The driver frowned, but at least he didn't order Chad out of his taxi. "What you lookin' for?"

"A woman."

"No need for a phone directory. I can take you to the right place," the cabbie assured him with a wink, and swung his taxi into the traffic.

Chad shook his head. "No, not that kind of woman. I mean, a specific woman. I just need to look up her address. Then you can take me there."

The driver shrugged his shoulders. As soon as the taxi exited the airport, he pulled into a drive-in grocery and motioned to the phone booth next to it. "There you go. But you gotta pay me something afore you get out."

Chad whipped out his billfold and removed a twenty-dollar bill. "Here, this will be my deposit." He almost left the taxi before the cabbie's happy smile reminded him. "But you'd better not drive off without me, 'cause I'll report you if you do."

"Hey, man, I wouldn't do that," the driver protested, holding up his hands in innocence.

With that, Chad rushed to the phone book hanging by a chain. M. C. Chase, M. L. Chase and Marvin Chase were three possibilities. With a silent apology to all future seekers, he ripped the page out of the directory and returned to the cab.

He selected the first Chase—M.C.—as the most likely.

The taxi stopped in front of some expensive condos. "You want me to wait?" the driver asked hopefully.

Chad considered the question and then refused. Somehow he felt sure he'd found Megan's address. He paid the driver.

After checking the mailboxes, Chad raced up the stairs to the last apartment on the second floor. He rapped on the door and was relieved when Megan opened it and looked out at him through the small opening afforded by the chain.

"Megan, I need to talk to you," he said, but she stared at him in astonishment. When she didn't move, he said, "Megan, let me in."

"No!" she gasped, and slammed the door in his face.

He knocked again.

"You're not coming in, Chad," she shouted through the door.

"I just want to talk, Meggie. What's wrong with that?"

"I believe that's what you said last night before you came into my bedroom," she reminded him coldly.

Guilt filled him. She was right. That was exactly what he'd said.

He leaned against the door. "Megan, please."

"No!"

"Why? Why are you mad at me?" He felt ridiculous having a conversation with a closed door, but his choices were limited.

"I'm not mad. I—I don't want to see you anymore."

"Until you come back to the ranch?"

Silence. Panic gripped him.

"You're not planning to come back, are you?"

"Go away, Chad!"

"No, I won't." He wasn't sure exactly what to do. He only knew Megan was the most important person in the world to him.

He decided to wait.

WHAT WAS WRONG with the man?

Megan peeked out the front window for the tenth time, only to discover Chad still leaning against the wall, his arms crossed over his chest.

He must be freezing.

Finally she grabbed her coat and purse. She had to buy groceries. There was nothing in the house to eat. When she opened the door, he eagerly turned to face her.

"Go away!"

"No."

"I'm leaving."

"Where are you going?"

"To the grocery store."

"Mind if I come along? I'm kind of hungry."

She didn't say anything, but he must've taken her silence as a yes since he followed her down the stairs.

When she unlocked her car, he slid into the passenger seat and clipped his seat belt in place. The only sign that he'd been standing in subfreezing temperatures for half an hour was his appreciation of the heater.

"I'll run you back to the airport if you're ready," she said softly as he warmed his hands.

He looked at her sharply. "I'm not going anywhere."

"Chad, this is pointless."

"Is it?"

She turned in at the grocery store, not answering him.

Pushing a cart, she hurried up and down the aisles, not watching Chad. She didn't have to—as if by radar, she knew exactly where he was most of the time. He picked up a few items in one of the small carryalls and checked out before she reached the cash register.

He was waiting to carry her two bags when she was finished.

They didn't speak all the way back to her apartment. At her door, he handed her the two bags without saying a word, taking up his sentinel position against the wall.

"Chad, it gets almost as cold here as it does in Wyoming. You're going to freeze."

"I'll manage. I'm not going anywhere until we talk, Meggie. This is important."

"I don't want to talk," she insisted, trying to make her voice sound firm. But she was afraid he'd heard it waver. She slammed the door extrahard to convince him.

After pacing her apartment for another twenty minutes, she

opened the door again. "You can come in and sleep on the couch. But I don't want to talk."

His nose was red, his hands were tucked under his arms and the collar on his jacket was turned up around his ears. But he shook his head no. "I'm not coming in to sleep on the couch. I'm coming in to talk…and then to sleep in your bed. It's all or nothing, Megan. That's the way it has to be."

"Why, you—you conceited, arrogant, stubborn cowboy! Fine! Freeze to death! See if I care!" She slammed the door again. And slumped against it.

How long could she keep this up? She was fighting Chad… and she was fighting herself. What if she let him in? She *wanted* to love him again, to have him love her until the rest of the world disappeared, leaving only the two of them.

It was the heartache afterward that she couldn't face.

Just one more time, an insidious voice inside her whispered. *What can one more time hurt?*

Again she paced the living room, arguing with herself, sending angry looks at the door, as if Chad could sense her mood through the wood.

Finally, with the argument that she couldn't have his death on her hands, she swung the door open again. Prepared to let him in, to accept another night in his arms, to have the right to touch him, if only for twenty-four hours, she was shocked to find he'd gone.

CHAD WAITED with impatience for the phone to be answered. When his brother's voice finally spoke, he hurriedly said, "Jake, it's Chad. I guess Red told you I'm in Denver. I'm not sure when I'll be back."

"You okay?"

"Yeah. I have to get things straightened out with Megan."

"Call if you need us, little brother."

"I will. Thanks, Jake."

He hung up and hurried up the stairs to Megan's apartment, thinking as he walked how fortunate he was to have his family. He was almost to the apartment door when he realized Megan had come outside and now was disappearing again.

"Megan!" he called, and she hesitated. "I went to call Jake, to let him know where I was."

"I thought you'd gone," she said, her gaze meeting his for one unsettling look before she turned away.

"I told you I'm not going anywhere. Have you decided to talk to me?"

"I—I don't want you to freeze to death."

"I'll be okay."

"You can come in." Then, without looking at him, she nodded and went inside.

Chad picked up the sack full of his purchases from the store and followed her in.

Megan took his jacket from him. "You're freezing," she said. "Would you like something hot to drink?"

"No, that's not what I need to warm me up." He stood still, waiting for her to give him permission to touch her.

She swallowed, licked her lips and took a small step toward him. "Are you sure that's what you want?"

"With all my heart."

She melted into his arms, heat meeting ice, and Chad warmed up right away. Her kisses drove him wild in nothing flat. "Where's the bedroom, Meggie?"

All thought of talk went out of his mind, and evidently hers, too, since she showed him the way. He swept her up in his arms and hurried through the door she pointed out.

He almost didn't remember the bag in his hand. But as he laid her down on the bed, Jake's warnings reminded him. He removed the condoms he'd bought at the grocery store.

Shoving aside his shirt, Megan didn't give him any time. Her hands roamed his cold skin, heating it up. Impatient, he ripped the buttons off her blouse and threw it aside. Megan didn't even complain as she worked on the opening to his jeans.

This time when he entered her, along with incredible pleasure he felt a sense of coming home. Thank God he'd come after her.

Afterward, when Chad pulled her into his arms and held her against him, dropping occasional kisses on her lips, Megan waited for the words that would wound her. Now he would talk about visiting her. An occasional rendezvous. The pleasures they would share.

"You know, I'd planned to visit you in a couple of weeks," he said, as if they were sitting across from each other at the kitchen table at the ranch instead of naked, wrapped in each other's arms in her bed.

She stiffened in spite of her efforts to remain relaxed. After all, she'd expected those words.

"Meggie? What's wrong."

"Nothing. You were saying?"

"That was my solution to your leaving."

"Ah."

He kissed her neck and then her lips again. "But that won't work."

"What—what won't work?"

He rose up on one elbow and stared down at her, his brown eyes almost golden. "I love you, Meggie. I can't wait a couple of weeks."

Had she heard him right? She blinked rapidly, unsure whether to believe him. And still unsure where the conversation was going.

"Aren't you going to say anything?"

What else could she say? "I—I love you, too."

She was rewarded with an incredible kiss that consumed her. Her arms went around his neck, and she clung to him, pressing against him. She discovered he was ready for her again, too.

Later, when she was again in his arms, her heart a little less frightened, he chuckled sleepily. "We're going to have to be careful what we say, or I may die from exhaustion before I reach thirty."

There was some comfort in his words, since he had four years to go before he reached the advanced age of thirty. Four years to enjoy what had just occurred. And four years to worry about the end of it.

But all the tension, followed by the two incredible releases of it, had left her exhausted and she snuggled up against him.

Like Scarlett, she'd worry about the future tomorrow. At least she could enjoy today.

HER BED WAS EMPTY when Megan awoke the next morning. Panic set in. He'd left her already? Had her happiness lasted only one night?

The sound of someone in her living room halted the ugly thoughts racing through her. She shoved back the covers and pulled on her robe.

She tiptoed to the door of the living room and discovered Chad sitting on the couch, writing. What was he writing, a letter? Was he writing her a goodbye note?

"Chad?"

"Morning, sleepyhead. Where's my morning kiss?" He grinned at her and held out his hand.

Only slightly reassured, she circled the couch and sat beside him, meeting his lips with hers. "What are you writing?" she then asked, holding her breath.

"Well, I've been up for a while, and I've been doing some thinking."

She tensed up, holding her breath. "You've got to go back to the ranch?"

His mouth covered hers, and his kiss was almost enough to make her forget what she thought he'd been trying to say. Almost.

"Woman, you're going to drive me crazy!" he muttered as soon as he got his breath back. "Haven't you figured out I can't survive without you?"

"What—what do you mean?"

"Why do you think I flew down here after you? For another night of good sex?" He kissed her again. "Hell, Megan, I want a lot more than that. You're coming back to the ranch with me."

She closed her eyes to gather strength. "I can't do that, Chad."

"Why not? Didn't you like living on the ranch?"

"Of course I did, but—but I can't just come live on the ranch. Jake wouldn't—"

"You think I'm asking you to live on the ranch as my lover?" Chad asked incredulously. "Sweetheart, you're out of your head."

She stared at him, irritated.

He didn't give her a chance to ask any questions. "You'll come as my wife. You'll come as Megan Chase Randall. And you'll never leave me."

His words were her dream, of course, but how could she believe him? He'd said he never intended to marry.

Some of her doubt must've shown in her eyes, because he leaned closer. "You don't believe me, do you?"

Not willing to admit he was right, she couldn't meet his gaze.

"I thought you might have a hard time believing me." The tenderness in his voice drew her to him.

"You did?"

"Yeah, and I don't want you to have any doubts. So I've drawn up a pre-nuptial agreement."

Stricken, she stared at him. Then she leapt from the sofa. "Get out!" she ordered, hoping to hold back the tears until he was gone.

The man was already planning for their divorce, just like her mother and each of her husbands. And he thought it would reassure her. She sobbed, almost hysterical at the irony of his actions.

"There you go, jumping to conclusions again," he said softly, not moving.

"The only conclusion I can see is that you're already planning for our marriage to fail. What do I get, a little money and my wedding band?" Her voice was vicious, but she didn't care.

"Nope," he replied, staring at her. "You should read it."

"I won't! I don't want any part of it. I don't want any part of you! I want you to leave!"

"That's not what you said last night."

She couldn't believe he was sitting there calmly on the couch. Opening her mouth to again insist he leave, she was stunned when he grabbed her hand and pulled her into his lap.

"What you get is my share of the Randall ranch."

"I don't care what— What did you say?"

He dropped a kiss on her lips and then laughed at her stunned expression. "Last night I got the feeling you still weren't sure about us, so I tried to think of some way to make you believe me. The most important thing in the world to me, after you, is the ranch. If I leave you, or betray you in any way, it's yours. We'll draw it up legally, and I'll sign on the dotted line."

"But, Chad—" she began, but she couldn't go on. He sat holding her against him, patiently waiting. "How can you do that?" she said finally. "How can you trust me with your most precious thing?"

"Because I've already trusted the most precious things to you, sweetheart. I've given you my heart…and my future. Without you, they all mean nothing." He kissed her again and then whispered, "With you, I have everything. And I'm never planning to leave you."

"Me, neither," she whispered, her heart at peace at last.

"HOT DAMN!" Jake exclaimed, turning away from the phone to face his brothers.

"What is it?" Pete asked.

"It worked! My plan worked. Chad and Megan are getting married."

"That's good news," Brett said, a big smile on his face. "Guess we'll be having those babies, after all."

Red frowned. "I'm not changing no diapers. I did enough of that when Chad was a little 'un."

"It'll be awhile before we have to worry about that, Red," Jake assured him. Then he looked at his brothers. "But we need to work on a few more marriages around here."

"Hey, Jake," Pete protested, joined in by Brett. "You got lucky with Chad. Don't press your luck."

Jake eyed them, a grin on his face. "We'll just see about that."

COWBOY DADDY

Chapter One

He was tall, broad shouldered, and his tan face was turned down in a frown. Janie Dawson had worked hard to prepare for this meeting, girding her strength. But one look at the cowboy standing in his living-room doorway told her no mental exercise could have toughened her enough to face Pete Randall.

"Hi, Pete," she croaked out.

He wasted no time on amenities. "What are you doing here?"

Her eyebrows rose at his directness. She'd been a neighbor of the Randalls since her birth. As a child, she'd been in and out of their house countless times. As a teenager, she'd followed Pete Randall around with all the adoration of a young girl for her idol. As a woman, she'd been his lover.

But now she evidently needed a good reason for being there. "I wanted to talk to you."

His hands rested on his trim hips, and his brown-eyed gaze stayed on her face. "As I remember, three weeks ago you told me you never wanted to speak to me again."

She felt her cheeks heat up. He was right, of course. Three weeks ago, she'd decided she'd made a mistake, a big mistake, believing Pete's desire for her meant he loved her. Instead, it had meant exactly what it was—lust.

As long as she could remember, she'd loved Pete Randall. When he'd finally noticed her as a woman, all grown up, she'd fallen into his arms, ready to follow wherever he led.

He'd led her straight to bed.

Six months later, when she'd finally woken up from the sexual haze his touch brought about, she'd realized she wasn't his love but his lover.

Her teeth sank into her bottom lip. "Yes, I did." She walked across the room to the front window and stared out at the cold Wyoming day.

From behind her, his voice deepened. "So, what's changed?"

She turned around before he could come too near, a fixed smile on her face. "I think I was a little hasty."

A flame in his brown eyes ignited, and a lazy grin lit his face. "You mean you want to come back to me?"

She'd had her game plan worked out, but the fluttering of her heart at his question almost shook her. With a deep breath, she clung to her goal. "No, that's not what I mean."

His gaze hardened again. "Then what?"

She stuck her fingers in the back pockets of her jeans so he wouldn't see them shaking. "I wanted to ask you a question."

He folded his arms across his chest. "Ask away."

Easier said than done. She swallowed and shifted her gaze from his. She could get the words out better if she wasn't looking at him. "I wanted to ask you—ask you to marry me."

The taut silence that followed her question forced her gaze back to his well-loved features. A mixture of shock and panic filled his face.

She wasn't surprised by his reaction. She'd been pretty sure he wouldn't consider her offer. The Randall brothers, all four of them, were notorious bachelors. They had all resisted marriage since the marriage of the oldest brother, Jake, had ended in divorce.

"Have I shocked you?" she finally asked when he failed to answer.

He nodded as he moved toward her. "Yeah, you have. Look, Janie, I told you from the beginning I wasn't— I had no intention of— I care about you, Janie."

"But you don't love me." She stated her conclusion with finality, having expected no less. It was a struggle to keep a smile on her face, but she did.

His big hand caressed her cheek.

"Sweetheart, I wouldn't do anything to hurt you but—but I'm not cut out for marriage. You know that."

His touch almost destroyed her composure. She stepped back from him. "Yes, I know."

An awkwardness filled the room. When she thought she could bear the silence no longer, she stepped around him and walked to the door. "Sorry I interrupted your work," she tossed over her shoulder, glad she didn't have to face him again.

"Janie, wait."

She ignored his command. If she stayed any longer, she wouldn't be able to keep her smile in place.

"Janie, why?"

That question stopped her in her tracks. Why not tell him? He'd have to find out sometime. And she already had the answer to her question. Turning, she stiffened her shoulders, pasted on her brightest smile and said, "Because I'm having your baby."

Then she left the room.

PETE STOOD without moving, stunned, like the time Joe Bob Daly had broken Pete's nose in his first fight. Only Janie's disappearance awakened him.

"Wait!" he called, but he didn't rely on his voice to bring her to heel. After all, he knew Janie well. Instead, he hurried after her into the entry hall, catching her by the arm and pulling her back when she would've left the house.

"Where do you think you're going?" he growled.

"Home." She flashed him that breezy smile she'd been using the past half hour.

"You drop a bombshell like that and then plan on waltzing home?" he demanded, outrage rising in his voice as the shock retreated.

"Well, it's a little early for a formal announcement. What else do you want from me?"

She sounded so reasonable, as if she'd announced she was dying her hair. Instead, she'd said she was…having his baby. It almost took his breath away.

"Well?" she said, her hands on her slim hips, her smile slipping a little.

"Why didn't you tell me?" he finally asked.

Her brows soared. "I just did."

"When did you find out? Have you been to the doctor?"

"I've suspected for a few days," she admitted, running a finger along the edge of the hall table, not meeting his gaze. "I saw Doc Jacoby yesterday."

Pete knew there must be a thousand questions to ask, but he was too overwhelmed. Finally he managed to say, "When…?"

"Is it due?" she finished for him. "August."

"And everything is all right?"

"Oh, yes. I'm healthy as can be." She didn't wait for any more questions. Turning toward the door, she said, "I have to go now."

"Wait!" he repeated, grabbing her arm again. "We have to make plans."

"For what?"

"For our marriage, for one thing," he said, wondering if pregnancy affected the brain. A discussion of future plans should've been obvious.

"No, that's not necessary."

That damn plastic smile was back in place, and she wasn't making any sense. "Of course it's necessary. We've both got family to invite…and friends…and…"

"There's not going to be a wedding, Pete," Janie said softly. "That's why we don't need to make plans."

He almost stumbled back at the second blow Janie had delivered. "What are you talking about? Of course there's going to be a wedding!"

She shook her head, her stubborn little chin rising as it always did when she was digging in her heels. Then she reminded him, "You turned me down, remember?"

Suddenly her earlier behavior made sense. "Yeah, but you didn't tell me *why* you asked me to marry you."

"In my book, there's only one reason to ask or accept. And it's not a baby."

"Well, it should be! I'm not having my son born a bastard, thinking I didn't care enough to marry his mother!"

"You do what you want…but I'm not marrying you," she returned rapid fire.

"Why?" Pete demanded.

"Because you don't love me, Pete. You want me…but you

don't love me. That's not enough for marriage.'' For the first time, her smile disappeared and unshed tears filled her blue eyes. This time, before he could stop her, she left.

He stared at the closed door, rational thought almost impossible. Janie's bombshells left him too distraught. After several minutes, he turned to the back of the house, automatically heading for the kitchen, the gathering place for his family.

Red, the cowboy-turned-cook who'd taken care of him and his three brothers since his mother's death twenty-six years ago, was working at the sink. ''Janie gone?''

''Yeah.'' Pete pulled out a chair at the long breakfast table.

''You okay?'' Red asked as he reached the table, two mugs of steaming coffee in his hands. He set one in front of Pete and then pulled out the chair across from him.

''I don't know.'' Pete studied the dark liquid and then looked at Red. ''Janie's pregnant.''

Red's eyes widened, but he said nothing.

''I don't understand women at the best of times, Red, but pregnant women don't make any sense.''

''Don't look at me for advice, boy. I've chased a few pregnant cows in my time, and there's not an ornerier animal alive. But pregnant women? I'm just as lost as you.''

The two men sat in silence before Red ventured another question. ''Is the baby yours?''

''Of course it is! We'd been— We started going out a few months ago.''

''No offense meant, Pete.'' Red sipped his coffee before grinning. ''Jake's gonna be ridin' high. Ever since he matched up Chad and Megan, he's been thinkin' how he'll find wives for you and Brett, too. Now the only bachelor will be Brett.''

Pete drew a painful breath. ''She says she won't marry me.''

The older man stared at him as if he'd lost his mind. ''What? That's crazy. If you don't marry her, her dad'll be over here with a shotgun!''

''I know.''

''Is she gonna marry that greenhorn?'' Red suddenly asked, sitting up straight in his chair.

Pete froze. He hadn't had time to think about why Janie had turned him down. At least not in terms of another man. After Janie had sent him away three weeks ago, she'd been seen around town with a man who had recently moved to Wyoming from Chicago. He shook his head. "She can't!"

"Well, sonny, I reckon she can. There's no law against it."

"Damn it! Some greenhorn isn't gonna raise my boy! I won't put up with that!" Pete leapt to his feet and began pacing the large kitchen. "That's just not gonna happen!"

"Don't rant and rave at me, boy. I'm not the one cramping your style," Red protested, scarcely moving.

"Who's cramping Pete's style?" Jake asked from the doorway as he shed his winter coat and Stetson.

Brett, the third of the Randall brothers, was right behind Jake. Before either Red or Pete could answer Jake's question, Brett asked, "Where's Janie?"

Pete felt an almost-unheard-of urge to lie to his brother, but Brett was the one who had brought word to the barn that Janie was here to see him. He wouldn't believe she'd been abducted by space aliens. "Janie's gone."

"What'd she want?"

Glaring at Brett, Pete mumbled, "Nothing."

"You gotta tell 'em sometime," Red said.

"Tell us what?" Jake asked, taking a step toward Pete.

Pete hated to face Jake. He recognized the concern in his big brother's face, heard the worry in his voice. Jake took his role as oldest brother and head of the family very seriously.

And he really wanted another generation of Randalls to carry on the tradition of the ranch.

"Janie—Janie wanted to talk to me," Pete began, trying to figure out how to explain his situation.

"No kidding, Sherlock," Brett drawled as he poured coffee for himself and Jake, who'd already taken a seat at the table.

Pete shot him another glare before returning to the table and sitting down. "Janie's pregnant."

A quick look at his brothers' faces made him think he should've broken the news to them more slowly. He cleared his throat to try again.

Jake beat him to the punch. Leaping to his feet, he grabbed Pete's hand. "Congratulations, Pete! That's great! Janie's a terrific girl. We've started building on the next generation. I didn't expect it to happen this fast. I mean, Chad and Megan just got married. The most I'd hoped for was a baby by this time next year. But already pregnant! When are you going to have the wedding? It should be soon so people won't talk too much.''

By this time, Jake had abandoned Pete's hand and was pacing the kitchen, excitedly making plans.

"Jake," Pete said.

"We can have the wedding here. Though I guess Hank and Lavinia might want it at their house. We'll need to call Chad and Megan so they can get back here in time. What about—?''

"Jake!" Pete roared.

"What?" Jake returned with a frown.

"She refused to marry me."

While Jake stared at Pete, shock all over his face, Brett asked, "Is it your baby?''

"Of course it's my baby!''

"Well, it could be that greenhorn's, you know. They've been going out."

"For just three weeks! She's seven or eight weeks along." Actually he was pretty sure of the exact night when she'd gotten pregnant. They'd had words, and the making-up had been passionate.

Jake slowly returned to his chair. "Then why won't she marry you?''

"She—she tricked me."

"Tricked you? You mean by getting pregnant?" Jake demanded.

"No! She didn't do that on purpose. And we used protection every time," Pete hastily added. Jake had made sure all his brothers understood their responsibilities. "She asked me to marry her before she told me she was pregnant. You know I don't—didn't—intend to marry. And—and I said no."

"So tell her you changed your mind," Jake said, impatience in his voice.

"I did. But she wouldn't listen."

"Man, old Hank is gonna be on your back tighter than a tick on a hound dog," Brett said.

"Yeah," Pete agreed. "But unless he can handle his stubborn daughter better than me, I don't know what we'll do about it."

"MOM, WE NEED TO TALK," Janie said as she entered the kitchen. She dreaded the conversation she had to have with her mother, but she needed to get it over with. Her stomach wasn't too happy right now, and tension only seemed to make it worse.

"Sure, hon. We can talk while I mix this cake. Betty Kelsey broke her hip, and I thought I'd take a few things over for their dinner."

"I'm sorry to hear about Betty." She'd tried to sound sincere even though it was hard to think about anyone else's woes right now when hers seemed so large. And the smell of that perfectly innocent cake batter was making her nauseous.

Lavinia frowned. "Is something wrong?"

Janie used the same smile she'd practiced on Pete. "I guess you could say that."

Lavinia abandoned her baking and sat down at the table beside her daughter. Covering Janie's hand with hers, she was the epitome of a concerned mother. Janie knew she was lucky to have her parents. Which made the disappointment she was going to bring them even more difficult.

"There's no easy way to tell you, Mom, except to say I'm sorry."

"Janie, what is it?" Suddenly Lavinia crossed her arms over her chest and grinned. "Did you gain a few pounds and that expensive suit you bought last week won't fit?"

"Not yet. But I probably will soon," she offered, a small laugh accompanying her words.

"Then what is it?"

"I'm pregnant."

Lavinia's hand tightened momentarily on Janie's before she put it in her lap to clasp her hands tightly together. "I—I see. May I ask who's the father?"

"Of course you can, Mom. It's Pete."

Relief filled Lavinia's face. "Oh. That's all right, then. Pete will do the right thing."

Janie heaved a big sigh. "Yes, he will, Mom, but I won't."

"What do you mean? Lavinia Jane Dawson, surely you're not thinking of an abortion?"

"No! I intend to have my baby. But I'm not going to marry Pete." She looked away from her mother's inquiring stare.

"I don't understand."

"I love Pete, Mom, but he doesn't love me. He offered to marry me when he found out I was pregnant. But five minutes earlier, he refused to marry me. I won't trap him into marriage just because—because I'm carrying his child."

Her hand rested on her stomach. Somehow the words hadn't seemed true until this moment. She was carrying Pete's child. Forever she would have a part of him in her life. She faced her mother with another smile, this one warm and real. "I don't know what you and Daddy want. I mean, I don't want to embarrass you. If you want me to go away, I will."

"You'll do no such thing, Janie," Lavinia assured her, reaching over to enclose her daughter in a hug. "You're our daughter and you'll have your baby here. If you choose to be an unwed mother, you'll need our help."

"I can manage, Mom. I'll move to Casper and get a job. People will talk if I don't marry." Janie didn't want to be selfish, taking her comfort while causing her parents pain.

"Absolutely not! I'm not having my grandbaby born in Casper! Raised as a city kid? Why, she'd probably grow up and join a gang!"

"Mother! In Casper?" Janie couldn't help laughing, though her eyes were clouded with tears.

"You just never know. No, we'll keep the Dawsons here on the ranch, all of us, where we belong."

"Mom, you're so wonderful. Are you sure?"

"I'm sure. Now, are you going to tell anyone who the father is? Or did you want to keep it secret?"

"I guess that's up to Pete. Dr. Jacoby asked me if I knew the father but—"

"He did what? Did he think you'd sleep with someone you didn't know? Of all the nerve! Wait until I get my hands on him."

"Mom," Janie said, touching her mother's arm, "you'll have to expect that kind of reaction. Are you sure you don't think it would be best if I went away?"

Lavinia settled back down in her chair. "No, you won't go away, and I don't want to hear another word. And I'll try to restrain myself, but I can't believe Fred Jacoby would—"

"Mom, it's okay. Anyway, I told him I knew who the father was but I'd rather not say."

"And did you and Pete discuss—I mean, what did he say?"

"He said he'd marry me." Janie closed her eyes, fighting the pain of turning him down.

"And you said no?"

She nodded.

"Did you discuss—?"

"Nothing. I—I had to leave. I didn't want him to feel sorry for me."

The two women sat in silence until the roar of a truck approaching the house roused them.

"Daddy! That's him, isn't it?" Janie asked. "What are we going to tell him?"

"Well, we'll have to tell him the truth sometime, sweetheart. You know he loves you."

"Yes, I know, but I don't think he'll take it too well. Could we wait just a little while? It won't matter. I'm sure Pete won't tell anyone for a while, if ever." She couldn't bear the thought of facing her father with her news.

"Okay, we'll wait…until an opportune moment arrives, when your father's calm."

Janie almost laughed. With that criterion, she'd have to keep her news from her father a very long time. She only hoped he had a calm moment before she started showing. Otherwise, the roof would come off the house.

The back door swung open, and Hank Dawson strode into the kitchen. In spite of her distress, Janie smiled at the energy that filled the room when he entered. Her mother was the center of the tornado, calm, cool, serene. Her father was the tornado, blustery, quick, powerful.

"Hello there, ladies!" he boomed as he walked to the wall phone. Without any other words, he dialed, then waited impatiently. Abruptly he hung up the phone.

"Damn, line's busy. Well, I'll be back in half an hour, Lavinia, and I'll be plenty hungry." He patted Janie's shoulder and dropped a kiss on Lavinia's lips before starting for the door.

"Where are you going?" Lavinia asked.

"To the Randalls'. I've got to talk to Pete. Some of his herd has escaped."

Before Janie could voice a protest at his destination, he was out the door, already getting into his pickup truck.

"I hope you're right about Pete keeping quiet, Janie. I sure would hate for your father to find out about the baby from Pete."

"You and me both," Janie agreed, rolling her eyes. The explosion such an event would occasion might make the citizens of Wyoming think they were experiencing their first major earthquake.

Chapter Two

The three Randall brothers and Red were still sitting around the kitchen table, trying to sort out the situation, when they heard a truck coming down the long driveway.

"Who could that be?" Brett asked, and stood to walk to the kitchen window. "Damn! It's Hank. Janie must've already told him!"

Everyone stood, though none of them seemed to know what to do.

Jake placed his hand on Pete's arm. "You'd better stay here. I'll go talk to Hank."

"Nope. It's my problem. I'll deal with it, Jake." He wasn't looking forward to this conversation, but Pete wasn't about to hide behind his brother's coattails. Besides, he'd offered to do the right thing. It was Janie who'd refused.

Pete strode to the door, reaching for his coat hanging beside it, but Hank opened the back door before he could intercept him.

"Howdy, boys. I woulda called, but your line was busy. Just wanted to warn you."

"Look, Hank, the others don't have anything to do with this."

"I know that, Pete, but—"

"Why don't we go outside and talk?" Pete suggested, desperate to avoid having an audience, even if it was his brothers and Red.

"Outside in the cold? You must have feathers for a brain,

son. It's twenty degrees out there. What we have to talk about isn't *that* world bending.''

Pete stared at him. The man didn't think his daughter getting pregnant was important? ''Hank, I promise I didn't intend for this to happen.''

'''Course you didn't. Accidents do happen,'' he assured him with a grin. ''I know you'll take care of it.''

''Well, I tried.''

''Oh, so you already knew about the problem?''

''Yeah. But just today.''

''Then everything's settled. And I won't protest if one or two of my little ones look a lot like a Randall brand.''

Pete couldn't believe what he was hearing. ''That's it?'' he asked.

''Well, if the little mama gets ornery, I may send her over to you to take care of until after she delivers. How about that?''

''Hank, didn't she tell you? I'm willing to marry her,'' Pete said in a strangled voice.

Hank's genial smile disappeared, and his brows lowered. ''What are you talking about?'' he demanded.

''Janie. What were you talking about?''

''Janie? Why were we talking about Janie? I was talking about your bulls getting into my herd and—'' Hank's eyes widened, and his face turned a mottled red. ''You got Janie pregnant?'' he roared, and started toward Pete.

Jake quickly moved between them. ''Now, Hank, wait just a minute. Pete offered to marry Janie. She's the one who said no.''

''She said what? Well, that don't excuse Pete. He shouldn'ta been messing with Janie! My little girl! How dare you, boy?'' He tried to push past Jake.

Brett joined Jake in his attempts to calm Hank. Pete almost wished they'd move aside and let Hank do his worst. Maybe it would assuage the guilt Pete felt.

''Hank!'' Jake protested. ''Pete didn't do it by himself. Janie's a grown woman. She didn't have to fight him off, you know.''

''Are you sure?'' Hank growled.

Jake stepped back, and Brett with him. ''You ought to know better than that, Hank.''

"Hell, I didn't mean any insult," Hank assured him, his gaze seeking Pete's over Jake's shoulder. "So why haven't you been to see me, to settle things manlike? That's what your dad woulda wanted."

"Because Janie just told me this afternoon, about an hour ago. As soon as she told me, I asked her to marry me, but she turned me down. We were just trying to figure out what to do." Pete paused and then added, "I'm sorry, Hank. I wouldn't have hurt you and Lavinia for anything."

"How about Janie? I imagine she's going to be hurt the worst," Hank said, sadness replacing his anger.

"Hank, I swear I'm perfectly willing to marry her and take care of her and the baby."

"Fine. Then we'll make the arrangements. And we won't have any hide-in-the-closet kind of marriage, either. Our Janie is our pride and joy."

"With good reason," Pete agreed, smiling slightly for the first time. "She's a wonderful woman."

"Yeah," Hank agreed. But his voice was faint, and he suddenly reached for a chair. "Janie pregnant," he muttered. Suddenly he looked up at Pete, his gaze sharpening. "I didn't even know you two were seeing each other." Before Pete could say anything, he asked another question. "Didn't you think about the consequences?"

"Of course I did. But, like you said, accidents happen."

Silence fell, and the Randalls and Red joined Hank at the table. Jake leaned forward. "Hank, Pete says Janie refused him. Are you sure you can change her mind?"

"Of course I can," Hank assured them, straightening his shoulders. "Janie always does what I tell her to do."

With that statement, Pete realized he knew Janie better than her father did. And he also came to the conclusion that the next few days were going to be difficult.

"Why'd she turn you down?" Hank asked, swinging his gaze to Pete.

He ran his finger around the collar of his shirt. "Uh, she asked me to marry her before she told me she was pregnant."

"And?"

"I said no."

"You've been sleeping with her but you didn't think she

was good enough to marry?'' From the sound of his voice, Hank's hackles were up again.

"Hank! You know better than that. It's not Janie who's the problem. She's—she's wonderful.'' He paused to clear his throat. "I never planned to marry. After Jake's—'' his gaze flicked to his older brother, hating the regret he read there "—divorce, I decided I didn't need that kind of pain. But the baby—'' Again he broke off. Just saying those words threw him for a loop. "The baby makes a difference.''

"Did you tell Janie that?'' Hank retorted.

Pete drew a deep breath and then exhaled. "She didn't give me a chance. I tried to make some plans, and she said they weren't necessary because she wasn't going to marry me. Then she left.''

Hank rose to his feet. "Well, I guaran-damn-tee you there'll be a wedding before my first grandchild takes a breath, so get your best suit pressed, boy. You're about to become a member of my family.'' Then he strode out of the room without saying goodbye.

Jake was the first to speak. "Do you think he'll convince her?''

Pete shrugged his shoulders.

"Well, I remember Janie's stubbornness,'' Brett threw in. "I have my doubts.''

Pete stood. "We'll find a way. My baby is too important.'' He left the kitchen in a hurry, as if he needed to be outside to breathe.

"Man, I hope he's right,'' Jake muttered. Then he looked at Brett. "And if he is, and he and Janie marry, you'd better start looking for a likely bride for youself, too, 'cause you'll be next on my list.''

"Hey, Jake, two out of three ought to satisfy you,'' Brett protested.

"Nope. I want all my brothers married with lots of little Randalls underfoot. And don't you forget it.''

JANIE HAD TROUBLE concentrating on any of her chores as she waited for her father's return. Even if Pete kept quiet, she needed to tell her father that she was pregnant.

He'd be upset. Unlike her mother's reaction, her father would explode. And his anger wouldn't all be directed at Pete. Rightly so. In fact, if she was honest with herself, she was probably more responsible than Pete.

After all, what single man, when faced with one hundred percent cooperation, wouldn't take a reasonably attractive, single young woman to bed? And she'd been totally cooperative. She'd loved Pete for so long, it had seemed natural to melt into his arms, to let passion surge between them.

But she'd been wrong.

Now she had to face her father and explain to him why she'd made this mistake…and why she wouldn't marry Pete.

The phone rang and Janie, in her father's office doing some of the paperwork that weighed down a rancher, stared at it. Was it her father? Had Pete told him?

"Janie?" her mother called from the kitchen. "Phone for you. It's Bryan."

Not her father, but almost as bad. Bryan Manning had dated her a few times after she stopped seeing Pete. He had recently moved from Chicago and didn't know too many people.

He was a nice man, but she couldn't continue to see him.

"Hello, Bryan," she said, trying to make her voice cheerful.

"Hi, Janie. How's life?"

If he only knew.

"Um, fine, Bryan."

"How about dinner tomorrow night? We could grab a steak in town."

"I can't." She should explain, but how could she?

"Then Friday night? I've thought about you constantly. You're the best thing I've found since I left Chicago."

The warmth in his voice was touching, as well as his words. She'd give anything to hear that sentiment from Pete. In fact, everything about Bryan was great. He was handsome, successful, warm, loving—but he wasn't Pete.

"I can't go out with you anymore, Bryan," she finally managed to say.

After a tense silence, he asked in a low voice, "What did I do, Janie? Whatever it is, I'll change. You mean a lot to me. I can't—"

"Bryan! It's not you. It's me. I—I can't date for a while."

"Problem with your parents? You could move out. I'll gladly share my digs," he offered with a laugh he couldn't quite pull off.

Trying to inject some lightheartedness into her voice, she replied, "Thanks for the generosity, but I can't do that. After all, I work here."

More silence. "What is it, Janie? Is there anything I can do?"

Tenderness. Concern. His reaction was soothing, but she couldn't take advantage of him. Maybe she should just tell him the truth. After all, she would tell her father as soon as he returned, so it wouldn't hurt to tell Bryan now.

"No, there's nothing you can do. I—I'm pregnant, Bryan."

She expected him to retreat at once. Babies tended to scare bachelors.

"So you're getting married?" he asked instead.

"Um, no," she replied. "I really have to go, Bryan."

"Wait. Did the father refuse to marry you?"

"No."

"Then why aren't you getting married?"

"Bryan, you really shouldn't—"

"I'll marry you."

She was speechless.

After waiting for her to respond, Bryan plowed on. "Look, I know it's too soon to tell you, but I love you. I'll love your baby. I'll take care of the two of you."

"Bryan, please. This is impossible. You can't— This doesn't make sense."

"Yes, it does. Think about it, Janie."

The urgency in his voice convinced her he was serious. But she still couldn't consider his offer. "No, I'm sorry, Bryan."

"Look, can I at least call you? Take you out? I mean, if you're not marrying the man, then we can still see each other. Give me a chance, Janie."

"I'll—I'll think about it." That was all she could promise him. She just needed some time.

"Janie!"

Her father's roar drew her attention away from Bryan.

"I have to go now, Bryan."

He was still protesting as she hung up, but she couldn't spare any time for him at the moment. She had to face her father.

When she entered the kitchen, she discovered her mother and father facing each other, hands on their hips. *Oh, great. Not only is my life a mess, I'm going to ruin theirs, too.*

"She will too!" her father shouted.

"Hi, Dad."

Her greeting drew his immediate attention. He didn't waste any time making his position clear. "Young lady, I'm very unhappy with you. But you *will* marry Pete Randall. Make no mistake about it!"

"No, Daddy, I won't," she replied softly, refusing to join him in a shouting match.

He gaped at her, as if she'd never opposed him before, though they had had some spectacular arguments in the past. After all, she was her father's daughter.

"What did you say? Janie, you have to! You're going to have his baby."

"I know that, Daddy." She knew it better than anyone. "But I'm not going to marry Pete. He doesn't love me."

"He wants to marry you!" her father insisted.

"That's not the same thing."

"Hank," Lavinia interrupted before he could speak again, "Janie's tired. She doesn't need all this harassment."

"Harassment? What are you talking about, woman? I'm her father, in case you've forgotten! It's my duty to guide her. I know what's best for her, and she'll do what I say."

Lavinia stepped to Janie's side and put her arm around her. "No. She'll do what she thinks is right."

"Surely you're not on her side? Lavinia, what are you thinking about?"

"I'm thinking about Janie," Lavinia said quietly.

It wasn't often her parents disagreed. They were a wonderful couple, as loving now as when they'd married. But neither of them gave in easily, either.

"Now, Lavinia…" Hank began, eyeing his wife warily.

"No, Hank. I will not have you browbeating Janie. She's not at full strength right now."

Janie's heart filled as her father spun around to face her,

panic and caring on his face. "You're not well? Is something wrong with the baby?" he hurriedly demanded.

"No, Daddy. I'm fine. Everything's fine."

"How dare you scare me to death!" he yelled, turning back to Lavinia.

"I was referring to her pregnancy, Hank. Surely, after all my difficulties, you know how delicate her condition is."

Janie's mother had miscarried twice before she'd given birth to Janie and once afterward. Then the doctor had ordered no more pregnancies.

One of Janie's hands stole to cover her stomach. Already this baby was so real that even the thought of losing it frightened her.

Her mother's words also affected her father. "Now, Lavinia, honey, you know I wouldn't do anything to upset Janie, but she has to marry Pete. Surely you can see that."

"No, she doesn't. She has to do what's best for her and the baby."

"That's what I said. She has to marry Pete."

"Daddy, I can't."

"Why not?" came a deep voice from the doorway.

"Pete!" Janie gasped.

"Sorry for not waiting for you to open the door, Lavinia," Pete apologized, but his gaze didn't leave Janie. He wanted her to tell him one more time why his child would be born a bastard. "I didn't think anyone was going to hear my knock."

"That's all right, Pete," Lavinia assured him.

To his relief, she offered him a gentle smile. Since his mother's death, Lavinia had watched over him and his brothers acting as surrogate mother on many occasions. He hadn't wanted her mad at him.

Now he turned his attention back to Janie. "Tell me again, Janie, why you won't marry me."

Her stubborn chin rose, and she looked away. "You know why."

"I want to be sure. I want to know why you're refusing to give my baby my name. I may have to explain it to him when he's older." He squared his shoulders and glared at her. He was a lot bigger and older than her. He wasn't averse to using intimidation if it meant she gave in.

He almost chuckled out loud as Janie reminded him that he was dreaming if he thought he could intimidate her.

"*You* won't have to explain anything to *my* baby." Her body language said he'd better think again if he thought he could take her down.

"*Our* baby will expect me to explain."

"Who said I was going to tell the baby who the daddy is?"

Pete's mouth dropped open. It had never occurred to him that his child might not know who he was. "*I'll* tell him, if you don't!"

"You're yelling, just like Daddy."

Pete cast a guilty look at Hank. He'd come because he'd known Hank wouldn't be able to persuade Janie. Not alone. He'd thought maybe the two of them could do the job. But now he looked for reinforcements. "Lavinia, talk some sense into her."

Before she could answer, Hank said, "She's on Janie's side. No use asking her for help."

"Lavinia?" Pete repeated, shocked by Hank's words. "Surely you understand that it will be best for Janie and the baby for her to marry me."

He held his breath as Lavinia considered her response. Finally, with an arm still around Janie, she said, "I'm afraid that has to be Janie's decision, Pete. I support whatever she decides to do." She looked at her daughter. "Perhaps you two should talk again without us old folks interfering."

Lavinia took Hank's arm and led him from the kitchen. Suddenly Pete found himself once again alone with Janie. What he said now might determine his child's future. He wet his lips and frantically sought for the right words.

"Pete," Janie whispered, speaking before he could. "Don't do this."

"What? Don't do what, Janie? Fight for the right to give my name to my son? To acknowledge him before everyone?"

"Why are you so sure it's a boy?" she demanded, turning her back on him.

He pulled her around to face him. "Boy, girl, it doesn't matter, Janie. What matters is this is my baby."

She stared at her toes, refusing to look at him. "I'm not denying the baby is yours, Pete."

"I don't see how you could!" he exclaimed. He knew the baby was his. But in the back of his thoughts was the man she'd been seeing. He didn't want any doubt at all in anyone's mind.

"I'll leave it up to you."

He frowned. What had he missed? "Leave what up to me?"

"It will be your choice as to whether or not you publicly claim to be the father."

He stared at her, totally lost by her words. "What are you talking about? Did you think I'd deny my own child?" His voice rose as outrage filled it.

"Not—not exactly but—"

"Damn it, Janie, I'll shout from the rooftop that this baby is mine! And don't you forget it!"

"You're yelling again," she protested, her gaze lifting to his.

"Damn right I'm yelling! You're driving me crazy!"

The stubborn look on her face, her eyes sparking with challenge, took his breath away. The fire in her always lit a corresponding one in him, one that quickly burned out of control.

Groaning, he pulled her into his embrace. "Aw, Janie," he crooned, his body shuddering as her softness went all the way through him. He tilted her chin, his lips descended to hers and he drank from the sweetest fountain in the world. He never wanted to let her go, to let her put the distance between them that had driven him crazy the past three weeks.

Her arms stole around his neck, and he pressed her even closer, wanting her to feel his arousal, to know that she made him ache with need. From the very beginning, she'd had that effect on him.

"I knew it! I knew Pete would talk her into it!" Hank shouted from the kitchen door.

Chapter Three

Her father's words ripped Janie from Pete's embrace. She was grateful for the intervention. Once again, she'd proved to herself how easily Pete could erase all her carefully constructed barriers.

"No! No, Daddy. Pete hasn't convinced me." She drew a deep breath and pasted that practiced smile on her face. "He was just...assuring me of his support." She couldn't quite bring herself to meet Pete's gaze, but she heard his snort of derision.

"That so, Pete?" Hank asked.

"Yeah, right," Pete said, but the tone of his voice didn't match the agreement in his words.

"Well, it seems to me that you shouldn't be kissing like that unless you're going to get married," Hank said, a frown on his face.

"Daddy! You're being ridiculous." Janie risked a quick glance at Pete and discovered his cheeks were as red as hers felt. As if they hadn't done a lot more. Otherwise, she wouldn't be pregnant.

"Hank," Lavinia said quietly.

"You know I'm right, Lavinia. They shouldn't be carrying on like that."

"I think that's what my father said when we told him I was pregnant," Lavinia said calmly, staring at her husband.

Hank's face reddened and he tried to speak several times. Finally he muttered, "I can't believe you said that."

"It's true."

"You mean you were pregnant when you and Daddy got married?" Janie blurted out, staring at her parents.

"I refuse to discuss this subject!" Hank roared, looking anywhere but at Janie or her mother.

"But, Daddy—"

"Whatever happened, your mother and I got married! Can you match that, young lady?"

Janie gave her father a rueful smile. "No," she said, shaking her head. "I can't. You see, you and Mom loved each other and—and that's not the case with us."

"Janie—" Pete began, but halted as someone knocked on the back door.

"Who could that be?" Lavinia wondered aloud as she hurried to open it.

"Good afternoon, Mrs. Dawson," Bryan Manning said, but his gaze flew over her shoulder, seeking out Janie. "May I speak to your daughter?"

Janie closed her eyes. Just what she needed. Another determined male wanting to make choices for her. She opened her eyes and stepped forward. "Bryan, this really isn't a good time."

"But it can't wait, Janie. I want to tell your dad that I'm the father of your baby. We can be married at once." He smiled at her, reminding her of a little boy expecting to be rewarded.

Instead, she wanted to bash him on the head.

Before she could protest, the other three in the kitchen burst into questions. The babble of voices made her cover her ears.

Pete immediately seized her wrists and pulled her hands away as he leaned down to face her, nose to nose. "What the hell is he talking about?"

"Take your hands off her," Bryan protested, advancing on Pete.

"Back off, greenhorn, before you find yourself flat on your back," Pete growled, turning to face him.

Janie immediately inserted herself between the two men. "Pete, don't start anything."

"You're warning *me?*" Pete demanded, his voice rising in protest. "I'm not the one who's sticking his nose in where it doesn't belong." He glared at Bryan.

Janie ignored Pete. Bryan was the problem, and she wanted

him gone as soon as possible. "Bryan, what are you doing here? I said I'd think about it."

"You'd think about what?" Pete demanded, even more outrage in his voice.

"Yeah, just what have you been planning with this man?" Hank chipped in.

"You really should explain, dear," Lavinia added.

"And how did he know about my baby?" Pete demanded. "Is that why you refused to marry me? You already were making plans with *him?*"

Bryan tensed even more and surged toward Pete in response to the scorn in his voice.

"No!" Janie yelled, extending her arms straight out between the two men. It had always looked so romantic in the movies when two men fought over a woman. In reality, it wasn't romantic—it was chaotic!

She drew a deep breath. "If you would give me a moment alone with Bryan, I'd appreciate it."

"You haven't answered our questions," her father reminded her.

"No, Daddy, I haven't. But I'd prefer to do that after I've explained things to Bryan. If you don't mind."

Even as her father opened his mouth—to protest, she assumed—Pete spoke up. "I don't think you should be left alone with him."

Janie gave a sigh of exasperation. "Right. He's certainly dangerous, isn't he? Come on, Pete, we're not dealing with a mass murderer here. Bryan is a friend. He made his offer out of—of friendship." She couldn't help sending a look of apology to Bryan. After all, she didn't mean to trivialize his feelings, but she *wanted* what they shared to be friendship.

Pete was watching her closely and settled his hands on his hips, his mouth tightening. Finally he said, "All right, I'll give you five minutes."

Janie's patience fled. A few minutes ago, she'd been in heaven in Pete's arms. But that didn't give him the right to lay down the law to her. "Listen, mister," she said, poking him in the chest with her forefinger, "I'll take all the time I need. And if you get tired of waiting, feel free to head on home."

She was quite pleased with herself, finally feeling she'd

gained control of the situation. But her stomach quickly erased her superiority. She barely made it to the sink before she threw up her lunch.

LAVINIA TOOK CHARGE, shooing the men away from Janie. "I'll take care of her," she said, leading Janie out of the kitchen. "She'll be just fine." Just before they disappeared, she added in a stern voice, "And we want no fighting down here."

As soon as the door closed behind the two women, Bryan spoke. "Look, Mr. Dawson, I love your daughter. I'll take care of her, if she'll marry me. And the baby, too."

Pete didn't wait for Hank to respond. He was too afraid. "The baby is mine, and I've already offered marriage to Janie. *I* will take care of both of them."

"When I talked to Janie, she said she wasn't marrying you," Bryan challenged.

"Things change. Janie will marry me." He only hoped he was right. But he wasn't going to show his fears to this man.

"Well, until Janie tells me differently, I'll be here, ready to take care of her."

"She doesn't need you," Pete growled, irritated that the man didn't recognize that he was treading on Pete's territory. It had torn him up that Janie was out with another man the past three weeks. That the man claimed to love her made him want to punch something…or someone.

Hank spoke up. "Boy, if you've got a lick of sense in your head, you'll say your goodbyes now. Pete's a little riled up as it is, and I'm worried about my little girl."

"But I want to talk to Janie," the man insisted.

Pete shook his head. This guy wasn't right for Janie. Why couldn't she see that? He flexed his hands, itching to show Bryan the door a little forcefully.

"You're not bothering Janie now. Just go," Hank insisted, and Pete nodded in agreement.

"Why does he get to stay?" Bryan pointed to Pete, just in case Hank didn't understand whom he meant.

"'Cause I want him to, and it's my house," Hank replied, his voice growing louder.

Both Pete and Hank took a step closer to Bryan, and he began backing toward the door. "Okay, okay, I'm going. But I'll be back. I won't abandon Janie."

As the door closed behind him, Pete and Hank looked at each other with relief.

"Son, I don't mind telling you, I'd much rather have you married to Janie than that Easterner."

"I'd get a big head about that statement, Hank, except that I don't think Bryan is much competition," Pete drawled, still scowling at the door.

"Maybe not, but at least he's willing to say the words Janie wants to hear." Hank gave Pete a steady look. "You may find him more competition than you think."

Pete refused to even consider such a thing. Janie was having *his* baby. He couldn't believe she wouldn't listen to him eventually. Then he turned his thoughts to a more important matter. "What about Janie? Is she all right?"

"Yeah, or Lavinia would've already been on the phone calling Doc. You'd better get used to her throwing up. Lavinia always did."

Pete shook his head. No question about it. The female was the stronger of the two sexes. He didn't think he could stand throwing up very often.

The kitchen door opened, and both men snapped to attention when Lavinia walked in.

"How's Janie?" Pete asked.

"She's fine. I've got her lying down. Don't we have some club soda around here, Hank?"

Her husband hurried to the pantry, and she turned to Pete. "Did Bryan leave?"

"Yeah, with a little encouragement."

"You two didn't come to blows, did you? Janie was worried about that."

"Of course not. I behaved myself." He ignored Hank's chuckle. "Can I see Janie?"

Hand returned with a bottle of club soda. "Better not, son. She's in no mood to be talked to now."

"I think it will be all right," Lavinia contradicted, but she gave Pete a warning look. "As long as you don't upset her. It was all that arguing and stress that caused her to throw up. It's not good for the baby.''

"Lavinia, I don't think it's a good idea," Hank said, frowning.

She turned to stare at her husband with that determined look that Pete had seen a thousand times, and he grinned at the older man. "I know who's going to win this argument, because I've seen that look on your daughter's face. You two can discuss it in private while I visit with Janie." He turned to go to the door and then added at the last minute, "I promise I won't upset her."

He knew the way to Janie's room, though he hadn't been there in a number of years, not since the summer he'd helped Hank paint the upstairs for some extra spending money. He rapped on her door and heard her faint permission to enter.

"Hi, Janie," he said quietly, his gaze roaming her pale face.

"Pete! I—I was afraid it was Bryan."

Her word choice did a lot for his morale. "Nope. We told him to leave." Immediately he held up his hand. "Nicely, we told him nicely." He grinned and sighed with relief when she grinned back.

"Yeah, I bet."

He crossed over to the bed and sat down on the edge of it. "I was as nice as I could be."

She raised her eyebrows. "That might not be saying too much."

He smiled at her but turned the conversation to her health. "How are you? Still feeling bad?"

She sobered and shook her head. "No. Just a little tired. It's been a—a busy day."

"I'll say." He reached over and took her hand. "I'm not going to argue with you anymore. I promised your mother. But I wanted to be sure you're all right, you and the baby, before I left."

Pete didn't know what he'd said wrong, but the darkening of Janie's blue eyes before she lowered her lashes told him he'd upset her. He tightened his grasp on her hand. "Is everything all right?"

"Everything's fine."

"So why won't you look at me?"

His question brought her gaze back to him, a challenge in those blue eyes. He'd known she'd respond to a dare. She always had. Once she'd broken her arm because Chad had dared her to jump out of a tree. Both of them had caught hell from Hank and Lavinia.

Without conscious thought, he leaned over and brushed her lips with his. "I wanted you to know I'm not going away. I'm not giving up. We're going to be married, Janie Dawson, and you might as well resign yourself to that fact. Okay?"

She tugged on her hand. "No, it's not okay. We've been through this already."

He held on, not wanting to break contact with her. "I'm not going to argue with you right now. Just think about what I've said."

"And you think about what I've said," she said, her chin rising.

"That's my Janie," Pete said, his grin returning. "Never give in."

"I was afraid you'd forgotten," she returned.

"Nope." His voice grew serious. "I've never forgotten anything about you, Janie, and I'm not likely to." He kissed her again and stood. "Don't you forget that, either."

Then he walked away, fighting the desire to crawl into bed with her and cuddle her against him, protecting and loving— no, caring for her. That's right. Caring for her. He didn't love Janie, of course. But he cared about her.

He just had to convince her that caring was good enough.

JAMIE STARED at the ceiling, biting her bottom lip to stall the tears that pooled in her eyes. Was she being stubborn for the sake of stubbornness? Should she give in to Pete's determination?

With a sniff of her nose, she answered those questions. No, she wanted the best for her baby…and for her. Pete would be a good daddy. But she wanted a husband, too. Someone like her father, who loved his wife more than anything.

She'd never doubted her father's love for her, his only daughter, but she had always known that he loved her mother even more. And that was as it should be.

When Pete loved her, not just their baby, then she'd accept marriage with him. Until then, she'd hold out. Even if it meant being alone.

"WHERE'D YOU GO?" Jake asked when Pete appeared in the big barn housing the indoor arena where they worked their animals away from the harsh Wyoming winter.

"I followed Hank back to his place. I figured he'd need help with Janie." He pulled his Stetson down farther over his eyes, hoping his brother wouldn't read the turmoil he knew was there.

"And?"

"And what?"

"Are we going to have a wedding?"

Pete looked anywhere but at Jake. He loved his brother, but he was going to have to disappoint him. "Not yet."

"So what are you going to do?"

"I don't know."

"Pete, you only have a few more months. Don't you think you ought to make some plans?"

He whirled around to stare at Jake. "I'm trying to figure out what to do. But you know how stubborn Janie can be."

Jake nodded. "We'll think on it together. There's got to be some way."

"Some way for what?" a throaty feminine voice asked behind them.

Both men spun around to face B. J. Anderson, the new veterinarian to the area. She and her aunt and four-year-old son lived in a house on the Randall ranch. Though she'd only been there a week or two, already she was fitting in well.

"Hi, B.J." Pete said, forcing a smile in greeting.

Jake simply nodded.

"Is there a problem I can help with?"

"Nope," Jake said emphatically.

B.J. didn't seem to take offense at his blunt dismissal of her offer, but Pete had another reason for apologizing.

"Don't mind Jake. He's not used to being around females."

"That's all right. I didn't intend to stick my nose in where it's not wanted."

"Well, actually I might ask you a question or two, if you don't mind. I mean, you being a female and all." Pete watched her carefully to see if she would mind offering advice.

Though her gaze fell first on Jake, as if to determine whether he would forbid any exchanges, she smiled at Pete. "Well, I'm definitely female, so ask away."

Now that he had someone to advise him, Pete didn't know exactly how to begin. He looked helplessly at Jake.

"Don't expect me to lead this discussion. It wasn't my idea to drag a stranger into it." Jake glared at B.J.

Pete saw B.J. stiffen, and he figured she'd walk away, but instead her chin rose just slightly and she turned a little more pointedly toward Pete. It reminded him of Janie's stubbornness.

"What's the problem? Something to do with a female?" B.J. asked encouragingly. "You have a cow with a problem?"

"No! No, it's not about a cow. It's not professional. I mean, for a vet. I—I'm going to be a daddy."

Though B.J. was momentarily stunned by his words, she quickly offered her congratulations. "That's wonderful, Pete. When's the wedding?"

Jake snorted, and B.J. looked at him in surprise. "Did I say something funny?"

"You could say that," Jake drawled.

"That's the problem," Pete hurriedly said. "She won't agree to marry me."

B.J. tilted her head to one side, as if seeing him for the first time. "Did you ask her?"

"Of course I did. She—she said no."

"Is there someone else she's going to marry? I haven't seen you dating anyone since I've been here, so—"

"No! She's not going to marry anyone else!" When Pete realized he was shouting, he drew a deep breath before explaining, "She's been seeing someone else, but the baby is *mine.*"

"She's not still seeing him?" Jake asked quickly, a frown on his face.

"I don't know. He showed up today and—and he proposed marriage. Told Hank the baby was his," Pete hissed, anger filling his voice.

"Oh, my," B.J. said with a sigh. "Wyoming is a lot more

interesting than my old stomping grounds in Kansas City. This sounds like a plot line on one of the soaps my aunt watches."

"So tell me what to do," Pete ordered.

B.J. looked first at Pete and then Jake. "About what?"

"How do I get her to marry me? I've told her she's going to, but Janie's as stubborn as a mule."

B.J.'s lips curved into a slow smile. "You *told* her she was going to marry you?"

"Yeah. And she is." Pete had to keep believing his words because if he didn't, he'd go crazy.

B.J. chuckled. "Pete, haven't you ever heard you catch more bears with honey?"

"What do you mean?"

"She means," Jake began, his voice laden with sarcasm, "you should waltz around Janie with flowers and candy in your hands."

B.J. shot a cool look at Jake before she spoke. "Flowers and candy are a start. But a woman agrees to marry a man when she believes that she matters to him more than any other woman in the world. Have you convinced her you love her?"

Pete's face turned red, and he looked away. Jake moved closer to his brother and muttered, "That's a useless emotion."

B.J. appeared even more stunned by that pronouncement than by Pete's imminent fatherhood. "I beg your pardon?"

"Look, B.J.," Pete said, desperate to explain things before Jake exploded. "Our experiences with females have left the Randall brothers a little scarred. I told Janie I'd take care of her and the baby. That's all she needs to know."

B.J. gave both of them a considering look that had Pete squirming before she smiled at him. "Then, Pete, I'm afraid you'll have a hard time convincing Janie to marry you. Women don't want to be taken care of—they want emotional commitment."

Pete didn't like the way this conversation was going.

"The woman isn't the only one who wants commitment," Jake intervened, his voice harsh with emotion.

Pete knew his brother was thinking of his own failed marriage. They had all suffered through the breakup. Since Chloe, Jake's ex-wife, had been the first female on the ranch since their mother's death at Chad's birth, twenty-six years ago, their exposure to life with a female had been an unhappy one.

To Pete's surprise, B.J. smiled at Jake. "Once bitten, twice shy?"

"You're damn right," Jake returned, for once appearing to agree with the vet.

"Well, then, boys, I have one bit of advice for you—you'd better get your snake-bite kit ready, because Pete here is going to have to stick his neck out if he's going to convince his woman to marry him." With a smile and a wave of her hand, she strode out of the barn.

Chapter Four

Lavinia insisted Janie take it easy the next day. After the high drama she'd experienced, Janie didn't argue. It was a relief to wake up without losing her breakfast. That was a start in the right direction.

She spent most of the day in her father's office. Though she participated in the actual running of the ranch, she also did a lot of the paperwork, using her computer skills to update the files.

After college, she'd considered moving to Casper to find a job, but her father had offered her a paid position with him. After all, he'd pointed out, it was her heritage. Who better to help him?

She'd agreed. Her heart was on the ranch. She loved the lifestyle. And it had kept her close to Pete Randall. That thought brought a big sigh.

"Janie?" Lavinia called just before she appeared in the doorway. "There's a flower delivery for you."

Janie was surprised. The florist in the nearest town charged a fortune to deliver to the ranches, so the thrifty ranchers seldom bothered with that city tradition.

To her astonishment, she had two deliveries, both huge floral arrangements. The deliveryman was waiting in the kitchen, the flowers on the table, a huge grin on his face.

"Hi, Buddy." She'd gone to high school with him.

"Hi, Janie. Looks like you got yourself two beaux."

She gave him the cash she'd pulled out of a desk drawer for a tip before she came to the kitchen and thanked him, not anxious to add to the rumors that would be flying around the countryside.

"Aren't you gonna open the notes before I go?" Buddy asked, lingering.

"Nope."

"Want to know who they're from?" he asked hopefully.

"Nope. But thanks for bringing them, Buddy," she added pointedly, walking him to the door.

"No problem. Thanks for the tip."

She waited at the door until she saw his truck drive away before turning to face her equally curious mother. "I guess I have no excuse to avoid reading those notes now. If those two put anything in them that will cause more rumors, I'll kill them both!"

"Maybe they're not from those two boys chasing after you. Could be from—from a business acquaintance," Lavinia offered, a smile on her face.

"Yeah, sure." Janie unpinned the first envelope and read it.

Dear Janie,
I wanted roses, but the florist said she didn't have any. But these flowers are to assure you of my love. Think about my offer.

                                        Love, Bryan

With a groan, she put the note down and unpinned the second.

Janie,
Don't forget what I said.

                                        Pete

Hysterical laughter bubbled up inside her. How typical of the two men. Both had been discreet. But what a difference.

"Well? Are they from Pete and Bryan?" Lavinia asked.

"Of course," she acknowledged with a sigh.

"Thoughtful."

"Mmm. Yes, but sure to cause a lot of talk. When I start

showing in a few weeks, everyone is going to remember these flowers, and gossip will spread all over the county.''

"Honey," Lavinia said, a rueful smile on her face, "when you start showing with no wedding ring on your finger, gossip is going to run rampant, flowers or no flowers."

"I know. Are you sure you don't want me to go away, Mom?"

Lavinia crossed the kitchen and wrapped her arms around her daughter. "No, I don't want you to go away. A little gossip is not going to splinter our family."

"Thanks, Mom," Janie whispered, hugging her tightly in return. "I think I'll go finish my work."

Two hours later, her mother again summoned her to the kitchen, where she found a grinning Mr. Jones. Ever since she could remember, as a child she'd visited his store, a modern-day general store, in Rawhide, clutching her allowance in her hands, eager to spend it on his motley collection of merchandise.

"Mr. Jones! How nice to see you," she greeted him with a smile, but behind that smile was a search for the reason for his visit.

"Howdy, Janie. Nice to see you, too. But I'm here on business."

"Business?"

Instead of answering, he nodded toward the kitchen table. For the first time, Janie noticed the two packages on the table, each with its own huge bow.

"What are those?" she asked, dread building in her.

"Gifts, with special delivery instructions. The biggest boxes of chocolate I had."

She assumed his broad smile meant the fees for special delivery had been handsome, in addition to his finally unloading merchandise that had lingered on the shelf too long. "I see. Well, thanks for making the delivery."

Her mother handed her some bills for a tip, but when she offered them to Mr. Jones, he refused. "No, no, that's not necessary. They paid me well. Enjoy the chocolates," he added before leaving.

Janie looked at her mother and sighed. "This is ridiculous."

"Yes, it is, but I suspect it's also amusing the entire community. It will take you a while to live this courting down."

"It will take a while to eat all those chocolates, too. And if I do, I'll have a new nickname, 'the Blob.'"

"Well, open them up. I feel like a chocolate break," Lavinia said, and poured them each a cup of coffee.

When Hank came in half an hour later, he found both the females of his family sitting at the kitchen table surrounded by their bounty. "What's going on?"

"Have a piece of candy, Daddy," Janie offered.

"What's the occasion?"

"Your daughter is being courted by her two suitors." Lavinia picked up another piece of chocolate. "And I'm enjoying it."

"Damn! What's wrong with those boys?" Hank fumed. "Don't they know it'll cause a lot of talk?"

"Oh, Hank, just sit down and have some chocolate."

Hank followed his wife's suggestion. But he suddenly wondered if he should've sent Lavinia chocolates every once in a while. She sure seemed to be enjoying Janie's.

WHAT DID HE DO NOW? Pete asked himself. He had sent flowers and chocolates yesterday. When he'd called last night, he talked to Hank, but Janie had refused to speak to him. Seemed like his gifts didn't help any.

What else could he send her?

What else could he do?

"Well?" Jake asked, walking up beside him.

"Well what?"

"Did you send the flowers?"

"Yeah, and candy, too."

Brett paused beside them, cocking one eyebrow. "Kind of expensive, isn't it?"

"Yeah, but Janie's worth it. Only, she wouldn't even talk to me on the phone last night." Pete frowned at the cowboys on the cutting horses in the arena as if it were their fault.

"Not a good sign," Brett said calmly.

Why not be calm? His future wasn't at stake, Pete thought glumly.

"Now what?" Jake asked.

"I don't know. I can't figure out what to do."

"Maybe something a little more personal. Anyone can order flowers," Brett stated.

"Anyone with a lot of money," Jake added.

"Manning sent her flowers and candy, too." Pete wasn't sure how much money the man had, but he seemed as determined as Pete in his pursuit of Janie.

One of the cowboys called from across the arena. "Pete? Telephone."

Jake had had phones put in all the barns several years ago. It saved them a lot of steps. Pete figured one of the rodeos he'd been in contact with had a question about the animals he was going to supply.

"Hello?"

"Pete, it's Hank. I figured you might like to know that Lavinia sent Janie into town to do some grocery shopping. If she won't talk to you on the phone, she can't refuse to speak to you over broccoli."

"Okay, I'll track her down there. Thanks, Hank." Whether it was in produce or dairy, she'd talk to him, all right.

JANIE NAVIGATED the streets of Rawhide with reluctance. She hadn't wanted to come to town so soon after the flowers and candy. But her mother needed some things right away. Besides, the weatherman said another snowstorm was moving in. It didn't pay to be short of supplies during the winter.

At least it was the middle of the day, when most people would be at work. She pulled into the almost-empty parking lot at the only grocery store in town.

Inside the store, she unbuttoned her coat, the sudden blast of heat thawing her out quickly.

"Hi, Janie," one of the checkers, Elizabeth Munger, called. Janie had gone to school with her, too. "Buddy said you've been getting some special deliveries."

Janie smiled and waved but kept on going. She hoped if she ignored those gifts, everyone would forget about them sooner. Pulling her mother's list out of her coat pocket, she began pushing the grocery cart up one aisle and down another, piling supplies in her cart.

"Hi, Janie. Figured you or your mother would be here," an older woman said. She was the wife of the rancher on the other side, opposite the Randalls.

"Hi, Mrs. Fisher. Stocking up?"

"You bet. When one of those storms hit, you know the menfolks will tend to the cows first and the roads last. Don't want to be caught short of the necessities…like chocolates." A big grin accompanied her teasing.

Janie smiled back, but she started pushing her cart again.

"Well, if that ain't a coincidence," Mrs. Fisher exclaimed, drawing Janie's attention. The woman was staring over Janie's shoulder, and she couldn't resist turning around.

"Hi, Janie, Mrs. Fisher," Pete said. "I just came into town to pick up a few things for Red."

"Really?" Mrs. Fisher said, her eyebrows soaring. "I thought Red always did his shopping on Mondays."

"He forgot some things."

Janie decided escape was the best plan while Pete was still talking to Mrs. Fisher. She resumed pushing her cart only to have one of Pete's big hands grab hold of the push bar.

"See you around, Mrs. Fisher," he said with a nod before turning to Janie.

"Turn loose of my cart," she whispered. To her surprise, he did as she asked, but he strolled along beside her.

"Why won't you talk to me, Janie?" he asked.

"We have nothing to talk about."

"You haven't thanked me for the candy and flowers."

"Oh, yes. How could I forget? Half the town has reminded me. Do you think they will have forgotten by the time I'm in maternity clothes?"

"Why the hell do I care? Do you still think I don't want to be known as the baby's father?"

"Shh!" It felt as if everyone in the store was following their progress, staring at them.

"Janie, what can I do to convince you—?"

"Hi, Janie."

They both whirled around. Janie recognized her second suitor's voice with a sinking heart.

"Hi, Bryan." She paused, sent an apologetic look to Pete and added, "Thanks for the candy and flowers."

Bryan beamed, and she could feel Pete tense beside her.

"I wanted you to remember what I said."

"I wouldn't forget. Now, if you'll excuse me, I have to finish shopping before the snowstorm arrives."

"Is it going to snow again? What's on the ground hasn't melted yet."

Pete snorted. "Well, it is Wyoming. If you don't like snow, come back in late spring."

Again Janie moved her cart, stopped and reached around Pete to pick up a large jar of peanut butter, her father's favorite late-night snack.

"Here, I'll get it for you," Bryan hurriedly said, and almost bumped heads with her to pick up her choice.

She drew back with a smothered sigh. "Thanks, Bryan, but really, I can manage."

"I like doing things for you," he assured her, an eager grin on his face.

Pete, beside her, scowled at the man before asking Janie, "What's next on your list?"

"Mother wants some cans of baked beans," Janie finally said. She sent him a look that said *Please back off.* But she knew he wouldn't. Not with Bryan hovering at her side.

For the next few minutes, they toured the grocery store, each man dashing from one side to the other to gather the groceries on Lavinia's list. All over the store, the other customers watched, gathering in twos and threes and whispering, big grins on their faces.

Janie felt as though she were leading the Fourth of July Parade. Only it was winter, they were in a grocery store, and there were only three of them. And she wished she wasn't one of the three.

Finally she reached the checkout stand. "Really, it was nice of you to help, but that's all my shopping."

"How about a cup of coffee?" Bryan asked.

"Sorry, the storm, you know."

"I'll follow you home to be sure you make it all right," Pete offered, but the caring that remark might have evoked was erased by the one-upmanship glare he sent Bryan's way.

"I could follow her home."

"No, Bryan, but thanks for the offer. You might have trouble getting back," Janie hastily said. The thought of Bryan having to stay at her house during a snowstorm was more than she could take.

During their discussion, Elizabeth, her old high-school friend, had been checking her out, ringing up each item and then staring at the three of them. Janie thought it must be the slowest checkout in history. The package boy, bagging the groceries, had to wait on the checker several times.

When Elizabeth pushed the empty cart past her toward the package boy, both men jumped into action, each grabbing a bag of groceries and stowing it in the cart. When the seven sacks were in place, Pete won the tussle over the cart.

Bryan immediately took advantage by taking Janie's arm. "I'll help you to your truck."

She couldn't meet Pete's hostile gaze. They both knew she didn't need any help getting to her truck. But she acquiesced to Bryan's offer, allowing him to draw her hand through his arm.

When they reached the truck, she pulled away from Bryan, who'd been filling her ears with compliments, to open the back of the vehicle.

Pete immediately began putting the paper bags in the truck, and Bryan joined in. As if they were in a race, they each grabbed a sack and then immediately wheeled around to grab the next. When there was only one sack left, she should've known what would happen next.

"I'll get it," Pete announced as he reached for the last sack.

"No, I'll get it!" Bryan said, trying to reach over Pete's strong arms. He managed to grasp a corner of the bag and pulled it in his direction. Pete, of course, had no intention of surrendering his hold. The rip of the paper announced the latest disaster.

Suddenly, canned goods were rolling across the parking lot. Potatoes landed with a plop in the unmelted mounds of snow surrounding the truck. The lettuce rolled over several times before coming to rest against the muddy tire of another vehicle.

She heard the laughter of those watching from the grocery store and covered her eyes. With both men apologizing, she picked up her groceries with a sigh. They weren't a parade. They were a freak show.

The package boy came out to help them retrieve the groceries, along with several other people in the parking lot. Mortified, Janie took their offerings with thanks and shoved them into the truck.

"Do you want me to go back in and get some more lettuce and potatoes? These got kind of dirty," Pete said.

"No, they'll wash. Just put them in the truck. They'll be fine." Anything to get out of there.

"I'm sorry," Bryan said again.

"It was an accident. And I appreciate your help." She paused and then shot a look at Pete, glowering beside her. "And yours, too, Pete."

"Yeah, I bet," Pete muttered, surveying their audience, still in place. "We made a spectacle of ourselves."

"Yeah, we were more exciting than the coming storm," she teased, breaking into a grin. It wasn't often she saw Pete Randall feeling sheepish. It was almost worth the embarrassment.

When he caught her smile, he returned it, and her spirits brightened. The man could bring sunshine to the gloomiest day ever. At least, he could for her.

"Come on. You'd better be on your way. I'll be right behind you."

She nodded and turned to tell Bryan goodbye.

"When will I see you?"

"I don't know. I'll—I'll call you in a few days."

Pete stiffened beside her, losing his endearing grin.

Bryan leaned toward her as if he would kiss her goodbye, but Janie ducked away. When they'd dated, she'd allowed him to kiss her good-night, but nothing more. And she had to admit that she hadn't particularly liked his kisses. She'd told herself to give their relationship time, but she had felt more than a hint of relief when the baby gave her a reason to stop seeing Bryan.

Now she had to tell him that.

But not today. She'd been through enough today. And she couldn't tell him the truth in front of Pete and all the other citizens of Rawhide who'd been drawn to the little trio's shopping trip.

All the way home, the sight of Pete in her rearview mirror was both a comfort and an ache. He'd always looked out for her, even when they'd been lovers. She corrected herself. Especially when they'd been lovers. He hadn't let anyone know about them because he was protecting her reputation, he'd said.

Well, everyone knew about them now. The candy, the flowers, the grocery shopping. She chuckled. From this distance, the grocery shopping was hysterical. But if the two men ever approached her again at the same time, she was going to run.

Reaching the turnoff to her house, she waved her hand in the back window to say thank you to Pete and braked for the turn. After she straightened out on the driveway, she checked her mirror, expecting to see Pete sail past her toward the Randall ranch.

Instead, he turned in after her.

Now what was he up to? Why was he following her?

She nibbled on her bottom lip, anxiety rising. In the grocery store, he couldn't bring up anything personal with everyone around. But here, at her house, she knew he could get her alone.

With a sigh, she parked the truck. By the time she got to the back of the vehicle to open it, Pete was beside her.

"What are you doing here? Don't you need to get home before the storm?"

"The radio said it might hold off for a day or two," he said, and reached past her for a grocery sack.

"I can carry the groceries in, Pete," she protested.

"I don't think pregnant ladies are supposed to carry anything heavy."

She heaved a big sigh. "I'm not an invalid."

As she reached for a grocery sack herself, Pete ordered, "Leave it, Janie, and go inside."

"Pete Randall, stop ordering me around!"

"Janie Dawson, use your head. There's no point in taking risks. And if you're good, I'll take the blame for the spilled groceries."

She stared at him, her mouth dropping open. Then she sputtered, "You'll take the blame? Like it's not really your fault?"

"That's right." He swooped down and kissed her before reaching for a second sack. "I figure it's your fault for flirting with that greenhorn. But I'll forgive you," he said magnanimously, a twinkle in his eye. "Now get inside."

Chapter Five

Chapter Five

Pete figured he had a big advantage over Bryan Manning. Lavinia liked him. He hoped to parlay that liking into an invitation to dine with the Dawsons.

"Howdy, Lavinia," he greeted her with a smile when he entered the kitchen with the first bags of groceries. Janie was standing beside the door, her arms crossed and her foot tapping.

"Well, hi Pete. What are you doing here?"

"Helping Janie with the groceries. I was worried about her lifting anything heavy."

Lavinia looked first at her daughter and then back to Pete. "That's real thoughtful of you, Pete. But why does Janie look so irritated?"

Pete cleared his throat. "Well, it could have something to do with one of the grocery sacks splitting. I think she's worried about the lettuce."

"I don't think so," Janie retorted, one eyebrow raised. At her mother's questioning look, she continued, "You should have seen the two of them, Mom."

"Two? I only see one." Lavinia pretended to peer around Pete for another person.

"Bryan showed up at the grocery store, too. And they created a spectacle."

Lavinia looked at Pete. "Should I hope the grocery store was empty?"

"'Fraid not, Lavinia. But I tried to be discreet."

"You wouldn't know the meaning of the word if it slapped

you in the face," returned Janie, but Pete was relieved to see a twinkle in her eye.

"I bet you never finished your shopping that fast." His broad grin won an answering smile.

"No, I suppose not. I was so embarrassed I would've run up and down the aisles if I could have."

"What did those two do?" Lavinia asked.

"They turned my shopping into a competition, dashing around, each one trying to fill the cart before the other one could. They almost turned old Mrs. Capelli upside down with their mad rush."

"That's not true," Pete protested. "We only turned her around a time or two. And I helped her find the canned tuna." His righteous tone brought a laugh from Lavinia.

"A true act of charity, Pete. Are you going to bring in the rest of the groceries before they freeze, by the way?"

"Yes, ma'am!" he said, snapping a salute and sailing out the door. At least he'd mentioned the torn sack without Lavinia being irritated. When he returned two minutes later, with two more bags, Lavinia was leaning against the sink, laughing.

"What have you been telling her?" he asked Janie suspiciously.

"I was just describing your expertise at putting the groceries *in* the truck."

The flash of Janie's eyes, accompanied by a broad smile, reminded him of happier times. The urge to pull her into his arms and kiss her until she melted against him almost overcame him. But the knowledge that she would resist made him hold back.

That and Lavinia's presence.

He headed back out for the other groceries. When he set these sacks on the counter, Lavinia fulfilled his hopes.

"You'll stay for dinner, Pete? It's the least we can do for your helping Janie at the grocery store."

"I'd love to stay, Lavinia, on one condition."

"And that is…?"

"You have to promise not to let Janie near the food before I eat," Pete said deadpan. "She's sure to poison my share if she gets the chance."

"LAVINIA," PETE SAID with a sigh, "don't you tell Red I said so, but you must be the best cook in the whole state of Wyoming."

"Thank you, Pete, but I can't take all the credit. Janie made the apple pie."

Janie wanted to stick out her tongue at Pete and assure him she hadn't made it for him. Instead, she received his praises with a nod of her head. But she lost her calm with his next remark.

"You don't have to convince me Janie would make a good wife, Lavinia. I know that already. She's the one who's being stubborn. Maybe someone should be praising *me* to the skies to change her mind."

"Maybe *someone* should accept the answer he's already gotten!" Janie snapped.

"Janie!" Hank protested.

More effective than her father's protest was Lavinia's steady regard. Dinner had been fun, like old times, and Janie immediately regretted losing her temper. Especially when she knew she'd disappointed her mother.

"Sorry," she apologized with a small smile.

Pete leaned across the table toward her. "My fault. I shouldn't have brought up such a personal topic here at the table."

"I don't see why not, Pete. It concerns all of us," Hank asserted, his chin jutting out in stubbornness.

"It may concern us, Hank, but the decision has to be Pete and Janie's." Lavinia stood. "Just to show you how generous I am, Pete, I'm going to let you and Janie do the dishes, which should give you half an hour alone. Then Janie might want you to leave so she can get some rest."

When Hank didn't move, instead staring at his wife in surprise, she prodded him. "Come on, Hank. These young people want to be alone."

"Thanks, Lavinia," Pete murmured as Janie's parents left the room.

Janie, on the other hand, promised herself to have a talk with her mother tomorrow. Lavinia *knew* her daughter didn't want to be alone with Pete.

Janie got to her feet. "I'll rinse and load the dishwasher. You clear the table."

"Let's talk first," Pete suggested.

"Oh, no. One or both of us will get upset, and you'll leave and I'll be stuck with all the work. You're not getting out of it that easy, Pete Randall."

"Well, I thought I'd give it a try," he said with a grin, and began stacking the dishes to bring them to the sink.

They worked in silence for several minutes. Janie was determined to leave any talking to Pete. But she dreaded what he might say.

"Did you really make that pie?" he asked, surprising her.

She turned from the sink to stare at him. "Yes, of course I did. Did you think Mom would lie about it?"

"Nope. I just didn't know you could cook."

Janie chuckled. "I'm not as good as Mom, but she made sure I wouldn't starve to death if I ever left home."

"Isn't that strange? If anyone had asked me, I would've said I knew everything there was to know about you. After all, I watched you grow up."

"There's lots you don't know about me," she assured him, amused by his words.

"Oh, yeah? Like what?"

"Do you know who gave me my first kiss?"

The sudden glower on his face tickled her, and she laughed.

"I don't find that question so funny," Pete said.

"I was just making a point."

He set a pile of dishes down beside her at the sink. "I need to ask you a question."

The sudden seriousness of his tone made her stomach clinch. "What?"

"Did you sleep with Manning?"

"I don't think that's any of your business."

"I know it's not, but—but he said the baby was his." Pete didn't look at her. He kept his gaze on the dishes in front of him.

"I thought you said you believed this is your baby. Have you changed your mind? If so, I bet you're glad I turned down your marriage proposal." She tried to keep her voice light, as if his answer didn't matter. Inside, her heart was breaking.

His hands, resting on the kitchen cabinet, clenched. "No, I don't think it's his baby. You wouldn't lie to me."

"Ah. Thanks for that, at least."

"What?"

"You think I'm a loose woman but an honest one."

"Janie! I didn't mean— You have every right to— I just wondered."

"Is that all of the dishes?" Maybe if they talked of mundane things, she could hold back the hunger that filled her.

"Uh, no. I'll get the rest of them."

She rinsed more dishes and was bent over, stacking them in the dishwasher, when Pete reached around her to catch her braid, hanging down in the open washer.

"Careful. You might get your hair caught on something."

The shivers that coursed up and down her body warned her again that Pete's touch had a tremendous effect on her. As if she could've forgotten. "Thanks. I'm—I'm thinking of cutting it."

"No!" Pete's voice was filled with horror.

She turned to stare at him. "It's just hair, Pete. It'll grow back."

A slow, sexy grin appeared on Pete's face. "Well, now, Janie, it may be just hair to you, but undoing your braid is one of my favorite memories. And when I'm holding you in my arms and those silken strands slide across my shoulders…" He paused and took a deep breath before finishing in a low voice, "I feel like I'm in heaven."

Janie fought the desire that filled her, that pleaded with her to turn into his arms, to feel his strength around her. She swallowed and licked her lips, playing for time.

"Aw, Janie, look at me."

She was powerless to refuse. Slowly she lifted her gaze to his, knowing that when she did so, he would kiss her. But she'd already expended her energy resisting him all evening.

When he pulled her against him, his big, hard body heating her skin even through their clothes, she gave in to her cravings and met him more than halfway. Still, the flash fire of desire that filled her was a surprise. Not that she hadn't always been sensitive to Pete's touch, but somehow she'd envisioned less interest in sex now that she was pregnant.

If anything, however, she was discovering her nerve endings were more finely tuned to the stimulus of his touch. When his lips left hers to trace the slender line of her neck, she gasped. Breathing became more and more difficult. Her hands roamed his broad shoulders as she clung to him.

"Janie, I need you," Pete muttered just before his lips returned to hers.

Her mind was racing as fast as her heart as she tried to respond to his words. She needed him, too, so much. But she needed more than his body. His heart was her goal, and she could settle for no less.

With a groan, she wrenched her lips from his. "Pete, we can't…. Mom and Dad—"

"If we're getting married, they wouldn't say anything," he said eagerly, his hands roaming her body with intensity.

"We're not getting married," she reminded him. She had to keep saying those words over and over again for her own sake as well as Pete's. It was too tempting to give in to his touch if she didn't.

"Damn it, Janie! How can you turn me down? We're good together. We're having a child. Marriage is the answer to everything."

"No, Pete. Love is the answer to everything. And you don't love me." She grabbed hold of the kitchen cabinet with both hands as she leaned against it, hoping to keep from reaching out to touch his tempting body.

"You know I don't believe in love."

"Why, Pete? Why don't you believe in love? Just because of Chloe? You're going to let one rotten apple spoil everything? Are you saying I'm like Chloe?" She stared at him, a challenge in her gaze.

"Of course you're not like Chloe! I never said that!"

"But you're lumping me in the same group as Chloe."

"Look, Janie, love doesn't last. People—people leave. It's better not to—"

"Who left you, Pete? Did you have a lover who left you?" She'd tried to follow his love life while he was on the ranch, but he'd gone away to college. And then he'd ridden the rodeo circuit.

He shrugged his shoulders. "I wasn't a virgin when we made

love, Janie. But I'm certainly not going to give you a summary of my past love life.''

Before her very eyes, she watched him withdraw, pull in, the eager lover disappearing. In his place was a withdrawn, hard man, protective of his secrets.

''Then how will I understand why you refuse to love me? Is it because I'm not lovable?''

''No!'' he barked, anger in his eyes. ''Janie, drop it! I want to take care of you and our baby. That's all you need to know.''

''No, it's not. How old were you when your mother died?'' She wasn't sure why that question popped into her head, but his reaction told her she'd touched a tender spot.

''My mother's death has nothing to do with us. Don't start talking like a shrink, Janie.'' Before she could say anything else, he turned toward the door. ''I have to go. Tell your mom I said thanks for dinner.''

Stunned by his abrupt about-face, Janie stood silent until he'd reached the back door. Then she remembered something she'd intended to tell him all along. ''Pete?''

''Yeah?'' he asked, but he kept his back to her.

''I didn't sleep with Bryan.''

He remained still, as if frozen in place, for a few seconds. Then he walked out. She stood there, unable to move or react. Then as the door closed, Janie thought she heard a loud cowboy yell split the night air.

ALL THE WAY HOME, Pete tried to concentrate on his happiness. Janie hadn't slept with Bryan. Since she was a virgin when they'd begun their affair, he knew he had been her only lover. And he intended to keep it that way!

As much as he celebrated the good news, even more did he try to avoid thinking about Janie's questions. He knew the problem wasn't Janie—she was more lovable than anyone he'd ever met. The problem was with him. But he didn't think it was unusual for a man to resist loving a woman.

And he didn't want to think about it.

Unfortunately Jake was waiting for him when he got home. Waiting to talk about the upcoming marriage.

"Well? You haven't been at the grocery store all this time, have you?" Jake demanded when Pete walked into the kitchen.

"If he has, he's bought out the store," Brett teased his brother.

"No. I had dinner with the Dawsons. Sorry I didn't call, Red."

"That's all right. You can eat the leftovers for lunch tomorrow," Red assured him. He was busy at the kitchen counter while Pete's brothers sat at the table, their customary cups of coffee in front of them.

"So I guess Janie talked to you at the store." Jake said. "Did she agree to marry you?"

"No. And—and we didn't do much talking. Manning showed up right after I got there."

"So what did you do?" Brett asked.

"We helped her do her shopping."

"You and Manning?" Brett asked, as if he wasn't sure he'd heard his brother correctly.

Pete grinned. "Yeah. It wasn't pretty."

"What happened?" Red asked, coming to the table.

Pete ran a hand through his dark hair, wondering how to explain the escapade at the store. Finally, he just stated the facts.

"Mercy," Red muttered. "It's a wonder the girl's still speaking to you, much less inviting you to eat."

"Lavinia invited me. But Janie and I made up."

As always, Jake got back to the heart of the matter. "Then why won't she agree to marry you?"

Pete was saved from answering by the sound of a vehicle coming down the driveway. Everyone looked up in surprise. It was a cold, dark night in Wyoming, not a good night for visits.

Red went to the window, but whoever was arriving had already turned off his or her lights. Jake stood to go to the front of the house, assuming whoever had come would knock on the front door. Before he could leave the kitchen, however, the back door opened. There were two people there, but only one walked in…carrying the woman with him.

"Chad! Megan!" Brett exclaimed, and all the Randalls, plus Red, conducted a group hug. When they eventually separated,

Chad, the youngest of the four Randall brothers, let his bride slide to the floor.

"Did we surprise you?" he asked.

"Yeah. Why didn't you call us to pick you up instead of renting a car?" Jake asked as he gestured to the table.

Chad and Megan sat down as Red poured two more cups of coffee. "We didn't fly. We drove," Chad explained.

"I wanted to bring a lot of things with me," Megan added.

"Of course, I hadn't thought of that," Jake agreed. "You'd need to move out of your apartment. Are you shipping the rest of it?"

Megan glanced at Chad before answering Jake. "I'm not giving up my apartment just yet, Jake."

"Why not? You two are living here, aren't you?"

There was a tense silence before Chad replied, "Jake, of course we're living here, but Megan wants to keep her job while her company does the work here, and she'll need to go back to Denver occasionally."

Pete watched the others, an amused smile on his lips. It was a relief to have someone else the center of Jake's attention. Ever since Jake had invited three decorators to redo the house, he'd been scheming to marry off his brothers.

When Chad and Megan, one of the decorators, fell in love and called to say they were marrying, Jake had been full of himself. Pete was as pleased as the rest of them for Chad's happiness, but he thought it might not be a bad idea for Jake to discover he wasn't in control of everything Randall.

"Keep her job?" Jake bellowed. He turned to his new sister-in-law. "Megan, you don't have to work. You and Chad will be wanting to start a family, like Pete here, and—"

Jake's words set off an uproar from Chad and Megan. Megan immediately protested Jake's dismissal of her job, and Chad wanted to know what Jake was talking about.

Questions flew around the table, but answers were in short supply until a sudden clanging got everyone's attention. Red was standing by the sink beating a skillet with a large spoon.

"Here, now! You all are gonna have to settle down or I'm kickin' you out of my kitchen."

Brett grinned at his oldest brother. "Guess Red's got a point.

Maybe you'd better stop laying down the law and listen to what the newest member of the Randall clan wants.''

Jake glared at his sibling, but he carefully wiped the frown away when he turned to Megan. She'd rapidly become a favorite with all of them even before they realized she'd be joining their family. "Megan, I didn't mean to step on any toes. I just assumed—"

"Sorry, Jake, but Chad and I haven't discussed—" her cheeks heated as she sought the right word "—starting a family. And I don't want to miss out on redoing the house. I'm looking forward to working with Adele." Adele, the second of the three decorators, was older, but she and Megan got along well. They'd decided to combine their ideas for the ranch house.

The other three brothers looked at Chad, as if wondering how he would react to his wife's response. Chad leaned back in his chair and grinned. "Boys, whatever makes Meggie happy is fine with me. Now, what's this about Pete?"

Pete immediately realized his time out of the spotlight had come to an end. But he left it to Jake to do the explaining.

"Janie's pregnant."

Talking about Janie and the baby made Pete tongue-tied, but even he could've done better than Jake's blunt statement.

Megan looked puzzled, but Chad put things together quickly and turned to Pete, a frown on his face. "Yours?"

Pete nodded.

"So, when's the wedding?"

With a sigh, Pete confessed, "I don't know."

"You offered, didn't you?" Chad demanded, tensing. "You can't treat Janie like some—some…"

"Of course I offered. Hell, I insisted. But you know Janie. She's as hardheaded as they come."

"You mean she turned you down?" Chad asked, astonishment on his face.

Pete studied his cup of coffee, and no one said anything.

Finally Megan reached out to pat Pete on the arm. "I'm looking forward to meeting Janie. I saw her the night you all took us to the steak house, but we weren't introduced."

"Maybe Megan could talk to her, woman to woman, you know?" Brett suggested.

Five pairs of male eyes focused on the only female in the room.

"Well," Megan said, before pausing to run her tongue over her lips, "I'd certainly like to—to talk to her, but I don't know—"

"Great!" Pete replied before she could finish. He was desperate for help. "I'll bring her over tomorrow."

Chapter Six

Chad settled beneath the covers with a sigh of satisfaction. Megan, emerging from the bathroom, noticed how much more comfortable her husband was here than in her apartment in Denver. "Happy to be home?"

He grinned, putting his big hands behind his head. "Yeah."

His muscular physique still took her breath away, but she tried to concentrate on other things. "You don't mind that I want to work on the house, do you?"

"Of course not. Like I said, whatever makes you happy."

"We haven't discussed children." She slipped off her robe and slid into the bed beside her handsome husband.

He chuckled and drew her into his arms. "Don't let Jake get to you, Meggie. I didn't marry you so we'd have another generation of Randalls. That's Jake's plan, not mine. I married you because I love you more than anything, even the ranch. Remember?"

She remembered. Afraid of marriage because of her mother's numerous trips down the aisle, she'd had a hard time believing Chad was serious about his commitment until he'd presented her with a prenuptial agreement promising her his share of the Randall ranch if he should ever leave her.

Offering her lips to assure him she remembered, Megan found herself wrapped in his powerful arms, his lips devouring hers.

When his mouth moved on to nibble on her neck, she asked, "But do you want children?"

He pulled back and stared at her in the night lamp's glow. "He really spooked you, didn't he?"

"No. But everything happened so quickly, I just realized we didn't discuss a lot of important things." She ran her fingers through the black hair on his chest, her gaze not meeting his until his fingers lifted her chin.

"You're not having regrets, are you?"

"No! Never!" Again she kissed him, with his complete co-operation. "But what do you think about children?"

Brushing back her silky hair, he said, "I think kids would be great, when you're ready. But Pete's taking care of the next generation, so there's no hurry."

"But what if she doesn't marry him?"

"She will. She's been in love with him forever." Then, with a laugh, he added, "Besides, Pete's got you on his side. You'll talk her into it."

Megan's eyes widened in panic just before Chad turned off the light and proceeded to distract her.

JANIE RODE OUT with her father the next morning, in spite of her mother's protests. "Mom, I'll be okay. I asked the doc, and he assured me any normal activities could be continued for a few more months. And Daddy needs me."

"I'll have a word with your father," Lavinia insisted.

"No, Mom. I'll be careful."

Lavinia knew her hardheaded daughter and gave up the fight, only saying a silent prayer that Janie was right. But she was relieved to find a like thinker when the phone rang about ten o'clock.

"Lavinia, may I speak to Janie?" Pete asked.

"She rode out with her father."

"What?" Pete roared. "What did you say?"

"Janie rode out with her father. She said he needed her help."

"Damnation! Crazy woman," Pete muttered.

Lavinia felt her regard for Pete rise until he asked his next question.

"Why didn't you stop her?"

"Pete Randall, you know Janie as well as I do. Do you think *you* could've stopped her if she'd made up her mind?"

"But the baby…"

"I *know*. She said the doc okayed it."

Pete muttered something else under his breath, but Lavinia didn't catch the words. And she decided not to ask him to repeat himself.

"Look, I called to see if all of you could come to dinner tonight," Pete finally said. "Chad and Megan are back home. I want Janie to meet her."

"I'm sure she'll want to meet Megan. But you don't have to include me and Hank."

"Janie wouldn't come without you." As if suddenly realizing how inhospitable his words sounded, Pete hastily added, "And we want you and Hank to meet Megan, too. After all, we're all going to be family."

"I hope so, Pete," Lavinia replied. "Shall we come about six?"

"That'll be great. See you then."

When Janie and her father returned for lunch, Lavinia repeated Pete's invitation.

"I don't think I'll go, thanks anyway," Janie said, sinking into a chair with a sigh of relief.

"Why not?" Hank demanded.

"Because I don't want to." She raised her chin and stared at her father.

"They're our neighbors, Janie Dawson. We'll all go. It's the neighborly thing to do." He joined her at the table as if the conversation were over.

"But, Daddy—"

"Janie, I think it's the least you can do. We've left the choice of marrying Pete up to you, but we shouldn't have to give up our association with the Randalls."

"Of course not, Mom, but I can stay at home, and you two—"

"We'll go as a family," Lavinia said firmly and sat down to dish up the food she'd prepared.

After a silent lunch, Janie decided not to return to the saddle with her father. Her mother let her help with the dishes and then shooed her upstairs. "You need a nap, young lady, and don't bother denying it."

With a weary smile, Janie shook her head. "I'm not a child, Mom…but you're right."

"I've been pregnant before. The most important thing now is your health."

"Yes, Mom."

As she started up the stairs, her mother added one more thing. "By the way, Pete was very unhappy that you were in the saddle this morning."

Janie was tempted to tell her mother what Pete could do with his concern, but she decided to save her words for the person who needed to hear them. Words she would deliver after a good nap.

HER AFTERNOON REST DID a lot to restore Janie's sense of humor. She could face Pete now and handle any arguments he threw at her concerning going about business as usual.

What she wasn't looking forward to was meeting the newest Randall. The bleached blonde who'd partied with the best of them that night at the steak house when she'd seen the Randall group from a distance hadn't impressed her.

The other decorator, an attractive young woman dressed in a classic fashion, had been clinging to Pete's hand. At least *she* wouldn't be there. Janie didn't want any competition for Pete's attention, much less competition that made her feel unattractive.

"Are you ready?" her father called up the stairs. "We don't want to be late."

He could speak for himself.

Janie joined her parents downstairs and apologized for keeping them waiting. On the drive over to the Randalls', she firmly kept the conversation on the running of the ranch. Her father loved to talk about business. According to him, the Dawson operation was the best in the state. He would allow the Randall spread, almost twice the size of theirs, to be second-best, but no better.

Light streamed out from the windows of the Randall homestead, welcoming them. The house was enormous, but it had become run-down over the years, under the care of only men. Janie hoped Chad's new wife did a better job with the house than she did with her own appearance.

The thought of Jake Randall facing chrome and glass at breakfast each morning, or relaxing in front of the fireplace in a lime green plastic beanbag chair, brought a chuckle to her lips. It might serve him right for his stupid matchmaking. Everyone in the county had heard the tale of his machinations.

And he'd intended for Pete to be the first married.

She drew a deep breath at such a scary thought.

"Everything okay?" Lavinia asked as Janie hesitated before getting out of the truck.

"Sure. I was just wondering how much Chad's wife would change the house."

Lavinia turned and stared at the stately home. "I hope not too much. It's always been beautiful."

"Come on, ladies. It's cold out here," Hank urged, placing a hand on each of their backs.

They allowed him to steer them toward the back door.

"Maybe we should go to the front door," Janie suggested. "After all, we're dinner guests."

Hank snorted but didn't change direction.

"I think we're okay at the back door. We've known them a long time," Lavinia said with a grin.

Since Pete emerged just then, they all knew they'd chosen the right door. He bounded off the porch and met them halfway.

"Hi. We're glad you could make it." He hugged Lavinia and shook Hank's hand. When he turned to Janie, she took a step back, but her hesitation didn't stop him. He hugged her close and brushed his lips across hers.

"Pete!" she protested.

"I was just saying hello. Come meet Megan. I think you'll like her."

Janie said nothing, but she wondered how men could be so blind. The bleached blonde she remembered, with her tight, suggestive clothing, might impress a room full of men, but Janie didn't think she'd appeal to either her or her mother.

When they entered the kitchen, only Red was there, busy at

the stove. He turned to greet them, then quickly urged them into the living room.

"We're not eating in the kitchen?" Hank asked.

"Nope, we're formal tonight in Megan's honor," Red assured them. "We invited the vet and her aunt and little boy, too. That's too many to get around the table in here."

"The vet? I like B.J. I'll be glad of the chance to talk with her," Hank said.

"Her?" Lavinia asked, startled.

"Didn't I tell you she's a woman? Nice lady, very knowledgeable."

Janie looked at Pete. "Isn't she living on the ranch?"

"Yeah" was his brief answer.

"So the Randall ranch, after having no women for a quarter of a century, suddenly has two?"

Red was the one who answered her question. "More'n that if you count Mildred—I mean, Miss Bates—and I think you should."

Pete nodded but had nothing to say as he led them toward the living room.

When they entered the large room, the family was gathered around the fireplace. Everyone stood and turned to greet them, and Janie received a shock.

The bleached blonde wasn't there. But the beautiful woman who'd clung to Pete's hand was.

Chad came forward to greet them, pulling the fashionable young woman with him. Janie tried to suppress the surge of envy over the woman's elegant hairstyle, her knit skirt and sweater in a heavenly blue, the look of adoration Chad was giving her.

"I'd like to present my wife, Megan," Chad was saying, and Janie managed a nod in greeting.

Lavinia and Hank shook her hand, and then it was Janie's turn. "Hello, Megan. Welcome to Wyoming."

"Thank you, Janie. I know we haven't met, but I saw you that night at the steak house. I'm delighted to finally meet you."

"Me, too. But I'll confess to being confused. You were holding Pete's hand that night. I thought Chad had married the other lady."

"Rita?" Chad asked before hooting in derision. "I'm insulted, Janie, that you would think I'd pick someone like her. My heart was set on Megan from the first."

Janie managed a smile. "Well, I think you've chosen well."

Megan must have realized her discomfort, because she leaned closer and whispered, "I was only holding Pete's hand because he seemed so distressed to see you with another man."

Janie smiled her thanks as Pete returned to her side to lead them to chairs by the fireplace. Red entered at that moment with some chips and salsa.

"Red, is there anything I can do to help?" Lavinia asked.

"Well, now, I could use a little help with the rolls, Lavinia, if you're sure."

"When I offered, he refused," an older woman said, sniffing in disdain at the man.

"Now, Miss Bates, this is your first time to dine with us, and I wanted—"

"Red, why don't Miss Bates and I both help you? I'd like to get to know one of our new neighbors." Lavinia sent an inviting smile to the lady, who immediately stood and joined Lavinia. The two walked out of the room, talking together, and Red followed behind, mumbling under his breath.

"Janie, that was Mildred, B.J.'s aunt, and here's B.J. and Toby," Pete said, gesturing to a tall woman a little older than Megan.

Janie shook hands and felt a lot more comfortable with B.J. than she did with Megan. B.J. was dressed in a denim skirt and blouse. She was one of their kind.

The little boy, adorable with his shyness, reminded Janie of the child she was carrying. Suddenly misty-eyed, she decided to sit down.

"You okay?" Pete whispered, hovering. "You shouldn't have ridden out with your dad today."

Janie glared at him. "You've always urged me on, telling me I didn't get any special privileges because I was a girl."

"That's when you were growing up. Not now. You're pregnant, damn it!" He'd stopped whispering somewhere in the middle of his protest, and his words rang out in the utter silence as he finished.

Janie tried to keep hold of her temper. "Thank you, Pete. I

guess now I don't have to send out announcements.'' Then she smiled at the rest of those in the room, determined to avoid heavy drama. "You're in the company of a sinful woman, so let me know if I need to leave."

B.J. became her friend for life as she chuckled and said, "Honey, if you're the only woman the Randall clan has tempted to sin, I'll be surprised."

Megan joined her. "I'm certainly not going to cast any stones. Something about glass houses."

Jake had the final word. "We want to celebrate the newest Randall-to-be, Janie, not condemn him or her."

"Thank you." She could've pointed out that her baby was a Dawson, but that would be like a Southerner firing the first shot of the Civil War smack in the middle of Central Park.

Pete pulled a chair up to the side of hers and sat down, but he didn't have anything to say. He'd already said too much.

THE DINNER WAS more enjoyable than Janie had thought it would be. She discovered that Megan, in spite of her elegant city appearance, was warmhearted. Even better, the love she felt for Chad was written all over her.

So when Megan announced that Red shouldn't have to clean up since he'd done all the cooking, Janie was able to join the dishwashing crew with no qualms.

Or so she thought.

When the rest of the company had returned to the living room, Janie found herself left alone with Megan and B.J. For a few minutes, the three of them divided up the labor and chatted about the evening and the neighborhood.

Then, just as Janie began washing the dishes and B.J. dried while Megan put away the leftovers, the subject matter changed.

"Janie, this is a personal question, but I can tell you care for Pete." Megan hesitated by her side, a worried look on her face. "So why won't you marry him?"

B.J., after a sharp look at Megan, added, "And I know he cares for you."

Janie didn't want to answer. She didn't want to defend her position again. Nor did she want to expose her pain to anyone.

Finally, however, she couldn't ignore the caring in their eyes and their words. "Does he?"

"I'd swear he does, especially since he learned about the baby," B.J. said. "I haven't known him long, but he seems to really want to take care of the two of you."

"Yes." Janie sighed and then turned to face the other two and said abruptly, "I asked him to marry me."

Megan gasped, but B.J. didn't show any reaction, so Janie assumed she already knew the story.

"You did? Then what's the problem?" Megan demanded.

"He turned me down."

After staring at her as if she could read the secret on Janie's face, Megan confessed, "I'm confused."

"He turned me down until I told him about the baby. He's willing to marry me for the baby's sake. Not because of me."

"I WONDER WHAT they're talking about," Pete whispered to Chad.

Everyone was gathered around the fireplace again, drinking coffee, while the three young women did the cleaning. Pete would've preferred being in the kitchen, even if it meant he had to wash the dishes. He didn't want Janie out of his sight.

"Don't worry. I told Megan to work on her. She'll probably talk her into marrying you before the table's cleared off."

"What makes you so confident Megan can succeed where I can't?" Pete demanded a little huffily. *He* should be the one to persuade Janie, not Megan.

"She convinced a stubborn bachelor to marry, didn't she?" Chad boasted, looking irritatingly content.

"Yeah, but those techniques won't work on Janie," Pete muttered.

"What are you two whispering about?" Hank demanded.

"Hank, that's none of your business," Lavinia warned.

"Hank's right," Jake intervened. "They shouldn't be whispering in company."

"It's no big secret," Chad said, ignoring Pete's whispered protest. "I asked Megan to help convince Janie she should marry this old buzzard." He slapped Pete on the back and chuckled.

"Good," Hank replied. "I'd like a wedding real soon."

"I won't have Janie pressured," Lavinia insisted.

"Pressured, hell!" Hank roared. "It's her duty. She owes my grandchild, if nothing else."

"The most important thing is Janie and the baby's health," Lavinia said.

Pete's heart contracted in fear. "Is anything wrong? The doctor didn't see a problem, did he?"

"No, Pete. But I had some difficulties, as you know. I want to be sure Janie's healthy."

Somehow, in spite of knowing Lavinia's history, Pete hadn't connected it to Janie. Now anxiety was added to his frustration. "When does she go back to the doc?"

"I believe he's scheduled her for a sonogram next week."

"A sonogram? That early? Are you sure he doesn't suspect something is wrong?"

Mildred spoke up. "I believe they're using those right away now. Even when B.J. was pregnant with Toby, she had one early."

"What's a sonogram?" Toby asked, stumbling over the unfamiliar word.

Jake, who was sitting next to Mildred and Toby, reached over to rub the child's head. "It's a picture of you while you were in your mommy's tummy."

"Oh. Can I see it?"

Jake looked at Mildred, his eyebrow raised in question.

"We'll have to ask your mommy," Mildred replied.

"I want to go with Janie to Doc Jacoby's," Pete said. He didn't want secondhand information about his own child.

"If you do that, everyone will know the baby is yours," Lavinia warned.

"Damn it!" Pete yelled, standing. "Why does everyone think I don't want my identity known? This kid is mine! Janie is mine! And I'll fight the first person who dares say otherwise!"

Brett chuckled. "Janie was right. With Pete around, she won't need to send out birth announcements." He was unperturbed when Pete glared at him. "Don't waste your energy on me, big brother. I'm all for Janie marrying you."

"We all are," Lavinia assured him, "if it's Janie's choice.

But if she doesn't marry you, Pete, I promise you we'll take good care of her and the baby."

Pete sank back into his chair, misery filling him. "I appreciate that, Lavinia, and I'm sorry I lost my temper. But *I* want to take care of my own. My family." Those two words filled him, making his heart swell with feelings he didn't want to admit to. He was only doing his duty, he promised himself.

"Don't worry. Megan will persuade Janie, I'm sure," Chad assured him with a grin.

At that moment, the door opened and the three young women entered the room.

"We've finished the dishes. Does anyone need a fresh cup of coffee?" Megan asked, smiling at everyone.

"No," Hank replied, rising. "What we need is a yes from Janie. Did you talk her into it?" His frankness rendered his audience silent.

Pete watched, holding his breath, his gaze glued to Janie, but she didn't look at him.

Megan, after drawing a deep breath, replied, "No. I didn't. In fact, I agree with Janie. She shouldn't marry Pete."

Chapter Seven

Pete paced the floor the length of the telephone cord while he waited for someone to answer the Dawsons' phone. When Hank finally growled into the receiver, Pete breathed a sigh of relief. If Janie or her mother had answered, either of them might have hung up the phone rather than talk to him after the brouhaha two nights ago.

"Hank, I need to know when Janie's going to the doctor."

"I don't think I'm supposed to tell you."

"Come on, Hank. I need to go with her."

"Look, boy, I'm already sleeping on the sofa because of you. I don't think—" He stopped, and Pete waited for him to continue. "Aw, hell, okay. She has an appointment at three this afternoon. She and her mother left the house about five minutes ago."

"Damn! Okay, okay, I'll drive into town and meet them there." As an afterthought, he added, "If it makes you feel any better, you're not the only one suffering from the other night. Chad is having problems, too."

"Good. That boy needs to learn a few things about women."

Pete thought that was pretty much a case of the pot calling the kettle black, but he didn't say so. "I guess we all need help understanding females, Hank."

Hank grunted his agreement before saying, "You'd better get moving if you're going to be there in time."

"Yeah. Thanks, Hank."

"You bet. We men gotta stick together. Besides, I'm already on the couch. How much worse can it get?"

Pete didn't attempt to answer that question. He only hoped Hank didn't find out.

Grabbing his coat as he told Red he was going into town, Pete rushed out the back door to his truck. He was grateful he'd called Hank when he had. He'd been tempted to wait a few more days, so that everyone's temper might have cooled a bit more. The dinner two nights ago had ended in a male-versus-female battle.

He wasn't sure Janie would even speak to him. How she would react when he showed up at Doc Jacoby's office he didn't know.

Squaring his jaw, Pete vowed nothing would stop him from taking care of his baby and his…Janie.

When he entered Doc Jacoby's waiting room and all eyes of the waiting patients focused on him, he had to remember his resolve. After pausing, he strode over to the window to announce his arrival.

"Well, hi Pete. What are you doing here? You got a touch of the flu that's going around?" asked Mandy Andrews, the doctor's receptionist who'd gone to school with all the Randall brothers and Janie.

"Uh, no."

She waited, looking at him expectantly, for more information.

"I need to see the doc."

Grinning, she said, "Well, I figured that. Otherwise, you wouldn't be here."

She continued to stare at him, and Pete realized he was going to have to explain his presence. Feeling his cheeks heat up, he sought for the least embarrassing way.

Mandy's eyebrows suddenly shot up, and she leaned forward. "Don't tell me you've got one of those diseases?"

"No!" The eagerness in her voice told him she was ready to broadcast the news to the entire town. So what? He'd said he wanted to claim his baby. Squaring his shoulders, he said, "Is Janie here? I want to be with Janie during the examination."

"Now, Pete, I know the Randalls and Dawsons have been friends a long time, but her mother is with her. Why, the only way I'd let you in is if you were the—"

"I am."

Mandy's eyes widened, but she said nothing except to excuse herself.

Only seconds later, as Pete stood at the window, not knowing what to do with himself, Mrs. Priddy, Doc's starchy nurse, appeared.

"Young man, are you claiming to be the father of Janie Dawson's baby?" she asked in a whisper that could've reached the back rows of any theater. There was a sudden hush around him.

Again he straightened and said, "Yes, I am, and I want to be with her during the examination."

"She didn't say you would be coming."

"I'm here." He certainly wasn't going to start explaining all the complications of his and Janie's relationship.

After glaring at him, Mrs. Priddy muttered, "Wait here."

Like I have a choice, Pete groused to himself. The door into the examining rooms was kept locked. He remained by the window, ignoring Mandy's surreptitious stares as she resumed her place in front of the computer.

Finally, when he thought he could stand the waiting no longer, the magic door opened.

"Mr. Randall," Mrs. Priddy called out, and he hurried to the door.

"This way, please."

Without saying another word, she led him down the hallway to a closed door. The smells of medicine and antiseptic surrounded him, reminding him of visits to the doc as a child. Mrs. Priddy seemed just as forbidding today as she had back then.

And he wouldn't get a lollipop today.

She swung open a door, and he stiffened his shoulders, prepared to face Janie's wrath.

Instead, he found himself in the doctor's office. Doc Jacoby was sitting behind a massive desk, a frown on his face.

"Come on in, Pete, and have a seat."

"I want to see Janie," Pete blurted out, not moving from the doorway.

"Yes, so Priddy told me. She also said you're the father of Janie's baby."

"Yes."

"Janie didn't mention to Priddy that you'd be coming." Bright blue eyes stared at him from beneath bushy white eyebrows.

To give himself time to think, Pete moved to the chair in front of Doc's desk and sat down. "I, uh, we've had some differences of opinion. She refuses to marry me, seems to think I'm ashamed of the baby," Pete announced, his voice rising with frustration.

"And you're not?"

"Hell, no! I've begged her to marry me. I told her I'd shout the fact that this is my baby from the rooftops. She keeps saying no."

"Hmm," Doc Jacoby muttered, one finger laid across his lips. Then he stood up and Pete did, too. "Sit down, boy. I'll go talk to Janie and her mother. You wait here."

"I'm tired of waiting. I'll go with you."

"You'll wait here as I said, or I'm turning Priddy loose on you with a syringe."

Pete collapsed in the chair.

"WHEN IS HE GOING TO COME?" Janie finally demanded. She'd been patient as long as she could be.

"Doc will be in as soon as he can, Janie. You know that. Just relax." Lavinia sat in a chair nearby the examining table, a magazine spread across her lap.

But Janie wasn't fooled. Lavinia had been turning the pages at random. Janie didn't think her mother had seen a single page.

"Mom, I wish you wouldn't be mad at Dad," Janie burst out. "Ever since dinner at the Randalls', life at home has been crazy."

"Don't concern yourself. Punishment won't hurt your father." Lavinia grinned. "And it's not the first time."

"But I feel so bad about everyone getting upset. B.J. called yesterday. She said Chad and Megan are hardly speaking."

"At least B.J.'s not having marital problems."

"Only because she doesn't have a husband. But what if Jake decides to take her house away?"

"Jake Randall may be upset, but he won't be unfair. You

know better than that. The Randalls are good men, even if they don't understand women.''

"Do you think it has anything to do with their mother's death?'' Janie asked, returning to the question she'd asked Pete after their grocery shopping.

"Possibly. Jake and Pete were at very impressionable ages. Pete was five and Jake eight. Old enough to realize that their mother had left them, even if they couldn't understand death.'' Lavinia frowned and then began, "Maybe—''

Doc Jacoby's entry stopped her.

"Hi there, young lady, Lavinia.''

Lavinia greeted her old friend, but Janie only smiled nervously.

"Janie, my girl, we have a small problem,'' the doctor began.

Janie covered her stomach with her hand. "My baby?''

"No, child, no. We haven't done the sonogram yet, remember? No, the problem is with the daddy.''

Janie stiffened and looked away.

"What do you mean?'' Lavinia asked.

"Well, Pete Randall is waiting in my office. He claims to be the father of this child and wants to be present during the sonogram.''

"No!'' Janie replied sharply.

"No what? No, he isn't the father, or no, you don't want him to be present?''

Janie didn't look at the doctor. She didn't want to face the kind man who'd taken care of all her physical ailments since her birth. With her head down, she finally muttered, "He's the father, but I don't want him here.''

Before Lavinia could say anything—and Janie could sense her intent as she stirred—Doc Jacoby responded. "Now, Janie, I believe a woman should have control over her own body. If you tell me to send Pete away, I will. But I think you ought to reconsider your decision. This is his child, too. Even if you don't want to have anything to do with him, I think he should know about his baby.''

Janie thought he should, too. But she didn't want to lie down on a table, her clothing removed, and allow Pete to stare at her stomach. Yet she guessed she didn't have any choice. Swallowing the sudden lump in her throat, she whispered, "Okay."

Lavinia reached out and squeezed her hand in support, and Janie dared lift her gaze to her mother and offer a weak smile.

"Good girl," Doc said, patting her on the shoulder. "You put on the gown Priddy left for you and lie down on the table. I'll knock before I bring Pete in."

As soon as the doctor left the room, Mrs. Priddy replaced him, leaving mother and daughter no time to talk alone. But Janie knew she'd pleased her mother with her choice.

The gown, pink crinkle paper, was different from those she'd worn in the past. This one had snaps down the front, which would allow the doctor access to her stomach without revealing much else, thankfully. When a knock came on the door, she squeezed her eyes closed.

"Just relax, Janie. The doctor will take care of you," Mrs. Priddy assured her.

It wasn't the doctor making her tense.

"All right, Janie, I think everyone is here. We'll begin the show," Doc Jacoby boomed. Janie didn't have to see him to know he was smiling.

"Actually," Lavinia said, "it feels a bit crowded in here. Why don't I wait in the reception room?"

Janie's eyes popped open, and she pleaded without speaking for her mother not to abandon her. But Lavinia carefully averted her gaze.

"Lavinia, I'll be glad to bring Janie home, if you want. I'll be real careful," Pete promised.

"Thanks, Pete, if you're sure you don't mind. I can go on home and start making dinner. You'll join us, won't you?"

"Mom!" Janie finally protested, but the other two ignored her.

"Thanks, Lavinia. I'd appreciate that."

Before Janie could think of anything to say, Lavinia slipped from the room.

"You don't mind, do you, Janie?" Pete finally asked.

"You mean now that it's too late, I get to voice my opinion?" she demanded.

"Calm down, Janie," Doc urged. "Your blood pressure is going to shoot through the roof."

"She has blood-pressure problems?" Pete asked anxiously.

"No, I don't have blood-pressure problems!" Janie retorted.

Doc Jacoby heaved a big sigh. "Pete, you go sit down in that chair," he said, pointing to the chair Lavinia had occupied. "You," he began, turning back to Janie, "lie back and relax. I have other patients waiting."

Janie did as she was told, allowing her gaze to roam to Pete, waiting tensely in the chair, before closing her eyes again.

"Okay, Janie, I'm going to open your robe so I can examine you," Doc said even as he unsnapped the gown over her stomach. Then he began pressing on her stomach, making her regret the two glasses of iced tea she'd had at lunch.

When he grunted after placing the cold stethoscope to her stomach, she felt movement and opened her eyes to find Pete standing over her on the other side of the table.

"Is everything all right?"

Doc frowned at him. "Hmm? Oh, yes, yes, everything's fine. Quit worrying, boy."

Pete picked up her hand and threaded his fingers through hers. Janie tried to pretend that she didn't like the touch, but she knew she was lying to herself. Pete's grasp tightened as she clung to him.

"Okay, Priddy, let's prep her for the sonogram," the doctor muttered.

Mrs. Priddy, her lips pressed tightly together, came into Janie's range of vision and began smearing some kind of petroleum jelly on her stomach.

"What's that for?" Pete demanded, asking the question Janie was wondering.

"It helps conduct the transmission." The doctor patted the small black machine on a cart. "This contraption is something else. With the doctor in the next county sharing the expense, we've improved the care for all our expectant mothers." He beamed at Janie as if expecting a thank-you.

But she remained silent, waiting for the examination. Thoughts of her mother's difficulties, combined with the tension of the past week, had her dwelling on the negatives of her situation.

Doc Jacoby took a ball connected with wires to the machine

and began rolling it around Janie's stomach. She even feared he might hurt the baby by pressing so hard.

"Doc—" Pete began, and then he stopped, but his hold on Janie's hand tightened. Since the doctor ignored him, he said again, "Doc, shouldn't you be more gentle?"

"You got experience with babies, son? Until you do, keep your advice to yourself." He watched the machine as he continued to move the ball. Then he exclaimed, "Aha!"

"What is it?" Pete demanded.

"See that? That's a heartbeat. That's your child, Pete Randall, alive and well."

"Doctor," Mrs. Priddy whispered, elbowing him and pointing to the machine.

"What? What?" Pete insisted, looking from the doctor to the nurse and back again. Janie followed his gaze, apprehension filling her.

"Well, well, well. I thought that might be true," Doc muttered to himself as he changed the position of the ball slightly.

"Doc, if you don't tell us right now what's wrong, I'm gonna—" Pete broke off, and Janie suspected he couldn't think of a threat Doc Jacoby would believe.

"Nothing's wrong. I told you that. But I do have some news. I don't know whether you'll think it's good news or bad, but—"

"Doc!" Pete roared.

"You're having twins."

PETE STARED AT THE MAN he'd known all his life as if he were a stranger. "What did you say?"

Doc Jacoby looked at both of them, a beaming smile on his face. "Twins. I said twins. I haven't delivered a set of twins in five or six years. The last ones were, um, what were their names? They moved right afterward. Remember, Priddy?"

"The Blackwells," Mrs. Priddy said crisply.

"Right, right. The Blackwells. Nice family. I remember—"

"Doc!" Pete roared again. "Forget the Blackwells. What about Janie...and the babies? Are they all right?"

"Well, a'course they are. Don't you see those strong heartbeats?" Doc pointed to the screen.

Pete stared at the dual thumping, finding it hard to believe that they represented his children. Children! He was having not one but two babies.

He lifted Janie's hand to his lips. "You okay, Janie?"

She, too, was staring in fascination at the machine. "Could there be some mistake, Doc? I mean, it's still early."

"No, Janie, no mistake. You've got two little buns in the oven. And I'm thinking you may be further along than I thought. Maybe closer to nine weeks than seven."

Pete watched Janie as she took in Doc's words. When her gaze flew to his face and then quickly away, he knew she was remembering their argument and the passionate making-up. The sudden longing that filled him to hold her again almost made him forget the news.

"I guess your mother is going to be surprised," he murmured, both his hands holding hers against his chest.

"Happily surprised, I hope?" Doc asked, his smile having gradually disintegrated. "You two are happy, aren't you?"

Janie stared at the doctor, seemingly speechless, and Pete squeezed her hand. "Of course we are, Doc. It's the shock, that's all."

As if realizing Janie needed some time alone, Mrs. Priddy urged the doctor to take Pete to his office while Janie dressed. The two professionals exchanged a look that Pete didn't quite understand.

"Janie will come to Doc's office when she's dressed?" he asked, wanting to be sure she didn't leave. "I'm taking her home."

"Yes, Pete, we know," Mrs. Priddy assured him, patting him on the arm. Then she pushed him and Doc out the door.

"That woman can herd people better than anyone I know," Doc muttered as he led Pete to his office.

Once they were seated, Pete leaned forward. "You didn't hide anything from us, did you, Doc? Janie's going to be all right?"

"As far as I can tell. A lot of things can happen in the next seven months. Maybe less. Twins usually come early." He smiled reassuringly at Pete. "What are you going to do about all this?"

"What do you mean?"

"I mean, are you going to marry Janie or not? Twins can be a heavy burden for a single parent."

"Damn it, Doc, I've been pleading with her to marry me. Both families are up in arms, the men arguing with the women, about our getting married. I don't know what else to do."

"Well, she must have some reason for turning you down. What is it?"

"It's personal," Pete snapped. He didn't intend to share his and Janie's private difficulties with the doctor.

Before Doc could question him further, making him feel he was back home facing Jake, the door opened and Janie slipped into the room.

"Sit right here, my dear," Doc said, gesturing to the chair beside Pete. "We need to go over a few things."

Pete couldn't stand the apprehensive look on her face. He reached out and took her hand again. To his surprise, she didn't protest.

"I'm giving you a prescription for vitamins that you are to take faithfully. Those two babies are going to need a lot of nourishment. Are you throwing up?"

"No."

"Janie, the other day you threw up," Pete reminded her.

The glare she sent him told him she didn't appreciate his help.

"That was because of—of tension, not morning sickness."

"Hmm," Doc said, watching her closely, "Okay, we won't worry about that so far. But if it starts happening, Janie, you let me know. Priddy says you've already lost four pounds since last week."

"She has?" Pete asked, straightening in his chair. "Should she be doing that? I thought women gained weight when they were pregnant."

"She'll gain weight, Pete. Some women lose early on, but we'll monitor Janie's progress. And you, young lady, I want you to get plenty of rest. Take a nap every afternoon and go to bed early. Once you get beyond the first three months, you won't be quite so tired, but don't push yourself."

"Yes, Doc."

Pete thought Janie sounded subdued, and he wanted to pull

her into his arms, to comfort her. Then he thought of something else he needed to ask.

"What about horse riding, Doc? Shouldn't she give that up until after—after the babies are born?"

"I told you Doc said it was okay!" Janie said, firing up at his interference.

"You're right, I did. But I think maybe it's not such a good idea now, Janie. Twins change things a little."

A little? Pete thought they changed things a lot.

After a few more last-minute instructions, Pete led Janie to his pickup. He helped her in and then hurried around to the driver's side. "Shall we go get the prescription filled before we go home, Janie? It will save you a trip tomorrow. And you probably should start the vitamins as soon as possible."

"Fine."

Pete headed to the drugstore, but he didn't give all his attention to his driving. "Are you upset about the twins?" he asked.

"No."

"Then what's wrong? You're not saying much. Did Doc hurt you? I thought he wasn't as gentle as he could've been."

"No, Pete, he didn't hurt me. It—it's just a shock, like you said."

He parked in front of the drugstore. "Janie, I know you don't want to marry me, but that doesn't mean I'm going to abandon you or forget that these babies are mine, too. I'll do everything I can to help you." Leaning over, he brushed her lips with his, aching to deepen the kiss, to celebrate the incredible news that they were having twins. But he did neither.

Janie said nothing.

"Wait here. I'll be right back."

And he was. There was no one waiting, and the pharmacist filled the vitamin prescription at once, even though he sent several curious looks in Pete's direction.

Pete hurried back to the truck. "Guess we'd better be on our way and tell your parents before gossip beats us to it," he suggested with a wry chuckle.

"We have something else to tell them, too."

"What's that, sweetheart?" he asked as he backed out of the parking space.

"I've decided to marry you—if you still want me after you hear my terms."

Chapter Eight

Even as she finished speaking, Janie was holding her breath.
But when Pete threw on the brakes, practically standing on
them, she had to forget her breathing to grab hold of the arm-
rest. Otherwise, she would've ended up on the floorboard.

"You'll marry me?" he demanded.

"Yes," Janie said, breathing deeply. "But only on one condition, Pete. And you won't like it."

She'd given her decision some thought since Doc had told
her she was having twins. Suddenly overwhelmed, she'd realized she would need Pete's strength, as well as her own, to
give her babies a healthy birth. And he deserved to be involved
in his children's lives.

And then there was the fighting in their families.

And the fact that she didn't think she could hold out much
longer between Pete's pursuit and her longings.

"What condition?"

Before she could answer, loud honking interrupted. They
both turned to see several cars lined up behind them on the
road.

Pete quickly pulled the truck into the same parking place.
"What condition?" he repeated.

"I'll understand if you say no, Pete. Really, I will. But I
can't—I can't sleep with you." After one look at the shock on
his face, she turned away and waited for his response.

One large hand snaked out to pull her chin back around to
him. "Let me get this straight. You'll marry me, but you won't
sleep with me?"

Her skin tingled from his touch, and she could understand his incredulity. She'd always responded to him like fire racing through deadwood. "Yes."

"Janie, that's absurd! If there was one thing right about us, it was the loving."

"But it wasn't loving, Pete. Remember? You don't love me. You just want me."

"Don't start that again, Janie. I want to take care of you and our baby—babies. That's enough."

What a hardheaded man. She wanted his love so badly, she'd been willing to risk giving him up. But he hadn't budged an inch. "Pete, you can say no. I won't tell anyone. Everyone will continue to think I'm being stubborn."

"You are!" he snapped.

She didn't think he had to be so quick with his agreement. "Fine. We'll just forget I ever offered."

"Nope, we won't. I'm accepting your proposal," Pete said firmly. "I'm marrying you. But I have a condition, too."

Such a jumble of emotions filled Janie. She was going to marry Pete Randall. But he had terms. Just like her. "What—what kind of terms?"

"I don't want anyone to know that our marriage isn't a normal one. I'll go along with your terms until after the babies are born. I'm not sure it'd be safe, anyway. Then we'll renegotiate. Okay?"

"Renegotiate?" she repeated, her voice wavering.

His eyes narrowed, and he reached out to encircle her nape. "That's right, Janie, my girl. You get your way now. I get my way later."

"Wait—" In one fluid motion, he pulled her close, and his lips covered hers. Instantly the longing that welled up in her was more than she could handle. She'd never realized before that life without Pete's touch was colorless.

Her fingers fluttered against his cheeks before sliding around his neck. She settled into his embrace with a sigh that shivered all the way through her. How she'd missed his kisses! When his tongue pressed for entry, she didn't hesitate. The taste of him was ambrosia to her.

His hands stroked her sides under her coat, then slid around to cup her breasts. Memories of their lovemaking overtook her.

Pete had never done anything halfway. When he'd taken her, she'd felt completely loved—and she longed to feel that way again.

Hazily she tried to remember why they'd stopped loving each other. It felt so good. *He* felt so good. She slid one hand down across his broad chest, her fingers seeking an opening so she could touch his warm skin.

But her tactile exploration was cut short when a rapping on the car window interrupted their embrace. Pete looked over her shoulder and grinned at the old gentleman passing by. But Janie couldn't even summon up a smile. Now she remembered why she hadn't felt Pete's arms around her for a long time—and why she'd agreed to marry him but not sleep with him.

Pete's loving might be magical, but reality hurt too much afterward. It was a lot safer to do without his touch, she reminded herself as she fought to stay in control of her emotions.

As if he were obliging her, he immediately set the truck in motion again, pulling out of the parking space with a squeal of tires.

"Slow down, Pete," Janie protested. "What's the hurry?"

"What's the hurry? I'm getting you home in front of your parents before you change your mind."

Janie drew a deep breath. The ramifications of her offer were beginning to sink in. "I—I won't change my mind, but we could wait awhile, to see if you do."

"I won't. And we're not waiting."

"Well, you don't have to be so dictatorial!"

Pete pressed down on the accelerator. "Dictatorial? Janie Dawson, I've been following you around like a dog begging for a bone for almost a week. And you wonder why I don't want to wait?"

"I'm not showing yet."

"No, but at least ten people heard Mrs. Priddy ask me if I was the daddy. So just how long do you think that secret will take to spread all over the county?"

"You said you didn't mind if people knew," she reminded him, her teeth sinking into her bottom lip.

"Hell, Janie! You're driving me crazy. I'm thinking about you, not me. People always blame the woman, you know that. If we get married at once, there won't be that much gossip.

But if we wait, after everyone knows, they'll think you forced me to marry you.'' He grinned, a teasing look in his eyes that reminded her of happier times.

"Maybe I'll tell them *you* forced *me*."

"And that would be accurate," he returned, and then puffed out his chest. "But no one would believe you."

Only the laughter on his face kept her from slugging him. He had always teased her. "A little full of yourself, aren't you?"

"Why not? I'm having twins…and I'm marrying the most beautiful girl in the world."

Before she could recover from such a wonderful compliment, he leaned over and kissed her again.

"Pete! You're driving!"

"No problem. There aren't any cars."

"And—and we aren't going to do that." She was becoming concerned about the way he kept touching her, throwing her hormones into overdrive…and her control out the window.

"You're wrong about that, Janie. We have to convince everyone that we're a normal couple, remember? That was my condition, and you agreed. We may not have sex, but we'll be doing a lot of kissing."

Oh, mercy, she was in trouble.

"PERFECT TIMING," Lavinia called out as they entered. "Hank is washing up, and dinner is almost ready."

"Good. I'm starved," Pete said with a grin. He gave Janie a significant look, warning her to wait until her father arrived on the scene.

"Everything's okay?" Lavinia asked with a slight frown, as if sensing some underlying tension.

"Fine," Pete responded, not giving Janie a chance to speak. Hank came into the kitchen just then, and Pete was glad. He wasn't sure how long he and Janie could remain silent.

"You're back. How's everything, Janie?"

Janie looked at Pete and then her parents. "We—we have some news."

Hank, who had just started to sit down, straightened quickly. "You mean you're—"

"Having twins," Janie said breathlessly, her gaze going from her father to her mother.

As if Samantha in "Bewitched" had twitched her nose, everyone froze. Then, with a small cry, Lavinia hugged Janie, while Hank gasped like a marathon runner on his last mile.

After they expressed their concerns and happiness, Hank turned to the next topic. "Now, see here, Janie, I don't care what your reasons are, it's time you gave in and married Pete."

"She has," Pete said quietly—and, he'd admit, with a little pride. While everyone had tried to convince Janie, or at least all the men in the two families, he'd been the one to persuade her. He set aside his disappointment that she didn't really want him. He'd deal with that emotion later.

For the second time, they stunned Lavinia and Hank. Then the real celebration began. Lavinia had tears in her eyes as she served dinner, constantly asking questions about their decision.

Hank, relief on his face, served himself large portions of the steak and potatoes Lavinia had prepared, ignoring the broccoli.

"Hank Dawson, you put back that second steak. It has too much cholesterol. You want to be around to play with your grandbabies, don't you?" Lavinia asked sharply.

Hank rolled his eyes and replaced the smaller of the two steaks. "You watch out, Pete. Don't let Janie get the upper hand. You never get it back."

Lavinia ignored her husband's comment. "Have you told Pete's family yet?"

"No, Mom. I wanted you and Dad to be the first ones to know," Janie replied.

Actually they hadn't even discussed whom to tell first. Pete, too, had assumed they would tell her parents first. Now he was anxious to inform his own family.

"I think we should all go to the Randalls'. There's a lot to discuss. Is that all right with you, Pete?"

"That's a good idea, Lavinia. I'll call." Pete excused himself and went to the phone on the wall. Brett answered. "Brett, would you tell Red I'm eating at the Dawsons again?"

"Sure. But he may be mad."

"I know. But we're all coming over there after dinner. Tell Jake, will you?"

"Yeah. What's up?"

"I'll tell you when I get there."

He hung up as Brett asked him another question. They'd all find out together. And hopefully the news would bring peace back to the Randall household.

B.J. RAPPED on the back door and waited in the cold night for someone to open the door. She smiled when Megan urged her inside. The two women had talked several times since the disastrous dinner to welcome Megan and Chad. B.J. felt she'd made a new friend.

"How's it going?" she asked as she passed Megan.

"About the same. It's colder inside than it is outside."

"That's pretty cold," B.J. returned, shivering as her body welcomed the heat.

"How about a cup of coffee?" Megan asked, gesturing to the coffeepot that was always ready in the Randall kitchen.

"I'd love one, but I really came to talk to Pete."

"He's on his way, according to Brett. If you have time, you can wait for him. And I can have someone to talk to."

B.J. sat down at the table. "Come on, Megan. Things can't be that bad. Chad speaks to you, doesn't he?"

"Sure. He says, 'Could I have more coffee?' or 'Please pass the potatoes.'" She shoved her hand through her chin-length light brown hair.

"Didn't you explain to him that Janie didn't feel she should marry Pete until he loves her?"

"Of course I did. And he assured me Pete loves Janie. I suggested he tell Pete he loves her so they can make up and get married before the baby's born." Setting two cups of coffee on the table, she joined B.J. "Then he tells me Pete doesn't want to say those words."

B.J. shook her head. "These Randall men are something else. Sexy as can be and as hardheaded as mules. God must've put them on earth as punishment for women."

"Tell me about it," Megan agreed with a sigh, thinking of her own struggles getting Chad to admit his love for her.

The sound of several vehicles arriving distracted them.

"Are you expecting someone besides Pete?" B.J. asked. "If so, I can see him tomorrow. It's nothing urgent."

Before Megan could answer, Jake hurried into the kitchen, but he paused when he saw B.J. "I didn't know you were here."

His frown didn't make her feel welcome, but then Jake had never acted pleased with her presence.

"I'm just on my way out," she offered pleasantly, standing, hoping he'd never know how his attitude hurt her.

Megan intervened. "Don't be silly, B.J. You needed to talk to Pete. I'm sure this is him. Sit back down."

Before B.J. could move one way of the other, the door opened to Pete, Janie and her parents.

After the initial greetings, B.J. cornered Pete. "Call me tomorrow when you have a minute. I need to talk to you about our inoculation schedule. Good night, everyone."

"Wait, B.J." He turned to Janie. "Do you mind if we tell her?"

Janie smiled at her rather than at Pete. "Of course not. She's become a friend."

"Tell B.J. what?" Jake asked.

"Our news. We wanted to tell all of you at once," Pete added.

"Okay," Jake agreed. "Shall we adjourn to the living room? Megan, would you knock on Red's door and ask him to join us? I'll get Brett."

"I really don't have to stay, Janie, if you want it to be just family," B.J. whispered.

"Stay, please. We won't keep you long."

After her last visit to the Randall household, B.J. had vowed to avoid any more family gatherings. But she couldn't leave now. Curiosity had won out over common sense.

JAKE CALLED for Brett and hurried to the living room. He hoped Pete's news was good. He wanted his brothers married— but he also wanted them happy.

Chad had married Megan with everyone's approval. And all the Randalls loved Janie, too. But if she didn't want to be married to Pete, everyone would be unhappy.

"Janie and I have a couple of things to tell you," Pete began once everyone had arrived.

By the grin on his face and the fact that his arm was wrapped around Janie's shoulders, Jake assumed the news was good, that Pete and Janie had resolved their difficulties. Pete certainly looked happy, but Jake wasn't so sure about Janie.

"Janie has accepted my proposal. We're going to be married right away."

There was a lot of whooping and hollering from Brett and Chad, and Jake grinned. Chad was probably hoping his problems with Megan would be at an end.

Suddenly Jake remembered that Pete had said they had two announcements to make. "Pete, what's the second bit of news?"

Pete's grin widened even more, and Jake sighed in relief.

"The second announcement will really bowl you over, Jake. We're getting two for the price of one. Janie's having twins."

The celebration for his second announcement was even louder than the first. Jake let the others gather around Janie and Pete. He sat still, taking in the news, happiness bubbling up inside him. Two new Randalls. Two sets of little feet running around the house. And both of them before next Christmas.

Santa was coming to the Randalls. Yee-haw!

JANIE SUCKED IN her stomach as Megan tugged on the zipper. "I think we should've gotten a larger size. My waist is already starting to go."

"Nope. This one is perfect," Megan assured her as the zipper reached the top. "You're going to knock Pete off his feet."

"Didn't I already do that by having twins?" Janie asked ruefully.

B.J., her second bridesmaid, answered in place of Megan. "Maybe. But this will be a different kind of blow. You don't look anything like a cowgirl, Janie. More like a movie star."

Janie turned to look in the mirror. Her dark hair wasn't in its traditional braid. Instead, it flowed over her shoulders in shiny curls. The antique satin wedding gown with its matching veil gave her the look of a princess in a fairy tale, waiting for her prince to rescue her.

"I think I'm jealous," Megan suddenly said, gaining the attention of the other two.

"What are you talking about?" Janie asked anxiously. After all, she and Megan were about to become family.

"Chad and I got married on our own. I wore a blue suit. He wanted to come back home and have a traditional wedding, but I didn't want to wait. But you're so beautiful, and everyone's so excited, I think maybe I made the wrong choice."

Since Megan was grinning, neither of the other ladies took her seriously.

"It's how you feel when you wake the next morning that matters," B.J. said softly, her eyes clouding with memories.

Janie hoped the other two ladies couldn't read her mind, because her morning would be the same as all the other mornings without Pete, even if they were married.

By her choice.

I must be crazy, putting myself through such torture.

Jake had suggested she and Pete take the two-bedroom suite near Megan and Chad. Since Pete didn't want anyone to know they weren't a normal married couple, one room had been designated the babies' room, but Janie had suggested a daybed be rigged up like a sofa, filled with pillows, in case she had to spend nights with the babies after they were born.

Megan, who was in charge of redoing the house, agreed. While the room didn't have cribs yet, it had a sofa bed.

"It's time," Lavinia said, sticking her head in the door. "Brett's going to seat me now. Everything all right?"

"Everything's fine, Mom." Janie gave her mother her best smile, a little tremulous but warm. Her mother had worked nonstop the past four days to create the perfect wedding for her only daughter.

"Your father's waiting out here," Lavinia whispered before disappearing.

"Ready, Janie?" B.J. asked.

She nodded and faced the mirror one more time. Was she making a mistake? Could she ever make Pete love her?

Megan opened the door and waited for Janie to go to her father. Then Megan and B.J., dressed in amber taffeta, took their places. Janie stared after them as each marched down the aisle in the small church. Though it was cold outside, the sun was streaming through the stained-glass windows, filling the church with rich colors.

The organ music swelled, and Janie realized her friends had reached the altar. Now it was her turn. She placed her hand on her father's arm and raised her gaze to his.

"You're beautiful, Janie, just like your mother," he whispered, and led her down the aisle.

PETE HAD FACED some dangerous situations in his life. The first time he'd ridden a bull, his insides had been all scrambled up *before* he'd gotten on the bull. But getting married was tougher.

Just when he thought he wouldn't last much longer, Janie, her hand tucked into her father's arm, appeared at the door to the chapel and took his breath away. He was suddenly glad Jake had insisted on a professional photographer. He didn't ever want to forget how beautiful Janie looked today.

There were a lot of things to worry about in this marriage, but today wasn't the time to concern himself with them. Now was the time to celebrate their union...and to celebrate the babies growing inside of Janie.

His babies.

"Dearly beloved, we are gathered here today to join this man and this woman in holy wedlock."

When Hank surrendered Janie's hand to Pete, he grasped it tightly, hoping Janie wouldn't realize how nervous he was. Then he looked into her bright blue eyes, and the fear that had been growing the past few hours left him. Everything would be all right.

Janie whispered her vows, her gaze pinned to Pete's strong features. He was a good man, even if he did have trouble loving her. She promised herself, even as she made her promises to Pete aloud, that she would find a way to make him love her.

When the pastor pronounced them husband and wife and suggested Pete kiss the bride, he did so with enthusiasm. So much enthusiasm, and so effectively, that Janie forgot they were in front of an audience. After all, he hadn't touched her since that kiss in front of the drugstore.

It occurred to Janie, as she enjoyed Pete's touch, she didn't have to hold back this once. She could kiss the boots off Pete if she wanted to, and he couldn't do much about it because they had an audience. With pleasure, she pressed against him, wrapping her arms around his neck, pretending, if only for a little while, that he loved her.

Pretending he loved her as much as she loved him.

Pretending happily-ever-after.

Only Jake's voice, reminding them they had a reception to go to, brought Janie back to reality. That and Pete's withdrawal. But she did feel some satisfaction when she saw the reluctance in his eyes.

Her cheeks bright red, she turned to face family and friends.

"Ladies and gentlemen," Jake announced, "it gives me great pleasure to introduce Mr. and Mrs. Peter Randall. I hope you'll all join us at the ranch for the reception."

Lavinia had wanted to have the reception at their house, but the Randalls' was so much larger, she'd agreed to Jake's offer. After all, most of the county would show up in spite of the short notice. She and Red, along with Mildred's help, had been baking nonstop.

Pete and Janie walked down the aisle, smiling at the well-wishers. Janie dreaded the drive to the ranch. She would be alone with Pete for the first time since they'd decided to marry. Life had been so hectic the past few days, she'd only seen him a few times, and always surrounded by people.

The photographer was waiting outside. "Give her a kiss, Pete, so I can get a good picture."

With a grin, Pete swept her to him, his lips covering hers. The man was incredible. Here they were in broad daylight, surrounded by a lot of people, and a warning that she wouldn't sleep with him, and she was longing for a double bed.

Thank goodness for the daybed in the babies' room.

"Janie," her mother called to her just as they started down the steps to Pete's truck.

"Yes, Mom?"

"Honey, I'm sorry, but we ran out of bedrooms. I hope you don't mind, but Great-Aunt Henrietta decided to make the trip after all, and there was nothing left."

A sense of foreboding came over Janie.

"Jake said she could sleep on that daybed you had put in your extra bedroom. It will just be for one night." Her mother looked at Pete, standing beside her. "I'm sorry, Pete. I know you'd prefer to be alone, but we don't have anywhere else to put her. You should have planned a real honeymoon.''

"Remember? Janie didn't want one. But don't worry about Aunt Henrietta. We Randalls are a hospitable lot." His grin was wide enough to cover Wyoming, and Janie wanted to punch him in his breadbasket.

"Well, there's one good thing," Lavinia added with a wink. "Aunt Henrietta is as deaf as a fence post. She won't hear a thing."

Chapter Nine

"Wipe that grin off your face, Pete Randall," Janie ordered in frustration as soon as the two of them were in his truck.

"I'm not supposed to be happy on my wedding day?" he asked, his brown eyes wide with innocence.

"That's not why you were grinning and you know it. You think we're going to sleep together tonight because of Aunt Henrietta!"

"I always did like that lady," Pete returned, still smiling.

"You've never even met her!" Janie's great-aunt Henrietta lived in Cleveland, and Janie had seen her a few times as a child.

His sexy chuckle was the only response.

"Pete," Janie said in a warning tone.

"Relax, Janie. You know I'm teasing you. I gave you my word, didn't I? Whatever else you may think of me, you know I keep my promises."

Janie sighed and sank back against the seat. What Pete said was true. She knew he was a man of his word. In fact, the only thing she'd ever found to complain about him was the fact that he didn't love her.

She was more worried about her own reaction. Sleeping in the same bed with Pete would be a test of discipline she wasn't sure she'd pass.

"Did I tell you how beautiful you look today?" Pete asked softly, drawing her from her depressing thoughts.

The rush of warmth that filled her brought a blush to her cheeks. "No. But I don't think I look as good as you." Pete had worn a navy suit, a blue-and-gold tie and crisp white shirt. With his broad shoulders and narrow hips, he was every woman's dream.

"Honey, you're wrong about that. If we have little girls, I hope they both look like you."

For the first time since Doc's revelation, Janie considered the future. "It won't bother you if we have girls?"

He grinned. "Janie, I've been living in an all-man world for a long time. I'm looking forward to having a few women around, even if they're in diapers."

"You already have Megan and B.J. and her aunt. Soon the women will outnumber the men."

"Not likely," Pete objected with a grin. "B.J. and Mildred really aren't part of the family. They just live on the place. And since I don't think Jake will ever marry again, and Brett hasn't shown any inclination in that direction, either, we've got a long way to go before females outnumber males at the Randalls'."

Pete turned the truck onto the long driveway leading to the ranch, and the proximity of the ranch house reminded Janie of her original concern. "Pete, what are we going to do about this evening?"

"What do you mean?"

She sent him a disgusted look. "I'm talking about the sleeping arrangements, and you know it."

"We've got a king-size bed, Janie. Surely we can both sleep on it one night without any problems."

Sucking in her breath as she pictured Pete, his broad chest bare, wearing only his briefs as he slid under the covers within her reach, Janie shuddered. Could she keep her hands to herself? Could he?

When she said nothing, Pete pulled the truck to a halt by the house and turned her toward him. "I won't make love to you, Janie, unless you change your mind. But remember, you have a promise to keep, too." With those words, he leaned forward to kiss her. "We have an audience," he added just before his lips covered hers.

He extracted one hell of a down payment.

MEGAN STARED at Pete and Janie from the back door of the ranch house, remembering those first few minutes after her own marriage, just a couple of weeks ago. At least *she* had known her husband loved her.

Poor Janie.

"Remind you of us?" Chad whispered in her ear, his arm sliding around her.

"Not lately," she said coolly, hiding her reaction to his nearness.

Chad pulled her around to face him. "I think it's time we buried the hatchet, Meggie. I've missed you."

"But I didn't go anywhere, Chad. You're the one who withdrew because I didn't agree with you." She felt it was important to work out what went wrong, not sweep it under the rug.

"Hell, Meggie, you sided against Pete. What was I supposed to do?"

"Allow me to have my own opinion? I'm not an extension of you, Chad. I'm my own person. I love Pete like a brother, but that doesn't make him—or you—always right."

He linked his arms around her waist. "If I promise to do better, will you forgive me?"

How could she resist his smile? With a sigh of agreement, she melted against him and their lips met.

"Hey, you two, get out of the doorway," Red grumbled. "You're not the only newlyweds anymore."

"I don't know, Red. I'm feeling pretty much like a newlywed right now," Chad said, still holding Megan against him.

"I can tell, but I need some help."

Megan pulled from Chad's embrace. "What can I do?"

Mildred bustled into the kitchen in time to hear Megan's question. "Lavinia thinks you and B.J. should serve the punch and cake. You both look so pretty in your dresses."

"Thanks, Mildred. We were fortunate to find two alike." When she started toward the dining room, where the cake and punch were located, Chad followed. Over her shoulder, she said, "You should stay here and help Red."

"But who's gonna protect you from all those woman-hungry cowboys?"

Mildred chuckled, but Red ordered Chad to get the hot rolls from the oven before they burned.

"I could've done that," Mildred said, eyeing Red.

"Now, Miss Bates—" Red began.

"He's used to ordering me around, Mildred," Chad intervened. He'd noticed some tension between the two older people, though he didn't understand why. "You can put them in the bread basket Red has ready."

Mollified, Mildred picked up a spatula.

"Where are those two? I thought their truck arrived five minutes ago." Red frowned toward the back door.

"I think they got distracted," Chad offered, a big grin on his face. He had similar plans for his bride as soon as they could escape the celebration. In fact, he'd been doing a lot of thinking about babies, ever since he'd heard of Pete's approaching fatherhood.

Tonight might be a good time for a discussion with Meggie. Or something.

Janie and Pete entered the kitchen.

"It's about time," Red growled. Then, to everyone's surprise, he stepped forward and kissed Janie on the cheek. "Welcome to the family, Janie."

"Oh, Red, thank you!"

"Hey, watch it, Red," Pete protested, but the grin on his face told everyone he wasn't serious. "I'm not letting anyone kiss my bride but me."

"From what I saw out the back door, I'd say you've already used up your quota," Chad teased, laughing as Janie's cheeks flushed.

"Don't mind these men, child," Mildred said. "Pete, you take your beautiful bride in the living room and show her off. The house is full of people waiting to congratulate you." Then she turned to Chad. "You should join them, young man. Half the county is waiting to be introduced to your bride, too."

Chad willingly headed for the dining room. As he was leaving the kitchen, however, he wondered if it was safe to leave Red and Mildred alone.

"Who put you in charge?" Red growled behind him.

"I'm just trying to be helpful," Mildred returned.

Love might be brimming in the living room, Chad thought, but it was in short supply in the kitchen.

"FEEL FREE to go upstairs whenever you want," Jake said, pausing beside Pete. "You and Janie have been good sports, and no one would mind whenever you want to call it an evening."

"Thanks, Jake, but we're enjoying ourselves, right Janie?" Pete asked, slipping his arm around Janie's waist.

"Right," she murmured, struggling to summon a smile. It wasn't that she wasn't having fun. Sort of. She and Pete had been the center of attention for several hours. The food had been delicious, and the cutting of the wedding cake suddenly brought home to Janie that she'd actually achieved her dream of marrying Pete Randall.

But she was tired. And anxious about the coming night. Every time she thought of sharing a bed, even a king-size bed, with the sexy man next to her, she grew more and more nervous.

"How about a dance?" Pete asked, surprising Janie.

Jake stared at his brother, too. "You want to dance? There isn't much room in here with all the guests."

"Everyone can't dance, but we've got a guitar player and a fiddler here. Janie and I could have our dance, and you and B.J. and Chad and Megan can join us."

Even as he said it, Pete was motioning to a friend across the room. Within minutes, he had arranged a cleared space in the center of the room and the two musicians ready to play. He motioned for Chad and Megan to join them.

"Where's B.J.?" he called.

"Over here," she returned, waving to him. "Do you need something?"

"Pete, B.J. and I don't need to join in," Jake protested in a low voice.

Janie watched him curiously. He seemed agitated. She supposed he was afraid B.J. might get the wrong idea.

When B.J. reached their side and Pete explained what he wanted, she agreed, after a brief glance at Jake. The three couples gathered in the cleared space, and Pete nodded to the musicians.

Janie, after a moment of resistance, collapsed against Pete's chest. She was too tired to resist. His arms wrapped her against him, and they moved slowly to the music. With her eyes closed, she could almost imagine them alone six months ago, just beginning what she'd hoped would lead to a long life together.

Instead, it had led to a pregnancy and a marriage—in that order. And not because Pete loved her.

"You okay?" Pete asked, leaning down to whisper in her ear. He followed his question with a kiss beneath her ear, and she shivered against him.

"I'm a little tired," she murmured.

"I've kept you down here too long, I guess. But…I was enjoying pretending that our marriage is real. When we go upstairs, I have to face the fact that it's not."

Janie reared back from his hold. "Don't try to make me feel guilty, Pete Randall. It won't work."

"Darn, Janie Randall. You're too smart for me." His lips captured hers for a brief kiss. "By the way, I kissed Aunt Henrietta, too. I thought it was the least I could do to thank her."

"I don't know why you want to thank her. It's not going to change anything," she assured him, but she figured she was trying to convince herself as much as him.

"At least I'll get to see you when I wake up in the morning."

"I just hope the first thing you see isn't me bent over the toilet."

Pete frowned sharply. "You're getting sick? Did you call the doc?"

"It's only happened once."

"Wait a minute. I think he's still here. I'll—" Pete began, and started to leave her standing alone in the middle of the makeshift dance floor.

Janie grabbed him by his lapels. "Stop, Pete. I don't need you to find the doctor. I'm fine. Throwing up before a wedding is commonplace."

"Yeah, but Doc said—"

"Pete! For heaven's sake, it's no big deal." She wanted to shake him, but he was too big. The only things that got a response from the man were sex or babies.

"Have you been taking your vitamins?" he asked, still staring at her.

She rolled her eyes. "How romantic you are, Pete Randall."

"You want romance?" he asked, pulling her closer, his lips trailing down her neck.

Pulling back, she muttered, "That's sex, not romance."

"Hell, I already sent you flowers and candy. Much more romance, and I won't be able to pay for the babies," he teased.

"I don't need candy and flowers. And whatever else you do, don't help me with the grocery shopping, either," she ordered.

"You won't have to do any grocery shopping. Red takes care of that."

It suddenly struck Janie that her entire life had been turned upside down. "What am I going to do?"

"What do you mean?" Pete asked, frowning.

"Tomorrow. What am I going to do tomorrow?"

Pete seemed confused, and he stopped moving to the music. "What will you do tomorrow?" he repeated. "You'll relax, do whatever you want."

But Janie wasn't comforted. Suddenly she felt disoriented, lost.

"Janie, you don't have to do anything you don't want to. Your job is to take care of yourself and the babies." For the first time since he'd discovered she was pregnant, he reached down and pressed his hand against her stomach, his fingers splayed against the satin wedding gown.

"Pete!" Janie squealed softly. "People are watching."

He gathered her back into his arms. "We're married, Janie. They haven't forgotten even if you have."

She laid her head on his shoulder. "I'm so tired, I don't think I can even remember my name."

"Randall. You're a Randall, Janie Dawson Randall, and I think it's time I take you home." She didn't even protest when he swung her up into his arms and headed for the stairs.

"Wait!" Mildred called out as Pete passed her. "Janie hasn't thrown her bouquet!" She thrust the flowers, which had been resting on a nearby table, into Janie's hands.

"Make it fast, Mrs. Randall," Pete whispered. He climbed the first two stairs and turned her toward the living room.

"Put me down, Pete," she whispered.

"Nope. Toss that bouquet, little lady, and toss it fast."

Somehow, doing as her new husband ordered seemed the

easiest thing at that moment. With one arm around his neck, she used the other to toss the bouquet over the balustrade.

Shrieks of laughter filled the air, and Janie looked down to discover a terror-stricken Brett clutching the bridal bouquet to his chest.

Pete didn't wait. He turned and headed up the stairs. Behind them, Janie heard Brett protesting.

"Hey! Wait! Throw it again, Janie. Not me! I wasn't supposed—"

"I think Janie did a fine job," Jake announced, and their guests burst into delighted laughter.

JAKE WATCHED Pete carrying Janie up the stairs. Before he could stop himself, he thought of doing the same to B.J. He'd have a harder time of it because she was a tall woman. Curvaceous.

He shook his head. What was he thinking? His first wife, Chloe, had been small, dainty, demanding. And he needed to remember that she was the reason he would never marry again.

The dance with B.J. had been more enjoyable than he'd expected. To fight the attraction he was feeling, he asked, "Are you sorry you didn't catch the bouquet?"

She looked at him, surprise on her face. "No, of course not, I'm not in the market for a husband." She chuckled as she looked across the room. "Though I can't say Brett thinks he is, either."

"He'll adjust. I've told him it's time he start looking around now that Pete's married."

"You're rather dictatorial about your brothers, aren't you?"

He frowned at her. "I'm the head of the family. It's up to me to see that they're all taken care of."

"Don't you think your brothers are old enough to figure things out for themselves?"

"No, I don't! And how I handle my family's business is none of yours." He regretted his burst of anger, knowing he should apologize, but he couldn't bring himself to do so.

After staring up at him in silence, she only said, quietly, "I think some of the guests are ready to leave now that Pete and Janie have gone upstairs. Perhaps you should go—"

"Yes. Thank you for reminding me of my duties." After giving a brief nod of his head, he strode to the door. Damn the woman. She always made him feel he'd been less than a gentleman.

"Looks like we're the last couple, Meggie," Chad whispered in her ear. "How about you? Are you exhausted?"

"It's been a busy few days," she said, smiling up at him. "But at least we're not angry with each other anymore."

"Yep. I've decided I've been pretty dense to waste even one day apart from you." He trailed kisses down the side of her face. "I think we may have more fun tonight than Pete and Janie."

"Do you think?" she asked, smiling at him.

"Yeah. And we could probably have triplets or quadruplets, if we tried, too." He closed his eyes and pulled her even closer.

Megan, surprised by his words, pulled away to look at his face. "What did you say?"

He smiled down at her. "I said we could— What's the matter? Don't you want to have kids?"

"Of course I do, Chad. But not right away. I'm going to redo the house with Adele, remember? Once I had a baby, I couldn't travel back to Denver or do all the work that's involved. You know that."

"Yeah, but I think our family is more important than a few couches."

He knew he'd made a mistake as soon as the words were out of his mouth, and Megan's glare confirmed his error.

"Is that what you think I do? Just buy a few couches? That interior decorating is one big shopping trip?"

"No, baby, I didn't mean that." Chad hurriedly retreated, whispering his words.

"'Baby'? I don't like being called baby."

"Meggie, come on. We just made up."

She sniffed, her body stiff.

"Look, I was wrong to bring up the subject tonight. I know you've got important work to do. We'll talk about this stuff some other time." Hell, he might never bring up the subject again if it meant Megan would be angry with him. He regretted the past week's coldness between them.

Tonight he had plans to heat things up.

"Let's go upstairs, too. We'll leave the bachelors to say the good-nights for the Randalls."

Relief filled him when she agreed.

THE REMAINING RANDALLS, assisted by the Dawsons, bade the last of the guests goodbye and did a brief cleanup.

"Man, I forgot weddings were such an ordeal," Brett said, flopping down on the sofa.

"Get used to it. Yours is next," Jake said, a weary grin on his face.

"It seems to me you may be asking for trouble, Jake," Lavinia said as she joined Brett on the sofa.

"What do you mean, Lavinia? You think there's no woman out there insane enough to take on Brett?"

The others chuckled, as Jake intended, but Lavinia explained. "No. There's the possibility that your brothers will decide what's good for the gander is also good for the gander's older brother."

Jake pretended he didn't understand her slightly altered version of the old saying. "I don't think you've got that story right, Lavinia."

Brett leaned forward. "I think she does. Good idea, Lavinia. If marriage is such a great idea, why isn't Jake looking around?"

"Because I didn't catch the bouquet."

"That was an accident," Brett scoffed, his cheeks turning red. "It doesn't mean anything. You should be looking for your own woman, not one for me."

"How do you know I'm not? Mildred Bates was flirting with me tonight."

Again everyone laughed, except Red.

"Mildred is a very nice lady," Lavinia said, in spite of her laughter.

"Yes, she is. Only the nice ladies will do," Jake assured her.

"That wasn't what you called Chloe," Brett reminded him.

Jake wasn't pleased to have bad memories of his ex-wife brought up. "Fortunately there aren't too many women like Chloe around. By the way, the other day I heard she remarried."

"Poor guy," Brett muttered with an exaggerated shudder.

"You two are too hard on Chloe. It must've been difficult to move into this male bastion," Lavinia said.

Brett burst into laughter. "Too hard on Chloe? That's amusing, Lavinia. That's like saying one of Pete's bulls is just mischievous."

Though Lavinia smiled, tears filled her eyes as she said, "I think it may be hard for both Megan and Janie. You will be kind to Janie, won't you?"

While both Jake and Brett rushed to assure Lavinia that Janie would be treated well, Hank moved over and put his arm around his wife. "Don't worry, boys. Lavinia knows you'll be good to our Janie. She's just experiencing post-wedding blues. Everything's happened so fast, she's just realized Janie won't be going home with us."

Hank pulled Lavinia up from the couch. "Time for us to go home, sweetheart. At least Janie's close, and you can come see her whenever you want."

"Yes, of course. Sorry, Jake, Brett. We'll—we'll call tomorrow. Thanks for all your work, Red."

"Happy to do it, Lavinia."

After the Dawsons had driven away, Brett looked at the other two men. "I'm glad Hank knew what to do when Lavinia started crying. I sure didn't."

"Well, I hope you paid attention," Jake warned him, "because the Randalls include two ladies now. And it's up to us to keep them happy."

Brett looked up the stairs. "Naw, Jake. It's up to Pete and Chad to keep them happy. Speaking of which, I hope you remembered to have that discussion with them about the birds and the bees."

Chapter Ten

The door was open to their bedroom when Pete reached it with Janie in his arms. A good thing, he decided, since he thought Janie had gone to sleep on the way up the stairs.

He'd kept her at their reception too long, and he felt guilty because of it. She'd been tired an hour ago. But he'd loved holding her against him, kissing her to everyone's applause.

And he'd known when they came upstairs she would withdraw.

Her eyes fluttered open as he laid her down on the large bed. "Pete?"

"Hi, honey. We're home." His grin invited her to find the humor.

She rose up and looked around her, her bright blue eyes wide as they lit on several vases full of flowers.

"Megan and B.J. brought in the flowers. They said it made the room look more romantic." He hadn't told them the only thing the room needed was Janie for him to think it was romantic. "They also left the negligee as a gift."

Janie's eyes widened even farther as she looked over her shoulder to the other side of the bed. There, spread out in all its glory, was a silvery silk negligee, in material that would only cast a shadow over the wearer's charms.

"I—I can't wear that."

"Good."

"You don't like it?" she demanded, sitting straighter.

"Don't like it? Am I alive? Honey, any man would like to see his woman wearing something like that, especially if she looks like you.'' He paused, but she continued to stare at him, waiting for an explanation. ''Unless he promised not to make love to her.''

She dropped her gaze. ''Oh.''

''You haven't changed your mind, have you?''

His heart stopped beating while she considered her answer. Then she whispered, ''No.''

''That's what I figured. So I hope you brought something a little less, uh, maybe I should say a little more...unsexy.''

With a weary smile, she stood. ''I did. Are—are my bags here?''

He pointed them out beside the closet door. ''Just get out what you need tonight. You can unpack tomorrow, after you've rested. I'm going down for a late-night snack while you get ready for bed.'' The relief on her face didn't make him feel good, but he tried to ignore his disappointment. ''Don't wait up for me.''

She nodded, avoiding his gaze.

Pete stepped out of the room, pulling the door closed behind him. Then he collapsed against it and breathed deeply.

Man, keeping his hands off Janie was going to be tough. Especially when she slept in his bed. He'd better stay gone until she'd fallen asleep. With a sigh, he loosened his tie, took off his coat to hang it on the doorknob, shoved his hands in his pants pockets and strolled to the stairs.

Hearing voices still in the living room, he came to an abrupt halt. Hell, he'd completely forgotten that everyone else hadn't gone to bed already. Now what was he going to do?

Every bedroom in the house was filled with guests spending the night. His old bedroom was off-limits. Their second room was filled with Great-Aunt Henrietta.

As he stood there thinking, he heard someone near the bottom of the stairs say, ''I think we'll go on up to bed, now, Jake. We're too old for such late-night shenanigans.''

Pete didn't know who was speaking, and it didn't matter. He didn't want *anyone* to see him lingering in the hall on his wedding night. He sprinted back to his bedroom door. Grabbing his jacket, he opened the door, slipped in and quietly shut it behind him.

Then he turned around in time to discover Janie coming out of the bathroom wrapped in a towel. A very brief towel.

"Pete!" she gasped.

"Janie!" he yelped at the same time.

She backed toward the bathroom, clasping the towel tightly around her. "I thought you wouldn't be back yet."

"I wasn't— I didn't mean to— I couldn't get to the kitchen without everyone downstairs seeing me. I didn't want them to know—"

She interrupted him, her cheeks red. "I'm through in the bathroom if you need it. My pajamas are in here."

He edged his way past, avoiding touching her, but he couldn't keep his gaze from tracing every inch of her pale flesh. He was panting by the time he closed the door behind him.

Deciding a shower was in order, he turned on the water, all cold, and stripped down. When he finally dried off a few minutes later, he felt a little more in control. As long as the door was closed.

When he finally got up the nerve to open the bathroom door, he discovered only a small lamp burning on his side of the big bed. Janie was curled into a tight little ball on the other side, almost falling off the edge.

"Janie?" he whispered.

No answer. Could she already be asleep? It would make life easier for him if she was. He crept over to gaze down at her beautiful face, pale with exhaustion but relaxed in sleep.

He reached down to caress her cheek, longing filling him. The desire to hold her against him, to protect her, to love her, filled him. Groaning, he stepped back and rounded the bed. Lifting the cover, he got in and pulled the blankets to his chin.

After several minutes of trying to ignore Janie's presence, he made a decision.

He'd promised not to make love to her. But he hadn't promised not to hold her. Turning, he reached out and slid her next to him. Though he feared she would awaken, he was delighted when she cuddled against him, her eyes closed.

With a sigh, he shut his eyes, too. He was tired. But he loved the feel of her against him. And, in spite of his promise, he was experiencing something new on his wedding night. He would wake up in the morning next to Janie.

Not a bad way to start the day.

JANIE WOKE the next morning slowly. *Must've turned off the alarm.* She struggled to open her eyes. When she did finally manage that simple task, she stared around her, the events of the past day slowly reinstating themselves.

She was pregnant.

She was married.

She'd shared the bed with Pete.

At that thought, her head whipped around to be sure she was alone. During their affair, they'd never spent an entire night together.

With a mixture of disappointment and relief, she discovered Pete was nowhere to be seen. She relaxed against the pillow…until she realized her pillow was in the middle of the bed. She distinctly recalled clutching the side of the bed last night.

The indentation in the pillow next to hers showed Pete hadn't sought the far reaches of the big bed, either. Had they spent the night together wrapped in each other's arms…and she'd missed it?

She groaned and swung back the covers. No use thinking about such a thing. It couldn't happen again. As soon as the other room was abandoned, she'd move in. Discreetly, of course, as she'd promised Pete, but she couldn't risk the temptation of sleeping with him again.

Fortunately her stomach seemed settled this morning. She set about getting ready to face the world, including her new family.

When she started down the stairs, the nervous tension in her stomach surprised her. She'd known the Randalls all her life. But things were different this morning.

Red stood by the sink and Megan sat at the table, working on a sketch, when Janie entered the kitchen. "Good morning."

Megan smiled and Red rushed to her side to take her arm as if she were unstable. "Here, Janie, come sit down," he urged.

She looked at him in surprise.

Megan chuckled. "You didn't know you'd suddenly become an invalid, did you?"

"Now, Megan, don't go talkin' that way," Red ordered. "We're just tryin' to be careful."

"About what?" Janie asked, still puzzled.

"Why, about you and the babies. Pete warned us all this morning."

"Pete warned you about what?" Janie asked.

They'd reached the table, and Janie sat down across from Megan as she asked her question. Red didn't answer, because he was hurrying across the room to the stove.

"Now, Janie, do you want eggs and bacon with flapjacks, or—?"

"Red, it's ten o'clock. Lunch is in two hours. All I need is a piece of toast, a cup of coffee and, I suppose, a glass of milk."

"But Pete said—"

"Yes, what exactly did Pete say?" she demanded, irritation building in her.

"That we were to take care of you," Megan explained. "He laid down the law to all of us that you weren't to lift a finger, and we were to feed you every time your mouth opened." Her grin told Janie she would understand her reaction.

Janie shook her head, a rueful smile on her face. "Red, just toast, coffee and milk."

"Are you sure you should have coffee? I read—"

"One cup won't hurt me."

"But Pete—"

Janie got up from the table and crossed to the coffeepot, reaching for the mugs stored just above it.

"I coulda done that, Janie," Red insisted.

On the way back to the table, she kissed his cheek. "I know, Red, but I'm not an invalid, in spite of Pete's warnings. But I will let you fix me some toast, just this once."

Though Red grumbled under his breath, he set about fixing her toast, and Janie sat back down across from Megan.

"I'm going to have problems here, aren't I?"

"Only if you want to do anything except breathe," Megan agreed. "The Randall men aren't used to having women around, much less a pregnant one. Pete envisions keeping you seated on a satin pillow, being waited on hand and foot, until the babies are born.''

''I'd go out of my mind.''

Megan nodded in sympathy.

Red brought over the toast and a glass of milk before refilling his own coffee cup and joining them at the table. ''Anything else I can get for you? Megan, you need more coffee?''

''No, Red, thanks. Besides, I'm not pregnant. I can get my own coffee.'' Megan's grin took the sting out of her words.

''As far as I know, being pregnant hasn't impaired my legs, either,'' Janie protested.

''Now, Janie, don't get all hot and bothered. Pete just wants to take care of you because of…well, past history,'' Red said, and then looked alarmed.

''I suppose he warned you not to talk about my mother's problems…or his mother's? Does he think I don't know?'' Janie stared at the other two in disgust.

''He doesn't want you to dwell on bad things,'' Megan assured her.

Again Janie rolled her eyes. ''I'm surprised he even let me out of bed.''

''Oh!'' Red jumped up as if something had bitten him. ''I forgot. He left you a note in case you got up before he got back.'' He hurried across the kitchen to the desk where he stored everything from recipes to receipts. He returned to hand Janie a folded piece of paper.

Prop your feet up and take it easy. Red will get you whatever you want.

Pete

Janie folded the paper and put it in her jeans pocket. Not exactly romantic, but she hadn't had too many notes from Pete. Unconsciously she sighed after sipping her coffee.

''Bad news?'' Megan asked.

''No. Just orders to do nothing.''

''You should give yourself time to adjust. You've had several big changes in your life recently.''

''And that's exactly the reason I need something to keep me

from going crazy. I've never sat around the house my entire life."

"You could watch some movies," Red suggested, "or read. The boys have lots of books around."

"Thanks, Red, but I'm talking about more than just today. I'm going to be pregnant for the next seven months. If all I do is sit around, I'll be as big as a house."

With a grin, Red said, "I reckon you'll get big as a house no matter what you do."

"Thanks for that depressing thought," she returned, but she was smiling.

"Want to walk down to the horse barn with me?" Megan suggested. "I love to check on the babies."

"Great! I haven't seen the latest foals. I'll go get my coat."

"I'll get it for you," Red offered, leaping to his feet.

Janie, already standing, stared at him. "Don't be ridiculous, Red. I haven't broken a leg." Then she rushed out the kitchen door.

"Tell that to Pete," Megan suggested, sharing a wry grin with Red.

NORMALLY PETE ENJOYED his time in the saddle, especially on a day like today, when, in spite of the cold, the sun shone and the wind was still. But today, all he could think about was Janie.

Had she gotten up yet? He'd debated staying in bed, holding her until she opened her eyes. Then he'd realized that might not be such a good idea. She might feel he hadn't stuck to his part of the bargain. Or that he was trying to tempt her into dissolving that agreement.

And that would be true.

But he worried that she might throw up this morning and not tell him or the doctor. She'd gotten irritated with him last night when he'd tried to find Doc Jacoby.

And what if she didn't take her vitamins? He'd forgotten to remind her in the note he'd left. She and the babies were his responsibilities now. He needed to take good care of them.

"You okay?" Jake asked, riding up to his side.

"Yeah. Fine."

"We're almost back to the corral. Why don't you make sure the gate is open and then go on up to the house? You probably want to check on Janie."

Pete gave him a grateful smile and nudged his horse to a lope. Jake was almost as anxious about Janie and the babies as he was.

His anticipation grew as he reached the house. The thought of seeing Janie again filled him with all kinds of emotions. "Hi, Red," he said as he rushed through the kitchen, heading for the stairs.

"Hey, Pete, where you going?"

"To check on Janie. Has she come downstairs this morning?"

"Yeah. She and Megan walked to the horse barn."

Pete came to a sudden halt, a ferocious frown on his brow. "What did you say?"

"She and Megan walked—"

"You let her go outside?" Pete demanded, slowly walking toward Red.

"How was I supposed to stop her?"

"She might catch cold," Pete said as he changed directions and sped toward the back door. "You should've told her to go lie down and rest."

By the time he reached the horse barn, he was muttering under his breath, so that little puffs of chilled air followed his progress. He should've known better than to leave Janie there on her own.

Throwing open the door, he roared, "Janie? Where are you?"

"Shh," Megan cautioned, leaning against the half door of one of the birthing stalls.

Automatically Pete lowered his voice. "Where's Janie?"

"Here, helping B.J.," Megan whispered as Pete drew closer.

"What?" Pete exclaimed hoarsely as he rushed to Megan's side.

The two women in the stall were concentrating on the mare and the just-born foal.

"Thanks, Janie. You were a lot of help," B.J. said as she and Janie helped the newborn to its feet.

"No problem. It was a pleasure to watch you work, B.J."

"Janie, are you crazy?" Pete demanded, steel in his voice.

His wife—he liked the thought of that word—wheeled to stare at him. "What's the matter, Pete?"

"Have you forgotten you're pregnant?"

Janie's hand stole to her stomach, still relatively flat. "No, I don't think so."

"You should be in the house, resting. You might hurt yourself helping B.J. Or you might catch cold."

"Or I might be struck by a falling meteor. What's your point, Pete?"

B.J. intervened. "Pete, I wouldn't let Janie do anything that would endanger the babies. But an extra pair of hands helped."

Pete stared at all three women in frustration. They didn't understand. "Come on, Janie. Get cleaned up, and I'll take you back to the house."

"You think I can't find it on my own?" She hadn't moved.

"No, but you might decide to stop and pitch a few bales of hay up to the barn loft. Or brand a few cows. Or round up the strays, for all I know." His frustration edged his voice.

Janie wanted to let her temper loose, to tell Pete what he could do with his coddling, but she couldn't. Not in front of the other two women. And not to Pete. As much as his concerns drove her crazy, she couldn't jump all over him. "I'll come with you, Pete, but we're going to have to talk."

"Sure, Janie, once you're inside and warm."

"Pete, it's not that cold in here." She couldn't help but protest. The man acted as if they were wandering around in a blizzard.

He stood patiently waiting.

Rolling her eyes at the other two women, she bade them goodbye and left the stall, crossing to the sink to wash up. Then she put her jacket on, with Pete's help, of course, and the two of them left the barn.

"Pete, I'm not made of Venetian glass. I won't break into a million pieces."

"I'm just trying to take care of you, Janie. You're my responsibility now. I don't want you or the babies to get hurt."

His responsibility. That wasn't what she wanted to be. She wanted to be the love of his life. His partner. Instead, she was his responsibility. "That's sweet of you, Pete, but millions of women are pregnant all the time. They still manage to get some work done.''

"There's no need for you to work. Red takes care of the house, and we take care of the ranch. All you have to do is take care of the babies.''

Janie came to a halt in the snow. "So for the next seven months, you expect me to sit and contemplate my navel as it expands to the size of a blimp?''

Pete blinked several times. "A blimp? Are you going to get that big?''

"Pete Randall! Quit trying to distract me. You know what I'm trying to say.''

"Yeah, I do, honey,'' he assured her, a warm smile on his face that reassured her even as it frustrated her. His arm came around her shoulders, and he urged her on toward the house.

"Well? I have to have something to do, or I'll go crazy. Megan is working on redoing the house. Red doesn't really need any help. What am I going to do with myself?''

"I don't know. We'll figure out something.'' He brushed his cold lips against hers, and Janie fought to keep her desire under control. This man could start a fire inside her in the coldest temperatures.

"Hey, Pete, Janie,'' Brett called as he made his way to the house. "Some honeymoon you two are having. You should go away to Hawaii or somewhere.''

Pete and Janie, having reached the porch, stood waiting for Brett to join them. "Maybe we will take a honeymoon, but it might be a good idea to go after the babies are born.''

Janie wanted to sock her new husband. He thought it would be easy to leave newborn twins? He had no idea how his life would change once the babies were born.

"I wish I had something like that to look forward to. I've got so much paperwork stacked up that I'll never get finished, even if I don't ride out this afternoon. And Jake needs me in the saddle.''

Like a light bulb in the comic strips, an idea jumped into Janie's head. "I can help you with the paperwork, Brett, if you'll show me how you have things set up.''

The rising pleasure on Brett's face died a quick death as Pete roared, "No!''

Chapter Eleven

"Pete, what's the matter with you?" Janie demanded, her hands on her hips.

"Don't you recognize the signs?" Brett asked, a comical look on his face. "I think he's about to blow."

"That's enough, little brother. You can do your own paper-work. I'm not having Janie worrying about all that stuff." Pete grabbed Janie's arm and tugged her toward the door.

"Pete Randall, I've just about had it!" Janie protested, pulling away from him. "You're acting like I'm a mummy, wrapped up and standing in a museum. I'm going to go crazy if I don't have something to do."

"Janie—" Brett began.

"You stay out of this, Brett," Pete ordered.

"*I* want to talk to Brett."

"You—"

"What's going on?" Jake asked, having walked up to the porch without the other three noticing.

All three tried to explain the discussion.

Jake held up a hand. "Can't we talk about it inside? I'm cold and hungry."

Janie suddenly exploded. "No, *we* can't! I may have married one Randall, but I didn't marry all four!" Then she threw open the door and stomped through the kitchen, ignoring Red's cheerful greeting. She didn't stop until she reached the bed-room she'd shared with Pete last night.

The sight of the freshly made bed enraged her even more.

In the hour she'd spent in the barn, Red had rushed upstairs to tidy up after her. Her mother would be ashamed of her.

And she could admit to herself, behind the closed door, that she felt like a guest at an expensive hotel.

But she wanted to feel like family.

"Janie?" Pete called softly, rapping on the door.

She tried to ignore him. But she couldn't. She'd already been more than rude. Reluctantly she opened the door.

"Janie, Jake didn't mean to interfere. We're all wanting to do what will make you happy."

"I apologize."

Pete's smile replaced the anxious expression on his face. "Good. Lunch is ready."

"I'm not hungry. I think I'll lie down for a while."

Her simple words immediately triggered Pete's overprotective urges. "Should I call Doc? What can I get you? Do you need anything? I'll bring a tray—"

"Pete!" Janie almost shouted, grabbing him by both arms. "I'm sulking! Okay? That's all I'm doing. Go eat your lunch and ignore me."

She stepped back and closed the door in his face.

Pete stared at the piece of wood that separated him from his wife, stunned by her words and her action. What did he do now?

He'd fix a tray for her, of course. She couldn't be allowed to skip meals. That wouldn't be good for her or the babies. Damn! He'd still forgotten to ask about morning sickness and her vitamins.

His mind filled with concern about Janie, he didn't remember that he had to face his family until he opened the kitchen door to discover them waiting at the table, all their gazes fixed on his face.

"Oh. Sorry I kept you waiting," he muttered, and sat down in his usual seat, ignoring the place set for Janie.

"Where's Janie?" Jake asked sharply.

"She decided to rest. I'll take a tray up to her before I go out again."

Megan leaned across the table. "Do you want me to check on her?"

"Should we call the doctor?" Brett asked.

"Is she mad at me?" Jake demanded, a frown on his brow.

Chad's hand reached for Megan's, as if talk of Janie's health made him appreciate his wife beside him.

Pete felt envy fill his heart. He wished he could claim Janie as simply. "No. No, she assured me she's fine."

After Red served the meal and they all began eating, Pete asked Megan quietly, "Did Janie get sick this morning? I mean, throw up?"

Megan's eyebrows arched. "She didn't mention it if she did."

"Did she take her vitamins?"

Shaking her head, Megan said, "I didn't see her take them, but Janie is an adult. And I'm sure she'd do whatever she needs to take care of the babies."

Janie might seem like an adult to Megan, but Pete had been keeping an eye on her all her life. Somehow he'd always felt responsible for her. And now that he'd gotten her pregnant, the feeling had only increased. "I'll check with her later," he muttered, unwilling to show how anxious he was.

"She probably just needs to rest," Jake assured him. "I've heard pregnant women need a lot of rest."

Brett raised his head and stared at his oldest brother. "You've heard?"

One would've thought Brett had questioned his sanity. Jake stiffened and stared down his little brother. "Yes, I've heard. You got a problem with that?"

Shrugging, Brett looked away. "Nope. I just never pictured you standing around talking about pregnant women."

"I don't, damn it!" Then, as if confessing a terrible sin, he muttered, "I bought a book."

Pete's eyes widened, and he felt incredibly stupid. Why hadn't he thought of that? Here he was the father, totally inexperienced in these things, and his brother had bought a book. "Reckon I could borrow it?" he asked Jake, a smile on his face to show his appreciation.

"Sure. You want to stay in this afternoon and read it?"

Nothing else could've shown Pete how supportive Jake was trying to be. They were shorthanded today because several of the cowboys had the flu. He knew Jake needed him in the saddle. He shook his head. "No, thanks. I'll read it this eve-

ning. I'll be down to the barn as soon as I take Janie some
food.''

"Um, Pete, why don't I take Janie a tray? She can eat and
then take a nap so she'll feel better when you come in this
evening.''

Pete thought of Janie's temper and decided Megan was right.
"Thanks, I'd appreciate that.''

"Well, ready to be on our way, then?'' Jake asked, standing.

As they moved to the door, after thanking Red, Chad leaned
over to Pete and whispered, "After you finish that book, do
you think I could borrow it?''

Both men looked over their shoulders to make sure Megan
didn't overhear them. Pete nodded his agreement.

Brett, behind them, saw no need for secrecy. "Damn! After
Chad, I guess I'm going to have to read it. And I'm not even
married yet!''

JANIE PLACED HER EAR against the door. No sound. Softly, she
rapped on the wood. Nothing. She reached down to turn the
knob but stopped when knocking sounded.

It took her a second to realize the knocking was coming from
the door to the bedroom, not the bathroom door leading into
their second room. She hurried back through the bathroom to
open the door, steeling herself to face Pete again.

Instead, she discovered Megan. Carrying a tray.

"Megan! What are you doing?''

"Bringing you some lunch. Pete was going to, but I offered.''

Janie took the tray from Megan and stood back so she could
enter the bedroom. "I'm ashamed of myself. I would've come
down if I got hungry. There's no need to wait on me.''

"I know that,'' Megan assured her, a smile on her face, "but
you just got married yesterday. A little pampering won't hurt
you.''

Janie didn't know why such behavior was easier to accept
from Megan than Pete, but it was.

"Would you like to come in and keep me company? Or I
could go back down to the kitchen....'' She trailed off, watching Megan.

"I'd love to keep you company. Do you want to get into bed to eat?"

"No. In fact, I was just thinking about unpacking. Has Great-Aunt Henrietta been downstairs yet? I didn't see her earlier." Janie set the tray on the bed and uncovered the steaming bowl of stew, the tossed salad and crisp rolls. "This smells delicious."

"Your mom and dad picked up your great-aunt and the couple from Denver and took them all to the airport this morning. Sorry I forgot to mention it earlier. Your great-aunt didn't want to be gone too long because of her cats. She said to tell you goodbye."

"Oh, thanks." At least she knew she wouldn't have to face another night in Pete's arms. She ignored the disappointment that filled her.

After she'd taken several bites, she looked at Megan. "I guess I owe everyone an apology. I'm usually not such a prima donna."

"Of course you aren't. These Randall men are a difficult lot. But they really only want to take care of you. Jake even bought a book."

Janie stared at her. "What? A book about what?"

"Pregnancy, silly!" Megan assured her with a chuckle. "Can't you picture Jake hiding in the barn reading a book about pregnant women instead of some girlie magazine? He admitted it at lunch, and I had a hard time not laughing."

"Jake?" Janie squeaked in surprise.

"Yes, and Pete's going to borrow it."

Janie joined Megan in some cleansing laughter.

THE MEN RETURNED at dark, cold, tired and hungry. But it cheered Pete to find Janie in the kitchen with Megan and Red, setting the table for dinner.

"You've got twenty minutes to clean up," she announced as they entered, smiling at all of them.

Pete wanted her smile just for him. He moved toward her, his gaze intense. Her eyes widened, but she didn't sidestep his embrace. "Hi, honey. I'm home," he whispered in her ear before he kissed her.

When he released her, he had to fight the desire to scoop her up in his arms and continue upstairs.

"You smell like horse," she complained, but she wouldn't meet his gaze. "Go grab a shower before we eat."

"Care to come scrub my back?"

"Pete!" Her reddened cheeks delighted him. He much preferred this homecoming to the one at lunch.

"We've got everything under control down here," Red added, his eyes twinkling. "Just don't take too long, or we'll eat without you."

"Newlyweds!" Brett exclaimed. Since Chad and Megan had already left the room, his complaint fell only on Pete and Janie.

"Jealous, little brother?" Jake asked. "If so, I know a remedy."

"Don't start, Jake. You've got Pete and Chad married. You should be satisfied." Brett started to the kitchen door, hoping to escape his big brother's attention.

"It's only a matter of time," Jake shouted after him as he followed him out of the kitchen.

"Skedaddle," Red insisted, moving around Pete and Janie. "I'm not letting my food go cold. Twenty minutes flat, no more, no less."

"I should stay and help—" Janie began.

"Nope. *Newlyweds* should go up together," Pete insisted, hoping she caught his message. After all, she'd promised to keep the state of their marriage a secret.

After staring at him intently, she turned without a word and headed for the stairs. When they arrived at their bedroom, he reached in front of her and opened the door. "After you, Mrs. Randall."

She entered ahead of him but then stood awkwardly in the center of the room.

Pete looked around, too. "You unpacked? You didn't overdo it, did you? Red or I could've helped you."

"No. I didn't need any help. And Red has enough to do."

Pete grunted as he began unbuttoning his shirt and headed for the closet for a fresh one. He'd carefully left half the closet space for Janie when he'd moved his things in. Somehow, their clothes sharing a space, even if he and his wife didn't, sent a thrill up his spine. He pushed back the closet door to discover the space inside didn't look any different than it had yesterday.

"Where are your things?" he asked, wheeling around to face her.

"In the other room," she said quietly, meeting his look.

He strode through the bathroom to the other bedroom, over to the closet and threw the door open. He stood there, staring at rows of shirts, skirts and dresses, feminine clothing, hanging pristinely in the closet.

She couldn't even share the closet?

Frustration rose up in him, and he reached forward and filled his big hands with hangers. Before Janie could protest, he had spun around, his hands grasping her clothes, and headed back to the other room.

"Pete, what are you doing?"

He ignored her.

"Pete, where are you going with my things? We're not sharing the same room, remember?" She tried to get between him and the closet door, but he wouldn't let her.

"Janie," he said softly, slowly, emphatically, "we may not be sharing the same bed, at least not now, but we sure as hell are going to share the same closet. Don't argue with me." His order didn't sit well with her, he could tell, but she stepped back, frowning at him.

He made a second trip. When he came back into the bedroom, she hadn't moved. But she spoke. "All my things won't fit in the closet."

"Then we'll *both* keep things in the other closet. But when Red puts our clean clothes away, I don't want him getting any ideas."

"But, Pete, I told Red I'd take care of our rooms. And our laundry. No one will know."

"I'll know," he insisted, whirling around to glare at her. "We're married, Janie. Get used to it."

Without waiting for an answer, an answer he feared he wouldn't like, Pete slammed shut the closet door and strode into the bathroom, closing the door behind him. Ripping off his shirt, he sat on the side of the tub and pulled off his boots, then shed the rest of his clothing.

The tension didn't dissolve even a little until steaming hot water splayed on his broad shoulders. But the water massage couldn't dissolve the raging hunger inside him. He wanted Janie so badly he could hardly concentrate.

But it wasn't just sex that fueled that hunger. He wanted her to be a part of him, emotionally as well as physically. He wanted the right to claim her. The wedding should have given him that right. But he knew, if no one else did, that Janie had only married him because of the babies. She'd made it clear she never would've walked down that aisle if Doc hadn't told her she was having twins.

A jarring thought brought him up short. Wasn't it the same for him? He wouldn't have married her if she weren't pregnant. After all, he'd refused her proposal before he'd known. What had changed suddenly? Pete refused to contemplate how his feelings for Janie had changed. There was too much else to think about. Like what would happen once the babies were born. Janie couldn't leave, could she? Taking his children with her? Such a thought almost stopped his heartbeat. Why hadn't he thought of it before?

Because he'd wanted to believe that once they were married, everything would work itself out.

So far, that hadn't happened.

He savagely shut off the tap and stepped from the shower, grabbing a towel from the linen closet. He rubbed himself vigorously, hoping to restore his belief in their future…together.

Then he swung open the bedroom door and discovered his wife sitting on the bed, staring at him as he stood in the doorway stark naked.

AFTER DINNER THAT NIGHT, Pete challenged Chad and Megan to a game of pool. He didn't want Janie to retreat to "her" room, locked away from his sight.

"Hey, good idea," Chad agreed. He took Megan's hand and led her toward the room that housed their pool table.

Pete kept his gaze on their locked hands, envy filling him. Every time he touched Janie, she pulled away. Maybe he could coach her on her playing.

Minutes later, after Chad racked the balls, Pete knew he'd have a better shot of getting Janie to coach him. They hadn't played together since she was eleven or twelve. Somewhere along the way, she'd improved her game. Not to mention a few other things.

Chad leaned over to kiss his wife. "Sorry, darlin', but I may have to trade you in for Janie. Especially if we ever get challenged by someone other than family."

Megan puffed up in pretend anger. "Only married a couple of weeks and you're already tired of me?"

Chad dropped his pool cue with no compunction and wrapped his arms around Megan. "Changed my mind," he assured her, burying his lips in her hair.

"Your shot, Megan," Pete said, hoping to bring the attention back to the game. Otherwise, he was going to die of frustration. "Good playing, Janie."

Chad picked up his cue stick and patted Megan on her rear. "Go get 'em, tiger."

"Behave, Chad, or Janie and Pete won't play with us again," Megan warned him, and then turned her attention toward the table.

A puzzled frown came over her face. "What do I do?"

Before either man could offer advice, Janie began explaining Megan's options and showing her how to shoot.

Chad stepped over to Pete. "Remember Rita? When I offered to help Megan when the two of you were playing us, she became enraged. She didn't want to lose."

Pete remembered. Rita was the third decorator who'd visited the ranch with Megan and Adele. Once she'd caught sight of the Randall brothers, though, her mind was on activities other than decorating. She hadn't been their kind. Like Megan. And Janie.

Janie bent over the table to demonstrate a shot for Megan, and his gaze unerringly traced her trim shape. Beautiful and kind. Smart. And hardheaded as all get-out. He grinned. When he'd come out of the bathroom, she'd looked her fill. And then opened the dresser drawer to toss him a pair of briefs. "You'd better hurry before dinner starts." Then she'd left the room.

He didn't think he could've mustered such sangfroid if Janie had been naked. In fact, even thinking about such a sight had his blood surging.

"Your shot, Pete," Janie called to him.

Surprised, he looked at the others. "Um, I think I need some help, too. Like Megan."

Chad stepped forward.

"Not you, bozo," Pete growled, and then smiled sweetly at Janie.

"Get real, Pete. You were an expert by the time I was born," Janie replied, lifting an eyebrow.

"Well, then, how about a good-luck kiss?"

To his surprise, she stepped forward and brushed her lips across his, one hand resting on his chest for balance. His immediate fantasy of taking her right there on the pool table didn't help his aim. He missed.

"I think Pete's trying to make me not feel so bad," Megan said, smiling at her brother-in-law.

Chad chuckled. "I think Pete's mind isn't on the game. And if Janie kisses him for luck every time it's his turn, we'll win."

"Maybe Megan will return the favor and do a little distracting of her own," Pete suggested, wrapping an arm around Janie's slim figure. His heart clutched when she leaned her head against his chest, her silky hair resting against his chin.

"Not a bad idea. I'll prove I can handle distraction better than you," Chad assured his brother. Then he pulled Megan to him and kissed her thoroughly. Casually he released her and bent over the table. And missed.

"Damn! Unlucky shot," he muttered, avoiding his brother's gaze.

Janie stepped up to the table for her turn.

"Wait a minute! She's been doing better than all of us. Give her a kiss, Pete. Let's see if she can handle distraction better than the rest of us." Chad grinned at both of them before he ordered, "And no lily-livered peck like the last one."

Pete eyed his wife, wondering if she'd protest. When she turned toward him expectantly, he took her response as a green light. And proceeded with great expertise. And a lot of heat.

"Wow!" Chad said as Pete released Janie. "Janie, if you can make a shot after that, you've got ice water in your veins."

Pete thought so, too. He knew he was on fire.

Janie stepped up to the table and studied the balls' positions. Pete looked for any flicker of distraction or lack of concentra-

he was. As if it would be proof that his wife cared for him, wanted him.

She lined up her shot, pushed her long black braid back over her shoulder and hit the cue ball.

Pete stared in dismay as the little white ball rolled across the table, smacked into the nine ball and drove it into the hole.

Perfect shot.

Chapter Twelve

When their heavy breathing returned to normal, and Chad lay relaxed with Megan wrapped in his arms, she whispered, "Do Janie and Pete strike you odd in any way?"

Chad frowned and raised his head slightly. "What are you talking about?"

"They don't seem...comfortable with each other. Janie even avoids Pete's touch. And he seems reluctant."

"You must've had your eyes closed when he kissed her before she made that last shot." As if the memory reminded him of what he liked, too, he kissed his wife again. "Mmm, but I like kissing now better than kissing while playing pool."

"Me, too, but—"

"Give 'em a break, sweetheart. They've only been married a day or two. Unlike us. We've been married two weeks tomorrow. We're old hands at this sort of thing." He kissed her again. "But don't you worry about old Pete. He'll kiss Janie off her feet in no time." He chuckled. "Silly remark, I guess, since she's already pregnant."

Megan lay pressed against her husband's heart, well satisfied with her lot in life. But she also still had doubts about Pete and Janie. She didn't want anything to be wrong, but she couldn't quell the feeling that something wasn't right.

But she wasn't going to say any more to her husband about it.

"In fact," Chad whispered, running a hand up and down her back, "we may have been married first, but Pete's one up on me. Or should I say two up?'' he added with a chuckle. "Maybe we'd better practice again."

"This isn't a competition," Megan protested but weakly. She was enjoying his suggestion too much.

WHEN JANIE WOKE the next morning, she didn't have any trouble remembering where she was. She was in another room, away from Pete, in a single bed, missing his warmth and touch.

The sound of the shower immediately filled her with the picture of Pete when he'd opened the door yesterday sans his clothes. It had been all she could do to speak straight. Then she'd had to play pool with the man, in front of Chad and Megan, and try to ignore her hormones.

No one had been more surprised than her when she'd sunk the nine ball. Especially since she'd been aiming for the number three next to it.

She'd been too embarrassed to confess to Pete. And then she'd been too alarmed. Pete had stared at her coldly, as if she'd slapped him in the face. That reaction had caused her to miss the next shot.

Chad and Megan had continued their kissing game, but Pete, when his turn came around, had glared at her before picking up his cue stick and running the table.

The game was over. Both games.

She'd gone to bed immediately.

With a sigh, she shoved back the covers and swung her legs to the floor. Her big toe stubbed the book she'd been reading. Dick Francis's latest mystery was on the floor beside the bed. She was going to have to stock her library if she was going to bed at eight o'clock each evening.

The door opened and she grabbed the blankets, clutching them to her chest like some virgin fearing ravishment. Pete stared at her from across the room.

"I didn't expect you to be awake," he said in a voice she couldn't read. "Are you okay?"

"I'm fine."

"Are you getting up?"

"In a few minutes. I was waiting for you to finish in the bathroom."

"If you want hot water, you'd better get in there before Brett." A smile broke out on his face. "He's notorious for long ones that leave the rest of us yelping when the hot water disappears. Jake makes him wait half an hour until the rest of us have finished." His grin was relaxed, letting Janie breathe easier.

"Thanks for warning me."

Pete looked at his watch. "You've still got five minutes."

Janie wondered if he expected her to parade past him into the bathroom. Not that her pajamas were X-rated. On the contrary, they were cotton flannel. Definitely unsexy. Even so, she didn't intend to build any intimacy between them.

"Shall I tell Red you'll be down for breakfast?"

Would a message to Red convince him to go away? "Yes, please, but I probably won't make it down until after you're gone."

Pete stiffened, as if she'd insulted him. Then he began walking toward her. "In that case, I reckon I'll collect my goodbye kiss now."

Janie stared at him, her mouth falling open. The man was insane. "But, Pete, we don't have an audience. There's no reason to—"

Before she could finish her protest, he'd lifted her up from the bed, holding her against his chest, his mouth stopping her words.

Bacon in a hot frying pan didn't sizzle as much as her body did at Pete's touch. His hands slid up her back, caressing her skin, warming it. When one hand moved to her breast, her mind shut down and the heat intensified.

Then she was sliding down his strong body, landing with a thump on her bed.

Pete drew in a deep breath and marched across the room. "See if you can make a pool shot after *that* kiss."

Then he disappeared from sight.

TRUE TO HER PREDICTION, Janie didn't make it to the kitchen until the men had left. She made sure of it.

As she was eating the breakfast Red insisted on preparing, she asked, "Red, are you going into town today?"

"I'm not sure. Why? Is there something you need?"

"I thought I'd catch a ride over to my parents'. There are a few things I forgot to pack, and I'd like to get my car."

"You can take one of the pickups," Red offered.

"But then I couldn't drive my car back."

Megan entered the kitchen.

"I know. Maybe I can talk Megan into helping me," Janie suggested, smiling at her sister-in-law. She explained her need, and Megan quickly agreed to drive her.

"I don't know," Red said, scratching his head. "I'm not sure the boys would want you running around like that. You might get stuck or something."

Megan laughed and crossed the room to kiss Red's cheek. "Dear Red. There's nothing you can do to stop us. I have my own car, remember? And we're their wives, not their personal slaves."

Red backed off. "Okay, okay."

"In fact," Megan said, excitement rising in her voice, "why don't we call B.J. and see if she can meet us in town for lunch?"

Janie was amazed at the excitement that filled her. She hadn't realized how trapped she'd been feeling. "That's a great idea."

"Here now, you two don't like my cooking?"

"Don't be silly, Red. We just need a day out. Janie, we can leave early and shop for the babies' room. Then, when you and Pete go shopping, you'll know where to direct him so he'll choose what you like."

Megan's enthusiasm spurred Janie on. After Megan called B.J. and made arrangements for lunch, they began making a list of what they intended to do with their day.

"What am I supposed to tell the boys when they come in for lunch?" Red asked a bit nervously.

"Sit down and eat?" Janie suggested, and giggled.

Red smiled back. "You know those two lovelorn coyotes will be lookin' for you."

"Tell them we've gone to spend their hard-earned money, so eat fast and go earn some more," Megan told him. "Now, I'm going to do an hour or two of work before we need to leave."

"Shall I help you with the dishes, Red?" Janie offered.

"Nope. Won't take a minute to clean up after you two."

"Well, then, I'm starting some laundry. I'll do a load of bath towels first." With a sense of purpose in her step, Janie headed upstairs to gather the morning's trail of laundry left by four handsome cowboys.

PETE WONDERED how Janie would greet him. His parting words had shown his irritation with the events of the previous night. He regretted revealing his vulnerability to her.

"You comin', Pete?" Jake called from the barn door.

"Yeah, I'll be right there. Lester has something caught in his shoe." He bent over to pick up his mount's hoof.

"Need any help?"

"Naw. I'm coming." What was he doing, anyway? Hiding from some female? Even if she was his wife, no woman was going to cause Pete Randall to turn tail and run.

"Where are Brett and Chad?" he asked Jake as he joined him.

"They've already headed to the house. I was surprised you weren't with them. You and Chad seem to have females on the brain lately," Jake teased.

"Yeah." She was still on his brain. But he was reluctant to face her. He didn't want her to know how much he wanted her.

Jake gave him a strange look, but they'd reached the porch. When the two men entered the house, Pete's gaze scanned the room, searching for the woman he'd just assured himself he didn't want to see.

Chad was slumped down at the table.

"What's wrong?" Pete demanded.

"Nothing. The girls went shopping," Chad said, shifting his chin to his raised hand.

Pete stared at him, stunned. "Shopping? What for? What did Janie need?"

"Didn't need nothin'," Red assured him as he handled a pan of biscuits. "They're just bein' female."

"Careful, Red. That sounds like a sexist remark," Jake said.

"Jake!" Brett exclaimed. "First you're reading about pregnant women, and now you're talking about sexist remarks? What's going on around here?''

Jake looked uncomfortable, but he muttered, ''We have to be more sensitive to—to things if we're going to have women around. I don't want any more divorces in the Randall family.''

Pete wondered if Janie's nausea from her pregnancy felt anything like his stomach right this moment. The thought of divorce, of Janie leaving him, was more than he could bear.

But that had been his problem all along, hadn't it?

The question stunned him. Was that why he'd never sought marriage or any permanent relationship? He feared he might not survive its ending?

He hurriedly dismissed such wayward thoughts. He needed to think about Janie's actions today. ''What do you think, Chad?''

Chad looked up at him in surprise. ''Megan's not leaving me. There won't be any divorce from my marriage.''

''No! No, I didn't mean that. I mean about today. What should we do about today?''

Chad still looked surprised. ''What do you mean?''

Pete was beginning to question his own sanity. Why was Chad so confused? ''I mean about them going off to town.''

Jake cleared his throat. ''There's no reason they shouldn't go to town, Pete. We're not holding them prisoners here.''

''No, of course not. I just thought maybe they might get stuck on the road, or have a flat tire, or...'' Pete didn't finish his sentence, because he couldn't think of any other disasters. He didn't like realizing he was being ridiculous.

''I do need someone to go into town and pick up the part for the snowplow before we have a new storm,'' Jake said, watching Pete. ''You want to take care of that this afternoon?''

''I can do it,'' Brett said. ''I've got an order of office supplies I need to pick up. And there are a couple of things I forgot.''

Jake frowned at him.

''What?'' Brett asked, bewilderment on his face.

''Pete needs to go into town, not you.''

''But I really do need to add to my list.''

''Give it to Pete. He'll take care of it for you,'' Jake insisted.

Brett snorted in derision. "Pete's computer illiterate. He'd get the wrong stuff."

"It's okay, Jake," Pete began, realizing how hard his older brother was working to provide him with an excuse to check on Janie.

"Maybe you should both go," Jake said, ignoring Pete's words. "That way neither one of you will do anything crazy."

"Hey!" Brett protested.

Pete didn't say anything. He was feeling a little crazy today. With Brett along, he'd have to pretend everything was normal.

"That okay with you, Chad?" Jake asked. "I really can't spare you if these other two go off."

"Sure. I know Megan will be back this afternoon."

Pete wished he had as much confidence. Somehow he feared Janie might have decided she'd made a mistake. But he was determined to prove her wrong.

THERE WEREN'T too many choices for lunch in Rawhide. B.J. had agreed to meet them at Marietta's Sandwich Shop, opened recently by a friend of Janie's mother.

Janie relaxed as she, B.J. and Megan chatted about fashions, food and gossip. B.J. was just getting to know her way around and had a lot of questions about her customers. Megan, too, wanted to know about some of the people she'd met. Having lived in the area all her life, Janie was supplying the information, among other things, while they ate their sandwiches.

"I love Red's cooking," Megan said, "but it's nice to eat something a little lighter occasionally. Living on the ranch, I'm afraid I'm gonna look like a cow!"

Janie laughed. "I know what you mean. But it takes a lot of calories to keep a cowboy in the saddle all day."

"Do you miss the work?" B.J. asked.

"Yes, but I guess I don't have a choice until after the babies are born."

"And after they're born, you won't have any time or energy for ranching," B.J. added.

"Really? I don't mean to sound naive, but I've never been around babies all that much."

"Me, neither," Megan added.

B.J. grinned. "I found one a challenge. I can't imagine dealing with two babies at once. I think part of the problem is that you don't get any uninterrupted sleep so you can regain your health."

"I'll be there to help you, though, Janie," Megan hurriedly assured her. "In fact, I'm planning on using your babies as a training experience. Chad is—is interested in having a family." Her cheeks pinkened, and she looked down at her sandwich.

"I guess we can learn together," Janie agreed, but her heart was envious of Megan's happiness. Pete hadn't had any choice about having a family, and Janie wasn't sure he would've chosen that option if given a chance.

Several acquaintances dropped by to chat with them, and Janie made sure her friends met them all. She was discovering the luxury of having friends nearby, and she wanted to be sure B.J. and Megan settled in happily.

When a warm hand rested on her shoulder, she turned with a smile, expecting another neighbor. Instead, she discovered Bryan Manning.

"Oh, hello, Bryan. How are you?"

"Fine. How about you? Liking married life?"

His penetrating stare brought a flush to her cheeks. She looked down at her plate. "Yes, of course. Have you met B. J. Anderson, the new vet, and Megan Randall, my sister-in-law?"

He barely spared the others a greeting but immediately turned his attention back to Janie. "I was surprised by your wedding."

"Yes, well, it all happened very suddenly."

"You told me you weren't marrying him."

Janie felt irritation surge through her. She had owed Bryan an explanation, and she'd called him the day before her marriage. He had protested her plans, and he didn't sound any happier about them now. But it was her business.

"I also called and told you I'd changed my mind, Bryan. That's a woman's prerogative."

"That's anyone's prerogative," Megan chimed in, smiling at the man. "I know because I'm an interior designer and my customers always change their minds. Usually just after I've purchased some outlandish piece of furniture that only they would want.''

Janie was grateful for Megan's lighthearted attempt. It had no effect on Bryan. He was undeterred.

"My offer still stands," he said insistently, putting his hand back on Janie's shoulder.

Her irritation worsened. Shrugging her shoulder so he would remove his hand, she said, "Thanks, but I've made my choice, Bryan. I'm not planning on changing my mind."

"Look, can I speak to you alone? We could move to another table for a few minutes, have a cup of coffee together...."

"No, Bryan. I'm sorry, but we have nothing to say to each other."

He seemed almost as irritated as Janie, but she felt no sympathy for him. He was a handsome man, but she wasn't sure what she'd seen in him. When she'd phoned him, he'd been difficult, but she'd thought he'd understood. Now all he was doing was harassing her.

"Janie, why don't we go pay our bill and meet you at the door in a couple of minutes," Megan suggested.

"I'm not sure—"

"Thanks," Bryan said, nodding to Megan in gratitude.

As soon as the other two left the table, Bryan sat down. "Janie, I know you felt you had to marry the father of your baby, but I was willing to adopt the baby, to let it be mine."

"Yes, and I appreciate that, Bryan, but I made my choice, and I don't intend to change my mind." Apparently he hadn't heard there would be two babies. But she thought she'd made the right decision even if there were only one baby. She now believed that Pete should have a role in his children's lives.

If only he wanted to have a part in her life, too.

"Can I at least call you, talk to you occasionally? I can't just walk away from you."

Janie almost gasped as she envisioned Pete's reaction to a call from Bryan, his chief competition. "I don't think that would be a good idea, Bryan. You need to get on with your life."

"But I love you!"

They were the words she wanted to hear from Pete. Not from

Bryan. "I'm sorry, Bryan, but any relationship we had is over. I'm married."

His hand reached out to cover hers as it lay on the table. Why couldn't the man understand what she was telling him? She tugged at his hold on her, but he didn't let go.

"Bryan—" she began, but an icy voice interrupted her.

"Take your hand off my wife."

She didn't need to turn around to know that Pete had arrived on the scene and that he was angry.

"Pete, I'll take care of this."

"You're my wife. I'll take care of it." Pete reached over her shoulder and grasped Bryan's wrist. "Turn her loose."

"You're acting like a caveman," Bryan protested even as he did as Pete asked. "In Chicago, we're a little more civilized."

"I'm sure. And if you want to live a long and fruitful life, I'd suggest you hightail it right back to Chicago. Hitting on another man's wife out here will get you a broken nose."

"Pete!" Janie protested. The last thing she wanted was a scene in front of half the town two days after her marriage.

"Listen here, cowboy, you're not going to tell me what to do!" Bryan unwisely responded.

"The hell I won't!" Pete said. He punctuated his words with a blow to the man's nose.

Bryan crumpled to the floor, and everyone stared at Janie and Pete.

Chapter Thirteen

Brett, Megan and B.J. rushed to the table, arriving about the same time Bryan hit the floor.

"Pete! What are you doing?" Brett demanded, grabbing his brother by the arm.

"Protecting my wife," Pete growled.

Janie closed her eyes briefly and then glared at her husband. "I wasn't in any danger."

B.J. helped Bryan to his feet. She felt his nose even as she offered him a napkin to staunch the flow of blood. "I don't think anything is broken, Mr. Manning. But I'm sure Pete will be glad to pay the doctor bill if you want to go see Dr. Jacoby."

Brett quickly seconded B.J.'s offer, but Pete didn't. Janie could still see anger in his eyes as he looked at Bryan. She tugged on her husband's arm. "Pete, let's get out of here."

Without a word, he took her hand and led her outside. Once they were apart from the others, he turned on her. "What were you doing with that man?" The anger dripped from his voice.

"Trying to avoid causing a scene," she replied in kind. "Wasted effort, as it turns out, since you decided to play Tarzan."

"You *wanted* to talk to him?"

"No, Pete, I don't ever want to talk to him again. He was being insistent, which I didn't like, but I didn't think I was in any danger."

Pete looked away, staring across the almost empty street. He removed his hat and ran a hand through his hair. "Probably you weren't," he said on an exhaled breath. He kept looking away as he continued, "But if I'm Tarzan, you are *my* Janie, and I won't have that man hanging around you."

Janie didn't know what to make of this man. He both infuriated her and turned her on—all at the same time. Then something occurred to her. "What are you doing in town?"

The guilty look on his face confirmed her suspicions. But he hurriedly said, "Jake wanted me to pick up a part for the snow-plow."

"You were here to check on me, weren't you?" she demanded. "Do you think I can't be trusted out of your sight? Do you intend to follow me all over creation?"

"Now, honey—"

"Did I need a note from you to have lunch in town?" She was shouting at him now, unmindful of the people in the parking lot. "Are you afraid I'll spend all your money? Damn it, Pete! I don't even know if you have money. You won't let me do anything. You just want to keep me wrapped in cotton and sitting in a corner somewhere!" She feared she might've gone too far, but it felt good to release some of her frustration.

"Janie, are you all right?" Megan asked behind her, putting a hand on her arm.

Janie turned to see Brett, Megan and B.J. watching her, and she promptly burst into tears.

PETE SWEPT JANIE up into his arms and carried her to his pickup. B.J. followed and opened the door to the cab, then closed it behind Janie.

"Pete, emotional swings are normal with pregnancy. Humor her, okay?"

"Don't you think I should take her to Doc?" he asked, surprised.

"Nope. Everything's fine. She probably got a little tired today. Let her take a nap, and pretend this crying jag never happened."

"But it's so unlike Janie."

"It's unlike a nonpregnant Janie. Things are different now."

You could say that again.

Megan and Brett joined them.

"Are you taking Janie home?" Brett asked.

"Yeah. She needs a nap."

"But she wanted her car from her parents' house," Megan explained.

"So she can run around and get exhausted again?" Pete demanded.

"So she won't feel trapped," Megan said quietly. "Pregnancy is new to Janie at the moment, Pete. Letting her have her car won't hurt anything."

"And it's not as if you have a choice," B.J. argued. "She's an adult. Adults get to make their own decisions."

He stared at Janie, sitting in the cab of his truck, wiping the tears from her eyes. She looked at him and then hurriedly turned away. *She hates me.* The thought struck him with such force, he almost reeled back. What was he going to do? Hate was definitely not the emotion he wanted from her.

"Fine. We'll go by her parents and let her pick up her car. But I'm getting her a cellular phone so she can call if she gets in trouble."

"Good idea. You take her on back home, and I'll arrange for the cellular phone," Brett said. "That is, I will if you can spare the time, Megan, 'cause I don't have my truck here with me."

"Of course I can. Why are you both in town, anyway? I thought you were shorthanded at the ranch."

Pete's cheeks turned red, but he confessed, "Jake thought up an excuse 'cause I was worried about Janie. I knew she wouldn't want me to check on her, but—but I was imagining all kinds of disasters."

"You mean like someone punching another person out and causing a scene?" B.J. teased.

Pete reluctantly grinned. "Something like that."

After telling them all goodbye, he circled the truck and got in. Janie stared straight ahead.

"Honey, I'll run you by your folks' so you can pick up your car. I didn't think about you needing it."

She turned to stare at him, surprise on her face.

Finally he'd done something right, thanks to Megan and B.J. Maybe he'd take his marriage problems to those two instead of his brothers. Women seemed to understand other women better than any man did.

JANIE TOOK A LONG NAP, something she never used to do. But she'd learned that everything had changed since she'd become pregnant. And married.

When she came down to dinner, Pete was waiting for her, a wary look on his face. She couldn't blame him. Her crying had been almost as awkward and bizarre as his scene with Bryan.

But she didn't want to talk about the afternoon's events. It brought her emotions too close to the surface. She had to keep her distance from the sexy man she'd married.

Which was hard to do when he took the seat next to her, his broad shoulders touching hers every time he passed a dish to her. It simply wasn't fair, she decided. Why did he have to be so attractive?

After dinner, she insisted on helping Red clean up. It would give her some distance from Pete. But when Megan volunteered, too, Pete assured her he would help Janie in a voice that brooked no argument.

"You really don't have to," she protested anyway. So much for distance!

"You let him be, Janie. He needs to do his share. After all, he didn't work this afternoon," Red added, chuckling. "Unless you call rounding up one little stray hard work."

"I hadn't strayed, Red. I was with Megan and B.J."

"And was it Megan and B.J. this old grizzly bear punched out?" Red was more amused by his own humor than his audience was.

"That's enough, Red," Pete warned sternly. "This afternoon is best forgotten."

"Good idea," Brett agreed, "but it won't happen around town very soon. Everyone was talking about it."

Janie groaned. She'd never want to venture into town again.

"I think it's sweet that he's so jealous just because another man wanted to talk to you," Megan said.

"I'd be just as jealous, Meggie," Chad assured her with a growl.

"Good." Megan patted his cheek, and he leaned over to kiss her temple.

Janie turned away with a stack of dishes. Megan was right. She should appreciate Pete's...interest. But she would've traded that possessiveness in a minute for just one caress given with love.

Pete arrived at the sink beside her. "Sure you're up to this? I can handle the dishes if you're too tired."

"No, thank you. I had a long nap today."

Polite. They were being exceptionally polite around each other tonight, as if they were strangers.

"Okay. I'll wash and you dry."

He handed her a dish towel, and Janie took a step back. When she got too close to him, she had to fight a ridiculous urge to throw herself at him.

Distracted, she began running water in the sink.

"I'll wash," Pete repeated. "There's no point in you getting dishpan hands." Without warning, he put his hands on her waist and shifted her over.

The warmth of his touch was wonderful but all too brief. She really was going to have to get her hormones under control.

They completed the dishes with only occasional words exchanged, all surface, all polite.

Pete invited her to come watch a special on television afterward, but she refused. She couldn't take more close contact with him without losing control completely.

Going upstairs, she ran some hot water in the tub and added bath bubbles. After the difficult day she'd had, she needed some soothing.

She would've preferred Pete's hands to do that job, but she couldn't ask him. He was treating her like a stranger, someone he didn't know. Not like his lover.

Of course, she wasn't.

But she wanted to be again.

By the time the water had cooled, she was sleepy. Changing into her pajamas, she slipped under the covers, ready to go to sleep.

A knock on the bathroom door did away with all that relaxation. "Yes?"

"It's Pete. May I come in?"

"Of course." She pulled the covers to her chin.

"You're really going to sleep?"

"Why, yes."

"Oh. I bought you something today while I was in town."

"I know. Megan told me. The cellular phone. I appreciate it, Pete, but I don't think I need it tonight."

"No. I mean, yes, I bought you the phone, but I bought you something else, too."

Curiosity filled her. "What?"

"I noticed you were reading Dick Francis. When we were in the bookstore today, I saw his latest in hardback and I bought it for you." He pulled his hand from behind his back and held out the book to her.

Janie's eyes filled. Drat the tears! She never cried, but right now she was so moved by his kindness. "Thank you, Pete. I'll enjoy reading it. That was very thoughtful of you."

He brought the book over to her. "I'll leave it here by your bed. I didn't realize I'd need it, but I guess it's kind of an apology for, you know, hitting Bryan."

"It's all right. He probably deserved it."

Pete seemed surprised by her words, but she'd long forgiven his actions this afternoon.

"Thanks. Then—then I guess I'll say good-night."

He bent down and kissed her brow. Janie, expecting a real kiss, like this morning's, found herself empty and unfulfilled as he left her room, closing the door behind him.

Now he was really being too polite.

But she couldn't blame him. The fault was her own. He was only complying with her request. His promise to renegotiate their agreement after the babies were born had made her believe he still wanted her. Now she wasn't so sure.

Had her refusal to let their marriage be a real one killed even his desire for her?

He was such a special man. His thoughtfulness proved that. And no matter how staunchly she tried to deny it, she loved him. In fact, she always had.

What was she going to do now? Seduce him? Tell him she'd changed her mind? Send out an invitation to her bed? Move back into his bed?

She fell asleep debating her alternatives.

THE REST OF THE FAMILY sat in the television room, watching a special. During advertisements, Megan told Chad about the baby cribs she and Janie had found that morning.

"They're the only matched pair in town, so it was nice that Janie liked them. I hope she and Pete buy them before one is sold."

Jake, sitting nearby, leaned forward. "Did you see them?"

"Oh, yes, we studied them for half an hour. Janie fell in love with them, and I did, too. She said when—I mean, if—Chad and I have a baby, we'd be able to use them, too."

Jake grinned. "That's right. Start a family tradition with special baby cribs. Where are they?"

"McAnally's. We looked at sheets and bumper pads, but the ones Janie liked have to be ordered."

"Did she place an order?" Jake asked.

"Well, no, she wanted to wait until Pete had a chance to look at them," Megan explained.

"Would you have time to go into town tomorrow afternoon with me? I'd like to buy that stuff as a surprise for them," Jake said. Looking at his two younger brothers and Red, he added, "A surprise. Got that, guys?"

With big grins, the others nodded their compliance.

THE NEXT MORNING, after breakfast, Janie called her mother. During their conversation, Janie realized what she needed to do. She would return to her parents' each morning and do half a day's work on her father's computer, keeping his paperwork up-to-date.

At least until the babies were born. Or until she got too big to get behind the steering wheel of her car.

Excitement filled her at the promise of having some direction to her days. She put in a load of laundry, as she had yesterday, and returned to their rooms to tidy up.

And, as she'd decided last night, there was one other chore she had to do.

When she left the house an hour later, she warned Red she wouldn't be there for lunch.

"Again? Does that mean Pete will lose another afternoon of work?" Red asked.

"No. I'll be eating at home with my mom and dad. Pete knows I'll be okay there. Then I'll come back here after lunch and take my nap. I'm a lady of leisure, you know," she added, grinning.

"Yeah. Right," Red snorted in derision. "That's why you've already started the laundry, isn't it?"

"Just trying to be helpful," Janie said with a smile, and kissed his cheek. "See you later."

PETE MISSED JANIE at lunch. But, as she had foreseen, he couldn't complain about her visiting her family. At least Red assured him she'd taken the cellular phone with her.

After eating, he paused to call the Dawsons. Lavinia answered the phone.

"Lavinia, it's Pete. Is Janie there?"

"Yes, she is, Pete. Just a moment."

"I'm not checking on you," he said immediately when Janie came to the phone. "I just wanted to be sure you were feeling all right."

"I'm fine, Pete."

"Well, I didn't see you this morning," he said, lowering his voice, hoping his family wouldn't hear. "So I thought..."

"Everything's fine except that I'm expanding at a rapid rate. I had a hard time fastening my jeans this morning. You'll think I'm fat."

Pete didn't need any advice on how to respond to her complaint. From his heart, he said, "No, I'll think you're beautiful, just like I do now."

When only silence was her answer, he thought he'd upset her again.

Then very quietly she said, "Thank you, Pete."

"Janie? You're not crying, are you?"

"No. But we need to t-talk."

His heart contracted with fear. Had she changed her mind about being married to him? Was she going to stay at her parents' house? "Do you want me to come over now?" he asked gruffly, trying to hide the panic he was feeling.

"No! No, I'll be home in a little while. We can talk this evening. It's nothing urgent."

Nothing urgent. What did that mean? After telling her good-bye, he hung up the phone and stood there, staring into space.

"Pete?" Jake called to him.

"Yeah?"

"I'm going into town for a while. Take charge, okay?"

"Sure. Is there anything I can do for you? Why do you need to go into town today?"

He was surprised when Jake avoided his gaze.

"Just something I need to take care of."

The last time Jake had acted so suspicious, he'd been trying to find wives for them all. "You going into town to find a wife for Brett?" Pete teased, hoping to lighten his own spirits.

"Hey!" Brett protested. "I'm happy being single. At least I don't have to go around punching anybody's lights out."

"Your time will come, little brother," Jake warned him with a grin, but he didn't give Pete any further explanation for his trip to town.

When Pete got back to the house about dark, he was tired, but he was pretty sure his lack of energy stemmed from the mental exercises he wrestled with all afternoon. What did Janie want to talk about?

When he opened the back door, he was relieved to see her in the kitchen. If nothing else, she'd come back this time.

With a sigh, he crossed the room and wrapped his arms around her. He couldn't risk a kiss that might destroy what little control he had, so he gave her a peck on the cheek.

"Hi. How was your visit with your parents?"

"Fine," she returned, but Pete noticed she didn't look at him as she stepped from his embrace. "I'm going to go over every morning and do some paperwork for my dad. He's going to continue to pay me a salary, too."

"You don't need a salary!" Pete protested. "I'm getting you a checkbook for my account."

"I like to feel that I'm contributing, and no one will let me do anything around here."

"You're doing laundry," Red called out from the pantry, "and helping out in the kitchen."

"And I appreciate your letting me help, Red. It makes me feel a part of—of the family," Janie said, smiling at Pete.

Like a flash of lightning in a summer storm, Janie's words suddenly illuminated a problem, and Pete realized he'd made a big mistake. In his attempts to care for her, Pete had shut her out. Or at least it seemed that's how it appeared to her. Frowning, he scrambled for ways to involve Janie in his life.

"Are you good at the computer?"

Over her shoulder as she carried silverware to the table, she said coolly, "Very good. Why?"

"Reckon you could teach me?"

That question stopped her in her tracks. She spun around to stare at him. "Are you serious?"

He licked his dry lips, anxious for her response. "Yeah. Brett says I'm helpless, but I thought maybe you'd be a better teacher."

She smiled at him with real warmth, and he felt it all the way to his toes. Janie had to be the only woman who could turn him on talking about computers. But then, she could turn him on anywhere, anytime.

"I'd love to teach you. Do you have your own computer?"

"Nope. Just the one in the office Brett uses. But if you know what to buy, we can go get whatever we need."

Jake, having entered the kitchen in time to hear part of Pete's response, said, "What are we buying now? This family is turning into shopaholics."

Pete remembered that Jake had gone into town. "Was that what you were doing today?"

Jake smiled but didn't answer as the rest of the family trooped in. "What were you talking about buying?"

"A new computer," Pete said.

Brett, sitting down at the table, groaned. "Come on, Pete, you don't need a computer. You don't even know how to turn one on."

"Janie's going to teach me."

Brett turned to Janie. "You have no idea what a gargantuan task that's going to be."

"Pete will do just fine," Janie assured her brother-in-law and then smiled at Pete.

Pete vowed to stay up nights studying if it pleased Janie. If learning computers made her feel more a part of their family, then he'd learn computers. If computers kept her there, a part of his life, then he'd build one from scratch. Whatever it took.

"So where will you put the computer?" Jake asked, frowning. "Not in the babies' room."

"No, of course not," Janie said calmly. "If necessary, we can put it in our bedroom."

Pete liked the sound of that, *our bedroom*. He only wished it were true.

"There's a small room, not much bigger than a bathroom, just down the hall from your bedroom. We've been using it for storage, haven't we, Red?" Jake asked.

"Yep. Lots of stuff that needs to be thrown out."

"We'll convert it into an office for the two of you," Jake offered. "After all, with Pete's venture with the rodeos, I imagine you'll have a lot of records and files."

"Yeah. More than I can deal with," Pete agreed, thinking about the fat files of papers he had stacked in a corner in Jake's office.

"We'll take care of that, thanks, Jake," Janie said. Then she launched into a discussion of computers and computer programs with Brett with more animation than Pete had seen since their marriage.

He relaxed a little. Maybe they were going to make it after all. If he made Janie happy, she might agree to stay with him. Him and the babies.

After dinner, before anyone could leave the table, Jake cleared his throat. "Pete and Janie, I want to explain why I went to town today."

Janie looked puzzled, but Pete felt a sinking feeling in his stomach. What was going on?

"Megan said you found the cribs you wanted yesterday, Janie, and we bought them today for you. I was afraid if we waited, they might sell one of them."

Janie's face lit up. "Oh, thank you, Jake. That's so thoughtful of you. Pete, you don't mind, do you?"

"No, of course not. I should've— I didn't realize we'd need to buy that stuff so early."

"We don't, but it will be fun to begin putting together our nursery," she assured him, beaming.

Whatever made her happy.

"Great. So, let's all go to the Randall nursery and put these suckers together," Jake ordered, and rose from the table, followed by the rest of the family.

They were going to the nursery! His family was going to the nursery that was Janie's bedroom. They were about to discover the truth about his marriage.

Pete stared at Janie, panic filling him.

She smiled back serenely.

Chapter Fourteen

"No!" Pete said, jumping to his feet.

"Why not?" Jake asked, pausing on his way to the door, the rest of the family following.

"Uh, you must have lots to do. There's no rush. I can put them together some other time."

"But I'd love to see them put together tonight, Pete, if you don't mind," Janie said, moving over to touch his arm.

Damn. He'd promised himself he'd do whatever made her happy. He shrugged his shoulders and muttered, "Okay." He was about to be humiliated before his brothers. He only hoped Janie appreciated the sacrifice.

He received a small reward. Janie leaned against him and lightly brushed her lips against his, then took his hand and led him up the stairs behind the others.

The sweetness of her gestures almost made him forget what was about to happen. Almost. But he'd have difficulty facing his brothers once they discovered that his wife wouldn't even share the same room with him. He thought about heading out to the barn instead of their rooms, but he couldn't do that to Janie.

"Uh, the rooms may be a little messy. Janie—"

"I straightened everything this afternoon," she promised, interrupting him. "Our bedroom isn't too messy."

Our bedroom. There was that phrase again. And she squeezed his hand.

"We don't even need to go in there," Jake assured him. "Just the babies' room. And since they haven't arrived yet, it shouldn't be too big a mess."

Pete weakly returned his brother's grin.

"I hope you like the cribs, Pete," Janie said beside him. "They're all white, but I thought we'd put sheets and bumper pads with a circus theme. And we could get that lady who lives near Rawhide to come out and do a mural on the wall."

"That would be so cute, wouldn't it, Pete?" Megan said.

"Yeah, cute." If Janie wanted a mural, he'd agree to every wall in the house being painted. But right now his insides were quivering as Jake opened the door to the nursery.

Several big boxes rested against one wall.

"We brought these up earlier while Janie was taking a nap," Jake explained, crossing the room.

Pete was several steps into the room, his eyes searching for anything that would betray their secret, when he realized what Jake had said. While Janie was taking her nap. Why hadn't Jake seen her on the daybed? He turned to look at Janie.

"You must've been quiet as can be…or I was sleeping like a log, because I never heard a thing."

Feeling befuddled, it took Pete a minute to realize that Janie must've been sleeping in the bedroom. *Our bedroom.* He stared at her. Why? Did she always take her naps in there while he was at work? He'd gotten the impression she was never going to darken the door to that room again.

She smiled at him as if nothing of significance had happened and crossed the room to watch his brothers start taking the cribs from the boxes.

"I figure if we divide up into two teams, we'll have these put together in no time," Jake said.

The men quickly turned their activity into a competition with bets on who would finish first. Janie, Megan and Red became the cheering sections.

"I only hope they don't leave something out just to get finished faster," Megan said loudly enough for everyone to hear.

"They won't," Janie replied confidently. "Pete wouldn't let them. He wants everything perfect for the babies."

Pete wanted to tell her how right she was. And the most perfect thing for his babies would be for their mother to want to stay there with him. To love him.

He heaved a sigh. He'd finally admitted it. He needed Janie to love him. And he needed to love her.

"You okay?" Brett asked, working alongside him.

"Yeah. It makes the babies seem more real to be putting these things together."

"It does, doesn't it?" Jake agreed. "Next year we'll be putting together trains and tricycles and stuff for Christmas." The spark lighting his eyes made everyone laugh.

"You mean dollhouses, don't you, Jake?" Janie teased.

"Okay, but only if they're girls. I'm not putting together dollhouses for my nephews."

"Maybe we'll have one of each," Janie said, wrapping her arms over her stomach.

Pete's mouth went dry, and he wanted to hold her against him, to feel the growth of his children in her, to love her.

Janie had been right about his being afraid any woman he loved would leave him. Whether it was his mother's death, several past romances or Chloe's leaving Jake, he'd been afraid.

But Janie had gotten under his defenses. He'd fallen in love with her without realizing it. When she'd broken off with him, he'd felt he was dying. But he hadn't admitted his love.

Then, with the babies, he'd gotten a second chance. This time he wasn't going to blow it. He wouldn't overwhelm her. He'd take it slow and easy, and keep her happy. And quite possibly die of sexual frustration. But that was a small sacrifice to keep Janie in his life.

"Come on, Pete. We don't have time for daydreaming," Brett warned, poking him in the ribs.

He took his gaze off Janie and returned it to the task at hand. In no time, both cribs were ready.

Janie walked over and smoothed her hand across the small mattresses, first one and then the other. Then she turned to Pete. "Do you like them?"

Pete would've claimed to like the ugliest cribs in creation to please Janie. But he did like these.

"Yeah, I do. They look great."

She turned to look at them again, beaming, and leaned back against him.

Pete couldn't help it. His arms came around to cradle her against him. He was in heaven.

"Thanks, guys," Janie said, her voice sounding a little weepy. "What a wonderful surprise."

Pete tightened his hold on her, loving the feel of her against him, wanting to comfort her.

"Our pleasure, Janie," Jake replied. "We want you to know how happy we are you married Pete and how excited we are about the babies."

The others nodded.

"And we hope to use these beds next," Chad added.

"Chad!" Megan protested.

"Well, we do. We're just not sure when." Chad winked at his brothers. "We're working on it really hard, though."

"Chad Randall!" Megan protested again, more vehemently.

Everyone laughed, but Jake suggested they get out of Pete and Janie's rooms and let them have some time to themselves.

The family filed out, but much to Pete's delight, Janie didn't move, staying wrapped in his arms. He leaned his head against her silky hair, loving the fresh smell of it.

"Chad's funny, but I'm not sure Megan was amused," Janie said.

"I don't think she really minded."

"No, probably not."

Unimportant dialogue, he knew. What was important was being said by their bodies. Pete only hoped Janie wasn't put off by the response he couldn't hold back.

"Pete."

"Hmm," he replied casually, rubbing his face against her hair, concentrating on the feel of her, the scent of her.

"Remember when I said we needed to talk?"

He felt as if someone had doused him with a bucket of cold water. "Yeah. You want to talk now?"

She tensed against him, and he let his arms fall as he took a step backward.

"I think we should," she said as she turned to face him. But her gaze didn't rest on his face. She quickly looked away.

When she didn't say anything else, Pete thought he would die from the suspense. "Tell me, Janie," he ordered roughly, taking another step back.

"I— This is difficult for me to say."

His heart contracted as he prepared for the worst. She had

decided to leave him. Why hadn't she told him before they'd put up the cribs? Why had she let him picture the two of them bending over the beds, watching their babies sleep, him holding Janie in his arms, as he had a moment earlier?

Closing his eyes, hoping to hide his pain, he waited for her to continue.

"I moved my things back into our bedroom."

Our bedroom. Pete's eyes shot open, and he stared at her. "What are you saying?" he demanded hoarsely.

She turned her back to him and walked to one of the cribs, running her fingertips over the smooth metal. "I want us to be really married." After a brief pause, she added, "If you want to."

He turned to stone. Having prepared himself for the worst, he found it impossible to speak or move.

"If you don't, it's okay. I can move my things back—" Janie began hurriedly, her head down.

"No!" Finally he came out of his trance and grabbed her by the shoulder, spinning her around. "Are you saying you want to sleep with me?" He didn't want to make any mistakes.

She nodded. "If you're not put off by my being fat and—"

Pete didn't waste words. He swooped down on her and lifted her against him, his lips covering hers in a heart-stopping, life-giving kiss. Her arms went around his neck, and she clung to him with an eagerness that fed his heart.

"Will we hurt the babies?" he asked, thinking he'd die if she said yes.

"No. Doc said there wouldn't be a problem about that for at least a few months."

With a heartfelt prayer of thanks, Pete carried her into the room he would forever call *our bedroom* now. He laid her down on the bed and began unbuttoning her shirt. "I want to see our babies growing in you, Janie. I want to touch every inch of you. I've missed you so much."

"Me, too," she whispered, her hands going to his shirt.

He unbuttoned her jeans and slid them down to reveal her stomach, reverently stroking her skin, feeling the slight mound his children had caused. Then he bent down to caress her stomach with his lips, each kiss a promise to love and protect his little family.

"Pete," Janie urged.

"Hmm?"

"I'm dying for you to kiss me. Please."

She didn't have to ask twice. Pete slid onto the bed beside her, and his lips joined with hers. His hands began the pleasant task of removing her clothes…and touching her to his heart's content.

"Your jeans," she finally whispered when his lips strayed once more, caressing first her neck, then her breasts.

He was willing to follow her urging. But he didn't want to stop what he was doing. She tasted so good…and he was so hungry for her. He stripped as quickly as possible and returned to her side. He was ready for her, and it appeared she was ready for him as she guided him to her.

Though he intended to go slowly and gently into her, he found his needs raging. Janie joined him, tempting him, caressing him, as she had the first time, and Pete couldn't hold back.

When they collapsed against each other, their breaths rasping, their hearts pounding, Pete wrapped his arms around her and held her against him. He never wanted her to leave.

JANIE LAY in Pete's arms, grateful for the decision she'd made. Grateful that he still wanted her. Grateful that she was here with him instead of in her single bed in the next room.

Last night she'd debated what she should do. She loved the big lug, but she'd tried to hold out for his love. Finally, she admitted to herself that he might never come to love her. But if there was a chance that he would, it would happen because she made him happy.

And she wasn't making him happy sleeping in the other room.

It didn't hurt that his loving satisfied the hunger in her for his touch. After six months of feeling him move inside her, of loving him with all her heart, she'd felt half alive apart from him.

So she was back in her lover's arms. Now all she had to do was convince him he loved her, as well as his babies.

She kissed his chest and snuggled closer. Combat duty had never been so comfy.

THE NEXT FEW DAYS whizzed by, filled with their loving and Janie's work at her parents' ranch. Pete was all consideration, helping her with anything she did when he was home.

When the two of them did the dishes the next night also, Jake decided to arrange a dish rotation. Chad and Megan, Pete and Janie, and Brett and Jake.

"Hey, I don't get female companionship," Brett complained. "I don't think I should have to do dishes."

"We have to train you so some woman will take you on," Jake assured him. "Women today expect a man to pitch in. Right, Janie, Megan?"

"Definitely," Janie answered.

"Of course," Megan agreed. "Are you in training, too, Jake?"

Pete, sitting next to Janie with his arm around her, saw Jake tense. Megan was a favorite with Jake, but her teasing had gone awry.

"No," he replied gruffly. "I've already tried."

"Don't you want children of your own, Jake?" Janie asked softly.

Pete's heart ached for his brother. The babies he and Janie were having meant everything to him. Well, almost everything. Janie meant the most. But Jake wasn't going to have anything.

"You're having two. I figured you'd share with me, Janie. How about that?" Jake tried to muster a smile, but he was still uptight.

"Okay. But I think you'd make some wonderful babies."

"Yeah, and you read that book," Brett added, a big grin on his face. "You ought to put all that knowledge to good use."

"What book?" Janie asked, pretending Megan hadn't already told her about it.

After glaring at his brother, Jake said, "A book about having babies. I wanted to be sure we were doing everything we needed to for you."

"That's so sweet of you, Jake," Janie said.

"Pete's reading it now."

Janie looked from Jake to Pete, smiling at him, and Pete wanted to make love to her at once. Which wasn't surprising since he wanted to make love to her morning, noon and night.

"Ready to go up?" he whispered in Janie's ear.

Her nod made his heart swell. He'd tried not to make too many demands on her, but she never said no.

"We're going to go on to bed now," he said, rising and pulling Janie after him.

"Now?" Brett asked in surprise. "But the movie's not over."

What Pete had in mind would be a lot more fun than any movie ever made. "Yeah, now."

"But—"

"Brett," Jake said softly, gaining his brother's attention.

"Yeah?" Brett answered, but he stared at Pete and Janie leaving the room.

Before Jake could speak, Megan and Chad said good-night and left the room.

"What's wrong with everyone?" Brett asked.

Jake sighed. Brett was twenty-nine. He hadn't thought he'd have to explain the birds and the bees again. "They're newly-weds, Brett. They're not interested in television."

"Yeah, but—but Pete and Janie have been together for a while. They're expecting already. Don't you—? I mean, I don't remember you and Chloe—" Brett broke off, as if suddenly aware that he might be stepping on his brother's toes.

"Nope, I don't, either. Which makes me hope these two marriages are a hell of a lot better than mine."

PETE WOKE JANIE UP with a kiss, not an unusual occurrence these days. "Hey, beautiful, want to go to town today?"

She ran her fingers through his chest hair, loving the feel of him. "Hmm, why?" Somehow she feared any change to their routine, as if it might make a difference in their marriage.

"It's Saturday. I thought we might go shopping for that computer you were talking about. I want to get started learning how to operate it. The paperwork is about to overtake me."

"Especially since you don't work on it in the evenings anymore."

"Yeah, you little seductress. You keep dragging me upstairs to seduce me."

"I believe," she said, putting a finger to his lips, "you carried me up the stairs last night. So who's seducing whom?"

"I only carried you up because I was trying to prove my manhood."

Pete's grin, so warm and inviting, had been in short supply the first few days of their marriage. It made Janie feel good to see him happy. "Um, I believe you have a better way to show your manhood than flexing your muscles, Pete."

"I don't know, sweetheart. I think I'm just making another muscle hard to please you." He nuzzled her neck.

"Well, it certainly is getting a workout," she whispered, reaching for him.

WHEN JANIE finally got down to the kitchen, after Pete had risen from their marriage bed late to work, she discovered B.J. at the table with Megan.

"Good morning. Good to see you, B.J."

"You too, Janie. You look a lot happier than you did at the boxing match in town."

"Shh," Megan said, a grin on her face. "We're not supposed to mention that, Pete's orders."

"Ah. Sorry, I didn't know the rules," B.J. returned with a grin.

"We're also not supposed to notice when Pete comes to breakfast very late," Megan added.

"Then I take it I shouldn't mention Chad's late arrival yesterday?" Janie said, her own grin in place.

Megan's cheeks flushed. With a chuckle, she said, "Probably not."

B.J. leaned back in her chair. "This place is a breeding ground for happy couples. Any sign of it spreading?"

"What do you mean?" Janie asked.

"I just wondered if Jake and Brett were showing any inclinations toward joining the happy throng."

"'Fraid not," Megan said with a sigh. "They're both staunch supporters of bachelorhood."

"Just as well," B.J. said with a shrug. "Their availability keeps half the women in the county hoping they'll look their way."

"True. And that's fine with me as long as they don't look at

Pete,'' Janie said with a sigh.

"Or Chad,'' Megan added. And they grinned at each other.

PETE GOT BACK to the house a little after ten. He bounded up the stairs, anxious to see Janie. "Sweetheart, are you ready?'' he asked as he opened the door.

She popped her head out of the bathroom, one bare shoulder enticing him forward.

"Almost. I just have to put on— Pete! What are you doing? You'll mess up my makeup,'' she warned him with a sexy chuckle as he pulled her against him.

"Okay, okay,'' he grumbled, moving back into the bedroom. Janie stared at him, as if he'd grown two heads.

"What?'' he asked, puzzled.

"Nothing.'' She turned back to the mirror.

He sat there drinking in her beauty, enjoying the slight hint of her pregnancy. It wasn't the same as making love to her, but it beat not being able to see her.

She came into the room and opened the closet door. The intimacy of watching her dress was new…and pleasurable. He hadn't had all that much experience with it. Usually he showered and left while she stayed in bed, recovering from their lovemaking.

"I'm ready,'' she said breathlessly, emerging from the closet as she slipped into a pair of pumps.

"You're kind of dressed up, aren't you?'' he asked.

"I haven't gone too many places with my husband,'' she said. "I wanted to look nice for you.''

He rose from the bed and took her in his arms. "Well, you sure succeeded, sweetheart.'' He kissed her until he realized he'd have to stop or take her to bed. She'd already nixed that plan.

So he'd take her to town to buy a computer. And show off his beautiful new wife. Whatever it took to make her happy.

And all the time, he'd be wishing they were back home, alone, making love.

Chapter Fifteen

He's already tired of me.

Janie watched her husband out of the corner of her eye as he drove the pickup to town. That had to be the answer to the puzzle. Before she'd gotten pregnant, Pete had never backed off making love to her.

Now all she had to say was stop, and he turned away.

She'd heard of married couples growing disinterested, but she'd never expected it to happen after one week.

"Something wrong?" Pete asked.

"No, why?"

"You were staring at me."

She smiled. "Just admiring your handsome mug," she said. "And wondering if our babies will look like you or me."

"You if they're girls. They'd be mighty upset if they looked like me."

"Would you be disappointed if they're girls?"

"You asked that before. All that matters is that they arrive safely, sweetheart. I'll be happy with either boys or girls. Or one of each." He reached out and took her hand in his, bringing it to rest on his strong thigh.

She shivered. Touching him made her want him all the more. She wanted to tell him she loved him. But that was a topic he didn't want to discuss. She wanted to beg him to love her as much as he loved his unborn children. But she wouldn't beg. She wanted to believe their future would be happy. But she couldn't.

All they'd had was sex. If he showed a lack of interest in

that, how would she hold him? With the babies? But even that hold would slip away.

Maybe she was getting carried away. After all, they'd just made love that morning before getting out of bed. And every night since she'd returned to their bedroom.

Yes, that was it. She was making a mountain out of a molehill. *Be patient. Take each day as it comes.*

She tried to listen to her own advice the rest of the way into town.

There was only one store in Rawhide that dealt in computers. Janie had discussed the right choice with Brett, and she had decided what to buy. But she wanted to browse first, see if there was anything new on the market.

As they entered the store, her hand still clasped in Pete's, a man hailed them from the back.

"Pete, Janie! What are you doing here? Usually Brett comes in if you need anything." Orry Brownell met them with his hand extended in greeting to Pete. They'd all gone to school together, and Orry had attended their wedding. He'd taken over the hardware store from his dad and updated his merchandise to include computers. From what Janie had heard, it was a booming success.

"We're here to buy a computer, Orry. Janie and me, I mean."

"You, Pete? I sure hope you know what you're doing, Janie. Brett says this guy won't even turn one on."

Janie smiled, but her irritation was growing with those who made Pete sound like an idiot. Just because he wasn't trained in computers didn't mean he couldn't understand. "I'm not worried. We're going to set up his records for the rodeo work."

Realizing he was going to make a sale, Orry got down to business. Janie listened to him and then asked a few questions that had him revising his sales talk.

"Wow. She really knows her stuff," Orry said in an aside to Pete that Janie could clearly hear.

"You're not going to get anywhere with flattery, Orry," she warned him. "I haven't forgotten who pulled my pigtail in kindergarten."

"Aw, Janie, that was years ago. I don't do things like that now."

Janie pointed to a computer and printer. "What's your best price on this combination?"

He quoted her a price and she nodded, making no comment. "That's really the best I can do."

She smiled and pointed to another. After several quotes, she was about to tell him her decision and ask for a better price, since she wanted the most expensive of the group, when the door to the store opened again.

Casually looking over her shoulder, she froze. Bryan Manning. Just what she needed when everything was going so well.

Orry turned and offered a greeting.

Pete stiffened.

"Pete, please," she whispered.

Bryan, having come in from the bright sunlight, didn't readily identify the other customers until he was almost beside them. Then he flinched and took a step back.

Much to Janie's surprise, Pete extended his hand. "I want to apologize for my behavior the last time we met, Manning. I overreacted."

Warily Bryan shook his hand. "I just want Janie's happiness," he said.

"Me, too. You here to buy a computer?" Pete asked, as if casual conversation with Bryan Manning were something he looked forward to.

Janie stared at her husband.

I was right the first time. Now she knew Pete had lost interest in her. He was showing no jealousy. Instead, he joined in an idle conversation with Bryan. Janie's spirits plummeted, and she wanted to cry. But she struggled to hold back the tears. After all, how could she explain them? She couldn't announce in the middle of a computer store that her husband didn't want her anymore.

She interrupted the chat going on between the three men. "Orry, this is the computer I want, with the printer, but you're going to have to give me a better price. After all, I've picked out the most expensive."

Orry, with the scent of a sale, immediately gave her his attention. With a great show of reluctance, he mentioned a figure.

"We'll take it," Pete said at once.

"But I think we could get a better deal in Casper," Janie said.

"Yes, you could," Bryan agreed. "I priced this exact same model just last week."

"Damn, you're ganging up on me," Orry complained. "Okay, here's my final offer."

Bryan grinned. "That's the exact price."

Again Pete said, "We'll take it."

"I've got all of it in boxes in the back. Give me half a sec, and I'll bring it out."

After Orry walked away, Pete turned to Bryan. "That was mighty decent of you, Manning. Of course, Orry may never speak to you again."

Bryan smiled. "He won't mind. I've come to buy a new unit for the office, so he'll come out okay." Then Bryan looked at her. "How are you, Janie?"

Janie assured him she was well, but she watched Pete. Not by even a twitch did he show any concern that Bryan was talking to her. What had happened to the jealous husband who'd slugged the man last week?

Orry returned, and Pete pulled out a credit card, telling Janie to gather up whatever supplies she needed. As she did so, Bryan followed her.

"Is everything really all right?" he asked insistently.

Janie turned to stare at him. "Of course it is. Did you think Pete would beat me every night? He's spoiling me rotten, Bryan. I'm very happy."

It heartened her a little to see that Pete was watching them, but he smiled, as if their conversation didn't matter. She hurried over with her purchases.

"This should take care of everything," she assured Pete.

In no time, they loaded their purchases in the pickup and headed back to the ranch.

"That didn't take much time," Pete marveled, smiling at Janie.

"Nope. You can spend a lot of money without even trying."

"If we can get control of all those papers, it will be well worth it."

Janie returned his smile, but she couldn't shake the doubts and fears from her mind. They kept replaying themselves until she thought she would go crazy. But one thought remained constant: Pete hadn't been faking his response each night in their bed.

"Something wrong?"

She looked at Pete in surprise. "No. No, of course not. Everything's fine."

"Is there something else you want? We can go back to town if you do."

"No, there's nothing. We've spent enough money today. But there'll be lots more things to buy for the babies."

Pete looked surprised. "Really? Like what?"

"Clothes, of course, car seats, bottles, diapers, all kinds of things."

"We'll get them all," he promised, and squeezed her hand.

And he would. Anything money could buy, he'd give her. But she wanted his heart.

"LIKE THIS?" Pete asked warily. He pushed the buttons Janie pointed out and watched the screen. Much to his surprise, the program Janie had described appeared on the screen. "Hey, I did it."

"Of course you did. All you needed was someone to show you how."

He leaned over to kiss her. "You can show me how anytime, sweetheart."

"I don't think you're concentrating on the computer."

Pete smothered his sigh and smiled. She was right. He was concentrating on making love to his wife. But he'd have to wait until bedtime.

In the meantime, he had to pay attention to a machine. He hated the whole business, but he was impressed with how fast Janie set it up and began working on his files.

"Are you sure you feel up to this, Janie? You didn't have a nap today. I don't want you to overdo it."

"Maybe I'll go to bed early tonight."

Go to bed early. Magic words. He couldn't wait.

At dinner, Janie bragged about his expertise at the computer. Brett hooted in derision, and Janie launched into him as if he'd insulted Pete's manhood.

"Whoa, Janie!" Pete said. "Brett's been teasing me about

computers for at least a decade. That's why I tease him about his roping. He can't rope a fence post, much less a steer on the move.''

Brett, of course, immediately protested such a scandalous statement. Then Chad and Jake pitched in, and a full-scale, rip-roaring shout-fest took place. Pete, however, kept an eye on Janie. He feared she might be upset, but she'd seen them in action before.

She didn't join in, but she smiled at him.

Megan, on the other hand, appeared stunned.

Pete elbowed Chad and motioned to Megan.

"Honey, what's wrong?" Chad quickly asked her.

She shook her head. "What are you all doing?"

"Aw, don't get upset. This is our version of roughhousing. We're too old to roll around on the floor," Chad explained.

"I see," she said, but she had a bewildered look on her face.

"Don't worry, Megan," Janie assured her. "They don't mean any of it. It's just…exuberant teasing.''

Megan's cheeks flushed. "I'm sorry. You see, when my mother began fighting with whichever husband she was with, it was a sign that we were about to move on, to change our lives.…'' She trailed off, staring at Chad.

"Nope, that's not gonna happen, Meggie," he said, putting his arm around her and pulling her close. "We may fight, even for real, but we're all Randalls. We stick together through thick and thin.''

"That's right, Megan," Jake said, his voice earnest.

"It's a four-musketeers mentality," Janie added.

"Six musketeers and growing," Chad said with a grin. "But we've got room for lots more in our house and our hearts, sweetheart, and we will be together forever." He ended his pledge with a kiss that had the others looking in a different direction, albeit with big grins.

Except for Janie.

She studied her tightly clasped hands in her lap. It was painfully obvious that Pete didn't second Chad's assurances. Coming on top of the earlier events of the day, it just underlined to Janie that Pete wasn't sure their marriage would last.

And it broke her heart.

After dinner, the men of the family got into a discussion about pasture management. Janie saw it as an opportune moment to excuse herself. She had something to do before she and Pete went to bed.

PETE WATCHED as Janie went up to bed early, his brow furrowed. Something was wrong. He'd felt a tension growing in Janie all day. Should he go up now?

Jake drew him back into the discussion, unconscious of Pete's indecision. With a sigh, he responded. He loved his brothers. He loved all of them living together. But it did cause some difficulties.

If he and Janie had a house all to themselves, he'd be free to follow her to bed. To demand an explanation. To plead for another chance to make her happy. Hell, he'd spent all afternoon with the stupid computer when he could've been in the saddle. What more did she want?

Almost an hour later, he trudged up the stairs. His gut feeling told him Janie wouldn't let him touch her this evening until whatever was bothering her was settled. He said a fervent prayer that he'd be able to clear it up at once.

With a rueful chuckle, he wondered if God answered prayers for sex. But it was more than that. He needed to hold her. Only when she lay in his arms, sleeping, breathing softly against him, did he believe that she would stay with him. That they had a future.

Tonight, when Chad had promised Megan forever, Pete had wanted so badly to say the same to Janie. But he didn't think she wanted to hear that kind of promise. Not yet.

With a sigh, he prepared himself for an argument and opened the door.

And discovered, once again, that he didn't understand women.

Janie was stretched out on their bed, wearing that silvery negligee she'd rejected on their wedding night. Her hair was unbraided, providing her with a cloak of shining velvet. It even seemed to Pete that she was wearing makeup.

"Janie?" he questioned hoarsely from the door.

"Aren't you coming in, Pete? I've been waiting forever."

It occurred to Pete that Janie was acting out of character. She seldom bothered with makeup even during the day. She'd never played the role of seductress. And she'd never worn anything so shamelessly revealing before.

He should ask her what was wrong.

After struggling several seconds between his conscience and his hormones, he admitted there was no contest. He'd ask questions later.

With his gaze never leaving her, as if he feared she'd disappear if he turned away, he began stripping off his clothes. When he joined her on the bed, her perfume swirled around him, the silk of the negligee enticed him and Janie, all Janie, drove him wild.

A few powerful minutes later, he held her tightly against him and waited until he could speak. The negligee was on the floor, but she lay content against him.

"Janie?" he whispered.

Her eyes were closed. He kissed one eyelid and then the other. "Janie? Are you asleep?"

She mumbled something, as if she was on the edge of drifting off. Pete rubbed his hand up and down her back, loving the silken feel of her skin, and debated his options.

He could awaken her and ask if anything was bothering her. She'd probably think he was crazy. After all, they'd just had the most wonderful sex they'd ever shared. At least, in his opinion.

He had no complaints.

Except that he held a different Janie in his arms. Not that he minded. As long as she wasn't unhappy.

He wanted his Janie to be happy.

Tomorrow. He'd ask her tomorrow if anything was bothering her. That plan satisfied his conscience, and holding her against him satisfied everything else. With a sigh, he fell asleep, too.

As WAS their Sunday ritual, the next day the Randalls, en masse, attended services at the small church where Pete and Janie had been married. Janie thought their row was the most impressive in the church. Exuding strength and determination, the four Randall men would catch anyone's eye when they were all together.

She and Megan, mixed in among the four men, were a real change. She could remember, as a little girl, watching Pete file into church with his brothers and his father. She'd dreamed of the day he would ask her to sit beside him in their row.

She'd finally achieved that goal.

But she felt dishonest about it. Her seduction scene had worked last evening. Incredibly. But she hadn't been herself. Pete didn't seem to mind or notice, but she had.

She'd vowed to herself that she'd keep Pete's interest, whatever it took. She wouldn't allow him to lose his desire for her. At least not this soon.

What happened when she could no longer use sex to hold him? When the doctor said their lovemaking had to stop because it might damage the babies' health? Or when she grew older and wrinkles appeared around her eyes and her waistline wasn't so trim?

She didn't have an answer to those questions, and it frightened her.

Pete took her hand in his. She smiled at him and then looked away, only to encounter her father's approving smile. Desperately she tried to believe that everything was going to be all right. That Pete, like her father, would remain beside her all her life, even if she couldn't always be beautiful.

And she said a few prayers.

RED INVITED Janie's parents and B.J.'s family to Sunday lunch. He'd put on a pot roast before they'd left for church. Everyone accepted, and dinner was a noisy affair.

Afterward, again B.J., Janie and Megan volunteered to do the dishes. Lavinia and Mildred helped them carry the dishes into the kitchen, but the younger women sent them into the living room to relax.

Janie waited until there was a lull in the conversation before she launched the discussion she wanted.

"Megan, do you have a lot of sexy underwear?"

Her sister-in-law seemed surprised by the question. "Some, I suppose. My mother always believed in that kind of thing, so she would give me negligees for Christmas."

"Oh. I love the one the both of you gave me. Where did you find it?"

B.J. grinned. "We had to drive all the way into Casper to buy it. Rawhide wouldn't have anything that scandalous."

Janie laughed with the other two. "What store?"

"You want some more?" B.J. asked curiously.

"Pete must've liked it," Megan said, grinning.

"Yes, he did. And I thought I might see if they had anything else…interesting."

Megan laughed. "Save your money, Janie. If he's anything like Chad, you don't keep it on long enough to get your money's worth."

They all laughed again, but Janie turned away so they wouldn't see the tears pooling in her eyes.

Chapter Sixteen

Pete scratched his head.

Damn if he knew what to do.

"Anything wrong?" Jake asked, riding up beside him.

"Nope, they're moving along just fine," Pete replied, speaking of the cattle he and several cowboys were moving to another pasture.

"I didn't mean the cows."

Pete look at his brother and then turned away. "What are you talking about?"

"I don't know, or I'd ask better questions. It just seems to me that you've been...unsettled the last few days."

Pete sighed. What could he complain of? Great sex? Jake would think he was crazy. "Maybe I have been. This marriage business takes some getting used to."

Jake shifted in his saddle. "Yeah, I guess so. But everything's all right between you and Janie?"

"I guess. But...she's working too hard at it," Pete finally said.

"What do you mean?"

"I don't know!" His frustration burst out of him. "Jake, she's driving me crazy. Every night, like she's putting on a show or something, she seduces me. Hell, the sex is great. But I feel like I've lost the real Janie. She doesn't argue with me anymore. Whatever I say, she agrees. You know that's not like Janie."

"Nope," Jake agreed with a chuckle. "Even when she was little, she could hold her own. Remember when she tipped you into the water tank because you were teasing her?"

Pete laughed with his brother, but Jake's words only increased the feeling that something wasn't right.

"Do you think it's the pregnancy? None of us knows much about that, even if we did read a book."

Pete could feel Jake's eyes on him, and he wished he had an answer. But he didn't. "I don't know. There wasn't anything in the book about someone losing herself...changing into another person. If anything, the book said the mother might get difficult, fussy."

"And she doesn't get that way when it's just the two of you? I'd wondered if living with all of us was too big a strain."

"No, it's not that. We don't talk when it's just the two of us. She goes up early. When I come up, she's ready to lure me into bed." He laughed self-consciously. "Not that she has to try very hard."

"Maybe you should ask her what's wrong."

Pete's cheeks heated up in the cold air. "I've considered that, but the minute I enter the room, my hormones go into overdrive. She even had a new nightgown last night. Some rosy pink thing that was made of a few ribbons and some sheer material." Pete shuddered just thinking of her appearance and his enthusiastic removal of the aforementioned garment.

"I don't know what to tell you, Pete," Jake said, frowning. "Maybe you need to talk to Megan or Lavinia."

Pete stared at his brother in horror. "You want me to tell Lavinia about my sex life with her daughter? Or Megan? Are you crazy?"

Jake laughed. "Sorry. I guess I wasn't thinking. But I don't know what to do to help you."

Jake smiled at his brother. "Don't worry about it, Jake. You can't take care of all our problems for us. I'll work it out...one way or another."

THAT NIGHT, Pete watched Janie slip away from the group and start up the stairs. Her steps seemed slower, her tread heavier, than in the past few days. He'd started to ask her several times if she was feeling all right, but in the past she'd always gotten irritated when he worried about her.

Reaching a sudden decision, he broke off the conversation he was having with Brett and got to his feet.

"What's wrong?" Brett asked in surprise.

"Nothing. I have to go upstairs."

Brett grinned. "Are you sure you're leaving her enough time to breathe?"

"What are you talking about?"

"Well, I've heard of nonstop sex, but I've never seen it in action before. You don't hardly let her out of your sight."

Pete started to sit back down, afraid Brett was right, that he'd been hounding Janie. Then he remembered that *she'd* been seducing him. "No, that's not it," he said distractedly, and headed for the stairs.

And it wasn't. He wasn't an animal. He could control his desires...he thought. He'd been prepared to do so when Janie had agreed to marry him. No, it was as he'd told Jake earlier. Something was wrong.

He hoped if he went up when she did, before she transformed herself into his very own painted lady, he could control his hormones and get her to talk to him. Talk had been in short supply lately, at least between the two of them.

Opening the door cautiously, he discovered Janie curled up into a little ball on the far side of the bed.

"Janie? Janie, are you all right?" he asked as he crossed the room and knelt down beside her.

She hid her face from him. "Go away."

He felt her face and found it warm to his touch. "Janie, are you running a fever?"

"No. Go away," she repeated.

"Janie, look at me," Pete commanded sternly. "I need to know if you're sick."

"I'm not sick. But I'm not interested in sex tonight, so you might as well go away. I'll sleep in the other room if you want."

She uncovered her face enough for Pete to see tears streaking down her cheeks.

"Why would you do that?" he asked, fear clutching his heart. "We've been sharing this bed for a while now. There's no reason we can't continue."

"Yes, there is!" she exclaimed, her voice breaking at the end.

Pete rolled back on his heels, staring at her. "What reason?"

"I can't keep this up."

"Keep what up? Janie, are you talking about our marriage? You're not thinking of leaving?" He couldn't keep the horror out of his voice. "You're not leaving, Janie." He may have missed the old Janie, but he wasn't letting either one of them go without a fight.

"Why not?" she cried. "You won't want me anymore."

"What are you talking about?"

"Later," she said with a sniff. "You won't want me later."

"Janie, you're not making any sense."

She sat up on the bed, a look of determination coming over her. "Yes, I am. You just won't admit it. And I'm not waiting around for it to happen." She rolled away from him to the other side of the bed, stood up and ran for the door.

"Janie, what the hell are you talking about?" he shouted, springing to his feet to chase after her. "What is it?"

"You don't love me, and I can't always be young and attractive," she wailed over her shoulder.

She reached the stairs while she was answering Pete's question and missed the first step. In horror, Pete watched her fall, as if in slow motion, and roll down the stairs.

"Janie!" Fear filled him as he raced down after her.

She lay silent on the floor.

The rest of the family came running out at the commotion.

"Janie," Pete crooned, lifting her up against his chest. "Janie, talk to me."

Jake snapped out orders. "Brett, call the doc. Chad, go get B.J."

"B.J.?" Chad asked. "She's an animal doctor."

"She's also the only female to have had a baby around here. Go get her." Then he turned his attention to Pete and Janie. "Did she break anything?"

Pete stared at him, a dazed look in his eyes.

Jake ran his hands over Janie's arms and legs. "Nope, I don't think so."

Pete held his wife against him, as if trying to share his strength with her. He didn't even notice the others around him.

"Pete, can you carry her to bed? With nothing broken, I think it will be okay to move her." Jake had to tell him a second time, but finally Pete heard him.

"I can carry her," he assured him gruffly, trying to hold back the tears that filled him. He couldn't bear the thought of Janie hurt.

He stood and lifted Janie high against his chest. With Jake at his back, as if offering support, he started up the stairs.

"Megan," Jake called over his shoulder, "as soon as Brett finishes talking to the doctor, maybe you'd better call Lavinia and Hank."

Jake hurried around Pete and his burden to strip back the covers on their bed. "We'd better keep her warm. She might go into shock."

Pete laid her down, reluctant to let go of her. He had the feeling that as long as he held her, she would be okay.

"Pete, you want to take off her shoes?"

He turned to stare at Jake, a blank look on his face. What had Jake said?

"Her shoes, Pete. Take off her shoes."

He did so and then drew the covers over Janie just as the bedroom door opened. B.J., with Chad right behind her, came into the room.

"How is she?"

"She hasn't regained consciousness yet," Jake said in a low voice.

B.J. gently moved Pete aside and felt Janie's pulse. Then she opened one of her eyes. After that, she gently patted Janie's cheek. "Janie? Janie, can you hear me?"

Pete wanted to protest. But Janie's groaned response stopped him. He pushed closer. "Janie? Are you okay? Janie, speak to me."

"My head," she said with a low moan.

"Doc Jacoby is on his way, Janie," B.J. assured her calmly. "Just lie still and rest."

Janie clutched her stomach instead. "Ooh!"

"Are you having pains, Janie?" B.J. asked, her voice again calm.

"My babies!" Janie cried, sending a chill through the room.

PETE PACED THE FLOOR, unable to contain himself. Doc, Lavinia and B.J. had been upstairs with Janie for at least half an hour.

The fear that he might lose her so consumed him that he didn't hear footsteps coming down the stairs.

Perhaps it was the concerted movement of the rest of his family that alerted him. By the time he turned around, Doc was almost to the bottom.

"Janie...?" he asked painfully.

"She's going to be fine. She has a mild concussion, and there will be an assortment of bumps and bruises, but nothing serious."

Pete bowed his head in relief.

"And the babies?" Jake asked softly.

Pete's head snapped up in time to see the doctor let out a long sigh. "I don't know. We'll know more after twenty-four hours."

"You mean she might lose the babies?" Pete asked in horror.

"I hope not. Babies are well cushioned. But I'm not promising anything right now. Lavinia is going to stay with her tonight. I'll be out first thing in the morning to check her again."

"You're not moving her to a hospital?" Jake asked.

"Nope. Lavinia is almost as good as Priddy. Janie will be better off here." He turned to Pete again. "You can go see her for a minute or two, but don't upset her."

Uncertainty and fear filled him. He was the reason she'd fallen in the first place. He'd already upset her. What if the sight of him disturbed her all over again?

With a nod to the doctor, he started up the stairs. He couldn't *not* see her. He had to see with his own eyes that she was all right. But he was afraid his presence wouldn't make her feel better.

"Lavinia?" he whispered from the door to the bedroom. "Doc said I could see her for a minute or two."

She motioned for him to come in. "Janie, Pete's here to see you."

Even Pete, from across the room, could see her body flinch at her mother's words. He and Lavinia exchanged looks of concern, but he walked to Janie's bedside.

"Sweetheart, I'm sorry. I didn't mean to argue with you." He could feel Lavinia's gaze on him, but it was no time to be dishonest. "I'll do whatever you want, I promise."

Even if it meant watching her leave. He wanted her—forever—but most of all, he wanted her safe and happy. Even if she went away. Or married someone else. But the thought of it was tearing him in two.

He brushed her lips with his, gently, softly, and then, without another word, left the room.

BY THE NEXT EVENING, Doc assured Pete the babies were fine, as would be Janie after some rest. While the relief was incredible, Pete's heart was heavy.

He was sure Janie intended to leave. She'd asked her mother to stay another night with her, after the doctor refused to allow her to go back to her parents' home.

He visited Janie once that evening, but she scarcely responded to him. As he left the room, Lavinia gave him a sad smile.

Yes, Janie was leaving.

"YOU CAN'T GO without telling him why," Lavinia said, frustration in her voice. "Janie, the man has been distraught with worry. He cares about you."

"He cares about his babies," Janie replied softly, one hand cradling her stomach. The scare she'd received, endangering her babies' lives, had made them so much more precious. And helped her make some decisions.

Unfortunately her mother was right. She couldn't leave Pete without telling him...without assuring him of a role in his children's lives.

"All right, Mom. We'll wait for him to come back."

"He's downstairs in the kitchen right now."

"He didn't ride out today?"

"Of course not. He's waiting to do whatever he can to help you."

Janie's eyes filled with tears, and she turned away. "Ask him to come up."

She moved to the window, hoping the bright winter sun would dry out her eyes. Reminded of that first meeting with Pete after she'd found out she was pregnant, Janie dug deep for the control she'd had then. She refused to let Pete know how painful this meeting would be for her.

"Janie."

That low, sexy voice that thrilled her announced Pete's arrival. She didn't turn around. "Pete, I'm going back home."

Silence greeted her announcement, but she didn't realize he'd moved until his hands fell on her shoulders and gently turned her around. "Why?"

She wasn't prepared to answer that question. "I won't keep you from seeing the babies or—or being their daddy."

"Why, Janie? Is it Manning?"

That question brought her gaze to his, filled with indignation. "Of course not!"

"Then why can't you stay? Why can't you let me take care of you? I'll sleep on the daybed if you want."

She ducked her head. "Pete, I can't continue to— I'd be living a lie."

"You once said you loved me."

Her heart contracted in pain. Once? She would always love this stubborn man. "Yes," she whispered.

"Janie, I'll try harder. I'll do whatever you want," he pleaded softly. "Give me another chance."

The tears reappeared, and she gasped, trying to hold them back. "Pete, it's me, not you."

He lifted her chin, staring at her, a frown on his face. One tear escaped and traveled down her cheek, and he erased it with his thumb. "What are you talking about, Janie?"

She tried to turn away, but he wouldn't let her. Finally she lifted her gaze to his and told him the truth. "I tried to be sexy," she explained with a hiccup, "but I can't hold you with sex the rest of my life. I won't always be attractive or young. And I can't live with the fear that you'll find someone else who is."

As if they were frozen in a lovers' tableau, they stood there, Pete's arms around her, their faces lifted to each other. Suddenly Pete lifted her in his arms and spun around.

"Dear God, give me strength," she heard him mutter.

"Pete, what are you doing?" she shrieked.

"Sorry, sweetheart, I forgot about your concussion," he muttered as he set her back down on her feet. Then, to her surprise, he tried to kiss her.

She shoved him away. "Pete, I'm leaving, remember?"

"Nope. Not in a million years."

"Pete Randall, you can't order me around. I'll do what I jolly well please, and you can just—"

He threw back his head in laughter, and she stared at him in surprise. Had he gone crazy?

"That's my Janie," he said as he chuckled. "I've missed you so much."

"What are you talking about?"

"Janie, the sex has been incredible these last few days—"

"I know, Pete, but I can't—"

"Would you let me finish?"

Irritation rose at his high-handedness, but she nodded grudgingly.

"Since when did I ever need seducing?" he asked, a grin on his face.

"When you began losing interest."

He looked as if she'd poleaxed him. "What?"

"You stopped wanting me all the time."

"Janie Dawson Randall, I have never stopped wanting you every minute of every day since the first time I made love to you. And I never will."

"What about the day we bought the computer?"

He shook his head in bewilderment. "What about it?"

"You acted like you wanted to make love to me before we left for shopping."

"I did. That doesn't prove I don't want you."

"But you didn't."

"You said I'd mess up your makeup!" he exploded.

"Such a silly excuse wouldn't have stopped you in the past. And—and…" She paused to restrain her tears. "And you were friendly with Bryan."

He leaned his forehead against hers. "Are you out of your mind, Janie? Do I have to punch out every man who even looks at you for you to believe I want you?"

She buried her face in his chest. "It doesn't matter, Pete," she said wearily. "I won't always look this way. Someone younger, prettier, will come along. I'm not strong enough to face that."

"Janie," Pete whispered, raising her head again, "I think I forgot to tell you something."

She blinked several times, wanting to ask if he'd already found someone else, but she couldn't bring herself to do so.

"What?"

"I forgot to tell you that I love you."

She stared at him. The words she'd always wanted to hear were now impossible to believe. "Pete, please—"

"Janie, I've always loved you. Only you. But at first, I was afraid to tell you, afraid to admit how much I needed you. Then, after we married, you seemed…unhappy with me. I realized how much I loved you, but I thought I had to—to woo you back. To convince you to love me again. So I was trying to do whatever would make you happy." He grinned. "Like spend all afternoon using that stupid computer."

"You didn't like it?" she asked, distracted by his hands. They were stroking her back in a rhythmic pattern.

"I hated it. I know computers are good, but I won't want to mess with them. I'd rather my wife take care of that end of our business."

"I could do that but, Pete—"

His lips covered hers before she could finish. The magic of his touch was still there even when she thought she was leaving him. When he lifted his mouth from hers, she tried again. "Pete, I'm not sure—"

He kissed her again.

This time he spoke. "I'm sure, Janie. I'm sure with all my heart. There will never be anyone else to tempt me. And I don't need a sexy lady every night. Even a crabby Janie will do me."

"Are you sure, because I can't—"

He silenced her with his lips. "I missed you, sweetheart."

"What?"

"The last few days, I knew you weren't being yourself. I wanted to argue with you just to find the old Janie. But every time I opened the bedroom door, well, other parts of me took over."

"Really, Pete? You're sure?"

"I'm more sure of my love for you than anything else in the world."

In a small voice, she said, "I was afraid if I lost the babies you wouldn't want to be married to me anymore." She felt ashamed to admit such a thing, but she wanted to be honest.

If—and she still wasn't sure—happiness was there waiting, within her reach, she didn't want it tainted with unresolved issues.

He tightened his embrace. "Janie, I would've grieved for our babies if we'd lost them. But you...I couldn't survive without you. Don't ever leave me."

Finally he'd convinced her. She had found the love she'd been seeking when she'd first come into his arms. And now she'd never have to leave them.

After several minutes of reassuring each other, Janie gasped. "What is it, sweetheart?" Pete asked with concern.

"Mom! I told her I was leaving you. We'd better go tell her."

"Good idea. Besides, if we don't get away from this bed, I may not be able to restrain myself, and I think it's too soon after your accident."

"Probably. At least until nap time this afternoon," she said with a grin.

They walked arm in arm down the stairs to the kitchen. When they opened the door, they found the full complement of Randalls, along with her mother, waiting for them, apprehension on their faces.

Janie let her husband speak for her. He beamed at their audience and simply said, "We love each other."

Everyone circled them, kissing Janie's cheek and patting Pete on the back. Relief and excitement filled the room.

Brett, after everyone sat back down, chuckled. "*I* could've told you that."

"Don't be too sure," Pete warned. "Love isn't as easy as it looks."

"And it's about time you found out," Jake added. "After all, you caught Janie's bouquet, remember?"

"Yeah, but I'm going to always be the bridesmaid," Brett joked.

"Uh-uh," Jake said, rubbing his chin. "We'll see."

**Beginning in March
from**

HARLEQUIN®

AMERICAN *Romance*®

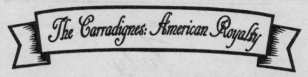
The Carradignes: American Royalty

A royal monarch's search for an heir leads him to three American princesses. King Easton will get more than he bargained for in his quest to pass on the crown! His first choice—Princess CeCe Carradigne, a no-nonsense executive who never mixes business with pleasure…until she gets pregnant by her rival, Shane O'Connell.

Don't miss:

THE IMPROPERLY PREGNANT PRINCESS
by Jacqueline Diamond   March 2002

And check out these other titles in the series:

THE UNLAWFULLY WEDDED PRINCESS
by Kara Lennox   April 2002

THE SIMPLY SCANDALOUS PRINCESS
by Michele Dunaway   May 2002

And a tie-in title from
HARLEQUIN®

INTRIGUE®

THE DUKE'S COVERT MISSION
by Julie Miller   June 2002

Available at your favorite retail outlet.

HARLEQUIN®
Makes any time special ®

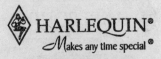

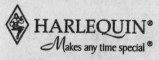